Eugene Vesey was born and bro
educated at a Roman Catholic gr
Roman Catholic seminary in t
University of Manchester, where
Literature, and the University ot
his teaching certificate. He lives and works in London, where he was a lecturer in English as a Foreign Language at private schools and Colleges of Further Education for many years. He now teaches privately as well as writing. His previous novels *Ghosters* and *Opposite Worlds* are prequels to *Italian Girls*. Both are available from Amazon, as is *Venice and Other Poems*, a book of poetry. You can contact Eugene at veseyeugene@hotmail.com or via Eugene's Facebook page.

Also by Eugene Vesey

Ghosters (Novel)

Opposite Worlds (Novel)

Venice and Other Poems

ITALIAN GIRLS

Eugene Vesey

Published by New Generation Publishing in 2014

First Edition

www.newgeneration-publishing.com

New Generation Publishing

for

Miriam

CHAPTER ONE

'This is for ju.'

She had been waiting for him outside the classroom, a tall, willowy, Spanish girl with black, waist-length hair, wearing gold-rimmed specs and a black leather jacket over denim dungarees, white socks and sandals. He didn't like leather jackets or women in trousers. She had a pale complexion, so didn't really look Spanish. Anyway, he preferred Italian girls. He certainly didn't fancy her.

'Oh?' he said, taking the envelope she handed him.

'But don't read it now,' she ordered. 'Go somewhere private.' Then she hurried off, flustered.

He slipped the envelope into his inside jacket pocket, hoping it wasn't a complaint about his teaching – not that there could be any complaint – and made for the gents. Shutting himself in one of the cubicles, he ripped open the envelope and took out a sheet of blue, Basildon Bond letter paper, on which was written:

Sometimes walking by the street you cross another eyes and you think: 'I would like to know this person' because looks interesting for you. It is possible that the phisique appearance don't be the best you would wish, but, never mind, you have seen any special thing in that person and you would wish to find out it.

This has happened to me and sorry because the 'victim' were you. You interests me like a person I would like to have the opportunity of to know you, to change opinions, ideas. To know another new person.

I wouldn't like to loose an opportunity by my fault. So I've done my best to get my wish, 'to communicate it'. If this idea don't suit you, don't worry, I'm a good looser (but don't laugh at this letter, please) forgive the letter and all is okay. If you agree with me, please telephone me and we can meet in any place. It would be nice. Tel: 5.50.04.13 (ask for DOLORES). Don't throw away the letter in any place with my telephone number, please!

Dolores

Wow, he thought. Well, actually, if you looked past the silly clothes and the geeky specs, she was quite attractive, with her long black hair, liquid dark-brown eyes and milky smooth skin. Nice tits too, though not exactly voluptuous. He was intrigued as well as flattered. And God he was lonely! Lonely and frustrated. It was ages since he'd had any female company. Since Mary, his wife, had left him. Well, since Cinzia had gone back to Italy and left him. Better go to the pub and have a proper ponder, he decided.

The trouble was, he thought, taking a first delicious sup of Guinness in the Bell, he wasn't sure if he fancied her enough to get involved with her. She wasn't really all that attractive. There were much more attractive women in his classes. God, some of them should never be allowed out, with their pretty foreign faces and sexy bodies! But they weren't exactly fighting each other like wildcats for his favours. Probably because they could sense he was a bit depressed. Even though he liked to think he always put on a good show of being cheerful and upbeat in class. But people – especially women – could probably sense that all was not well or not as well as it appeared.

Whereas this Dolores obviously fancied him. He'd never had a letter like that before. It was quite brave of her. She must *really* fancy him! Why not agree to meet her? Why not indeed, he thought, taking another sup of Guinness. Christ, he really had had enough of loneliness. Of living like a monk. He hadn't left the seminary to live like a bloody monk! He was poor, he had to obey the people in charge at college, as well as the laws of the land, but he damn well didn't want to be celibate as well – sod that for a game of soldiers!

How long was it now since Mary had left? Over a year. The memory went through him like a rapier. Nine years they had been together. *Nine* years! Exactly as long as he had been in the seminary. Funny coincidence! Or was it more than a coincidence? Was there something Freudian going on deep down in his subconscious? Oh, dear, black thoughts to accompany the black nectar, he reflected morosely, taking another sup. But it brought comfort to the soul as well.

What was Mary doing now, he wondered? He shouldn't think about her, because it always upset him, but he couldn't help it. He hoped she was OK. God, he had loved her! It had been the real deal. But obviously not enough. Maybe because the love was alloyed with pity, which according to Theodor Reik was incompatible with love. Even though he'd given her so much. Done so much for her. Been her knight in shining armour, as she had once told him. But he'd let her down. He'd hurt her. He'd been unfaithful. He couldn't limit himself to one woman for the whole of his life. In that sense their marriage had been a mistake. A tragic mistake. But she was the one who had wanted marriage. He had always made it clear to her that he didn't believe in it. It didn't alter the fact that he had been unfaithful to her though.

What she couldn't understand, couldn't accept, was that he wanted to have other relationships, even *though* he loved her, not because he *didn't* love her. No, he was kidding himself. Which he was good at. He hadn't really loved her. If he had loved her, he couldn't have been unfaithful to her, could he? No, he had liked her and felt sorry for her. Felt protective of her. But didn't love her. Not as a man should love a woman or a husband a wife.

Was that *his* fault though? He had tried his best. He had loved her at first. But then he had become bored by her, fed up with her, frustrated by her limitations. Even though he knew she was a diamond. Shine on! Not being able to have kids hadn't helped. That'd put an awful strain on the relationship. Been the final nail in the coffin. And she was the one who'd wanted kids, not he. As if her life depended on it. Which it did in a way. And he'd had the operation. He'd gone under the knife. He'd done his best. But it hadn't been enough.

The trouble was, he was too much of a free spirit, he supposed. Too much of a rebel. And he'd been damaged by the seminary. Not sexually. Not because Father Director had messed about with him. Not because he'd been madly in love with Mark Brown. And other boys with him. It'd been a real hothouse. And a hotbed. No. He certainly wasn't a homo or a paedophile, thank God. He was the very opposite. A sex maniac maybe. But better to be a sex maniac than either of those!

No, the seminary had been so like a prison, so like a living death, that now he couldn't bear being bound by rules or regulations. He couldn't bear being in an institution of any kind, including the institution of marriage. Well, he'd always been a bit of a rebel. A fully-paid up member of the awkward squad. Even in the seminary. It was one of the reasons he'd had to leave. He couldn't accept half the Church's teaching. About contraception for example. Even though it took him about three years to make the decision. Christ, the most difficult decision he'd ever had to make in his life! It'd nearly killed him. Literally.

He took Dolores' letter out and read it again, just to make sure he hadn't imagined it or misunderstood it. *You interests me like a person I would like to have the opportunity of to know you* ... That was clear enough, wasn't it, even if the syntax was dodgy? She obviously fancied him. It was very flattering. *But do I fancy her?* He couldn't make his mind up. He shouldn't go with her just because he was lonely. That'd just be using her, wouldn't it? Not if it was what she wanted. She was obviously lonely too. In a foreign country. No friends. Mutual need fulfilment.

It wasn't like Cinzia though. With Cinzia he'd had no doubts, no scruples. Except that he was still married when he'd met her. But his wife had left him, so he was justified in having a relationship with someone else. He was free. He'd been crazy with loneliness and frustration. Anyway, he'd fallen in love with her. He was still in love with her! He remembered the first time he'd met her properly. She'd been waiting at the bus stop outside the college one afternoon when he was on his way home after teaching. Waiting not for a bus but for him, as she'd later confessed …

'Hello,' he had said, stopping when he saw her at the bus stop. She was wearing a glittery black summer dress which revealed her nicely-tanned skin.

'Ees thees the righta stopa for one two three-a?' she asked him, in her charming Italian accent.

He had a thing for Italian girls, in spite of Grazia, or maybe because of Grazia, who he had fallen in love with the very first moment she had walked into his classroom last year, but who had resisted all his advances. 'Yes,' he said. 'Where are you going?'

'Woodforda,' she said.

'You don't live in Woodford, do you?' he asked.

'I 'ave moveda,' she told him.

'Oh. This is the right stop then. Are you still an au pair?'

'Yes. Where are you goinga?'

'I'm going to the pub,' he said, on the spur of the moment – he didn't normally go in the afternoon.

'Do you go to the pub after class every daya?'

'Yes. I'm usually thirsty after teaching!' he smiled. 'What about you? What do you usually do?'

'Nothinga. I never do anythinga.'

'Do you want to come for a drink?'

'I 'ave no money.'

'That's all right – I'll treat you.'

'Thank you!' she said, her dark-brown eyes lighting up. 'Where are you goinga?'

'Just down the road, to the Bell. Come on.' He walked off before she could change her mind and she hurried beside him.

'Ees eet true you are marrieda?' she asked, in the pub.

'Yes, but my wife's left me,' he said, taking a sup of his Guinness. It pained him to say it, but it also gave him a certain vindictive satisfaction.

'I'm sorry,' she said. 'Why 'as she left you?'

'Problems,' he shrugged, taking another sup of Guinness. She was drinking orange juice.

'Do you 'ave children?'

'No,' he said, sadly. 'That was one of the problems.'

'I'm sorry,' she said again.

'What about you? Have you got a boyfriend?'

‘Yes,’ she said, but with a sigh.

‘Tell me about him. Is he Italian?’

‘Yes. ’e is a sailor. ’ees name is Luciano. ’e is quieta. ’e don’t talka. ’e ees too quieta. I ’ave changed ’eem a bita, but eet’s not gooda.’

‘You don’t sound very happy with him.’

‘I only see ’eem every three monthsa.’

‘That could be a good thing!’ he laughed.

‘Eet’s no gooda,’ she said, serious. ‘If ’e gets a job on dry landa, I weel marry ’eem.’

‘What about children? Do you want children?’

‘I only want one childa. More would be too much trouble and expense.’

‘With your husband?’ he teased.

‘Of course weeth my ’usbanda! ’ow otherwise?’

‘Do you love him?’

‘‘Love’? What ees ‘love’?’

‘Good question!’ he laughed. ‘I’m not sure I know.’ Maybe that was the wrong answer. Maybe it had been a cue for him to say to her, ‘I love you.’ What was the Italian for it? He wasn’t sure. But he had a feeling he’d find out.

‘My landlady says she loves her ’usbanda,’ she continued. ‘’e is dying of multiple sclerosis in ’ospital. But she can’t love ’eem, because she ’as a boyfrienda, sometimes two boyfriendsa. All time she is in front of the mirror. Ugh! You can’t love two people. Eet’s impossibile.’

‘In some societies and cultures it happens,’ he observed, just for the sake of argument.

‘I don’t care about other societies and cultures,’ she declared, so he decided not to pursue it – he was starting to fancy her in spite of himself, so didn’t want to antagonise her.

There was a pause in the conversatione while they both sipped their drinks, she her orange juice, he his Guinness.

‘What do you do in your free time?’ she asked.

‘I read. And I write.’

‘What do you write-a?’

‘Novels. Poetry.’

‘You must be clever.’

‘Not necessarily,’ he laughed, flattered nonetheless.

'You must be patient.'

'Oh, yes, you have to be patient,' he agreed.

'Yes, I think you are patient. You don't show any anger in class, for example. Me, I prefer let out my feelingsa. If I'm angry, I must show eet. Then eet's over.'

'So you're an au pair. Do you have a day off?' he asked, deciding to change tack.

'Sunday is my day offa.'

'What do you usually do on Sundays?'

'I stay out all day. Alone. Last Sunday I slept all day in Saint James Parka.'

That sounds really sad, he thought. But good for me. She must have seen it written on his face.

'I know, it's sada. And all the time I was bothered by Japanese men.'

Fucking perverts! But then I quite fancy her myself. But I wouldn't pester women in public, in the park.

'That's horrible.'

'Si. But it's OK. It's my first time away from 'ome-a. My first time to be independenta. Usually my mama is on top of me. I 'ave already learnt a lota. I 'aven't enjoyed so much, but I 'ave learnt a lota.'

'Have you only ever had the one boyfriend?'

'I 'ad another one before Luciano. I was with 'eem during two yearsa. But I know 'e was fed up weeth me. So 'e left me.' She sounded doleful.

'Why did he leave you?' There were tears in her eyes. 'I'm sorry. You don't have to tell me if you don't want.'

'It's OK. I don't mind to talk to you. I like to talk to you. I think I can trust you.'

'Thank you. Yes, you can.' This was progress, he thought.

'I don't know why 'e 'as left me. We were together two yearsa. I was 'appy. One day 'e invited me to Venice. My mama didn't want to let me go. But I insista. I thought 'e was going to ask me to marry 'eem. On the first day in Venice, we was walking along the streeta. I stopped to look in a shop window. When I turned round, 'e 'as disappeared.'

'What? You mean, he just disappeared without saying anything? You never saw him again?'

'Si. I never saw eem again.' The tears welled up.

What a cowardly swine, he thought. 'I'm sorry. That's a very sad, strange story,' he said, putting his hand on her thin brown arm. His heart went out to her. Suddenly she wasn't just a girl he fancied. She was a real, live, sentient, sensitive human being with a heart of her own, a broken heart. He must try not to cause her any more pain. He still fancied her, yes, but if she let him, he'd look after her, take care of her, be good to her, he resolved. He took his hand off her arm, even though she hadn't resisted it.

Suddenly she seemed to brighten up. 'I'm 'aving a drink with my teacher!' she exclaimed. 'I can't believe eet! Wait till I tell Christine.' Christine was a French classmate.

'Are you friends with Christine?'

'Si. We talked about you so much. One day, before class, we wrote a list of points on the board for you.'

'Go on, tell me,' he laughed, not sure if he really wanted to hear.

'Are you sure?' she asked.

'You've got to tell me now,' he insisted. 'I'm not letting you go till you do.'

'OK, I tell you. Interesting. Intelligent. Extrovert. Intellectual. Funny. Polite. Kind. Nothing bad.' *Extrovert? That doesn't sound like me!*

'What about handsome?' he laughed, taking a sup of Guinness.

'Christine thinks you are not 'andsome.'

'Oh,' he said, crestfallen. 'Why not?'

'She likes the John Travolta type.'

'Oh, well, I can't compete with John Travolta,' he laughed, slightly put out, silly as it was. 'Do *you* think I'm handsome?' *God, that's a leading question!*

'Si. I think you are 'andsome. But I am not in love with you.'

I might fall in love with you though. But no. Not a good idea. Not on the rebound. And yet, she is quite pretty, in her own quiet way. And she is Italian. With that Italian accent that gets me, that I can't resist.

'You're not in love with me?' he asked, pretending – but not entirely pretending – to be offended.

'I'm not in love with you. But I like you.'

'You like me? Why?'

'I like you because you're Francis. And you look exactly like my boyfriend who deserted me in the street in Venice.'

'I see.' He wasn't sure how to take this, as a compliment or …

He felt deflated. But it didn't matter. She liked him and he liked her. He more than liked her. It was a start.

'I 'ave to go-a,' she said suddenly, looking at her watch.

'Why?' he asked, even more deflated.

'My landlady wants me 'ome-a. To worka.'

'Oh. OK. That's a pity. You look sad.'

'Not sad. Tired.'

'Not tired of me, I hope.'

'I can never be tired of you. Can I ask you somethinga?'

'Sure.' He took a swig of Guinness.

'Do you think I am a good studenta? Do you think I am wrong to go for a drink with my teacher?'

That was the easiest question he'd had for a long time. 'I think you're the best,' he said, impulsively stroking her cheek with the back of his hand.

To his alarm, she took hold of his hand, but only to hold it, not to rebuke him. Then he noticed she was crying, tears rolling down her brown cheeks.

'What's wrong?' he asked, putting both of his hands around hers. It was so small, so fragile, so *cold* …

'I don't want to fall in love with you,' she said, removing her hand from his, taking out a little embroidered hanky from her bag and drying her eyes with it.

'And I don't want to fall in love with you,' he replied, smiling. *Though I think I've already started to.*

'OK, let's not fall in love,' she laughed, to his relief, sniffling back the last of her tears.

'It's a deal,' he laughed. But it was a deal he knew he might not be able to keep.

'I 'ave to go,' she gasped, looking at her watch again and standing up.

'Shall I go to the bus stop with you?' he asked, when they were outside, though he knew it wasn't a good idea.

Wagging tongues.

'No, I want to go alone,' she insisted, running off back along Forest Road towards the college before he could even give her a peck on the cheek.

And that was how it had begun. At the 123 bus stop on Forest Road, right outside the college. 'Request Stop.' That was where the bus of love had arrived, he chuckled to himself, turning and sailing homewards on the crest of a wave, even though he hadn't requested it or even expected it.

CHAPTER TWO

She was at the bus stop again the next afternoon, as he had hoped. She was wearing a cheap-looking, sleeveless, flowery blouse, navy-blue culottes and pop socks. She smiled winsomely at him.

'Buon giorno!' he exclaimed, as if surprised. 'Would you like to go for a drink?'

'I 'ave no money again,' she said.

'Don't be silly – I'll buy the drinks,' he said. 'Come on, if you want.' He walked off, not sure if she would follow, but to his relief she did, without hesitation.

'I couldn't sleep last nighta,' she told him, when they had sat down, at exactly the same table as yesterday.

'Why not?' he asked, taking a first delicious sup of Guinness.

'I was thinking about you.'

'What were you thinking?' he asked nervously, not sure he would get the answer he wanted.

'I don't say. I will be red-a.'

He laughed. 'I hope they were nice thoughts.'

'They are always nice thoughts when I think about you.'

'I was thinking about you, too,' he admitted.

'*You* were thinking about *me*?' She sounded astonished. He wondered if she was acting. But no, she seemed too genuine.

'What were you thinking?'

He had been thinking about making love with her, of course, as well as other stuff, but didn't dare to say that. He didn't know her well enough yet. After all, they'd only met once. They weren't actually lovers. Not yet. If ever.

'Oh, about what you told me yesterday. About your boyfriends, for example,' he answered. 'And about spending all day alone in the park.'

'What did you think about it?'

'I think it was very sad. I felt sorry for you.'

'Grazie.'

He took hold of her hand and held it. Like yesterday, he noticed how cold it felt. But also feminine. She didn't pull it away. His heart fluttered. 'I don't want you to be lonely,' he said.

'I'm not lonely now.'

'You're not?' Oh, God – she hadn't found a boyfriend since yesterday, had she? That Turkish boy in the class, Hassan, liked her, he'd noticed.

'No. Because I am with you-a.'

He laughed, relieved. 'I'm happy to be with you.'

'*You* are 'appy to be with *me*?'

Again, she sounded surprised, as if she wasn't pretty and cute and sexy and *Italian*. Well, pretty in a mousy sort of way. That's what he would call her one day maybe, he decided, "my little Italian mouse". But he mustn't rush things. He didn't want her to get hurt. Or to be hurt himself. He'd had enough of that lately.

'Of course I am,' he laughed.

'Why?'

'Because I like you.'

'Francis, remember what we said yesterday.'

'What did we say?'

'We said we wouldn't fall in love with each other.'

'Oh, yes. I forgot.'

'Why do you like me?'

'You're pretty. And you have a nice personality. You seem sweet. Sincere.'

'You think so? Really?' She blushed, seemed surprised and delighted, as if she really didn't know how attractive she was. Unless she was a really good actress …

'And because you're Italian,' he laughed. 'I like Italian girls.' An image of Gina Lollobrigida flashed into his mind – he had had a secret crush on her even as a seminarian. Not to mention Grazia.

'You know Italian girls are colda, don't you? Everybody thinks they are hota, but they are not, they are colda.'

'I know,' he said. 'Your hand is cold.' He put both of his hands on hers and rubbed it gently between them, excited by the contact.

'I like your 'andsa,' she said. 'You 'ave beautiful 'andsa.'

'Thank you,' he said. 'Why are you so cold though?'

'I am always colda.'

'Perhaps you have a cold heart, that's why.'

'Per'aps, yes. All my body is cold. Always.'

'I'll give you a massage if you want, to warm you up.'

She suddenly pulled her hand away and he immediately regretted saying it. Damn, he'd gone too far, he thought, annoyed with himself. It was the alcohol. It always loosened him up. It was one of the reasons he liked it so much. But it was only a joke. If she couldn't take a joke …

'What's wrong?' he asked.

'We must not 'ave any more drinksa,' she said.

'Why not?' he asked, alarmed.

'It's too dangerous.'

'Why?'

'I don't want to fall in love.'

'Neither do I.' *Even though I'm already half in love with you.*

'I 'ad better go.' He was glad to hear her get the construction, which they had done recently in class, correct. *Had better plus zero infinitive.*

'Very good – 'I had better go'!' he congratulated her, with a shake of his index finger, but not bothering to correct her pronunciation. He found her Italian accent sexy. 'Why do you have to go? Oh, I know. Your landlady wants you home to slave over a hot ironing board while she gallivants about with one of her fancymen. Would you like to meet at the weekend? On Sunday?' He thought he'd better get it in quickly, before she ran off. It was Thursday and he didn't want to be alone again all weekend. Not again …

'Si. If you like-a.'

Thank goodness, he thought. He hadn't frightened her off. 'Can I have your phone number?'

'No!' She sounded horrified.

'What's wrong? Why not?' God, what had he said now?

'My landlady won't allow me to 'ave phone callsa.'

'Oh.' That fucking landlady! He was starting to seriously dislike her. 'Well, let me give you my phone number.' He scribbled it down on a beer mat and handed it to her. To his relief she accepted it and they went outside.

'Ciao,' she said, going. 'Thank you for the orange juice.'

'Don't forget to phone me!' he shouted after her, just as three colleagues approached the pub to go in for an afternoon bevy.

'Ah, the au pairs' delight!' declared one of them, Tony Holloway, who taught A-level history, and the others laughed good-naturedly.

He laughed himself, embarrassed, but didn't mind too much – Tony was a good fellow, he liked him, they got on well together, saw eye to eye about college politics and, indeed, world politics. Anyway, he didn't care – he had a date for the weekend, a date with a pretty, cute, sexy Italian girl. That was worth any amount of embarrassment! And he had a feeling that there would be more dates, that this was serious, that she really did like him …

Roy Bunting was in the staffroom when he arrived back for his evening class, smoking as always. He taught French and German. He dressed exactly like an old-fashioned teacher straight out of central casting: tweed jacket with leather elbow-patches, baggy grey flannel trousers shiny with wear and scuffed leather brogues. He was about fifty-five and unmarried. That was possibly because he was probably the most boring man in the world. But Frank liked him for that very reason and always made a point of being friendly, treating it as a challenge to try and find something interesting in what he had to say. Even when it was politically incorrect, as it often was. And also because other colleagues tended to avoid him and even make fun of him.

'Bertha's typically Jewish, isn't she, Frank?' he started up as soon as Frank entered the room, which was clouded with cigarette smoke, as if he had been waiting for him. 'She's just asked Catherine to type a reference at going-home time. Poor old Catherine's still at it now at five-thirty. Would you have the nerve to do that? There's no excuse for what Hitler and his cronies did to the Jews in Europe and that, but they do tend to attract a lot of this by the way they behave. I'm sorry, but I can understand it. Did you know 'h' is never not pronounced in German? Whereas the Russians have no 'h', so they pronounce it 'g', so for example they say, 'Tottengam Gotspur'. That Geoff Walker's a nice chap, but you can't push him too far. It was his decision to buy that language laboratory, but it's a bad buy in my humble. Oh, dear, this place! Life's not going to get any better here for me. It might for you, but not for me. Did you hear about the civil servant who wrote 'round objects' on some document? Explain that to your class! Of course, you'd have to explain what 'balls' means first, but it might embarrass one or two of them. That Sister Whatsername, for example. Can't understand any woman – '

'Sorry, Roy, I've got to go and do some photocopying for my evening class before the rush,' he said, cutting him off and making his escape, hoping he might be gone by the time he got back. All the time Roy had been chunnering on, he had been thinking about Cinzia, which made it bearable. But there were limits to even his patience.

He had hoped that Serena, another personable, easy-on-the-eye Italian girl, would be in class, but to his dismay she wasn't. That meant she was probably baby-sitting, so wouldn't be in the bar afterwards. He was disappointed, but it didn't matter too much. It was Cinzia he was really interested in. Anyway, Serena was with Terry, the good-looking geography student he had become friends with. And he had a date with Cinzia for Sunday to look forward to.

The town hall was a large, impressive building made of white Portland stone, set back from the main road by gently sweeping lawns and flower beds full of pretty May blooms, topped by an imposing green clock tower and fronted by an elegant fountain. Frank sat on one of the benches by the fountain at the appointed hour of three p.m., reading a paperback novel, gazing occasionally at the glittery cascade of water, the pretty flowers, the shiny building, the blue sky, and daydreaming about her and about life in general, while he waited for her. And waited. And waited …

By four p.m. she still hadn't turned up. He was seething with anger and frustration, especially because he couldn't even try to phone her, she'd refused to give him her phone number. But why hadn't she phoned him earlier, if she couldn't make it? Must be that damned landlady of hers, he thought furiously. Well, he wasn't going to wait around for her any longer. Fuck her! Fuck all of them – Marina, his Yugoslav girlfriend who'd jilted him and run off back to Yugoslavia, Mary, his wife who'd left him after nine years, Grazia, the Italian girl who'd rejected his advances last year, Sophie, the French girl he'd met on the summer school in Dublin, who'd given him the push after playing with him – and fuck this Cinzia for messing him about like this! Fuck the whole lot of them! As for Cinzia, she could fuck off! She wasn't worth it! There were plenty of other fish in the sea. He'd never speak to her again. Never mind a woman scorned – Hell had no fury like a man scorned!

There was only one thing to do, he decided angrily, jumping up and striding off, and that was to go for a drink, though he'd better not get drunk, he told himself, since he was working tomorrow. He'd go to the Robin Hood on the Marshes. A walk across the Marshes would do him good, especially on a sunny spring afternoon like this.

The Marshes were part of Lee Valley Park, a vast tract of open, semi-wild grassland on the edge of London that at this time of year would be embroidered with multi-coloured wildflowers and decorated with snowy, headily-scented, hawthorn blossom. It was intersected by the River Lea on its way down to the Thames and in the middle sat a reservoir with a little wooded island, which always reminded him of The Lake Isle of Innisfree. It was like a slice of countryside – Arcadian, bucolic, pastoral – in a London suburb, reminded him nostalgically of both the Lake District and County Cavan. Yes, it'd do him good, he told himself, to get away from buildings, traffic and the madding crowd; to smell the flowers, the grass, the earth, the river; to see the gaily-coloured houseboats and the herons, swans, mallards, coots, moorhens ...

It was a long walk from here, would probably take him an hour or more, so by the time he got to the Robin Hood he'd deserve a pint or two of his favourite tipple, he told himself, a vision of the cream-crowned, liquorice-black nectar in its glass chalice hovering like a beacon of solace before him as he strode angrily away, through the town hall gates, right along Forest Road, left at the Bell into Hoe Street, then right down the long, now-deserted market street and along Coppermill Lane, past the waterworks, past the reservoirs and across the railway level crossing onto the fields.

'What happened to you?' he asked her on the following Tuesday, trying to sound casual, though inside he was still fuming with her.

She was at the bus stop again as he had hoped. He had sworn to himself not to speak to her if she was, to walk right past her and blank her, but something about her melted his heart. She looked fragile and vulnerable, standing there on her own in the same navy-blue culottes and a sleeveless gingham blouse, with a scruffy-looking anorak around her thin shoulders. The culottes had silver buttons down the sides, he noticed. Her legs were bare as usual. Like her arms. Bare and brown. And sexy.

'I am sorry,' she said. 'I couldn't come because – '

'I know. The landlady. She wanted to go out with her boyfriend so she asked you to babysit at the last moment.' Was it possible to hate somebody you'd never even met, he wondered?

'Si. 'ow do you knowa?'

'I'm a mindreader.' He had to explain what that meant.

'So now you don't like me,' she said, forlornly. The 253 bus approached. 'I go 'ome-a.'

'You don't want to come for a drink?' he asked, swallowing his pride. He liked her too much – that was the problem!

Her eyes lit up. 'You still want to see me? You are not angry?'

'I was angry, but I'm not now, now that I've seen you. Do

you want to come?' He'd be devastated if she said no!

'I still 'aven't no money,' she said.

'It's OK, I'll put it on the bill,' he joked.

'You are too kinda, Francis,' she said.

'I know,' he laughed, delighted to hear her use his first name for the first time. 'Come on, let's go.'

They sat at the same table again, but this time next to each other on the bench, rather than opposite. It was turning into a tradition!

'You seem down,' he said, taking a first sup of Guinness with the customary gasp of pleasure.

'I am confuseda,' she said, nursing her orange juice. He still couldn't persuade her to drink anything alcoholic.

'What are you confused about?'

'I don't know whether I love Luciano or not. I 'ave been in Englanda since January to sort myself outa, but I still 'aven't.'

'If you have to ask yourself, it means you don't love him.' Of course, he had a vested interest in telling her that, but he believed it.

'You are righta,' she said, after thinking about this pearl of wisdom for a few moments. 'I can't love 'im.'

'So you should leave him,' he said.

'If I left 'im, everyone in Italy would say it was my faulta.'

'Why?'

'Lignano is a small town. Everybody knows your business. It's always the woman's faulta. Italy is a man's country. I 'ate it. I want to run away and 'ide-a.'

'Why don't you stay and hide in England then?'

She laughed. 'If I told my mama I was staying in England, she would say, "Cinzia, I am coming to get you. There is something wrong with your 'eada. You need a doctor".'

He laughed and took a swig of Guinness to fortify himself for what he was going to say. 'You can stay with me, if you want. You can be my au pair.'

To his relief she wasn't offended. 'I'll be your au pair if you 'ave one bedroom where no one can come ina.'

'Not even me?' he grinned, taking another swig of Guinness.

'No, not even you,' she smiled impishly.

'I might sneak in in the middle of the night,' he joked, even more daringly, but to his relief she didn't slap him across the face.

'Why would you want to see me in the middle of the nighta?'

'Just to say hello,' he laughed, wondering if she was really so innocent. Anyway, it was an amusing game to play with a pretty Italian girl.

'Francis, I am starting to think you are a playboy,' she remarked.

He was surprised she knew the expression. He couldn't help feeling offended too. Even if it was half-true. 'Why do you say that?' he asked.

'I know you like girlsa. I think you 'ave 'ad lots of girlfriendsa.What number am I? Twenty-nine?'

'No, fifty-nine,' he laughed, enjoying the joke, even if it wasn't entirely a joke.

'Do you bring all your girlfriends 'ere? To this seata?'

'No, I only bring very special ones to this seat,' he said. Suddenly he wanted to put his arms around her and kiss her, but didn't dare, not yet. But he could feel her leg against his, closer and closer.

'Francis, you know this is a new situation for me. I've never been in this kind of situation before.'

'What kind of situation?'

'Sitting in a pub next to my teacher. Look, the other customers – they are all watching us. They think we are lovers. It's what I would think. I would think – that couple, they must be so in love! But I'm not in love with you. Are you in love with me?' She turned her gaze on him.

'You know I'm in love with you,' he murmured, gazing back into her deep brown eyes. 'That's why I'm here with you.'

They gazed into each other's eyes for a few moments and he noticed hers moistening with tears. That was the cue for him to take her in his arms and kiss her. She let him, but after a moment or two she pulled away.

'What's wrong?' he asked.

'I can't kiss in public,' she said. 'Even though that's what I like best, kissing.'

‘Is it?’ he laughed. ‘That’s OK.’ He took her in his arms again and pressed her close to his chest, so that he could feel her breasts against it.

‘Oh, Francis, why are you so lovely?’ she asked, when he released her, gazing into his eyes again, hers still teary.

‘Am I?’ he asked, pretending to be surprised.

‘All the girls like you.’

‘Do they? Why?’ He was genuinely surprised and flattered.

‘You seem so sincere.’

‘Only “seem”?’

‘Yes. You’re so lovely on the outside, but so bad inside.’

‘You’d better escape now, while you can then,’ he laughed, letting go of her completely for a moment.

‘I can’t escape now. I’m in love with you. You know it.’

‘Me too,’ he laughed, pulling her back towards him.

‘Show me ’ow you kiss againa,’ she said.

He pressed his lips to hers, parted them gently with the tip of his tongue and their tongues touched. This time she didn’t cut it short, but seemed to melt further into his arms. While they kissed, she put one of her legs over his and he stroked the inside of her thigh. Then he moved his hand upwards and softly squeezed one of her breasts under the anorak she was still wearing around her shoulders. He could feel her nipple as stiff as he was himself. God, he wanted her! He wanted her *now*! Should he suggest she go home with him, he wondered?

‘You see,’ she said, gently breaking off the kiss. ‘I am not like other Italian girlsa. I am not so colda.’

‘You’re like a ray of sunshine,’ he said, continuing to squeeze her breast softly beneath the anorak.

‘But my ’ands are always colda,’ she said.

‘Yes, I’ve noticed,’ he said, removing his hand from her breast and holding her hand. It was like ice. ‘Let me warm it for you.’

‘I love you, Francis.’

‘I love you, too. How do you say it in Italian?’

‘Ti amo.’

‘Ti amo. It sounds better in Italian somehow.’

‘Are you sure you love me? I can’t believe it!’

‘Of course. As I said, that’s why I’m here with you.’

'I think I love you more than you love me.'

'Why do you say that?'

'I can feel it.'

'I'll prove it to you.'

''ow?'

'You tell me how.'

'Could you marry me?'

Wow, that was quick! 'Are you asking me to marry you?' he laughed, taking a swig of Guinness.

'No. I know you are marrieda already. I'm asking you if you *could* marry me.'

'I could marry you and I would marry you if I was free,' he said. Even as he said it, he felt guilty, but he *was* free, Mary had left him, even if they weren't actually divorced yet.

Then she asked him a really personal question. ''ow often do you make love with your wife-a?'

'I don't,' he laughed, embarrassed despite himself. 'I told you, she's left me.'

'But before. 'ow often?'

'I don't know – twice a week maybe,' he laughed again, taking another swig of Guinness. In fact, it wasn't true. *More like once a month. With no end product.*

'That's not often,' she commented.

'How often do you make love with Luciano?' he shrugged.

'Two or three times a nighta. Before we sleepa and when we wake up in the morninga. And sometimes 'e wakes me up in the middle of the nighta.'

'My God!'he laughed, taking another swig of Guinness to help the thought go down. 'Do you like doing it so often?' It was exciting having such an intimate conversation with a pretty Italian girl. He imagined doing it with her himself …

'Yes, I like to do it,' she said, matter-of-factly.

'We can do it this afternoon if you like,' he wanted to say, but didn't have the nerve. Anyway, although he was so excited, he wasn't sure if he wanted to actually make love with her yet. He really did want to get to know her better, to make sure he didn't hurt her. He really did care about her. He slipped his hand under her anorak and squeezed her breast gently again.

'Do you want to make love with me, Francis?' she

whispered.

'Yes, of course,' he said. 'I love you.'

'We can't do it today.'

'I know. You have to go home. Your landlady wants you.'

'Si. I am sorry.'

'It's OK. It's not important. It can wait. I'm happy just to be here with you.' Well, that was half-true, he thought.

'You know, my landlady is angry with you,' she said.

'*She* is angry with *me?*'

'Si. She is angry with you for taking me away from her. She warned me about English men.'

'Well, first I'm not strictly-speaking English. And second, you can tell her *I'm* angry with *her.*'

'I know you are Irish. Why are you angry with 'er?'

'For keeping you away from me.'

'I love you, Francis.'

'Say it in Italian.'

'Ti amo.'

'Ti amo,' he replied, pulling her close and kissing her again. Oh, God, he wanted to take her home right now!

'But you know I can't stay with you,' she said, ending the kiss. There were tears in her eyes again.

'Why not?' he asked, though he hadn't actually asked her to stay with him yet.

'I 'ave to go 'ome to Italy. And when I go 'ome to Italy, I will go to my bedroom and cry-a.'

'Cry? For me?' he asked, wiping away the tears from her cheeks with his finger.

'Not only for you. For London. But for you as well. I'm not ashamed to admit it. Then I will go to the beach, swim out, lie on a lilo and dream about you, my English dreama.'

This touching, romantic little speech filled him with a mixture of pleasure, because she seemed to genuinely like him so much, and sadness, because it seemed that he wouldn't be able to keep her. He wondered if he should end it now, before it had properly begun, to minimise any grief to both of them. Yes, that's what he'd say, he decided – *let's end it now, let's not go any further* – and took a slug of Guinness to fortify himself. But when he opened his mouth, something else came out instead: 'I'll follow you to Italy.'

And maybe I will. It might not just be romantic bullshit. I'm really starting to think I love this girl. It's serious. I think I've really got the bug. How ironic! I thought we'd just have a bit of fun with each other and then say arrivederci.

'You will come to Italy for me?'

'If you want me to.'

'But you 'ave your wife 'ere, your job 'ere.'

'My wife and I are finished,' he said, with a spasm of pain. 'But my job – well, I could get a job in Italy, I suppose.'

'Oh, Francis, I love you, but it's not possibile.'

'Why not?' He was crestfallen, even though he knew himself it wasn't really practical.

'I will 'ave to marry Luciano.'

'What, even though you don't love him?'

'I will 'ave no choice-a. My parents, everybody expect it. I will 'ave no choice-a.'

'That's very sad,' he said, writhing inwardly – she might as well have stuck a dagger into him.

'But you can come to Italy to see me.'

'You mean when you're seventy?' he laughed ruefully.

'No, not when I'm seventy. It doesn't matter if I'm marrieda. You can still come to see me.'

'Luciano might not like that!'

''e will 'ave no choice-a.'

'I don't know about that,' he said, shaking his head. 'So you're going to marry him?'

'I will come to London, too,' she said. 'I love London. I am free in London. I am independent. I 'ave sorted myself out 'ere. I know I don't love Luciano. I don't want to go back. Too many responsibilities.' A tear rolled down both of her cheeks.

'Don't worry,' he said softly, brushing the tears away with a finger. 'You can stay here with me if you want. I'll look after you.'

'I want to stay with you for ever,' she said with a little sob.

'You can if you want,' he said. 'For ever starts now.' He looked at his watch. 'One thirty-seven precisely, Wednesday the twenty-sixth of May, nineteen eighty-two. The Bell Pub,

Forest Road, Walthamstow, London E17. We have to remember this moment for ever too.'

'One thirty-seven! I 'ave to go! I 'ave to be 'ome at two o'clock!' she exclaimed, letting go of him and jumping up.

'That's not very romantic!' he laughed, standing up. *That bloody landlady of hers!*

'Shall I go to the bus stop with you?' he offered, outside the pub.

'No – I think it's better if people don't see us together,' she said. 'People will talka.'

'Yes, I suppose so,' he agreed, reluctantly. He didn't want to let her go though. He couldn't bear the thought of not seeing her again for twenty-four hours. Suddenly he couldn't be happy without her. He was in love, to his own surprise! It was like a fever …

'Ciao,' he said, giving her a peck on the cheek.

'Ti amo,' she smiled wistfully, turned and hurried off.

CHAPTER THREE

'That woman. Honestly, if she dropped dead tomorrow, I'd breathe a sigh of relief. I wish someone would put a bullet in her head. I might do it myself one of these days. I've still got a weapon from when I was in the paras. Got no ammo though, that's the trouble. Need a fucking elephant gun for her anyway.'

Frank laughed. Mark, a hard-nut South African ex-paratrooper, was talking in the staffroom about their boss, Bertha, whom nobody liked much. For one thing, she was always asking you to do her work for her, with the excuse that she was so busy. Only yesterday, she had said to him when they were invigilating an exam: 'Frank, would you mind hanging on here alone, so I can go and get on with some admin work?'

'OK, Bertha,' he had said, through gritted teeth. He was in a benevolent mood because Cinzia was doing the exam and they were exchanging secret glances. But he was still irritated.

'I had to give her a bollocking myself the other day,' Chris Hanson said. 'Gave her a metaphorical knee in the goolies.' Chris was a short, softly-spoken, mild-mannered chap – Frank couldn't imagine him giving even a teddy bear a kick in the goolies.

'I'm furious with her,' Geoff Walker chirped up. 'She left the staffroom door open the other day and all my keys were stolen. I had to pay twenty-five quid for a new barrel on my front door and get the car locks changed. That's going to cost nearly a hundred quid. Have to go to the garage tomorrow to collect it, but she's asked me to teach a class for her. I will, only so as not to let the students down.'

'The woman's fucking impossible,' Chris said.

'She's certainly a pain in the arse,' Frank said.

'And this EFL's a load of horse shit,' Mark said. 'I've got to get out. Do something meaningful. Something with content.'

'Such as?' he laughed, only slightly offended by Mark's estimation of his chosen profession, since he half-agreed.

'I've started a degree in psychology at the Open University,' Mark informed him.

'Interesting,' Frank commented.

'Only thing I like about EFL is the women,' Mark observed.

'That's true,' he laughed, thinking happily of Cinzia.

'You screwing any of them?' Mark enquired.

'Not at the moment,' he laughed, thinking again of Cinzia.

He hadn't 'screwed' her yet, as Mark in his laddish way put it, but he was hoping to later. Not that he saw her as just a potential 'screw'. He really loved her, he had decided. But love was something he knew Mark didn't believe in from previous conversations. For Mark 'love' was just 'mutual need fulfilment'. Or as he had summed it up once: 'You lend me your crotch, I'll lend you mine.'

'Anyone in your sights?' Mark asked.

'There's this Italian one I quite fancy,' he said, cautiously – he didn't want Mark to pour any cold water on his ardour.

'I haven't had a woman for months,' Mark moaned. 'I'm going crazy with frustration. I've almost wanked my dick off. Might just go out and rape one tonight.'

'Nobody in your class you fancy?' Frank laughed.

'There are plenty I fancy, but they don't seem to reciprocate,' Mark said bitterly.

'Maybe you're not romantic enough,' he was tempted to say, but bit his tongue, even though it was probably true, because Mark was quite good-looking physically – short but muscular, with a leathery, tanned complexion and rugged features. However, the bull neck and shaved head made him look somewhat menacing.

'Maybe you need to soft-soap them a bit more,' he risked saying.

'I know where I'd like to put some soap,' Mark riposted in his usual cynical way. 'Trouble is I can't get near one of them.'

'I think they're probably afraid of you,' Frank suggested. He was a bit afraid of Mark himself – you wouldn't want to get on the wrong side of him. He could probably kill you with one chop of his hand …

'Afraid of little old *me*?' Mark said in mock-surprise. 'I'm a teddy bear.'

Frank laughed. 'Anyway, I've got to go. I'm meeting her now.'

'The Italian one?'

'Yeah.' He wasn't sure he wanted Mark to know.

'You jammy bastard. Give her one for me. And ask her if she's got a sister.'

'What are you doing this evening?' he laughed.

'Going to see if I can find some ammo somewhere. Put a bullet in Bertha's head. Then maybe one in my own if I don't find a woman soon.'

Frank laughed nervously, opening the door to leave. He didn't like Mark much, but enjoyed his company, because he was so amusingly acerbic, cynical and unsentimental.

'Hello, old chap! Your associate lectureship go through all right?' Dr. Stewart Mackay enquired, passing by in the corridor as he was closing the door behind him. Stewart was Scottish, but you would never have known it from his English public school voice and manners.

'Oh, hello, Stewart. Yes, thanks. Didn't enjoy the interview with Jack Fullofhimself though. He's a pompous prat, isn't he?' He was referring to the college principal. 'I heard him actually say on the phone to somebody during my interview, "The tragedy is, this has been forced on us." Can you believe it?'

'Oh, don't worry about him – he's just a jumped up yobbo,' Stewart commented, to his amusement. 'Anyway, have a jolly weekend. Toodle-pip!'

He had arranged to meet her in the Chequers, a pub half-way down Walthamstow market – there was too much chance of being seen by colleagues in the Bell, he had decided. He didn't want Tony Holloway bursting in and announcing to all and sundry, 'Ah, the au pairs' delight!', amusing and flattering as it was and much as he liked Tony. Also, the Chequers was on the way home, so they wouldn't have quite so far to walk. That was, if she agreed to go home with him …

When he got to the pub, she was already there, sitting at a

table, writing in what looked like a diary. She was wearing a black dress, in which she looked very fetching. When she saw him, she smiled, a smile that made his heart flutter. He smiled back at her and without speaking sat beside her, took her in his arms and kissed her, the tips of their tongues touching playfully. Shakin' Stevens was on the jukebox, singing 'This Ole House'.

'They're watching us,' she said, ending the kiss.

'It doesn't matter,' he said. There were only two or three old codgers in the bar this early and nobody he knew.

'It's awful,' she said, drooping a bare leg over his thigh.

'I know, it's disgraceful,' he grinned, pulling her close and kissing her again. To his relief, she didn't resist.

While he kissed her, he caressed her thigh, letting his hand go just a little bit under the dress. Then he moved his hand to her breast and squeezed it, but she pulled it away.

'Francis, they are watchinga,' she said. 'Not 'ere.'

'OK,' he agreed, frustrated, taking hold of her hand, which was cold as usual. 'Can we go somewhere else later though?' He had to have her tonight, he thought. And try to make her his.

'Where shall we go?' she asked, ingenuously.

'To a night club?'

'What night cluba?'

'A night club called "My Flat",' he joked.

'OK, but just to see it,' she said, teasingly.

'Of course,' he said. 'Let's get something to drink? Will you drink something alcoholic today?'

To his delight, she agreed, so he went to the bar and came back with the ritual pint of Guinness for himself and half a pint for her. It was time to start educating her taste buds, he decided.

'Ugh, it's disgusting!' she spluttered, when she tasted it.

'I know it is first time,' he laughed. 'You have to practise. It's what we call an acquired taste. I'll get you something sweeter next time.'

'No, I want to learna.'

'Good girl!' God, he was in love big time! If she took to Guinness, they could be drinking companions as well as lovers!

'Now, can I ask you some questions?' he said.

'What do you want to ask me abouta?'

'About everything. Your family, for example. One of my colleagues wants to know if you have a sister.'

'Why?'

'I told him I was going to meet a pretty, sexy Italian girl today and he asked me to ask her if she had a sister. I think he's a bit lonely. He's not married and he's got no girlfriend.'

She told him she had one sister who was 'very nice', but she was only sixteen, so 'too young' – not that that would stop Mark, knowing him, he reflected wryly.

'Have you got any brothers?'

'No. The only man in my family is my father.'

'What's he like?'

'What does it mean?'

'It means, tell me about him.'

'My father used to be very 'arda, very jealous of me, when I was thirteen, fourteen. But 'e is OK nowa.'

'I don't blame him being jealous. What about your mama?'

'My mama is very kind and very sweeta, but she is too – 'ow do you say ..?'

'Too protective?'

'Si. She always wants me to be with 'er. Never to go anywhere. She tried to stop me coming to Englanda. She fought me so 'arda.'

'I'm glad you came.'

'I am 'appy too, because I 'ave met you. My baby.'

He laughed uncomfortably at the expression, which no girl had ever used to him before.

'Now I ask you some questionsa,' she said.

'OK, fire away,' he agreed, taking a swig of Guinness.

'Why are you unfaithful to your wife-a?'

'I'm not unfaithful. She's left me. I told you.' He was a bit irked by the question, but tried not show it.

'She left you because you were unfaithful. Because you are a bad boya.'

'Maybe I am a bad 'boya',' he laughed, imitating her accent. 'But she was unfaithful to me once.' He was thinking of the time Mary had publicly taken sides against him in a meeting of the summer school staff in Dublin. That had hurt him as much as if she had had it off with another man – not that he could imagine her ever doing that.

'She 'ad a boyfrienda?'

'I don't want to talk about her, to be honest.'

She could see that he was upset, so didn't pursue it. 'My poor baby,' she crooned, stroking his face. 'I think you need a lot of love-a.'

'Why do you say that?' he asked, impressed by her perspicacity.

'I just feel it,' she replied. 'I don't knowa. I feel you 'ave been very 'urt in life some'ow. Like something 'appened to you. Are you going to tell me?'

'It's a long story,' he said, quaffing some Guinness. 'I don't really want to talk about it now. Any more questions?'

'OK. What do you like doing best in your free time-a?'

He laughed – it was a question he often asked students in class, when he was 'interviewing' them. Just the other day, a sexy French girl had answered, 'Going to bed with my boyfriend,' to everyone's hilarity, but he resisted making the obvious joke. 'Writing, I suppose,' he answered, truthfully.

'Yes, I think you are some kind of intellectual,' she said.

'I don't know about that,' he laughed, but couldn't help feeling slightly flattered. Women were always impressed if you told them you wrote, he had noticed. And rightly so, perhaps.

'What do you write-a?' she asked.

'Novels mainly. And poetry sometimes, too.'

'Are you going to write about me-a?'

'Maybe, one day, if you're good,' he teased. 'I'll write a poem for you anyway.'

'I will be so 'appy if you write a poem for me. Nobody 'as ever wrote a poem for me before. It will my first time-a.'

'Written is the past participle,' he corrected her, playing teacher. 'I don't believe it. There must have been lots of boys who fell in love with you at school and wrote poems for you. A pretty, sexy girl like you.'

'Nobody 'as done that.'

'Luciano?'

'Luciano could never write a poema,' she laughed emptily. ''e never says or writes anythinga.'

'Well, I'll write one for you,' he said, giving her a hug and kissing her on the forehead.

'Oh, Francis, my baby, I love you so much, I don't know what to do now,' she said. 'I never wanted it to 'appen, but it 'as 'appened. I can't 'elp it. I'm in love with my teacher.' There were tears in her eyes, tears of happiness he hoped.

'And I'm in love with my student,' he smiled, wiping her tears away from both cheeks with a finger.

'I never want to leave you, but I will 'ave to leave you,' she cried.

'Ssh, don't think about that,' he whispered, kissing her on the ear, where he noticed she had a small mole. 'Let's just enjoy the present and not worry about the future.' He wasn't sure if it was good advice really, but it suited the moment. 'Do you want another drink?'

'I want to go.'

'Where?'

'To the nightclub called My Flata.'

'OK, let's go,' he said. It was what he had hoped she might say.

'But only to see it,' she smiled impishly.

'Of course, only to see it,' he laughed, pulling her up from the seat. 'Come on, let's go.'

He had intended to walk home across the Marshes, which would have been romantic on such a sunny May evening, but decided it would take too long, so they took the train. She was worried about how she would get home. He told her he'd get a taxi for her. He asked her if she wanted something to eat – fish and chips for example. There was a good chippy near his place.

'I'm not 'ungry,' she said. 'I'm too nervous. Too tight in my tummy.'

He laughed at the expression, which he supposed came from Italian. He was glad she didn't want anything – it would give them more time together. He was too nervous to eat himself.

When they entered the flat, she went straight into the room he used as a study.

''ave you read all these booksa?' she asked.

'Most of them,' he shrugged.

'I think you are definitely some kind of intellectual.'

'I don't know about that,' he laughed, amused but flattered again, leading her by the hand into the living room. 'Would you like a drink?' he asked

'I'm all right, grazie,' she said and started looking at the postcards on the mantelpiece. 'Are they from all your girlfriendsa?'

'Some of them,' he grinned, standing behind her with his arms around her waist, cupping her breasts and squeezing them softly.

'You 'ave a girlfriend in Bolzano?' she asked, picking one up.

'No, she's just an ex-student from a couple of years ago,' he said, taking it off her and replacing it, secretly annoyed with himself for not removing such 'incriminating evidence', hoping it wouldn't upset her. In fact, it was from Grazia, the Italian girl he had been crazy about last year, but who had rejected his advances, so he wasn't telling a lie, or only a half-lie.

'It's all right, my baby,' she said. 'I know you like girlsa. I don't minda. I'm not jealous.'

'You've got nothing to be jealous of,' he said, taking her by the hand and leading her to the settee. 'Let's sit down, shall we?'

He sat on the settee, pulled her gently down beside him, put his arms around her and they kissed, a long, slow, leisurely kiss, tongues touching, hands caressing each other.

'Baby, I'm too warma,' she said after a while.

'I'll open the window more,' he said, standing up and doing so. It was a hot, sunny evening, the bright orange sun beaming straight into the top-floor flat from just above the City skyline a few miles away.

'Is that better?' he asked, sitting down beside her again, whereupon to his surprise she stood up and sat straddling him.

'Do you really love me, Francis?' she asked, looking straight into his eyes.

'Yes, I love you,' he said, kissing her face and slipping his hands under her dress.

'I'm still too warma,' she said. 'Take my dress offa, please.'

He didn't need to be asked twice. He pushed it up and pulled it off over her head. Her body was beautifully tanned all over and she was wearing red, sexy, 'baby doll' underwear.

'You're beautiful,' he said, caressing and kissing her greedily, while she held his shoulders.

He placed his hands on her breasts, fondled them for a while, then started to take her bra off.

'That's enough, baby,' she said, trying to stop him, but she didn't try very hard and soon her breasts were bare. She tried to cover them with her arms, but he gently pulled them away and kissed them tenderly.

Her nipples were very brown, he noticed with surprise, just like the rest of her body. She must do a lot of sunbathing, he supposed, rubbing the nipples, stiff and hard, as he was himself, between his fingers, then pulling her towards him so that he could suck them. While he did so, she grabbed his hair and started moaning softly.

After a while, he slipped his hands under her French-style knickers. He noticed she was wet, as he was himself. He tried to pull her knickers off, so she stood up to help him and he did so, so that she was now completely naked. He put his hand on her buttocks, pulled her naked body towards him and planted kisses on her brown belly.

'Francis, aren't you warma?' she asked, after a while.

'Mmm, yes,' he murmured and to his delight she started to undress him, pulling off his trousers and underpants, then kneeling in front of him, taking him in her hand, kissing and licking him …

'Do you like him?' he asked.

'Si. I love 'eem. 'e ees so biga. 'as he got a name-a?'

'Yes, Fred,' he said off the top of his head, laughing.

'Do you like thees?' Her tongue was licking his cock as if it were an ice cream, a cornetto perhaps, while she held it between her sexy fingers.

'Oh, yes!' he gasped. 'Do you want to suck it?'

'Ugh! I don't do that!' she exclaimed, taking her mouth away and spitting.

'It's OK,' he laughed, grabbing her and pulling her down onto the settee with him, where they started to make love properly, exploring each other's bodies with their hands, caressing, kissing, squeezing … When they were both ready, she sat on top of him and started to push him inside her.

'Is it safe?' he asked, hesitating.

'Yes, my baby, tonight it's safe, yes, yes, yes, I want you inside of me,' she declared.

He pushed himself all the way in and she started bouncing up and down on top of him, yelping with pleasure.

'Can they hear me?' she asked, stopping suddenly, referring he supposed to the neighbours.

'No, don't worry, it's all right,' he assured her – as if he cared – and they carried on until until she let out a long, loud squeal of ecstasy and collapsed onto him.

'Did you come already?' he whispered in her ear, stroking her hair, her back, her bum.

'Yes, baby,' she whispered, stroking his face. 'Ti amo.'

'Ti amo too.'

'Did *you* come, baby?' she asked, putting her hand on his still erect cock and starting to massage it.

'Not yet,' he murmured, having struggled to restrain himself, but hardly able to do so any longer.

'Do you want it like this?' she asked, moving her hand up and down faster and faster.

'Yes, please,' he gasped and came almost immediately in a convulsion of pleasure mixed with joy, joy that he was with her, that he had found her, that he had found love again.

Afterwards, she wiped some of his semen up with her finger and held it to her nose, sniffing it, to his amusement. Then she put her finger into her mouth, licked it and swallowed it.

'What are you doing?' he laughed.

'I want you inside me,' she said. 'I want all the little baby Francises inside me.'

'Funny girl,' he laughed, pulling her back down onto him and kissing and caressing her joyfully. *God, she's wonderful! I'm so lucky. But I deserve a bit of luck. I deserve something good.*

'Where is your wife-a?' she asked, a few minutes later, to his discomfort, spoiling his mood somewhat.

'I don't know,' he replied. 'I don't want to talk about her.' Why was she so interested? Did she feel guilty about having sex with him, because he was still technically married? Why did she ask that right now? Because she thought he would be off his guard, having just made love?

'Why are you unfaithful, my baby?' she asked, stroking his face.

'You asked me that before,' he smiled, trying not to be annoyed, not to let it spoil the mood. 'For experience maybe.'

'But now you are experienced enougha. You should stop nowa. You should change-a. You know enougha. You're clever enougha. You are a playboya. You play with love-a.'

He couldn't really be annoyed, even though it was annoying, because she was caressing his body tenderly as she said it.

'You're making one mistake, my little Italian mouse,' he smiled indulgently at her.

'What ees eet?'

'You're confusing love with sex.'

'Oh, yes, I am,' she smiled back, kissing him eagerly. 'You are righta. You are too clever for me!'

'You don't think I'm playing with you, do you?' he asked, pleased with himself at having outsmarted her.

'I don't know, Francis. I don't really know you. I 'ope not. I think you are different from other men. I 'ope so.'

'Listen, Cinzia,' he said, seriously, kissing and caressing her, deciding it was time to straighten this out once and for all, it was time for a little speech. 'You may think I'm a playboy. I know some people think that about me. Colleagues at work, for example. There's one colleague who always calls me "the au pairs' delight". I let them think it. It amuses me and flatters me. But I'm not really. I know a lot of the girls like me, partly just because I'm the teacher, and a good teacher, but I don't chase them. I mean, I don't have sex with them. I may flirt with them, that's all. You may think I'm playing with you. You may think I'm going to have some fun with you, then throw you away and move on to another girl. But I'm not. I'm serious about love. Love is serious. I'm serious about *you*. I don't just want to have sex with you – though it's great, it was great. I love you and I want you to stay with me. I want you to stay with me for ever. I'm looking for a girl for ever. Not just for one night. If you stay with me, I promise I'll love you for ever. And I'll be faithful to you.'

'Oh, my baby, I love you!' she exclaimed, kissing him all over his face passionately. 'But you know I can't stay with you. I can't stay in Englanda. I want to stay with you, but I can'ta.' Then she started crying.

'Don't cry,' he said softly, kissing her tears away. 'Don't worry about it. Let's just enjoy it while we can. The future will take care of itself.'

'I love you, I love you, I love you.'

'Can you stay with me tonight at least?' he asked, unhopefully.

'Oh, baby, I can't, I 'ave to go 'ome-a. She will be waiting for me. I 'ave to work tomorrow morninga. What time ees eeta?'

'Nearly eleven o'clock,' he said, checking his watch.

'Oh, God, she will be worrying. 'ow will I get 'ome-a?' She jumped up and started dressing.

'I'll call a cab,' he said, disappointed. 'Don't worry, I'll pay for it.'

'She will pay for it,' she said.

'Don't be silly – I'll pay for it,' he insisted, getting dressed himself and dialling the number.

They went downstairs to wait for it. When it arrived, he gave her a last big hug and she got in. He offered her a five-pound note to pay for it, but she refused, so he threw it in and closed the door. He noticed the cab driver smirking, but didn't mind.

'Call me tomorrow,' he ordered, miming a telephone call through the cab window.

'Si. Ti amo,' she mouthed back at him.

'Ti amo,' he said, blowing her a kiss as the cab moved off and out of the estate, leaving him in freefall from ecstasy to agony until he saw her again.

CHAPTER FOUR

Next morning he was writing on the balcony of his flat, enjoying the sun and entertaining pleasant memories of the night before with Cinzia, when the phone rang. He ignored it, not wanting to be disturbed, but it rang several times and kept ringing. In the end, he climbed back into the living-room through the window and answered it. To his surprise, it was Cinzia.

'Where are you?' he asked.

'I am near you,' she said.

'What do you mean?' Alarm bells started ringing in his head.

'I am in the phone box near the traffic lightsa. My landlady is angry with you for keeping me out last nighta.'

'Your landlady hasn't thrown you out, has she?' he asked, seriously alarmed now.

'No, I ran away from 'er because she was shouting at me.'

'Oh, dear. You should go back. You can't afford to lose your job. Go back and say you're sorry.'

'Do you want to 'ave lunch with me?'

'Er, I'm a bit busy,' he stalled – he hated being interrupted when he was writing or doing anything for that matter. Even by a sexy Italian girl!

'Don't you want to see me?' she asked, and he could hear the hurt in her voice. 'If you don't, it's all righta. I'll go back 'ome-a.'

'No, it's all right, darling,' he said, sorry for having sounded so hard. 'Of course I want to see you. It's just that I was in the middle of something. Give me – give me a few minutes and I'll come and meet you. Wait downstairs.'

'OK. It's a nice area.' She pronounced it 'aria'. 'I'll go for a walk first and look arounda.'

When he met her, at the entrance to the estate, she was wearing the same dress as yesterday and a purple, hairy, woolly cardigan. Her auburn hair looked unkempt, he noticed, with a cheap-looking plastic hairband on it. She had a packet of Farley's Rusks in her hand and was eating one.

'You wanta?' she offered him one.

'They're for babies,' he laughed, giving her a kiss and a hug.

'You are my baby,' she said.

'No, thanks, I haven't had one of those for over thirty years,' he shook his head. 'Shall we go for a walk?'

'I'm so 'ungry.'

'We can have lunch in a pub. Come on.'

He took her to the Robin Hood. It was his favourite pub, because it had a panoramic view over the river and Marshes, and though a bit scruffy inside was decked out with nautical memorabilia, such as ships' helms, oars, anchors, portholes, lifebelts, fishing nets and even a racing skiff hanging from the ceiling, all of which he found appealing. He sat her at one of the tables on the patio, then bought two pints of Guinness and a ham sandwich for her, a cheese for himself – he had decided to go completely vegetarian.

''ow much do I owe you?' she asked, pouncing on the sandwich.

'You don't owe me anything, you silly girl,' he laughed. 'I love you. Maybe a kiss later ha ha.'

'I love you, too, my baby. But I think you are mada.'

'Why do you say that?' he laughed again, taking a first quaff of the black nectar.

'Your ideas are mada. We are both mada. For doing this.'

'You mean, for being in love with each other?'

'Si. You are marrieda and I will 'ave to go back to Italy and marry Luciano.'

'Hey, I keep telling you, my wife has left me. We're getting divorced. So I'm free.' As always, it pained him to say it, and the thought of Mary made him feel guilty, even though in his mind their split wasn't entirely his fault. 'If I wasn't free, I wouldn't be here with you. I wouldn't have been with you last night.' He wasn't sure how true that was, but wanted to believe it.

'I am not free-a,' she sighed.

'Why not?'

'When I go 'ome-a, I will 'ave to marry 'im. It's like, you know, arranged marriage. It's like I am a prisoner. But I want to be free-a. I want to decide for myselfa. I want to be myselfa.'

'You must,' he said, putting his arm around her. 'It'd be a mistake not to decide for yourself. You may please other people in the short term, but you will both be unhappy in the long term.'

'I know, my baby. You are righta.'

'I know it's a painful decision, but it's necessary, like surgery sometimes. You've got two basic choices. You can go home or you can stay here. You can stay with me if you want. I'll help you. I'll look after you. I love you.'

'I feel so 'appy with you, Francis. You are so understanding, so intelligent. I wish you could come to Lignano.'

'I don't think I'd be very welcome there!'

'No, you wouldn't, my baby. Except to me. I 'ave made a big mistake falling in love with you. Now when I think of going back, I feel so depresseda. When I think of Luciano, I feel like crying! 'e is too quieta. 'e never wants to do anythinga. 'e never speaks to me. Not like you.'

'Does he drink?'

'No, 'e thinks it's bada. 'e thinks everything is bada. 'e doesn't do anythinga.'

'He seems to like making love,' he chuckled.

'Si. But even then 'e is not romantic. Not like you.'

'You think I'm romantic?' He didn't really think of himself as 'romantic', but perhaps he underestimated himself.

'Si. You talk to me. Even when we were making love last nighta, you talked to me. You tell me things.'

He couldn't quite remember what if anything he'd said to her while they were making love, but he was happy to hear it and added it to his list of points under 'How To Please Women', which so far read: 1. Flatter them. 2. Make them laugh. 3. Buy them presents and now 4. Talk to them.

'I only really like talking when I have a drink,' he said, which was true. 'So I'd better get another beer if you want me to keep talking. Do you want one?'

'Francis, you spend too much money on beer,' she admonished him.

'Cinzia, can I ask you something?' he said, seriously.

'Yes, baby?' she said, startled.

'How do you think I managed my life before I met you?'

For a moment she thought he really was serious, but then, to his relief, she laughed and kissed him. 'I love you,' she said.

He went to the bar and bought himself a second pint of Guinness. It wasn't his habit to drink during the day, certainly not more than a pint, but he was enjoying himself too much to resist a second one. After all, he assuaged his conscience, it wasn't every day you could have a drink and a chat with a pretty Italian girl, knowing you would probably spend the rest of the afternoon making love with her, if you played your cards right. Carpe diem! Carpe potationem!

'Do you bring all your girls 'ere too?' she asked, as he took a first sup of Guinness. She was still working on hers.

'Only very special ones,' he joked, licking the froth from his moustache.

'You are such a bad boy,' she laughed, kissing him. 'But you make me 'appy.' She put one of her legs over his and he secretly stroked the inside of her thigh under the table.

'Did I make you happy last night?' he asked, mischievously.

'It was the 'appiest night of my life-a,' she said, kissing him.

'So I've got the job?'

'Maybe,' she laughed. 'Were you 'appy?'

'Very, but I think we need some more practice, don't you?'

'When?' she laughed, kissing him again.

'This afternoon? You don't have to go back yet, do you?'

'I won't go 'ome until midnighta. I don't want to see 'er.'

'So we've got all afternoon and all evening to practise. Great! I love you.' He kissed her, continuing to caress her thigh under the table, and their tongues met, sending ripples of unbearable desire through him. He could hardly wait to make love to her again.

'Can I ask you a question, Francis?' she said, eventually.

'Yes, my little Italian mouse,' he agreed, kissing her nose, her ear, her head, her neck, expecting something personal, private, intimate, romantic …

'What is your favourite animal?'

'That's a strange question!' he laughed.

'Answer it, baby,' she ordered.

'The horse, I suppose,' he said.

'Good boy,' she said.

'So it's the right answer?' he grinned.

'Why?' she demanded, ignoring his question.

'Why the horse?' he repeated. 'Because horses are big. Strong. Fast. Handsome.'

'Ti amo.'

'And they only eat grass,' he added. 'Which is why I've decided to go vegetarian myself. I want to be big, strong, fast and handsome.' He laughed.

'You are already 'andsome,' she said. 'And biga.'

'Carry on,' he joked. 'Don't stop there.'

'Oh, I love you so much, my big baby,' she said, laying her head on his chest.

'I love you too,' he said, kissing the top of her head and stroking her hair, which seemed to have reddish highlights in it.

Ah, this is the life, he thought! When he was an old man, he'd probably remember this afternoon as one of the happiest of his life. Should he tell her that, he wondered? It was a rather odd thought perhaps. But yes, he decided, he should tell her – women liked you to talk to them, to tell them things, especially personal, private, intimate things …

'When I'm an old man,' he started, but she interrupted him.

'Don't talk about being old, Francis,' she said.

'Why not?' he laughed – that idea had misfired somewhat! 'We all grow old one day. If we're lucky.'

'Yes, but I don't want to think about it,' she said.

'Why not?'

'When you are old, you can't enjoy yourself.'

'That depends,' he shrugged. 'I suppose you can't enjoy certain things any more. Sex for example, maybe.'

'You can't enjoy anythinga,' she insisted. 'Our bodies are like machines. They grow old, they break down – '

'And then we die.' It *was* a depressing thought.

'I don't want to talk about dying.'

'Sex and death,' he laughed. 'Two of the most interesting

subjects in the world!'

'My grandfather died last year.'

'Did he?' He hoped he hadn't touched a raw nerve. 'Did you love him?'

'I 'ated 'im.'

'You *hated* him?' He was shocked. 'Why?'

''e tried to stop me coming to Englanda. 'e tried to make me to marry Luciano. Once I wanted to punch 'im, I was so angry with 'im! I wanted to kill 'im!'

'I'm glad you didn't,' he laughed nervously, not sure how serious she was.

'Why are you glada?'

'You'd be in prison now.'

'I wanted to kill myself, too, I was so fed up with life-a.'

'Well, I'm glad you didn't,' he said again, hugging her tight, shocked, starting to realise how depressed she seemed to have been, excited but also worried to think that now perhaps her happiness depended on him.

'Why?' she asked, looking up at him.

'Because now you'd be in Heaven,' he laughed, trying to lighten the conversation a little. 'And I don't think they'll let me in there! So I'd never have met you!'

'Pah!' she exclaimed. 'I don't believe in 'eaven.'

'You don't? Neither do I.'

''eaven must be 'ere on eartha.'

'I agree,' he said.

'And 'ell is 'ere on eartha.'

'Yes,' he agreed. 'But let's concentrate on Heaven, shall we? This is Heaven for me. Being here with you.' *Talk to them. Flatter them.* But it wasn't just flattery – he meant it. He really would remember this afternoon for ever. 'Shall we go?' he suggested, finishing off his pint, resisting the temptation to have a third and knowing she wouldn't let him anyway.

'Where?' she asked.

'Let's go for a walk on the field over there,' he suggested. 'Then we can go back to a very good nightclub I know. If you want.'

'I want to go everywhere with you, Francis,' she smiled, kissing him.

‘Come on then,’ he said, gently removing her leg from his lap, taking her hand and pulling her to her feet.

They strolled upriver along the towpath, arms around each other’s waists, admiring the wildfowl and long, gaily-coloured houseboats as they went. He taught her some new words, such as ‘swan’, ‘goose’ and ‘coot’ and the expression ‘as bald as a coot’. He grabbed her and pretended to throw her into the water, making her shriek with terror. At the metal footbridge by the marina – a word he didn’t need to teach her – they crossed to the other side of the river and wandered into one of the meadows where the grass wasn’t too high, but high enough to give them seclusion from the few other people around.

The sun was still hot, but there was a lively, cool, susurrant breeze blowing through the poplars, making them sway sensuously. He sat down and invited her to sit beside him, but instead she suddenly started throwing grass and flowers at him and ran away laughing merrily. She must be slightly drunk on her pint of Guinness, he thought, jumping up, chasing her, catching her and pulling her down, so that they both fell onto the grass laughing. Then he pushed her over his knee and pretended to spank her.

‘This is what happens to naughty au pairs!’ he laughed, excited by her sexy bum, wondering if he *was* in Heaven.

‘Stopa! Stopa!’ she shouted, giggling, but made no attempt to escape, obviously enjoying the game.

‘That will do for now,’ he said, eventually stopping, unable to bear the excitement any longer, in danger of coming.

She rolled away from him, sat up and removed her sandals, so that her feet and her legs were bare. For some reason the sight of her bare legs and feet excited him so much that he had to look away. Well, they were shapely and beautifully tanned.

‘Ti amo,’ he murmured, taking her in his arms, kissing her and slowly pulling her down into the long grass …

A couple of hours later, they went back to his flat and made love properly on the settee.

‘Fred is very biga,’ she commented, as soon as he undressed. ‘And weta. Why?’

'He wants to go in,' he said.

'Where?'

'Into you. Can he?'

'Why not?'

'Is it safe?'

''ave you got an envelope?'

'A condom? Yes. Do we need one?'

'It's better, baby.'

He went into the study to fetch one and she followed him, both of them naked.

'Why must I always follow you, Francis?' she asked, her arms around him.

'Maybe you think I'm going to run away,' he laughed.

They went back to the settee and he tried to put the condom on, but kept losing his erection.

'Can I 'elpa?' she said, taking hold of Fred and doing so.

Eventually they got the condom on and he tried to enter her from above, but he kept losing his erection and the sheath kept coming off. He'd had too much sex lately, he decided – more than usual, anyway. However, she didn't seem to mind and kept encouraging him, caressing him and trying different positions. Eventually, he was able to do it by entering her from behind and came all too quickly.

'Are you all right?' he asked, kissing her, worried that she didn't seem to have enjoyed it as much as last night.

'Yes, my baby,' she crooned. 'I am very 'appy. I 'ave never done it like that before.'

'No?' He was genuinely surprised, because she seemed very uninhibited sexually, more than he. But that wasn't surprising, he told himself, considering his background.

'Luciano never does it like that.'

'Doesn't he?' he asked, fondling and kissing her breasts. He wasn't sure if he wanted to hear any more about Luciano's sexual habits or indeed any of his habits, but they did have a morbid fascination for him.

''e always does it the same way. We never even see each other, because always the light must be outa. And 'e never kisses me or speaks to me. Not like you.'

He was almost starting to feel sorry for poor old Luciano,

but at the same time pleased that he seemed so inadequate.

'Maybe he doesn't really love you,' he suggested, cautiously.

'I know 'e loves me, but 'e doesn't know 'ow to show it. Not like you. Already you 'ave given me so much, Francis. I 'ave learnt so much from you. I don't agree with all your ideas, but I 'ave learnt so much from you. I understand you, why you think like that. You are my 'ero. But I think you 'ave read too many books. You should burn them! When you were young, a child, you must 'ave been so simple and lovely. Now you are lovely, but bad too, because of books, ideas. Did you get married in churcha?'

'Of course,' he said. 'She was a Catholic. I used to be a Catholic.' If only she knew, he thought! He hadn't told her about his shady past as a seminarian yet. I *used to be* a Catholic*?* God, it still hurt him to say that! *Once a Catholic ...*

'Did she wear a white dressa?'

'Yes, why?' He really wished she wouldn't keep reminding him of her, especially at moments like this. She must feel really guilty, he thought, and yet if so, why was she here?

'It's the first time I've ever been in this situation.'

'What do you mean?' He was drawing invisible patterns on her tanned, sweaty tummy.

'It's the first time I 'ave ever been unfaithful.'

'You mean, to him?' He didn't want to use his name.

'Si. I must be mada. We are both mada.'

'Well, maybe love is always mad,' he said, a bit fed up with being told he was mada. And bada.

'I left Luciano once, but I went backa. I shouldn't 'ave gone backa. It was a mistake-a.'

'You can leave him again.' He kissed her ear.

'My sister approves of me going out with you,' she said, ignoring what he had said. 'But not my mama.'

'What about your father?'

'My father knows nothinga.'

'So you've told your sister and mother about me?'

'Si, they know all about you, my baby. There is a picture of you in my kitchen!'

'Really? You've sent them a picture of me?' He felt vaguely

disturbed to hear this.

'I told them you were getting divorceda,' she carried on. 'But they could never accept divorce-a. Luciano doesn't believe in divorce-a.'

'Is he religious? Catholic?'

'Si. 'e goes to Mass every Sunday.'

'Do you go with him?' He stroked her face with his fingers.

'I wait outside.'

'You'll never get to Heaven,' he laughed. 'You'll have to join me in Hell.'

'I told you, I will follow you everywhere, my baby.'

'What, even to Hell?'

'I want to be with you. And I don't believe in those things.'

'Does he?' He really didn't want to talk about Luciano, but …

'Of course-a. 'e believes everything the Papa says. If I say something unconventional, like I tell 'im I don't believe in Goda, 'e goes away and comes back in two 'oursa and says: *Are you all right nowa?*'

'My God!' he laughed. This guy sounded like a real plonker. He really did feel sorry for him!

'Do you believe in Goda?' she asked.

'No, not any more,' he said, nervously.

'You used to?'

'Yes. I was brought up as a Catholic. But I think it's all nonsense now. I think *all* religion is nonsense. Superstitious nonsense.' He was careful not say anything about almost becoming a priest – he didn't want to get into that now.

'Is your wife religious?'

'Yes. She's a traditional Catholic. It's one of the problems between us, I think. Though she denies it.'

'Did you tell her about yourself before you got marrieda?'

'Yes, of course. We lived together several years before we got married. She knew me very well, knew my opinions and beliefs. I even told her I didn't believe in marriage. But she still wanted to get married. More or less forced me to marry her. Blackmailed me into it, you could say. I mean, emotionally.'

'You don't believe in marriage?'

'Not really. Not until I met *you*. I could marry *you*.' He kissed her on the cheek and continued to fondle her breasts.

'I am completely in love with you, Francis. I wish I could put you in my luggage when I go backa. I feel sleepy nowa. I wish I could stay all night with you. Wake up in the morning with you. Why are you so sweeta? Your eyes are so sweeta. The way you look at me. I can tell you love me. I can see the love in your eyesa. Do you want to come againa?'

'I'm OK, thanks,' he smiled, kissing her.

'You're soft,' she said, putting her leg across his his and taking hold of him anyway.

'Let's just relax a bit longer,' he said, kissing her forehead. 'We don't need to do anything.'

'You are so gooda,' she said, removing her hand and caressing him. 'I better not go 'ome late-a. She will be angry. She disapproves of you, you know.'

'I gathered that.'

'But she can't say anything. She sleeps with two or three men every weeka.'

'She sounds like a bit of a tramp,' he said and had to explain the expression for her.

'She says she made an agreement with my mother to look after me, but I don't believe 'er. It's a lie, because my mother can't understand one word of English, not one worda. All the girls in the class like you, you know, including Marie-Claire.' Marie-Claire was a French girl he'd had a small clash with the other day.

'Do they? How do you mean?'

'They like you as a teacher, because you're a good teacher, but also as a mana.'

'Really?' he laughed, flattered, especially by the latter.

'Yes, even though in the classroom you seem a bit cold sometimes, a bit distanta.'

'Do you think so?' he said, surprised, deflated.

'It's OK, baby, I know you 'ave to be. You're the teacher. Promise me you won't go out with one of the other girlsa.'

'Of course I won't, you silly billy,' he laughed, kissing her face. 'I'm not interested in any of them. I'm only interested in *you*. That's why I'm here with you. I love you.'

'I love you so much, my baby. What time is eet?'

'Nearly nine o'clock,' he said, picking up his watch from the floor.

'I'd better go 'ome-a, or she will be angry. I better not be late againa.'

'Yes,' he agreed, pulling her naked body close to his own, kissing and caressing her.

'Do you want to make love againa?' she asked.

'Just a little bit,' he said.

'Come to me, my baby,' she said, putting her arms around him and pulling him on top of her …

On the way to the minicab office, they bought some fish and chips and ate them walking along, though he only ate the chips. He felt so euphoric that when they passed a small, hungry-looking lad, he held out his packet of chips and said, 'Do you want a chip, son?'

'No, fanks, I've just 'ad samfink,' said the lad.

'You are so kinda,' she said, as they walked on. 'Why are you so kinda? Is your mother like you?'

'My wife thinks so, but I don't,' he laughed. 'My mother's a very good woman, but very narrow-minded. I'm a very bad man, but very broad-minded.'

'You are a treasure,' she said, pleasing and surprising him with the word, but added something that didn't please him so much: 'But there is something wrong with you.'

CHAPTER FIVE

He spent the following day, Sunday, as usual, reading the newspapers and writing. The phone rang several times, but he ignored it, in case it was his wife, whom he didn't want to speak to, and even though he knew it might be Cinzia, whom he did want to speak to, especially as they weren't going to be able to meet today. Eventually, though, he gave in and to his relief it was Cinzia.

'I was thinking of you,' she said.

'Me too, I was thinking of you,' he replied, though it was only half-true and added in a whisper in case the dreaded landlady was eavesdropping: 'Ti amo.'

'Ti amo,' she whispered back in her sexy Italian accent. 'I miss you.'

'I miss you, too,' he said and it was true. 'What are you doing?'

'I'm writing you a letter. But I might not give it to you.'

'Cinzia, will you do me a favour?'

'Si?'

'Give it to me?'

'All right, baby. Vivien wants to meet you.'

'Why?'

'To see what you look like, what you sound like.'

'I don't think it's a good idea,' he said.

'It's OK. My mama rang today. She asked if I enjoyed myself last night.'

'What did you say?'

'I said yes, all right.'

'I hope you didn't tell her what you were doing!'

'If I told 'er that, she would come 'ere and take me 'ome-a!'

'*Did* you enjoy yourself yesterday?'

'I'm always 'appy when I am with you.'
'Me too. What are you going to do this evening?'
'I'll probably just watch TV. I 'ave to go. Ciao. Kiss.'
'See you tomorrow. Ti amo.'

The next day was Bank Holiday Monday or International Workers' Day – as the English establishment didn't want it to be known. He had hoped to have the whole afternoon with her, but to his annoyance she could only escape 'Vivien' for a couple of hours in the afternoon. He met her at Walthamstow Central and they went to visit the William Morris museum in Lloyd Park – which was appropriate, since Morris had been a staunch socialist, though the establishment tried to play down that aspect of his life nowadays, especially in these Thatcherite times.

Afterwards, they went for a walk in the park, which apparently had once been William Morris's back garden. They had agreed earlier on the phone that they didn't have enough time to go to the flat.

'Anyway, I've got a cold,' he had said, 'so we can't make love.'

'I don't minda,' she had said. 'I want your colda. Give me your colda! It will be another part of you.'

He had laughed, but they opted for the museum and a walk in the park, which he thought would be romantic, and so it proved. As well as flower beds riotous with spring blooms, lush green lawns, including a bowling green, trees in full blossom and a miniature aviary, it contained a small lake populated with ducks, geese, swans, coots and moorhens and had a verdant island in the middle.

He felt proud to be with her, as they strolled around the lake with their arms around each other. She was wearing green trousers, tied just below the knee, a check blouse and sunglasses. There were lots of women lying around sunbathing on the lawns, but she was definitely the prettiest girl in the park and she was his!

'You haven't been here before, have you?' he asked her.

'I came here with Hassan,' she told him.

'Oh,' he said, surprised. 'He fancies you, does he?' Hassan was a good-looking lad, but very young, about eighteen.

'Si. 'e tried to kiss me!'

'Really?' He couldn't help feeling a pinprick of jealousy, even though he knew there was no contest.

''e asked me why I like you. 'e told me 'e 'as seen your wife-a and she is beautiful. 'e tried to take me to 'is 'ouse-a.'

'You didn't – didn't let him kiss you, did you?'

'Of course not – 'e is only a little boy. And I was in love with you. I was waiting for you.'

'Waiting for me?'

'Waiting for you to notice me.'

'Ah, yes,' he smiled, giving her a hug as they walked. 'Waiting at the 123 bus stop!' Why hadn't he noticed her earlier, he wondered? But he hadn't.

'I fell in love with you from the first daya,' she said.

'Really?' It was flattering. He wanted to tell her he had fallen in love with her at first sight too, but it wasn't true – he had hardly noticed her in the class. There was definitely something mousy about her. 'You should have told me before.'

'I was waiting for you to notice me. But you didn't. I was afraid of you.'

'Afraid of me?'

'Si. I thought you wouldn't be interested in me, because you were marrieda or because you 'ad lots of girlfriendsa. And because you were my teacher.'

'You're not afraid any more, I hope,' he laughed.

'I think I 'ave been waiting for you since I was two years olda. I 'ave been looking for someone like you since I was fourteena. You're different from Italian people. You're different from English people. I'm different too. Everyone tells me that.'

'You *are* different,' he said, hugging her and kissing her quickly. 'That's why I love you.'

'Vivien is so angry with you.'

'She's jealous.'

'She's a bitcha! She told me I 'ad to be 'ome by four, but I refuseda. But I will 'ave to be 'ome by sixa.'

He led her away from the lake and onto one of the large

fields at the back of the park, where they sat down on the grass, as far away as possible from other people, though to his annoyance it was impossible to find any real privacy, because it was such a sunny day and a bank holiday, so there were people everywhere, strolling about, playing, sunbathing, snogging …

They lay back, he took her in his arms and they kissed and snogged themselves for a while, but neither of them felt comfortable doing so with so many people around and they sat up again.

'I never want to see Luciano again,' she declared suddenly.

He was getting used to her making these sudden, seemingly irrelevant remarks, especially about Luciano. It was obviously a major issue for her and he realised she was using him to try to resolve it, to decide whether to go back to Italy or stay in England. But he didn't mind – he was in love with her and wanted her to stay, more than anything in the world, and told her so.

'I love you, my baby,' she said, tears in her eyes, 'but I know I can't stay with you. I 'ave to go backa.'

'You can live with me,' he said, wiping the tears away from her cheeks.

'I ask you only one favour,' she said.

'Yes, what? You can have anything!'

'I would like to live with you just for one week before I go backa.'

'I want you to live with me for ever.'

'You're so sweet, my baby, but I can'ta. Just one weeka. After my exam, I 'ave a few days before I go backa. Can I live with you then?'

'Of course you can. I love you. We can go for a little holiday if you want.'

'Oh, you're so sweet, my baby! I love you! I never want to leave you!' she cried, throwing her arms around his neck.

He put his arms around her and hugged her tight. And that was the moment when he decided that he really did love her and would do everything in his power to make her stay with him for ever.

After she had left, he went to the Bell, bought himself a pint of Guinness, sat at their usual table, took a first sup, opened her letter and read:

London, Sunday 30.5.82

Francis,

I can't stop thinking of you for two reasons: the first reason is that I'm fond of you and the second one is that nobody takes care of me here. I remember your knack for explaining me things in clear, concise and logical concepts. You encourage me right from the start to save for a rainy day and you want me to stand on my own two feet. I need to be taught to accent the positive side of my nature. Yet, this doesn't mean that I'm an uncertain girl!

I have my organised system for living, but it's better if I have a neat example to follow, that's you. At the moment I would like you to keep me with you, it's my last time and it would be nice to spend these days together.

Then, after my arrival to Italy, I will live somewhere on my own or with somebody else, but you will always be by my side. Anywhere, in any place, your eyes will look at me and my hands will look for yours. You will be on my mind for years.

And now let me give you a little kiss as sweet as you.

Don't forget me!

Cinzia

In fact there were two letters in the envelope. The second one had been written only this morning:

It's Monday morning, ten minutes to eight and the radio creates a warm atmosphere around me. A simple room full of life. I always remember my past day: we used to look at each other and no one could never foresee the new reality. Your approach to me has been as much natural as possible, because of the gradual development of our knowledge. Francis and Cinzia have helped each other in many ways: that's why they shouldn't forget their friendship!

There are so many things to discover during our life and

I've discovered some of them with you: you said to me how to achieve rich and productive life (by developing our thoughts and our hidden capacities). I was afraid of something indefinite and you taught me how to overcome my fear of love. You've been able to conquer my anxiety and now I know that love can become the most interesting, rich experience of our life.

You know, Francis, my initial experience was of falling in love with you and now after few weeks I'm still in the permanent state of standing in love with you. We have been strangers for a long time and yet it hasn't been hard to let the wall between us break down. I feel close with you and an intimacy depends probably on the fact that we're living near each other. Yet I don't see any miracle and there isn't infatuation between you and me. I feel well living with you because I can see you or your shadow by my side and this is what makes me happy. Your pleasant manners, interesting conversation, your helpful, modest nature influence my mood in a positive way. Wherever you are, I'll be with you. This is not just an exciting experience of my life ...

I need to meet you again once more at least!

'Once more at least' – those words were like a dagger through his heart. How ironic it was, he thought, taking a swig of Guinness! He'd never expected or planned to fall in love with her. He certainly hadn't set out to seduce her. He had hardly even noticed her in the class! She was always very quiet. Shy. Mousy. There were lots of other better-looking girls among his students. At first, yes, if he was honest, he'd thought he'd just have a bit of fun with her till she went home, back to Italy. No harm in that. But somehow or other, he'd fallen in love with her! Exactly how or when he couldn't work out. It had just happened. As if by magic! Well, love was a kind of magic, wasn't it? A kind of black magic maybe. She'd definitely cast a spell on him, anyway. And he was happy to be under her spell. He'd been so lonely. He hadn't fully realised how lonely he'd been. Not just lonely, but wounded, by the loss of his wife, the break-up of his marriage. Even if it was largely his own fault. His own fault mixed with some bad luck. But now he was healed. By love! It was like a medicine. An antidote. To all the sadness and pain. And loneliness and boredom. Like a drug! Like alcohol for example. Such euphoria! Such sheer happiness! Such joy! But it'd last longer than the high from alcohol, he hoped, taking a another swig of Guinness. A lot longer. For ever! How to keep her though? How to stop her going back to Italy? Back to that plonker Luciano? Whom she didn't even love. Who didn't deserve her. Though he felt sorry for him. For being such a plonker! Felt a bit guilty. But why should he feel guilty? All was fair in love and war. He loved her. She loved him. That was all that mattered, wasn't it? He wanted her. He wanted to keep her, now that he'd found her. Or she'd found him. *I 'ave been waiting for you since I was two years olda.* What a funny thing to say! But beautiful. Like a dart to the heart. No, not a corkscrew, a dart. Straight from Cupid's bow. *I 'ave been looking for someone like you since I was fourteena.* God, how he loved that accent of hers! Another dart to his heart. A dart dipped not in poison but love. Like some secret magic recipe or potion. Would any girl ever say anything more beautiful to him? Anyone at all? She was a magician! Her voice was enough to put a spell on him. It was like a music that went straight to his stomach. Straight to his soul. Italian girls! *You know Italian girls are colda, don't you?* Such a funny thing to say. He smiled to himself, took another swig of Guinness and shook his head. Nothing could be further from the truth! Not if she herself were anything to go by. Cold hands though. Hot heart. Mind you, Grazia had been cold. No, just uptight. Hung up. Because he was 'marrieda'. God, how he'd fancied her! He'd been crazy about her! But now she was a zero. It was as if she didn't exist. There was only the one now. Only one girl in the whole world who mattered. Funny. The millions, billions, of others meant *nothing* to him. Even his heart-throb Gina Lollobrigida meant nothing to him now! The most beautiful women from every country in the world could line up in front of him right now and he wouldn't be the slightest bit interested in any of them. How strange was that? But that's how it was. He was in love with her. He was under her spell. He couldn't imagine ever being in love with anybody else. If he lost her, he'd be – no, he couldn't even bear to think about it. The very thought crushed him. He had to find a way to keep her. He suddenly had an idea. Yes! Yes, that was what he'd do, he decided, finishing his pint. Maybe he should go and do it right now. Yes! Why not? Do it *now*. Yes yes yes! Except it was a bank holiday. He'd nearly forgotten. Damn! Tomorrow then. But what about tonight? Tonight he'd write that poem he'd promised her. He already had the title and a few lines in his head. He'd go back to the park and do it there, sitting where they'd sat only a few hours ago. Her ghost would be there beside him to inspire him. He felt the lines flowing almost fully-formed already into his mind as he walked back to the park. Flowing like rivers from the mountains to the sea. The sea of love. Flowing naturally from the title:

Ti Amo

CHAPTER SIX

'Please make a point of coming to see me at least once a week,' Bertha ordered him as he collected his register from the office.

'I do pop in occasionally, Bertha,' he said, biting his tongue. 'But you're not always there.'

He rushed out, pretending to be in a hurry for his class, cursing her under his breath: *Bossy, fat bitch!* How dare she speak to him like that, as if he were a schoolboy and she the headmistress? He was annoyed, not only with her, but also with himself, for having been caught by her – he usually managed to give her the slip, though in view of her bulk that wasn't always so easy.

'Ah, the au pairs' delight!' Tony announced as usual, when he entered the staffroom.

'I saw you got nobbled by the dragon,' Mark said, a smirk of schadenfreude on his face.

'I think she was hiding behind the door, waiting for me,' he laughed grimly.

'Was it a barn door?' Roy piped up, in between puffs on his cig, which he held in a tortoiseshell holder. 'No other kind of door would be enough to conceal that mass, would it?'

'At least she didn't try to press you to her bosom,' Mark said. 'Which is what she tried to do to me the other day.'

'What a horrific thought!' he laughed. 'How did you escape?'

'It took me several minutes to fight my way out of the pneumatic folds of flab.'

'By the way, how's the writing going?' Roy asked, exhaling. 'Have you finished that novel yet?'

'Nearly,' he said, not wanting to talk about it.

'Are you going to dedicate it to Bertha?'

'Dedicate a book to Bertha?' Mark chipped in. 'I can't imagine dedicating anything to Bertha except a kick up the arse.'

'Well, I'm off to the chalk face,' he laughed, gathering his books to go.

'Who've you got this morning?' Mark asked.

'Upper Intermediates.'

'I tell you, you've got some good-looking chicks in that evening class of yours,' Mark commented, sticking his tongue out and panting like a dog on heat.

'Yeah,' he laughed, opening the door. 'See you in the bar tomorrow evening maybe.'

'Make sure some of those chicks are there!'

'They always are,' Tony declared. 'He's the au pairs' delight, isn't he?'

He laughed and left quickly, not wanting to get into a laddish conversation about women – there was only one woman he was interested in now, and that was Cinzia.

She was waiting at the bus stop as usual. They went to the Bell and sat in their customary place. She gave him a get-well card.

'My cold's gone,' he laughed, taking her in his arms and kissing her, touched. 'I hope I haven't given it to you!'

'I want it,' she said. 'I want everything of yours. I love you. You don't know how much I love you. You're different from all the other men I've ever met. You're so special. I'll never forget you.'

'I'll never forget *you.*'

'Promise?'

'I promise. Because I want to keep you for ever.'

'Will you write to me?'

'Are you definitely going back?'

'I 'ave to go on seventeenth of June. It's my return flighta.'

'That's only two weeks away.'

'I know. I should never 'ave fallen in love with you. I'm sorry for falling in love with you, my baby.'

'Don't go. You don't have to go. Stay here with me.'

'I want to, but I 'ave to go. I 'ave to see my family. Even

though they are stupida.'

'What do you mean, 'stupida'?' he laughed.

'All they think of is work, sleep, money, food. They never read a book or think or discuss ideas. Stupida!'

He laughed. 'You can come back.'

'I will 'ave to marry 'im. I don't want to, but I will 'ave to.'

'You can marry me instead.'

'Can I stay with you for a few nights before I go? Are you sure? I would like to sleep with you all nighta.'

'Of course. I want to sleep with you *every* night.'

'I'll give one week's notice to Vivien, so I can spend my last week with you.'

'I might kidnap you. I might not let you go.'

'Oh, my baby, I love you so much.' She threw her arms around his neck and they kissed. 'And now I 'ave to go to worka.'

He would do everything he could to keep her, he resolved, as he held her. He wouldn't kidnap her physically, but he would kidnap her emotionally, so that she wouldn't be able to get on that plane.

The next day he was nobbled again by Bertha, who harangued him about 'departmental duties' next year, insinuating that he didn't do enough for the department. 'And next year I hope to see more of you,' she concluded, to add insult to injury.

'What was Bertha on about?' Geoff Walker asked him in the corridor, when he came out of the office. 'Anyway, don't worry, I had to listen to that spiel when I started here back in seventy-three. I went home and said to my wife I didn't think I was going to enjoy working here. But she's so inefficient she'll forget all about it. It's just her chance to play the section leader. I could see you were inwardly gnashing your teeth!'

'You bet,' he laughed.

'How are you?' Mark asked, when he went into the staffroom, having been greeted in the usual way by Tony.

'I've just had to listen to a load of crap from Bertha about departmental duties next year.'

'You should've told her to fuck off,' Mark commented.

'One of these days I will. You doing anything this summer?'

'I've got to put up with another month of this EFL shit. Just agreed to do a month of summer school to pay for my Greece trip. At least there'll be some new women around.' He did his panting act.

'I see Catherine's thrown a big wobbly again,' Roy remarked, exhaling a cloud of Gauloise. Catherine was the departmental secretary, a somewhat neurotic, harassed, middle-aged woman who was out of her depth and overworked.

'What's happened?' he asked.

'Bertha asked her to take minutes at the meeting tomorrow and she refused. Said it wasn't her job. Said everyone was making too many demands on her. So she's run off home. Then Harriet Jenkins said Frank is the only one who gets on well with her, because he doesn't make any demands on her. Likes to put you down subtly you see, Frank. Said Catherine's a very delicate lady and has to be handled with kid gloves. She's a real stirrer, that Harriet Jenkins. That's the only thing I don't like about working with women. They all yap about one another. Bertha should take the minutes herself. She doesn't do anything else. She's always asking other people to do her work for her. The other day she asked me to carry a box full of tapes to the lang lab for her. I refused. I told her I wasn't a porter.'

'I think the women staff around here are all sex-starved, just like me,' Mark observed. 'But I handle it better. Nothing a bottle of Johnny Walker can't deal with.'

'Maybe you should proposition Bertha,' Frank joked. 'I saw her chatting up a Turkish student the other day. I think she fancies him. Actually, I think she fancies you.'

'I'd rather fuck a hippopotamus,' Mark said. 'Can you imagine actually doing it with Bertha?'

'No, please don't go there!' he laughed, holding his hands up in horror, collecting his things and leaving for his class.

It was Saturday afternoon. There was a knock at the front door. He was in the bathroom, washing clothes. He ignored it, because he wasn't expecting Cinzia till later. Then there was another knock, but he ignored that too.

‘’ello! Is anybody ina?’ a familiar Italian voice came through the letter box.

It was Cinzia! As he approached the door to open it, he heard her talking to the kids next door, which he was uncomfortable with – he didn’t really want neighbours to register her. He opened the door quickly and signalled her in, closing the door equally quickly and giving her a kiss. She was wearing her glittery black summer dress and carrying a Barry Manilow record. She looked cute.

‘I want to play it,’ she enthused. ‘Do you like ’im-a?’

‘Not really,’ he shrugged, but could see she was disappointed. ‘He’s OK, I suppose,’ he added to mollify her. ‘Maybe I’ll learn to, if you like him.’

He put the record on the stereo, took her in his arms and they waltzed around the living room for a while to the strains of ‘Can’t Smile Without You’. They had planned to go for a walk on the Marshes, have a drink, then come home and cook spaghetti together, but suddenly he couldn’t wait to make love with her, so a few minutes later she was sitting on the settee and he was kneeling in front of her, slipping his hands under her dress, exploring her body, then taking her black glittery dress off over her head, kissing her all over as he did so. She was wearing a camisole top, which he also removed, and started to remove her bra.

‘What are you doing, doctor?’ she smiled, ruffling his hair.

‘I think a full examination is necessary,’ he joked, removing her bra and kissing her breasts.

‘But I am not sick-a,’ she objected.

‘I think you’re lovesick,’ he joked, continuing to kiss her breasts.

‘It’s too early to make love-a,’ she laughed. ‘It’s only six o’clocka.’

‘Who said it’s too early?’ he demanded, slowly removing her purple, lacy French knickers.

‘I don’t know who said it first,’ she replied.

‘So when is the official time for making love then?’

‘Later. Nine o’clock,’ she laughed. ‘Now I’m ’ungry.’

But she didn’t stop him – indeed she pulled his head even closer to her breasts and soon they were lying together on the settee, where she whimpered with pleasure as his hands travelled over her, caressing, tickling, pressing, squeezing, probing …

Afterwards, she put his shirt on, went into the tiny kitchen, closed the curtains and started cooking. He had all the ingredients prepared: spaghetti, tinned tomatoes, garlic, onion, purée, spices. While she cooked she looked at his wedding album, which to his discomfort she had found in the study.

'She's nice,' she commented about his wife. 'But she doesn't smile much. She's nice when she smiles.'

'Mm,' he mumbled uncomfortably, standing beside her.

'I prefer you now to then,' she observed. 'You look un'appy on your wedding daya. I can tell. Were you un'appy?'

'Yes,' he admitted, wincing inwardly.

'Why were you un'appy?'

'I didn't really want to marry her,' he said, not wanting to talk about it, finding it too painful.

'Why did you marry 'er?' she pursued.

'She wanted to get married. I resisted for a long time. I wanted to make her happy. It was a mistake. I shouldn't have.'

'Did you love 'er?'

'I don't know. I think so. At first. But …' He trailed off. He really didn't want to discuss his absent wife with her or anybody. Especially with her, since technically he was being unfaithful with her. Not that he regarded himself as married any more. 'I'll go and get some beer and coke from the off-licence,' he said, as an excuse to escape from the questioning, and slipped out.

When he got back, the meal was ready and they ate, with the beer and for her coke. Afterwards, they made love again, listening to Barry Manilow, who actually had quite a good voice he decided, though the songs were far too schmaltzy for his taste. After she had come, noisily as usual, she took hold of him. He had restrained himself with the greatest difficulty.

''ow is Fred-a?' she asked, stroking Fred lightly.

'Very happy when you do that,' he smiled.

'What is the real name for it?' she enquired innocently.

'The technical name is "penis". But there are other, colloquial words.'

'I'll call him Fred-a,' she said. 'But I don't like 'im really.'

'Why?' he asked, miffed.

''e looks funny. Women's bodies are better than mensa. More beautiful.'

'I can agree with that,' he laughed. 'But human bodies are funny altogether. For example, noses.' He place a finger on the tip of her nose. 'For example, this nose.' She had a slightly big nose, but he liked it, because it stopped her looking too pretty.

'You don't like my nose-a?' she asked, pretending to be offended.

'I love your nose-a,' he laughed, mimicking her, kissing it. 'I love all of you. I mean noses in general. And ears.' He wanted her to make him come and must have shown it.

''ow are you, Fred-a?' she asked, teasingly.

'He's very hungry,' he said, struggling to keep from coming.

'Can you move 'im?'

'Yes,' he laughed, demonstrating. What sort of game was this?

'Any other way?'

'No,' he laughed, enjoying the game, but getting desperate.

'When you write to me, I want you to tell me 'ow Fred is,' she said.

'He'll miss you.'

''e will?'

'Yes. I mean it.'

'Does 'e like this?' She started massaging Fred more vigorously.

'Yes, he loves it,' he groaned, stroking her hand.

'Where does 'e like it most?'

'There. At the top.' He moved her hand to the top.

'My baby,' she cooed, moving her hand up and down faster and faster until he came in a spasm of pleasure and relief, spunk squirting all over.

'Oh, you're messy!' she exclaimed. 'I'll wash you.'

'There are some tissues there,' he gasped, pointing to the coffee table.

'No,' she insisted. 'I'll wash you properly.'

She went to the bathroom and came back with a wet sponge, with which she wiped him. Then she went back to the bathroom and brought a towel, with which she dried him off. Finally, she returned with some talc, which she sprinkled liberally all over the target area. He tried not to remember what had happened at the junior seminary …

'Why are you so sweeta?' she asked, caressing him with her fingertips as they lay together in post-coital languor.

'I don't know. Am I sweet?' he smiled, not sure if he'd ever describe himself as 'sweet' exactly.

'I must find outa,' she murmured, trailing her fingertips over his face. 'Do you feel more English or Irish?'

'Irish,' he said. 'My soul is Irish. Even though I was born and brought up in England.'

'Are you worried about something, my baby?'

God, she's perceptive, he thought! But most women seemed to have a sixth sense. It was quite disconcerting!

'Nothing really,' he said, as always reluctant to share his worries.

'Tell me, baby,' she coaxed, caressing his face.

'It's just that my boss at work – I don't mean Bertha, the one above her, the Head of Department – wants to see me on Monday, I don't know why. It's a bit odd.'

'You're not in trouble because of me, are you?'

'No, I shouldn't think so. I'm just worried Vivien may have told the college about you and me. To take revenge because you've given her your notice. And she's jealous. Not that it's any of their business. Anyway, there's no law against teachers having sex with students as far as I know. Why should there be?'

'Vivien wouldn't tell the college – I know too many secrets about 'er. She's a liar. She's a witcha.'

'Are you sure?'

'Yes, my baby. I'm sure. Don't worry.'

'I hope you're right. Anyway, we haven't done anything wrong. We're both adults, both free agents.'

'Don't worry, baby. Everyone knows you are a good teacher. Even though you're a bad man sometimes.'

'Hey, don't be cheeky!' he laughed, spanking her bum and making her squeal in delight.

'If I come back to London and you've moveda, 'ow will I

find you?' she asked, a little later. She knew he was looking for a house to buy.

'You can always find me through the college.'

'Oh, yes. You're so clever!'

'Anyway, I don't want you to go. I want you to stay with me.'

'Baby, I 'ave to go, but I'll always remember you.'

'Maybe I should go and live in Italy with you.' The idea appealed to him, though he knew he would probably never do it. It would really be burning his boats. Maybe he didn't love her enough? Maybe he didn't love her at all. Maybe he was just playing a game, without realising it. It didn't matter. She was happy and he was happy. For now.

'I will 'ave to marry 'im.'

'Maybe I'll have to fight him for you. In a duel.'

'Oh, baby, I love you so much,' she laughed. 'You 'ave made me so 'appy. Yes, I will always remember you.' She started crying.

'OK, don't cry, my little mouse,' he hugged her and kissed away her tears. 'We'll work it out.'

'Soon I will disappear back to Italy,' she sniffled, while he held her. 'Just one and 'alf 'ours on the plane and my life will be completely differenta. It's frightening. My life is in crisis now.'

'Sometimes I think life is one long crisis,' he said, his natural pessimism surfacing for a moment.

'No, don't tell me thata!' she exclaimed, sniffling back her tears.

'OK, OK,' he hugged her. 'Don't worry. Let's be happy while we can. We can discuss it another time.'

'I know I 'ave to be rational. Cool. Calm. To make the right decision.'

'Don't worry, darling. Whatever you decide, whatever you do, I'll always love you.'

'Oh, baby, you're so wonderful. You are so special for me. You 'ave given me so much. Thank you.' She kissed him.

'You've given me a lot too. More than you realise. Thank *you*!'

'You mustn't see me at the exam on Monday. If I see you, I

won’t be able to think about anything else-a! I’ll be shy.’ She was doing her First Certificate Intermediate oral exam on Monday.

‘I might be invigilating it,’ he said. ‘But don’t worry, I won’t look at you.’

‘But you mustn’t look at the other girlsa.’

‘We always look at the girls!’ he laughed. ‘And talk about them.’

‘Yes, I’m learning that all men are bad. Just like you. What do you say about them?’

‘We give them marks out of ten for how sexy they are. And discuss whether we’d like to make love with them or not.’

‘Bad man! Promise you won’t look at the other girlsa on Monday.’ She raised an admonishing finger at him.

‘I promise. I’ll wear a blindfold.’

He had to explain what a blindfold was. In fact, it would be easy for him not to look at the other girls – he was already blind to them, because he was in love with her.

‘Actually, I don’t need to wear a blindfold,’ he went on, warming to his theme. ‘You see, I love you and, as we say in English, love is blind.’

‘What does it mean?’

‘Well, for me it means that because I love you, I’m blind to all other women.’

‘Oh, baby, I wish I could stay with you all nighta. I love you so much. What time is it?’

‘It’s nearly eleven.’

‘I ’ave to leave you. She will be mad if I’m not ’ome before midnighta.’

She started to get up, but he pulled her back and climbed on top of her. She threw her arms round his neck and pulled him down. He didn’t go inside her, because he didn’t want to risk making her pregnant. But he didn’t need to go inside her – he was already inside her and she inside him and he intended to keep her there for ever, hearts as one.

CHAPTER SEVEN

After teaching on Monday morning, he invigilated the Cambridge First Certificate oral examination. Cinzia was there, but he pretended to ignore her, apart from an occasional exchange of knowing glances, secret smiles and a few pleasantries. He didn't want it to be general knowledge that he was having a relationship with her – because he didn't want it to be a subject of gossip – and also he was nervous about his meeting with the Head of Department, scheduled for four-thirty. He still wasn't sure that her witch of a landlady, Vivien, hadn't complained about him – not that she had anything to complain about, he told himself.

He enjoyed seeing Cinzia and knowing that she was his, she loved him as he loved her. There were lots of other girls attending the exam, some of them very attractive – for example, Véronique, a French girl in a white blouse and tight blue jeans, whom he would have fancied like mad if he hadn't already been in love with Cinzia. And Eva, a willowy, blonde-haired, milky-skinned German girl in a sexy blue summer dress. There was also Tiziana, another Italian girl, who obviously liked him, and he liked her, though he didn't fancy her – she was a bit chubby for his taste, dressed like a punk in scruffy leather jackets, printed T-shirts and ragged denim miniskirts and smoked like a chimney. She also had green hair. Well, she did play bass in a punk rock band at home in Italy, apparently. And at least she didn't have any rings or safety-pins impaled in her anatomy, as far as he could see. But he wasn't interested in any of them – he had eyes only for Cinzia and he was going to do his best to persuade her to stay with him in London and marry him rather than Luciano – who was a bit of a prat from what she had told him.

The interview with the Head of Department – a somewhat

dry, grey – grey suit, grey hair, grey personality – Scotsman from Edinburgh – turned out to be only a 'staff development' interview, to his relief. His name was Rob Roy. No, it wasn't – it was Ken Cameron, but they sometimes called him Rob Roy. SDIs were the new flavour of the month, all pretty pointless, he reflected afterwards, because he didn't consider he needed to be 'developed' or was happy to develop himself, but it was pleasant and positive enough and best of all he wasn't in any kind of trouble. Quite the reverse – in fact Ken actually said, in his soft Edinburgh burr, 'I never hear any complaints about you. You do your job quietly and efficiently. Nobody has a bad word to say about you. The students certainly like you.' He went on to tell him how he could 'develop' himself and should perhaps 'diversify' by teaching literature or 'straight English' as well as English as a Foreign Language, but he politely explained that he was happy as he was.

He found it all patronising, but at the same time couldn't help feeling pleased. And it was a very accurate description of his modus operandi, he thought – 'quiet and efficient'. Towards the end of the interview, Ken asked him what he did in his free time and impulsively he said he wrote. He regretted it immediately and wondered why he had said it. Just for the sake of something to say, he decided later, a little like how he used to make up sins to tell in Confession.

'Oh, what do you write?' Ken enquired.

'Novels, mainly,' he said, wishing he hadn't mentioned it, because he hated talking about it.

'Ach, I don't read modern novels – I can't take them,' Ken opined, which somehow didn't surprise him.

'I write a bit of poetry too,' he added, hoping this might redeem him in Ken's eyes.

'I can't take modern poetry either,' Ken pronounced. 'Although I've got a cousin who's a poet. Robin Bell, if you've heard of him.'

'Mmm … I can't say I have,' he said, pretending to dig into a deep trove of knowledge about modern poetry.

'Have you published much?' Ken asked.

'Nothing yet,' he admitted, embarrassed, but emphasising the word 'yet' slightly.

'You're not really a professional teacher at all, are you?' Ken remarked, somewhat cryptically.

'Well, I try to balance both teaching and writing,' he replied, offended, though he knew no offence had been intended.

'There doesn't seem to be anything I can do for you, then, does there?' Ken said, the ghost of a smile flitting over his grey, heavily-bespectacled features.

'No, thanks,' he smiled, wondering if it was the right answer.

'Well, good luck with the writing,' Ken said, rising to shake hands with him. 'Let me know when you get published.'

'I will, thanks,' he said, standing and shaking hands, then letting himself out of the office quickly.

'Ah, the au pairs' delight!' exclaimed Tony, who was waiting outside to go in, no doubt to be 'developed' as well.

As usual when the weather was fine, he went for a stroll around the playing field at the back of the college before his evening class and sat on the sward for a while, admiring the lush midsummer verdure all around, the green-robed trees, the white-blossomed hedges and the heavenly blue sky, across which trailed the occasional plane like a silent, spectral spaceship sailing from one world to another.

He watched a few children, mostly Asian, playing cricket, enjoying their simple, innocent pleasure in the game, wondering wistfully if he'd ever be able to have children himself, reminded nostalgically of playing the game on Wednesday afternoons in summer at the junior seminary, but reminded too of something else that happened on Wednesday afternoons in summer … He switched the memory off quickly. Think of Cinzia, he told himself! She was the perfect antidote to all such thoughts, all such memories. How lucky he was to have found her, after several months of loneliness and the pain of his wife leaving him! But he also wondered anxiously if he'd be able to keep her, was afraid of losing her, of suffering another broken heart …

After class he went to the bar as usual, though he wasn't really in the mood – he was missing Cinzia too much. Mark came in as usual, though he didn't teach in the evening, just to chat up the girls. Fortunately, several of the girls – mostly French – were there as well, so he didn't have to spend too long talking lad's talk with Mark, who quickly made a beeline for them. He ended up chatting most of the time to Albert, a plump, short, bearded German student from Trier, who regaled him with the tale of how he had got drunk at a beer festival in Trier last weekend, in between puffing on his pipe, and informed him that Karl Marx also came from Trier.

'What position did he play?' he asked waggishly, knowing that Albert had a good sense of humour – even though he was German – and like himself was a football fan.

'Left wing,' Albert riposted.

'Very good,' he laughed and they talked football for a while.

At closing time – he and a few of his students always stayed till closing time – Albert gave him a lift to the station in his sports car – an 'Owstin Sprrite', as he called it. On the way, they were stopped by a motor-cycle cop for speeding, but to his relief the cop let Albert off, 'in the interest of Anglo-German relations', as he pompously put it, having interrogated him for what seemed like ages.

'Fucking Nazi!' he thought to himself, as they drove on, but didn't say it out loud to Albert, and couldn't help recollecting that forty years ago Albert would probably have been wearing a coal-scuttle on his head and shooting at him rather than giving him a ride in a British sports car in north-east London. He might even have been ordering him about here in the streets of London, if that evil megalomaniac Hitler had won the war!

He wanted to talk to Albert about the war, but had never quite had the nerve to broach the subject, which was stupid, he told himself, but just went to show how it still constituted an invisible barrier between them. Maybe next time they met in the bar he'd mention it, he thought. Or maybe not. *No, don't mention the war!* Better not to spoil a pleasant friendship and stick to football, beer and women, even though he was interested in only one woman now …

'I can't stay out tonighta,' Cinzia said, when he met her

after his afternoon class at the front of the town hall. 'She wants me to babysita.' She had an elfin look about her, dressed as she was in brown cord dungarees and a red shirt, with a polka-dot bandana on her head.

Damn, he thought – what a bitch that landlady was! 'Never mind,' he said, giving her a kiss. They were sitting on one of the benches, in front of the fountain. It was yet another sunny June evening, the light bouncing blindingly off the white stone of the town hall.

'So, are you coming to stay with me tomorrow then?' he asked. It was her last week in London – unless he could change her mind.

'Si, but I must 'ave my own rooma,' she said.

'Sure,' he agreed, put out, not sure if she was joking or not.

'And you must let me to sleep late-a.'

'*Let me sleep late*,' he corrected her. 'Zero infinitive with 'let'.'

'Grazie, my baby,' she said, kissing him. 'Ti amo.'

'Ti amo,' he reciprocated. 'You can sleep late if you want. You'll be free to come and go as you please.'

'Thank you. Now I 'ave to go.'

They hugged and kissed and he took her to the bus stop and put her on the 123 bus. Then he walked home across the Marshes, as he usually did on summer evenings, having a pint of Fuller's in the Anchor and Hope on the way.

He felt a mixture of emotions as he sat down to enjoy his pint. On the one hand, he was annoyed that she wasn't here with him, as he had expected her to be, though he knew it wasn't her fault, it was her bitch of a landlady's. On the other hand, he was happy that she would be coming to spend her last week with him, but offended by her saying she wanted her own room. Was it a joke? If it was, he didn't find it very amusing! Did being in love meant he had lost his own sense of humour?

However, these minor anxieties were soon soothed away by the alcohol as it started to circulate around his system, as well as by the sight of the sun sinking in a firework-like display of golden effulgence over the Marshes, so that he soon slipped into a familiar mellow mood in which he felt that all was well with the world and all would be well and love would conquer all …

'She wants me to stay one more nighta,' Cinzia informed him on the phone next morning.

'Why?' he asked, angrily. *Fuck her!*

'She wants to go outa.'

'Again? Just tell her you're leaving today as arranged.'

'She 'as my money.'

'She has to give it to you.'

'She won't if I don't staya. She's a bitcha.'

He felt like going there and giving the landlady from hell a piece of his mind, but of course knew he couldn't. Then a horrible thought crossed his mind. 'You haven't changed your mind, have you?' he asked her.

'I 'aven't changed my minda. I want to stay with you. I will come to you tomorrow nighta. 'ave you changed your minda?'

'Of course not. I love you. I want you to stay with me. For ever.' God, it was so easy for misunderstanding to arise when emotions were high! And it was all really because of this awful Vivien woman.

'Are you teaching tonighta?' Cinzia asked.

'Yes,' he said. 'Why?'

'Because yesterday you said you were free.'

'But I usually teach on Thursday nights. You know that.'

'You know you mustn't lie to me, Francis. Never lie to me. You can do anything, but don't lie to me. You are free. I don't mind where you go or who you go witha.'

'Are you accusing me of lying?' he asked coldly, shocked and wounded by this outburst. 'Do you think I'm going out with somebody else? Is that it?' If only she knew how uninterested he was in anybody else. But she *should* know! God, she should know by now!

'No, my baby. I just want to say, never lie to me. It will kill me. I love you! I love you! You know, I didn't want to die before, but now I don't mind. I still don't want to die, I want to live a nice long life, but now I don't mind so much if I die, because I've met you. God has sent you to me. I 'ad to wait for you. Don't die yet, baby. Come to Italy once and I will come back to London once. Oh, please, baby! Promise me! We may never see each other again. I love you! I love you!' She was crying now.

Well, that took the wind out of his sails! Now he suddenly felt bad for having been angry with her. It was all a misunderstanding, he realised. It was because she was so wound up about going back to Italy, when she didn't really want to, and because he was so afraid of losing her, so confused about why she couldn't stay with him for good, they both knew they were living a dream, a dream from which they would soon be forced to wake up to the cold, lonely light of day.

'I love you, too,' he said to her, softly. 'Shall I pick you up tomorrow morning?'

'Si. I will be ready.'

'What are you going to do this afternoon?'

'I'm going to London, my London. I love it. To see everything for the last time. I'll walk and walk till I'm tired outa.'

'I'm sorry I can't go with you, darling. Maybe we can go together next week. We can make next week our honeymoon if you like.' It'll be a funny honeymoon though, he thought. A honeymoon to mark the end of our relationship instead of the beginning. Except that he was still determined somehow to keep her …

'Oh, baby, I love you so much,' she said, crying. 'I love you so much, you don't know how much.'

'Me too,' he said, almost in tears himself.

When he arrived home that night, he got a shock – Mary, his wife – or ex-wife as he thought of her now – was in the flat. She was wearing a black anorak over a pink top, a pink top that he remembered with a pang buying for her.

'What are you doing here?' he asked, thinking how lucky it was he didn't have Cinzia with him after all – not that he had any reason to feel guilty, since Mary had left him and wanted a divorce.

'I came to give you your poetry book back,' she said 'Don't worry, I'm not snooping.'

'Do you want a cup of tea?' he offered, doing a quick scan

to make sure there was nothing of Cinzia's lying around, though it was probably too late. Thank goodness he hadn't used the marital bedroom or bed with Cinzia, so there shouldn't be anything in there. Not that it was a marital bed any more …

They had a cup of tea and made strained small talk. It was strange and unsettling, because in a way it was as if she'd never left, as if it was a Thursday evening like hundreds before, when she would be waiting for him when he got home from evening class, they'd have a cup of tea and a chat, watch the news on telly, then go to bed together.

But this woman here tonight, although she was technically still his wife and had been his partner for nine years, was a stranger. She even looked a bit different, because she had had her fair hair, previously waist-length, cut short in a pageboy style. She might almost as well have been some stray woman who had wandered in off the street. He felt no love for her any more – that had died months ago. He felt sorry for her, especially as she looked washed-out and fragile, and guilty about the pain he had caused her, but he also felt extremely uncomfortable, especially now that he had Cinzia. It was almost as if he was being unfaithful to Cinzia, just being here with her. How ironic!

'I'm going now,' she said, when she had finished her tea, to his relief, but she didn't stand up. 'Would you look at an essay for me?' She was studying A-level English, at his prompting.

'Sure,' he agreed, surprised by the request and though he was reluctant – he didn't want any more contact with her, wanted a clean break. 'Isn't it a bit late to be handing an essay in?' he asked, hoping it didn't sound as if he was looking for an excuse not to look at it. After all, he had helped her with all her essays, not just English but also history and religious studies, and spent many hours of his time doing so, essays on F. Scott Fitzgerald, Robert Frost, Eugene O'Neill, Robert Lowell, Rudolf Otto …

'I've got an extension,' she said, taking several papers out of her bag and handing them to him.

'What's it about?' he asked, to show interest.

'T. S. Eliot.'

That should be straightforward enough, he thought. 'Do

you want me to type it up for you as well?' he offered, realising she was under pressure and feeling sorry for her again in spite of himself.

'If you don't mind,' she said.

'That's OK. How did the O'Neill essay go, by the way?' He had helped her a couple of months ago with an essay on 'Long Day's Journey Into Night'. In fact, he had half written it for her.

'It got a C+.'

'Is that all?' He felt offended, though it had only been half his work.

'I know I couldn't have got where I am without you,' she proffered, to his surprise. 'I'll always remember you with appreciation.'

'That's OK,' he shrugged, wanting her to go, not wanting to talk about what had happened.

'We had nine good years, didn't we?' she said.

'Yes,' he agreed. '*I* think so, anyway. I'm sorry it had to end.' Why the heck did he say that, he remonstrated with himself?

'I never thought it would end. I suppose I was naïve.'

He shrugged again, wishing she would go. He really didn't want to talk about it and was shocked that she seemed to. It re-opened the wounds, which had at least started to heal. Was she trying to get back with him, even at this late stage, he wondered? Was that why she had come? Was the poetry book just a pretext? Was the essay just a ploy to keep in touch with him? Oh, God, he hoped not, because it was too late, too late, he had moved on. Images of Cinzia and himself making love on this very settee flicked on and off in his mind …

'Where are you staying?' he asked, to try and steer her away from the subject of their failed marriage – the marriage he had never really wanted.

'I prefer not to say,' she said, to his annoyance – not that he was really interested.

'As you wish,' he shrugged.

'What do your family think about what's happened?' she asked, staring at him accusingly. She had always had slightly bulging eyes, caused by her medication for epilepsy.

'They don't sit in judgement on me,' he replied pointedly.

‘Why didn’t your mother tell me before we got married?’

‘Tell you what?’ he asked, needled. He really didn’t want this conversation. He didn’t want to talk about his mother or his family or anything else. And apart from anything else, he was tired after teaching. She could be very self-centred when she wanted to be!

‘Tell me you weren’t ready for marriage.’

‘I tried to tell you myself. It’s you who wanted to get married.’ He felt bad reminding her, but it was she who had started it.

‘I felt sorry for you. I knew you’d been deprived of love and affection, what you’d gone through with the Ghosters and all that.’

This was ironic, he thought – *she* telling him she had felt sorry for *him*, when he had always worried that his feelings for her were based on pity! Which according to Theodor Reik was not the same as love or even a good basis for love …

‘I don’t think there’s any point going over all this again,’ he said. ‘Anyway, I’m very tired.’ Hint, hint.

‘So what are we going to do?’

‘What do you mean? We’re getting divorced, aren’t we?’

‘We don’t have to get divorced.’

‘You mean, you want to get back together?’ This was totally out of the question as far as he was concerned. ‘It would have to be on my terms and conditions.’ He knew she wouldn’t accept.

‘What are they?’

‘You know what they are.’

‘You mean, you want to have other relationships?’

‘Yes.’

‘I can’t accept that.’

‘Why not?’

‘It builds up inside me. The jealousy. The insecurity. I just can’t accept it.’

‘So what do you want to do? Do you still want to get divorced?’

‘Yes, but can’t we remain friends?’

‘I don’t know. I’ll have to see how I feel.’ In fact, he knew that he never wanted to see her again, wanted to make a brand new start with Cinzia.

'Why are you learning Italian?'

So she *had* been snooping! Or at least she'd seen the Teach Yourself Italian book on his desk in the study. Or was it just that uncanny female intuition again? 'That's none of your business, is it?' he said, resenting the question, seriously fed up now.

'Is it because of that Italian girl? Cinzano or whatever her name is.'

Very funny! Why was she interrogating him like this, as if he had committed some crime? What right did she have at nearly midnight on a working day? Of what interest was it to her now who he was with? It was none of her business! He was going to tell her that again in no uncertain terms, but bit his tongue and decided to be candid. He didn't want to hurt her unnecessarily, but she had asked for it – literally.

'No, I was already learning it before I met her,' he said, semi-truthfully. 'I am interested in languages, as you know.'

'What's your relationship with her?'

'You could say it was intimate, I suppose.'

'How do you mean?'

'Physically and emotionally.'

'Have you made love with her?'

'Yes.' He was going to add 'of course', but didn't.

'How many times?'

'Three or four times, I suppose,' he shrugged. She really was making him feel like a criminal now. And making him feel bad about Cinzia, as if she was somehow a criminal, too. But he had decided to play along, so he carried on, answering her questions bluntly.

'Where?'

'Not in your bed, I assure you.' He said it as a sop. Though that might change next week. If Cinzia didn't start acting funny. Women!

'It doesn't matter to me any more.' The comment went through him like a dagger and he realised that his feelings for her, for what they had had, weren't as dead as he had thought. Not that he wanted to know that.

'So you were learning Italian before you met her?'

'Yes.'

'So it's just a coincidence?'

'Yes, maybe. I've always been interested in Italy.' *Especially Italian women.*

'I don't think so.'

'You can think what you like,' he said, reaching the end of his tether, and she must have sensed it.

'I'd better go,' she said, getting up. 'I have to catch the last train.'

'Do you want me to walk to the station with you?' he offered, at the front door.

'No, I can manage,' she said, categorically. 'Thank you for doing the essay for me.'

'When do you need it back?' He'd have to make sure Cinzia didn't find out about this. It was going to be tricky!

'I have to hand it in first thing Monday morning. You can call me when you've done it and I'll come and collect it. If that's all right. Good night.' And she was gone. Gone gone gone …

'OK, good night,' he said with relief, but stayed on the balcony to watch her leave the estate, worried about her safety, a woman on her own in this rather rough, working-class area this late at night, and wondering *why* he was worried. After all, she wasn't his responsibility any more, was she?

Oh well, he thought, going back inside – maybe it wasn't so easy to eradicate every last vestige of love. Maybe true love was indestructible. And he had truly loved her once. Hadn't he?

He remembered the question Cinzia had put to him in the pub the first time they had met: What is love? He wasn't sure he knew or would ever know. He hoped they would find the answer together. He would spend the rest of his life trying to find it if necessary, preferably with her. But maybe there was no simple, easy, glib answer. No secret, magic formula. Maybe love was something you had to *create*, like a piece of music or a poem or a painting. Create *with* someone. And only when you had created it together, only then would you know what it was.

CHAPTER EIGHT

At eleven o' clock the next morning he collected her from outside the town hall, having got up at seven and spent most of the morning editing and typing his wife's essay on Eliot. All about 'recurrent images and themes'...

Cinzia was agitated because she said she had been pestered by a 'black man'. 'Don't worry, you're safe now,' he said, giving her a big hug and they kissed. God, he thought, he loved her more than he would ever have thought possible. The thought of a 'black' man or anybody else pestering her or annoying her in any way aroused all his protective instincts and made him feel angry, even violent – he who was a vegetarian pacifist!

'Ti amo,' she said, as he held her in his arms.

'Ti amo,' he replied. 'You're mine now!'

'For a weeka,' she smiled sadly up at him.

'For ever!' he corrected her, picking up her suitcase and leading her to the bus stop.

'For ever,' she agreed, wistfully.

'Promise?'

'Promise.'

'You'll stay with me for ever?' he asked, forlornly.

'I will stay in your heart for ever. And you will stay in mine.'

It wasn't quite the answer he had wanted. 'Oh, you will stay in my heart for ever,' he assured her. 'But I want you to stay with me for ever too.'

'Baby, don't make me cry,' she said, her eyes moistening. 'Let me be happy just for this weeka. I think I'll never be happy again in my life-a. But I will be happy if I can remember you and this weeka. It will be my golden memory.'

'OK,' he said, pulling her tightly towards him as they sat on the bus and kissing her on the top of the head. But he almost felt like crying himself at the though that he had only one more week with her, when what he wanted was a lifetime. He had to find a way to make her stay, he resolved. He would give her so much love this week that she wouldn't be able to leave him! And he had another card up his sleeve.

When they got to the flat, they had a hurried lunch – pasta of course, which he had pre-cooked – and then he had to rush off to work, though he would have much preferred to spend the afternoon making love with her. He had been tempted to call in sick, but was too professional to do that. Anyway, he consoled himself, they had tonight and the next six nights to make love ...

'Oh, Frank, darling, do you think you could man the phone for me this afternoon?' Bertha accosted him, to his horror emerging suddenly from the ladies' loo next door to his staffroom as he was about to go in. He suspected she had been lurking in the ladies loo, waiting to ambush him.

'Sorry, Bertha,' he said, annoyed at being caught. 'I've got a hospital appointment.' The fib popped out of his mouth without him even thinking – it was how you had to deal with her, he told himself, or she'd have you running around her like a lap dog. If that's what lap dogs did.

'You're not sick, are you?' she asked, as if being sick were a crime. He was never sick.

'Yes, I'm sick of you,' he felt like retorting, but bit his tongue. 'No, it's just a routine check-up sort of thing,' he said. *You nosy cow!*

'Can't you change it?' she demanded, peremptorily.

'Well, I've waited three months for it, Bertha, so I don't want to wait another three months. I'm sorry.' He opened the staffroom door to go in, hoping he hadn't sounded too sarcastic.

'Oh, I'll ask Mark then,' she said. 'Is he in there?'

'He's not here, I'm afraid,' he shook his head, trying to sound disappointed and thinking: *I'll have to warn him*. 'Sorry.' To his relief Bertha then betook her great bulk off in a huff and he went into the room.

'Ah, the au pairs' delight!' Tony proclaimed, looking up from his desk.

The following day, Saturday, they went into London, had lunch in an Italian restaurant and did a tour of the sights, taking photos as they went: Buckingham Palace, St. James's Park, Whitehall, Trafalgar Square, Leicester Square … At first her mood seemed good. 'Oh, I love London so much!' she exclaimed several times. 'There are so many things for everyone. I don't want to leave it. I never want to leave it.'

'You don't have to leave,' he reminded her, giving her a hug. 'You can stay with me. I'll marry you.'

'Baby, don't remind me,' she reprimanded him. 'Let me just enjoy this time-a.'

He felt offended, even jealous, ridiculous as that was – it was almost as if she was more sad about leaving London than leaving him! But he was careful not to show it, was determined to remain upbeat, friendly and affectionate. He knew there was a certain tension in the air between them, because of the situation, and he didn't want to let anything spoil this day out together or any of the days to come.

But then it started raining and suddenly her mood became more subdued. She wasn't responding to his jokes or his gestures of affection. Then rain turned into thunder and lightning and they were forced to take refuge in a pub, the Sherlock Holmes at Piccadilly Circus – not that he ever needed much forcing to enter a pub.

'You seem a bit down,' he observed, bringing her a cappuccino and himself a pint of Guinness, pulling a sympathetic face.

'It's the only thing I don't like about London,' she said. 'The rain. Why does it 'ave to rain todaya? My last daya?'

'Apparently it rains more in Rome,' he informed her.

'But we are in London. It's my last daya!' she wailed.

'I'm sorry. I'll have a word with my uncle. See what he can do.'

'Francis, you are so funny, but I can't laugh any more todaya. I'm too sada.' She looked somewhat bedraggled, since she wasn't wearing anything waterproof – hotpants and a light cardigan over a yellow blouse. His heart went out to her.

'You should go and dry your hair in the toilets,' he suggested.

'I don't want to dry it. I want to keep it. As a souvenir. London raina. Even though I 'ate it!'

'I love you,' he smiled.

'I don't love you,' she replied.

'You don't?' he asked, alarmed, even though he knew she must be joking.

'I 'ave to stop loving you, because if I don't stopa, I can't leave you.'

'I don't want you to leave me.'

'I 'ave to go 'ome-a. I 'ave no choice-a.'

He was tired of hearing this mantra, but again tried not to show any annoyance. As far as he was concerned, she did have a choice, even though he knew it was a very difficult one. Maybe she just didn't love him enough? Maybe she didn't love him at all? Oh, no, he mustn't let any such negative thoughts into his head, he told himself, taking a slug of Guinness to try and wash them away. He had to stay positive. He had to find a way to make her stay with him. Or at least make her promise to come back …

On the way home, after they got off the bus, she said she was hungry and wanted fish and chips, which she loved. He resisted, firstly because they had both had a large, late lunch of pasta, so he didn't understand how she could be hungry, secondly because he had decided to become vegetarian and didn't even want to go into a fish and shop ever again and thirdly because he was impatient to go to bed with her. He was also worried about his wife turning up unexpectedly again, even though he had taken her key off her. 'I'll make you a sandwich,' he told her, but she went into a sulk.

It was the first time he had experienced such behaviour from her and it shocked him, but he excused it because he knew she was upset about going home. Maybe it was also her period, though she hadn't said anything. As soon as they got home, she went into the bathroom, then into the living room, where they had left her luggage, and closed the door, shutting him out. Was she joking or playing a game of some sort, he wondered, suppressing his annoyance?

'What, not even a kiss goodnight?' he asked, opening the door again, still not sure if it was a game or not, unable to believe she wouldn't let him sleep with her, on only their second full night together, only the second night of their 'honeymoon'. Last night, their first full night together, she had been so sweet, so loving, so sexy …

'No more kisses tonighta,' she said, shutting the door in his face.

He stood outside the door for a few minutes, bemused, still thinking that at any moment she would open it again, laugh and throw her arms around him. But she didn't. He heard the switch click and the light went out. He struggled to suppress his anger and bewilderment, tired from the day out, tired of this silly game – if it was a game. He wasn't in the mood for silly games.

'Goodnight,' he called through the door and waited a few seconds for a response but there was none, so he went to bed, in a turmoil of emotions.

What was wrong with her, he wondered, as he lay in bed alone, unable to sleep? Why was she behaving like this? Just because he hadn't wanted to go for fish and chips? How petty, how childish! No, there was more to it than that. It was because she was so unhappy about going back to Italy. She wasn't in her right mind. She wasn't herself. This wasn't his Cinzia, his little mouse. He mustn't be angry with her. He loved her. He had to let her work through her emotions. She'd be all right tomorrow. Everything would be all right tomorrow.

But what if it wasn't? What if she didn't let him sleep with her or make love with her again? What if she didn't love him? Maybe she was just using him! Maybe he was a fool to have fallen for her. Maybe he'd been taken in. If she carried on like this, he'd throw her out tomorrow! No, no, he couldn't do that. He loved her. He could never hurt her. He didn't want to lose her. But it seemed he was going to lose her anyway. Maybe he should go into the living room and get into bed with her? No, he wouldn't. It was *she* who had shut *him* out. Anyway, she might refuse to let him in. He was too proud and too stubborn to suffer another rejection. Even if he was cutting off his nose to spite his face. Even though he felt so lonely, so rejected, so bewildered by her behaviour.

Oh, God, how had it come to this? All because of fish and chips! Here he was, lying alone and lonely in his bed, his wife having left him, his girlfriend having rejected him, his girlfriend whom he loved and desired so madly just on the other side of the wall! What had he done to her to deserve this? Why was she doing this to him? Was it her way of killing their love, of alienating him, so their parting wouldn't be so painful? Maybe that was it. But it was silly. It was cruel. For him the pain of parting, if it had to happen, would be less painful if they could just have six happy days and nights together beforehand. That was what he had hoped for. That had been his dream. But now she had smashed the dream. And she was going to go away and leave him in five days. And then he would really be alone again. Alone again naturally. Or unnaturally. He might never even see her again. That thought sent such a wave of grief over him that tears came to his eyes …

He was woken up in the middle of the night by somebody yelling. It was coming from the living room. 'Francis, I need help! Come and help me!' Still half-asleep, he checked his clock – it was five a.m. What was wrong with her? She was probably just having a nightmare. Should he go to her? No! Let her scream! It served her right, after the way she had treated him. She didn't want him last night, so why should he go to her now? Let her suffer! Here he was, all on his own in the middle of the night, a grown man having cried himself to sleep like a baby, all because of *her*. Let her suffer! Let her learn how proud and stubborn he was. Then maybe she'd never do it again. Anyway, he was too tired, too lazy to get out of bed, having lain awake for so long.

He woke up again at eight o'clock as usual, wondering for a moment if it had all just been a bad dream, but quickly realising it hadn't, feeling guilty about not having gone to see her, worried she might be ill, might even be ... He got out of bed, slipped on his dressing gown and opened his bedroom door, intending to peep into the living room. She was standing there, still dressed as she had been the day before. Before he could say or do anything, she threw her arms around him and pressed her head against his chest, sobbing, 'Oh, baby, I'm sorry, I'm sorry, I'm sorry'.

'It's OK,' he whispered, putting his arms around her, thrilled to feel her body against his again, kissing the top of her head, rubbing her back. 'How long have you been standing here, you silly billy?'

'For three hoursa,' she sobbed. 'Waiting for you.'

'Why didn't you come in, you silly girl?'

'I was afraida,' she sobbed. 'I thought you would be angry with me.'

'I *was* angry,' he said, 'but if you'd come in, I'd've been happy. I was lonely. It was one of the worst nights of my life.'

'I'm sorry, my baby,' she sobbed. 'Can you forgive me?'

'Of course I can forgive you, you silly girl. But why did you behave like that? Not just because I wouldn't let you have fish and chips, I hope!' He gave an ironic little laugh. 'I just don't understand. '

'I'm sorry, Francis. I'm so confuseda. I'm so sad, so un'appy. I don't want to go 'ome-a, but I know I 'ave to go 'ome-a. I love you too much. I don't want to leave you, but I 'ave to leave you. I should never 'ave come 'ere. I should never 'ave fallen in love with you.' She started crying again.

'OK, OK, don't cry,' he whispered, hugging her tight. 'We'll work it out somehow. Why don't you come in here? Come to bed. I'll give you some spanks for being so naughty, ha ha.'

'Oh, Francis, you're so good, I love you so much, you've no idea 'ow much I love you.'

'Well, come and show me then,' he laughed, leading her, with tears streaming down her face, back into the bedroom.

They stayed in bed till two p.m., making love, sleeping, talking. They didn't make love properly, because she said she was too tense and her period was starting, as he had guessed, but that was no problem – he was happy because he had her back, she was back in his arms again, she was his again, even if only for another five days. Not that he was going to let her go after five days. He was more determined than ever to keep her, to make her his for ever, even if he had to follow her to Italy. The main problem was her boyfriend, Luciano. Somehow he had to dissuade her from marrying him. That was going to be difficult. And one way or another, it was going to be painful. But no pain, no gain, he told himself, and all was fair in love and war.

'Why are you so good?' she asked, gazing up into his eyes while he leant over her, playing with her breasts and kissing her tenderly.

'Am I?' he asked, still feeling guilty about last night.

'Si. Maybe you are Jesus Christa.'

'I don't think so!' he laughed.

'Maybe you were Jesus in a previous incarnation.'

'Well, if I'm Jesus,' he laughed, 'you must be the Virgin Mary!'

'If I was the Virgin Mary, I don't think so I would be 'ere in bed with you.'

'No, I suppose not,' he laughed. 'And anyway, you're not a virgin, are you?' His hand travelled up and down her body.

'Oh, baby, I love you so mucha!'

'Also,' he continued, amused by the conceit, 'if I was Jesus, I don't think I'd be here in bed with you. He didn't have sex, did he?' *What a strange conversation!*

'No, but in some ways you are like 'im.'

'In what ways?'

''e was a revolutionary, wasn't 'e? You are a bit of a revolutionary, aren't you?'

'Am I?' he laughed. It sounded vaguely flattering, but he wasn't sure if it was true. More of a rebel maybe. 'How do you mean?'

'You don't keep the rulesa. You break the rulesa.'

'Only if I don't agree with them. If I think they're wrong or stupid.'

'Not like Luciano.'

'Ah, Luciano.' He wasn't sure he wanted to talk about Luciano, but on the other hand it was an opportunity to build the case against him. All was fair. 'What about Luciano?'

'Luciano is so strict, so rigid, so narrow. 'e doesn't smile or laugh mucha.'

'He sounds what we would call in English "uptight",' he

said, guiltily. It was something of an unfair duel, since he wasn't here to defend himself. But, all was fair!

Then she asked him a question that really surprised him. ''ow shall I be'ave when I see 'im?'

'But I don't want you to see him,' he said sternly.

'I know 'e will be angry with me for going to Englanda,' she said, ignoring his comment. 'And for meeting you.'

'Are you going to tell him about me?'

'I will tell 'im. I want 'im to know about you.'

'What will he say?'

''e will say you are nothinga. You are just an aberration. 'e thinks 'e is better than everybody. 'e is arroganta. That's why 'e 'as only one frienda.'

God, the guy sounded like a total prick! Surely she couldn't go back to him, could she? But she seemed determined to.

'You shouldn't marry him,' he said. 'You're going to be miserable if you do. And so am I. And don't say you 'ave no choice-a. I want you to stay with me. I want you to marry me.'

'Oh, baby, I love you so much!' she exclaimed, kissing him wildly, running her hand up and down his body, taking hold of him. 'What does Fred think about me?'

'He loves you,' he groaned with pleasure. 'Just like me.'

'Does 'e want to come?'

'Yes, please,' he groaned and she started to excite him.

'Do you know 'ow many things a couple can do?' she asked, caressing his body with one hand while she played with Fred with the other.

'No,' he laughed hoarsely. 'Tell me.'

'One thousand and one.'

'Really? What are they?'

'This is one,' she said, kissing and licking his cock, putting it in her mouth and sucking it till he came in an ecstasy of relief.

'Wow, that was good, darling,' he gasped into her ear.

'It's my present to Fred, before I leave 'im,' she said.

'Mm, thank you,' he murmured, pulling her down on top of him and holding her close, so that their hearts were beating in unison, like Siamese twins. She still hadn't said she'd stay with him or marry him. But how could she leave him when they were so happy together? How could she throw such happiness as this away? It'd be a crime against nature! They fit together perfectly, in every way. But maybe that was the problem. Maybe it was too perfect. Maybe such perfection was impossible or couldn't last. Maybe that was what was unnatural. But he'd fight to keep it. He'd do everything he could to keep it. He couldn't imagine ever finding such happiness again.

'What are you thinking, baby?' she murmured.

'Nothing,' he replied, holding her even tighter and caressing her back. 'Let's just be happy together for as long as we can, shall we?'

'Oh, baby, I love you so mucha,' she sighed, tears moistening her eyes. 'When I go 'ome-a, I'll speak to the sea about you.'

After his morning class the next day, he met his wife in an Italian café in the shopping arcade, mainly to give her back her T. S. Eliot essay, which he had edited and typed up as promised. He felt guilty about the meeting, because he had to keep it secret from Cinzia, telling her he had a departmental meeting, so he'd be late home for lunch, which she had offered to cook. He felt uncomfortable about it anyway, because he didn't want to see his wife again – as far as he was concerned, their marriage was over, though he had tried his best to save it. He didn't love her any more. He wasn't even sure if he had ever truly loved her. And meeting her now made him feel as if he was sullying his relationship with Cinzia, as if he was being unfaithful to her.

'So, tell me what you want,' Mary said, after they had sat down in the crowded café, in the starchy, schoolmarmish voice she adopted with him lately. She was wearing a pink top that made her look skinny, with no make-up or jewellery of any kind. She looked washed out, drawn, pale, peaky. He tried not to feel sorry for her.

'You mean to eat?'

'I mean what do you want to do?'

'About what?' he asked, as if he didn't know.

'About us.'

'I think we'd better order first, hadn't we?'

To his relief a waitress came over and he ordered cod and chips for her and a salad for himself. He reckoned that if he only had a salad, he would still be able to eat Cinzia's lunch when he got home. *What a silly situation!*

'Is salad enough for you?' she asked.

'I've gone completely vegetarian now,' he shrugged.

'I don't think you should stop eating all meat.'

'You know me,' he laughed. 'The whole hog or nothing, ha ha.' *Why is she talking to me about my diet? Of what interest is it to her any more?*

'You should at least eat chicken and fish.'

'Why?'

'For protein.'

'You can get protein from other sources. You don't need to kill living creatures. I hate cruelty.' He knew that with the last remark he was setting himself up for a riposte and she duly delivered it.

'You don't mind cruelty to women though.'

'Besides which,' he said, ignoring her barb, not wanting to get into an argument or say anything to hurt her, 'meat and fish these days is full of crap such as antibiotics and growth hormones and God knows what else. Not to mention caesium probably, at least if it comes from the Irish Sea.' *You're probably eating some caesium or some sewage right now,* he felt like adding, watching her fork a chunk of cod towards her mouth, but didn't.

'I don't see anything wrong with killing animals,' she said, ignoring his point. 'People have always killed and eaten animals.'

It was strange – here she was, obtusely advocating something that he now regarded as little short of murder, and yet she looked so fragile, so delicate, so vulnerable herself, sitting in front of him in her flimsy, pink cotton T-shirt, as if she wouldn't hurt a fly. Which she probably wouldn't. Not that he would ever call her 'delicate' to her face. She hated being referred to in that way and had once burst into tears when he had used it about her. But why was he so scared of hurting her, if that was her attitude to animals? Maybe she didn't deserve any pity, if she was so unwilling to give pity to other sentient creatures.

'Could you kill a cow? Or a sheep? Or a pig? Or even a chicken?' he demanded, but she declined to answer. Anyway, he knew the answer. 'It's not so much the killing of animals I object to. It's the way they're kept these days. Factory farming. It's barbaric.' *Shouldn't we be talking about T. S. Eliot, not vegetarianism? Or about us? Not that I really want to talk about either. Not that I want to be here at all. Cinzia will be cooking my lunch now. I should be going home.*

'So what do you want to do?' she asked, again ignoring what he had said.

'Do you want me to go through the essay with you?'

'No. I'll go through it myself later. I mean, what do you want to do about us?'

'I thought you wanted a divorce,' he said, squirming inside – he would prefer to talk about T. S. Eliot, vegetarianism or anything rather than this.

'Is that what you want?'

'It's not what I *wanted*. It's what you said you wanted.' He couldn't understand why she was asking him these questions. She couldn't possibly want to get back with him, could she? Not after all they had said and done to each other, not after all the water that had passed under the bridge and the bridge itself been swept away. And anyway, he had Cinzia now. Or did he? 'Have you changed your mind?' he quizzed her.

'No.'

'So why are we discussing it?' Had her parents or somebody put her up to this? Had the whole divorce business just been a bluff? Or was she realising she had made a massive mistake? Whatever, he didn't want to discuss it, wanted only to pay for the lunch, say goodbye, preferably for ever, and go back to Cinzia. If Cinzia was still there. It was getting late, he noticed, glancing at his watch. What if Cinzia saw him here or somehow found out he had been meeting his soon to be ex-wife? The thought terrified him.

'I don't think there's any point discussing it,' he said.

'So you want a divorce?'

'I think we've crossed the Rubicon now, haven't we?'

'What does that mean?'

'It means we've gone too far to turn back. It's too late.' He knew it sounded harsh and possibly wasn't what she wanted to hear. But it was the truth of how he felt. And he didn't want to give her any false hopes or illusions of any kind. Any sort of reconciliation was impossible now. Whatever love he had felt for her had died. All that was left was pity and yes, remorse. This was just re-opening the wound.

'So I should instruct my solicitor?'

It sounded comically pompous, coming out of her mouth, possibly the least pompous person in the whole world. She had probably picked it up from that social worker sister of hers, Mona, like some of the social-worker speak she had used in her letters to him after she left. He almost felt like laughing. He hardly knew whether to laugh or cry. Cry for both her and for himself. For the pain they had inflicted on each other. Especially the pain he knew he had inflicted on her.

'You do what you have to do,' he said, putting the ball back in her court, unfairly perhaps – but he hadn't engineered this meeting or this conversation. 'I'm afraid I have to go. I'll get the bill.'

He called over the waitress, who brought the bill. Mary offered to pay, but he knew she was almost penniless, so he insisted on paying. It wasn't the only bill he was paying today, he reflected wryly, handing the waitress the plate with the money on it.

CHAPTER NINE

In the college bar that evening a disconcerting rumour was circulating that it was going to be closed down. He asked the bar manager about it when he was ordering a drink and to his dismay the manager confirmed it. 'On grounds of cost,' he said.

'Huh,' Frank said. 'If the bastards didn't spend so much money on carpeting their offices so nicely and having so-called training sessions in posh hotels, there wouldn't be any problem.'

'Yeah, dead right, mate. Facking bastards! It's up to you lecturers and students to get together and keep it. I'd start a campaign if I were you. A petition or something. Keep me in a job too.'

'Good idea – I'll do that,' Frank agreed, collecting his pint of Abbot.

When he told the others, they were all immediately up in arms, especially Mark. 'Let's barricade the door and have a sit-in,' he suggested. 'Get pissed while we're at it.'

'Yeah,' he laughed. 'But let's start with a petition. We can start it right now.' He took out a sheet of A4 and together they wrote at the top:

'We the undersigned wish to vehemently object to the closure of the bar at this college. The bar is a very popular social amenity much used by both staff and students. It affords both staff and students a congenial location in which to socialise with each other and indeed often serves as an extension of the education process. It would be a very sad deprivation for all if it were to close.'

They sent it round and collected several signatures there and then, including Cinzia's. She was sitting next to him, in a tweedy skirt, rather closer than he wanted, because he didn't want people to know they were together. But then he thought, well she's only here for a few more days – what does it matter if people know? Besides, he couldn't help feeling a touch of macho pride to be seen with such a pretty girl by his side. On top of that, it might make one or two of the other girls jealous, such as Rosalia from France and Tiziana, the other Italian girl, both of whom he knew liked him. Not that he wanted to make them jealous really – they were nice girls. He just didn't fancy them. He had eyes only for Cinzia. But it would be good to keep them interested, he thought – he might just need one of them soon, if Cinzia really did leave.

'Are you screwing that one, you sly dog?' Mark asked him, when Cinzia went to the loo.

'You could put it like that,' he laughed uncomfortably, realising that Mark had rumbled him. Well, it was rather obvious, he supposed, from Cinzia's body language. She was sitting with her leg almost across his, the way she used to do when they were in the pub together, and making sure none of the other girls got his ear. 'Trouble is, she's going home in a few days,' he added.

'You must be fucking mad if you let her go,' Mark opined.

'What can I do?' he shrugged, pained indeed at the thought of losing her.

'I'd tie her to the fucking bed. On a chain just long enough to reach the kitchen and the bathroom. And I'd shag her so silly she'd never want to leave me anyway.'

'I'm working on it,' he laughed.

'I thought you had a bit of a smug look on your face lately! How long's this been going on?'

'Only a few weeks.'

'You jammy bastard! Well, I'm going to work on that blondie over there,' Mark said, standing up. 'One of yours?'

'Yeah. German. Name's Steffi. Nice-looking, but a bit of a bimbo.'

'As I've told you before, mate, it's their bodies I'm interested in, not their minds. If I want intellectual stimulation, I go to the library. Look, I'm desperate. I haven't had a woman for months. I'm sick of wanking. I've nearly wanked my dick off! She looks like a goer to me. Wish me luck. See ya.'

'Good luck,' he laughed, as always horrified but amused by Mark's macho, cynical, jack-the-lad attitude to women. 'And good night! I'm going home in a few minutes, when I've finished this pint. See you tomorrow.'

'That's an early finish for you, isn't it?' Mark said, turning back.

'She's got her exam tomorrow,' he explained. 'I've promised to take her home early so she can get a good night's sleep.'

'Yah, and pigs will be flying all night too,' Mark shot back as he made for his quarry.

The next day was Tuesday, the fifteenth of June, the day of the Cambridge First Certificate examination written papers, which Cinzia was taking and he was invigilating, held as always in the Main Hall. This was an intermediate level examination which he expected her to pass easily, possibly with a grade A, especially after the extra bit of coaching he had given her. As at the oral examination, he pretended to ignore her while he was invigilating, apart from a few pleasantries and frequent surreptitious glances while she was reading and scribbling away.

As usual, once the sixty-odd candidates had settled down to work and they had completed all the initial admin, his two colleagues – Mark and Geoff – and he proceeded to play the ratings game to pass the time. This meant giving marks out of ten for looks and desirability to various female students as they sat scribbling, chewing their pencils or just frowning at the paper. As most of the candidates were girls, there were plenty to choose from, including Cinzia.

'What about that Italian in the hotpants, row three, seven back?' Geoff asked, to his discomfort indicating Cinzia.

'That's Frank's piece of totty,' Mark said. 'She's out of bounds.'

'Really, Frank? Are you doing a line with her?' Geoff asked.

'We are very friendly, let's say,' Frank admitted, slightly embarrassed but at the same time flattered.

'He means he's screwing the arse off her day and night,' Mark said.

'Not quite,' he laughed uncomfortably.

'You lucky sod,' Geoff commented. 'But we can still give her a mark, can't we? Frank?'

'If you like,' Frank laughed uncomfortably again.

'I'd give her an eight,' Geoff said. 'She's very pretty. Lovely tan. Nice tits.'

'I'd give her a ten,' Mark said, 'but that's just because I'm so fucking desperate. I'll give anything with tits a ten.'

They both chuckled as surreptitiously as possible while the candidates beavered away. He felt sorry for them as always, remembering examinations in the study hall at the junior seminary long ago. But at least they wouldn't have to go and say the Rosary in front of a grotto in the college grounds afterwards, to be followed by an evening of study in the study hall under the beady eye of an irascible, maniacal Dean of Studies …

'How did you get on with that German one last night?' he asked Mark, keen to divert attention away from Cinzia.

'Steffi? She gave me the bum's rush.'

'Why?'

'I asked her what her father did in the war. Not exactly the most romantic of chat-up lines, I know, on reflection. But I thought it'd be better to get the subject of the war out of the way early on. Rather than having it crop up in mid-fuck or something.'

'What did she say?' Frank asked, shocked but amused.

'She said her grandfather and grandmother were both killed in the bombing of Dresden by the RAF.'

'Oh, dear! To which you replied?'

'Let me take you home tonight and fuck you silly to make up for it.'

'You bloody didn't!' Frank laughed, shaking his head.

'Well, not quite in so many words. Suffice it to say, she didn't fall for my numerous charms. Not the least of which is a nine-inch dick.'

Frank and Geoff chuckled quietly. One of the candidates put a hand up.

'I'll get this one if you like – she's one of mine,' Frank offered, standing up, not enjoying the laddish banter as much as usual.

'What, another one of yours?' Geoff chipped in.

'Not like that,' Frank laughed, moving towards the candidate.

'They don't call him the au pairs' delight for nothing,' he heard Mark say to Geoff as he moved away to help the candidate, not as flattered or amused as he used to be by the Tony Holloway-conferred title, because he was head-over-heels in love with Cinzia.

When he had fetched the candidate some extra writing paper, he walked up and down the row, just for the excuse of pausing at Cinzia's desk to see how she was doing. On a piece of scrap paper, in large capital letters for him to see, she had written:

TI AMO

Oh, God, he couldn't let her go, he told himself. Mark was right – he'd be a fool. For him she was ten out of ten and all the other girls in the room were zeros. He'd tell her that later, he thought, going back to sit down with his colleagues. He had arranged to meet her in the college foyer later that afternoon, when the examination had finished. He could hardly wait.

The next morning they stayed in bed till ten o'clock, making love. It was their last full day together. Unless he could persuade her to change her mind and stay with him. Or at least promise to come back to him.

'You never fail, you always do it,' he said, after she had made him come with her hand for the third time.

'What?' she asked, playing with him, pretending not to know what he meant.

'You know,' he laughed, wrapping his arms around her and hugging her tight, still slowly floating back down into the earth's atmosphere after the high of orgasm. 'Make me come. That's three times in one night! I think it's a record!'

'Because I love you, my baby.'

'And I love *you*. What about you? Are you happy? Have you had enough?'

'Si, grazie. You make me very 'appy. Anyway, I think Fred is too tireda.' She was still playing with the aforementioned Fred, but Fred was definitely played out now.

'Tonight then,' he whispered, kissing her.

'Si. Our last nighta,' she said, sadly.

'It doesn't have to be,' he replied, caressing her tenderly.

'What shall we do tonighta?' she asked, ignoring what he said.

'I think we should get drunk and make love all night,' he laughed.

'I love you so much, my baby. I don't know 'ow I can live without you. I don't know 'ow I can leave you.'

'You don't have to.'

'Maybe I should just suicide myselfa.'

'Hey, don't talk like that!' He smacked her on the bum.

'Maybe we should both suicide together tonighta.'

'I said don't talk like that.' He smacked her on the bum again, harder. 'This is not Romeo and Juliet, you know.'

'Ouch!' she laughed and he hugged her tightly to him.

'Can we go to the forest tonighta?' she asked.

She was talking about Epping Forest, near where she had lived in North Chingford. He knew it was one of her favourite places, as it was one of his, where they had gone for walks a few times.

'Good idea,' he said. 'Maybe I should murder you and bury you there. Then I can visit your grave every day.'

'I would be 'appy to stay there, if you visit me every daya.'

'Hey, I *was* only joking!' he laughed.

'You can kill me now if you want. Then I will always be yours.'

'You mean like this?' he laughed, putting a hand on her throat and pretending to squeeze, kissing her on the lips at the same time. In fact it was quite erotic and he felt himself becoming aroused again, so took his hand away, slightly shocked by himself. 'No, I think I'll just fuck you to death instead,' he said, easing himself on top of her …

Later he made her breakfast in bed – cornflakes accompanied by crisps and Treets, her favourite chocolates, which he had bought specially for the occasion. ‘This is the best breakfast of my whole life-a!’ she declared. ‘Baby, I’m in ’eaven with you. You make me so ’appy. You are so good to me.’

‘I love you, that’s why.’

‘I’m just a little girla. What you need is a woman.’

‘Well, in some ways you’re a little girl, that’s true, but in other ways you’re a lovely woman.’

‘You ’ave made me a woman. I feel like a woman with you. Tell me what you like sexually. I’ll do it for you tonighta.’

‘You know,’ he said, and whispered in her ear, too embarrassed to say it out loud: ‘Blow job.’

‘Ugh!’ she said. He knew she didn’t really like doing it, even though she had done it once before for him, but only once. ‘Do you want me to do it nowa?’

‘Not now,’ he laughed. ‘You haven’t finished your breakfast. And I have to go to work. I’m invigilating again. Tonight.’

‘OK, maybe we do it again tonighta,’ she agreed.

‘You don’t mind?’

‘I don’t minda. My girl friends all talk about it, what they do. They say to me, “Oh, ’aven’t you done that yet?” I’ve never done it before I met you. Did I do it righta?’

‘You certainly did,’ he laughed, excited already.

‘It’s funny. I’m so inexperienced. I ’ave only made love with one man. And ’e only wants to do it one waya. I ’ad my first kiss when I was thirteen, no, twelve-a. With the boy downstairs. ’e said, “Do you like it?” I said ‘Yes!’ But really I am shy. But I’m not shy with you. I used to ’ave sexa with my boyfriend in the bedroom when I was supposed to be studying and my mum was downstairs. I can’t believe it nowa. Just kissing and touching.’

‘Didn’t you take your clothes off?’

‘Clothes off? No! But it was my first time to ’ave sexa. Is kissing sexa?’

‘Kissing like we do is, yes,’ he laughed. ‘It’s called French kissing.’

‘Why do they call it French kissing? It’s like a school for sex with you!’

He laughed. ‘I don’t know. The French are supposed to be good at it perhaps. Maybe I should start a school for sex. That’s a good idea. English and Sex instead of English and Business. Much more fun!’

‘Promise me you will not ’ave sexa with another girl for one month after I go.’

‘Hey, I don’t even want to think about that. You’re the only girl I want to ’ave ‘sexa’ with ever again in my whole life-a.’

‘Promise me, baby,’ she said seriously, ignoring his mimicry of her accent. ‘So I can at least dream about you for one month.’

‘I promise.’

‘’ave you ’ad much discipline in your life?’

‘What a funny question! Yes, I suppose so.’ He remembered all those years in the seminary, which he hadn’t told her about. God, he had a bloody honours degree in discipline!

‘From your parents?’

‘They were quite strict. More at school really. The teachers used to hit us a lot. Some of them were psychopaths.’ He shouldn’t have said it. It was a subject he didn’t want to go near. It was like a big black ugly cloud on the horizon of his memory. ‘Maybe that’s why I like spanking girls,’ he laughed, giving her a playful spank on the bum again, making her squeal. Then he kissed her.

‘Luciano slapped me once.’

‘He *slapped* you?’ He stopped in mid-kiss, shocked.

‘On the face-a.’ *Bastard!*

‘Why?’ he asked, stroking her face tenderly.

‘I said something cheeky. It was only once-a. ’e never did it againa. ’e apologiseda.’

‘It doesn’t matter. That’s disgusting! For a man ever to hit a woman. It’s unforgiveable. You should have left him there and then. And if you marry him, how do you know he won’t do it again? Or worse? He might think because you’re married, he has the right. You mustn’t let him. I can’t bear the thought of anyone hurting you, darling. Promise me, if he does, you’ll leave him.’

'I promise, baby. I love you. You don't speak much, but when you do, it's concentrated. I love you so mucha. I love the way you speak to me. I love everything about you. Will you promise me something?'

'Of course. I love you.'

'Will you come to see me in Italy? Just once-a?'

'OK.' He felt his heart contract with pain at the thought of her leaving in twenty-four hours. And he wasn't sure he wanted to go to Italy if she did leave, because it would only prolong the pain.

'Will you write to me too?'

'That's two promises,' he laughed, trying to put the previous thoughts out of his mind.

'Please, my baby. I can't live without you completely.'

'OK.'

'Often?'

'Often.' He kissed her. 'But I don't want you to go.'

'If you write to me, I will keep all your letters,' she said, kissing him.

'Where will you keep them?'

'In a special box 'idden in the cellar of my 'ouse-a.'

'In the cellar? But couldn't somebody else find them there? Why not in your bedroom?'

'My mum would find it if I kept it in my bedroom. It's in a secret place in the cellar. And only I 'ave the key. It's a special box where I keep all my private thingsa.'

'All your love letters from other boys, eh?'

'I'll throw them all outa. I'll keep only your letters.'

'You have to write to me too,' he said, touched.

'I'll write every day,' she said. 'Even if you don't reply to my letters, I'll write every daya. Even if I don't send them. It will be my – 'ow do you say, life – '

'Lifeline.'

'It will be my lifeline-a.'

'Oh, God, my darling, I love you so much,' he exclaimed, taking her in his arms again, suddenly touched almost to tears. 'Why don't you stay with me? I'll love you for ever. I'll make you happy for ever.'

'I 'ave to go 'ome, my baby, but I'll always remember you.

I'll never forget you. You will always be my lifeline-a.' Seeing the tears in his eyes, she embraced him and held his head to her chest, stroking it. 'Don't cry, my baby, don't cry. I'll always love you. I'll love you until the day I die. I'll never forget you, I promise.'

Suddenly, he couldn't hold in his emotion any longer and he felt tears running down his face. For the first time in his adult life he was crying in front of another human being! Even as the tears ran down his cheeks, he felt embarrassed and tried to fight them back but couldn't. It wasn't manly to cry! *Big boys don't cry!* That was what they had always been taught. But he decided to let the tears flow. Maybe if she saw how much she meant to him, how much he loved her, she'd change her mind and stay. So he let the tears flow freely while she held his head tight to her chest and stroked it, as if she was his mummy and he her little boy.

'Ah, the au pairs' delight!' Tony declared, when he rushed into the examination hall that afternoon, slightly late, which was unusual for him.

'Hi, sorry I'm a bit late,' he laughed, embarrassed. *I've been screwing my girlfriend all morning.* 'What are you doing here?' Tony was a history lecturer, not EFL.

'Bertha twisted my arm into doing it for her. Said she had interviews to do or something.'

'Lazy cow. You should have refused. Told her to 'fuck off', as Mark would say.'

'Oh, I don't mind too much. I can do some work on my book. In fact, it's the best place, once they've all settled down. Nice and studious. Better than the staffroom. Not so many interruptions.'

'Oh, good,' he said and started to help putting the exam papers on the desks. It was the Cambridge Advanced exam, Use of English, which would be followed by the listening paper.

'What's your book about?' he asked Tony when the students had settled down to work and they had completed the register and seating plan.

'Oh, modern European history. Second World War. Hitler

and his cronies. That's my main area of interest, you know.'

'Roy seems to be a fan of Hitler, at least as far as the Jews are concerned,' he observed.

'That's because of Bertha, Bertha being a big Yiddisher momma,' Tony said.

'And because I think he's got some sort of Austrian girlfriend. In Austria, I mean. Not here. He goes to visit her. So he tells me.'

'Really? I didn't know that. But you're the only one who really talks to him. Is she an ex-concentration camp guard?'

'I don't know,' he laughed. 'I'll ask him.'

'What he and his ilk forget is that it wasn't just the Jews Hitler went after. It was gypsies, the mentally and physically handicapped and homosexuals as well.'

'Really?'

'Yes. That's what my book's about. The Other Holocaust is the working title.'

'Sounds fascinating. I hope I'll get a complimentary copy.'

'You're one of the few people who will.'

'You'll have to give Roy one as well!'

'He can damn well put his hand in his pocket, the skinflint. He doesn't half chunner on. I have to say, Frank, I do admire the way you handle him. I don't know how you do it.'

'I sort of feel sorry for him, actually. And he is quite interesting, once you get talking to him. We have lunch together sometimes. Over at the town hall. He knows a lot about German and Russian languages, for example. And politics. Even though he's pretty reactionary.'

'Come to think of it, he looks a bit like Hitler. Especially with that toothbrush moustache.'

'You're right!' Frank laughed. 'But he's certainly not a vegetarian. Eats a steak for lunch every day.'

One of the candidates put their hand up and Frank went to deal with them while Tony carried on with his book.

'A few nice-looking birds in here today,' Geoff whispered, when he sat down at the front again, having done a tour of the room.

'As always,' he replied, not really wanting to talk laddish.

'Any of them yours?'

'Most of them, actually. In a manner of speaking.'

'Is Véronique Gauthier one of yours? She was in the exam yesterday.'

'Yes. In a manner of speaking,' he grinned. What was Cinzia doing, he wondered? Was she packing?

'I fancy her like mad.'

'She is very attractive.' He felt guilty even saying that, thinking of Cinzia.

'Never noticed her all year, but our eyes met at the exam yesterday. I had a little chat with her at the end, invited her out. But it was too late. She told me she was leaving today. Was meeting some friends last night. She'll be gone now. Could kick myself. That ever happened to you?'

He thought again of Cinzia, who had been in his class for several weeks before they 'met' at the bus stop that first time. But he didn't want to talk about Cinzia, not in that way, not as if she was just a casual fling. He was serious about her! She would be packing now, he supposed, not that she had much to pack. Strangely, the thought didn't bother him. It was too unreal, like a dream. He couldn't believe she would really go tomorrow. How could she leave him, when they loved each other so much? She couldn't! She wouldn't! Surely love conquered all?

'No, not really,' he replied. He hoped he didn't ask him about Cinzia.

'Mind you, about five years ago, I noticed a girl who was leaving next day. I went home with her and we had what you might call a 'refined grope' on the couch. But it was too late. That was the last I saw of her.'

'You never kept in touch?'

'No. I think she was a bit ashamed of what she'd done, actually.'

'Oh, well, there are plenty more fish in the sea,' he said. 'A few fanciable ones in here, aren't there?'

'Indeed. That black one right in front of us, for example. What a pair of knockers! But I've had a few successes since. Are you really, you know, with that Italian one who was at the exam yesterday?'

'Yes,' he admitted somewhat sheepishly. 'We've been

together a few weeks. But she's leaving tomorrow.' It sounded unreal, even as he said it. He could hardly believe it himself. In a way, the whole thing was unreal, like a dream.

'I'm sorry to hear that. I mean, I take it you don't want her to leave?'

'No. It's quite serious, actually. I'd like to marry her in fact.'

'Oh, that serious? But she doesn't?'

'She says she has to go home to marry this berk of a boyfriend she's engaged to.'

'Oh, dear. I am sorry. There's no way you can persuade her not to?'

'I've tried, believe me. I still can't believe she'll actually go, to be honest. It seems unreal. Like some sort of bad dream.'

'Maybe she won't, when it comes to the crunch.'

'I don't know what I'm going to do tomorrow night, if she does. Get smashed, I suppose.'

'I'll be watching England in the World Cup.'

'Who are they playing?'

'Italy.'

'Oh, no! I think I'll give that one a miss!'

That evening, after teaching, he took a bus to Chingford to meet her as arranged at the Queen Elizabeth Hunting Lodge on the edge of Epping Forest, where they went for a walk as planned. The forest looked resplendent in its mid-June livery of greens of different shade: oak, beech, silver birch, chestnut, hawthorn, holly and other trees he couldn't identify. As well as the trees, there were open areas of grassy heath and several ponds. What a miracle that it had been preserved from property developers and speculators over the centuries, for ordinary people like them, he thought! It was like stepping into a different world from that of hustling, bustling, modern London. It was like stepping into a different time too – it was easy to imagine one of the Tudor kings with their retinue on horses hunting wild boar or deer. Not that he would have wanted to be around then and certainly not that he would have wanted to be involved in shooting deer or boar any other animal …

'Oh, baby, it's so beautiful!' Cinzia exclaimed, as they

strolled through the arcades of trees.

'Yes,' he agreed, trying not to think that by this time tomorrow she would be hundreds of miles away.

'There's a lake too!' she exclaimed, as Connaught Water came into view with its little wooded islands.

'Yes, I was keeping that as a surprise for you,' he laughed. 'Lovely, isn't it? Let's walk round it. "You have been to Derrinrush: you know how mystic and melancholy the lake is, full of hazels and Druid stones".'

'What are you talking about, baby?' she asked.

'It's a quotation from a novel called 'The Lake' by an Irish writer called George Moore. The novel's a bit boring, to be honest, but I think that sentence is beautiful. I always think of it whenever I'm at a lake.' *Especially if I'm with a girl I fancy and I think it might impress her.*

'You are so clever, my baby,' she said. 'It's why I love you.'

'Not because I'm handsome and charming?'

'I love you because you're you,' she replied.

'Thank you, darling,' he said, hugging her. 'That's what I wanted to hear. Anybody can be clever. The world is full of clever people. And handsome men. And pretty girls. It's not so important really, is it?'

'You see, you are so intelligent, my baby. You say intelligent things. Not like Luciano. He is so stupid!'

'Oh dear!' he laughed. This was music to his ears, though he actually felt sorry for the hapless Luciano, who again wasn't here to defend himself. Which was stupid of him, he thought, since it was Luciano who would be with her this time tomorrow. The thought sent a stab of pain through him. He didn't want her to go! He didn't want Luciano to have her! It had almost become personal – even though he had never met this Luciano – a sort of love tug-of-war, unless he could say or do something to make her change her mind. And he had something that might just do that, a surprise that he would spring on her later tonight or in the morning, his last throw of the dice.

'I can never walk slowly like this with Luciano,' she observed. ''e is always in 'urry.'

'Let's not talk about Luciano or anybody else, darling,' he

said, hugging her, wanting to rid Luciano from his mind. ‘Let’s just enjoy being together. In our own little world. At least for tonight.’

‘I’m sorry, baby. You are righta! Let’s pretend there is no tomorrow. Let’s pretend today will last for ever.’

‘I want it to last for ever,’ he said.

‘Me too, my baby,’ she agreed.

‘Or at least as long as these trees,’ he said, stopping for a moment to gaze up at the towering beeches all around.

‘Are they very olda?’ she asked.

‘Hundreds of years, some of them, I should think.’

‘They are so simple and basic,’ she observed.

‘How do you mean?’

‘They’re born, they grow, they live, they die-a.’

‘Yes. They’re so – dignified. That’s what I like about them.’ He patted the trunk of one. ‘This one for example. Here it is. Just standing here, strong and silent. Stood here for hundreds of years maybe. Just carries on being a tree, season after season, hail, rain, shine, snow. Doing what it’s supposed to do. Fulfilling its destiny. Bothering nobody. If only we could be more like that.’

‘Oh, baby, you’re a philosopher, I know,’ she crooned. ‘And a poet.’

‘Now I’ll have to write a poem about it,’ he laughed. ‘Sonnet to a Tree. There was a famous poet who lived around here, you know. In the forest, I mean. At a place called High Beach. We’re going there.’

‘What was his name?’

‘Edward Thomas. Apparently he lived here in the forest during the First World War. But sadly he was killed in the very last year of the war. He was only thirty-nine – only four years older than me. He wrote a lot of poems about nature and the countryside. But they weren’t published till after he died. So he never knew he was famous. He was very poor, actually. He’d be rich if he were still alive, I suppose, from royalties.’

‘How sad! Do you know any of his poems?’

‘His most famous poem is called ‘Adlestrop’.’

‘What is it abouta?’

‘It’s about a tiny village in the middle of the English

countryside where his train stops unexpectedly one hot June afternoon. Just like today! Except it was late June, not mid-June. We used to have a proper railway system in this country, until the stupid Tory government closed half of the stations, because they didn't make a profit. It's a very simple but lovely poem:

> Yes, I remember Adlestrop –
> The name, because one afternoon
> Of heat the express-train drew up there
> Unwontedly. It was late June.

I'll give you a copy if you like.' I'll give her my little anthology of Edward Thomas, he thought. As a farewell present. *No, don't think about it! Don't think about tomorrow ...*

'Thank you, baby. You are so clever. You know so many thingsa.'

'Not really,' he smiled, with a shrug. 'I just happen to be interested in poetry. Reading it and writing it.'

In fact it was his colleague and friend Roger who had put him onto the connection between Epping Forest and Edward Thomas. Roger, whose knowledge of literature was ten times his, who made him feel like an ignoramus, even though he had an honours degree in English Literature! Roger, who had taken him one day to see an old man called Ernie Miller in Loughton, who claimed to be the seventeen-year-old telegraph boy who had delivered the telegram with the news of Edward's death to his wife, Helen, right here in High Beach, which they were now approaching, with the setting sun, still fire-hot and fire-bright, bathing the treetops in a golden benediction of dazzling light and the fiery air full of sweet incense-like scents of flowers, and he with the girl he loved, so that suddenly, secretly, for a moment or two, he felt transfigured, transported to a state of bliss, as if he had taken a drug and entered a paradise, a garden of Eden, a state of bliss he often imagined and dreamt of ...

Enraptured, he put both his arms around her and pulled her close. 'I love you,' he declared, solemnly. 'I've never been so happy in all my life. I'll always remember this moment. For ever and ever.'

'A – a – achoo!'

'Oh, dear!' he laughed. 'Is that all you have to say? Very romantic!'

'A – a – achoo !' she sneezed again. 'Scusami.'

'Have you got a cold?' he asked.

'I 'aven't got a colda. I 'ave got – 'ow do you say, grass allergia?'

'Ah, allergy. Hay fever we call it.'

'What is 'ay?'

'It's grass. Dry grass. What horses eat. Here, use my hanky.'

She took his hanky and blew her nose.

'I'm sorry, darling. I usually have hay fever, but not today for some reason. I think this is a good excuse to go in the pub here for a drink. Get you away from the pollen. Not that we need an excuse, do we?' They had arrived outside the King's Oak in High Beach, in the middle of the forest, one of his favourite places, now to be associated for ever more with this his last evening with her. If it *was* to be the last.

'Grazie,' she said, giving him his hanky back.

'Perhaps I should keep it and never wash it,' he laughed, putting it in his pocket.

'You are so funny, my baby. I will give you a piece of my 'air to keep if you wanta.'

'I do wanta,' he mimicked her.

'Achoo!'

'Here, have my hanky again,' he said, giving it back to her.

'Bellissima!'

'What? My hanky?'

'Achoo! Bellissima vista.' She held out her arm.

'Ah, the view! Yes, it's beautiful.'

From this high point in the forest they could gaze across a green sea of trees and meadows stretching far into the hazy distance, a green sea illuminated to an almost unearthly radiance by the still brilliant, sinking sun. Again he felt that euphoric sensation of transfiguration that he had felt a few moments before, as if this were some secret paradise and he had been suddenly transported here from his normal humdrum life by some magnificent and munificent god.

'What are you thinking, my baby?' she asked.

'I'm thinking, it's funny, isn't it?' he said, holding her close to his side, enraptured. 'That poet, who's dead now, lived here seventy years ago, where we are now. It makes me feel an extra connection with him. Little did he know that you and I would be walking here one day, over sixty years later, perhaps exactly where he walked once, and I'd be quoting one of his poems to you, an Italian girl. So you see the connections: me, Manchester, Ireland, Waltham College, London, you, Italy, Epping Forest, High Beach ... Strange! It'd make a good short story. Maybe I'll write it one day.'

'Will you give it to me?'

'If you stay with me.'

'Baby, you are breaking your rule-a! We are not going to talk about tomorrow. Only todaya.'

'Yes, I'm sorry. There's no tomorrow. Tomorrow has been cancelled. Maybe we can just skip tomorrow and go straight to Friday. Then you will still be with me. How about that?'

'Sssh! You mustn't say anythinga!' she put a finger on his lips.

'OK,' he laughed, pulling her away from the view. 'Come on. Let's go in the pub and have a drink and something to eat. You should splash your face with cold water. It'll help to stop you sneezing.'

CHAPTER TEN

'Am I doing it right?' she asked, looking up at him.

'Yes! Yes! It's lovely! Carry on!' he panted.

'Does Fred like it?' she asked, in between licks.

'He loves it!' he gasped.

It was Thursday morning, the day of her departure. They were in bed, having woken up at eight o'clock and started making love. The night before they had both been too drunk and too tired to do so – after arriving home, they had both drunk some more, he had put her Barry Manilow record on, she had started dancing in her bra and knickers and they had fallen into bed in each other's arms, but both conked out almost immediately.

She was doing what he had requested the other day – holding him with one hand and alternately licking and sucking him as she crouched on the bed between his legs, her breasts hanging provocatively as she did so. He was trying to make it last as long as possible, because it was so good, but he came with a loud groan all too quickly.

'Ugh!' she exclaimed. 'The liquid is in my mouth! Shall I swallow it?'

'You can if you want,' he laughed, still panting from the exertion. 'Some women do, apparently.'

'I 'ave already swallowed it!'

'Is it OK?'

'Si, it's OK. I want it inside me. It's from you. It's your children. I will take them with me to Italy.'

'I don't want you to go to Italy,' he said, grabbing her and pulling her down on top of him. 'I love you. I want to keep you.'

'I love you, too, my baby, but I 'ave to go-a.'

'I've got something for you.'

'What 'ave you gota?'

He reached over to the bedside cabinet, opened the drawer and took out a little purple box. 'Sit up and close your eyes,' he ordered her and she did so. Then he put the box in her hand. 'You can open your eyes now.'

'What is it?' she asked, opening her eyes and looking.

'Open the box,' he ordered.

She did so and burst into tears.

'Oh, dear!' he laughed, kissing her. 'That's not the reaction I was expecting!'

'What is it?' she asked, tears rolling down cheeks.

'It's a ring. An Irish ring. It's called a Claddagh ring. It's a love ring. A wedding ring, if you like.' It looked lovely in its box, a gold circle with a heart clasped by two hands and surmounted by a crown.

'Is it for me?'

'Of course it's for you, silly billy. Here, let's put it on, shall we?' He took the ring out of the box and slipped it onto the ring finger on her left hand, making sure the point of the heart was towards her fingertips with their bright red nails, to show she was engaged. The gold looked good against her slender, brown finger.

'It's beautiful. Why 'ave you got me a ringa?'

'Because I want you to stay here and marry me. Will you?'

She burst into tears again and threw her arms around his neck. 'I want to stay 'ere and marry you, my baby,' she blubbed, 'but I can't. I 'ave to go 'ome-a. I 'ave to go. I know I should never 'ave fallen in love with you. I knew it was a mistake-a. I'm sorry, my baby. I'm so sorry. I know I 'ave 'urt you. Please forgive me.'

'It's OK, darling, it's OK, I understand,' he whispered, holding her tight, kissing her head and caressing her, thinking: *This is the last time I'll be able to hold her like this.*

'Thank you for the ring, my baby. It's the most beautiful gift I 'ave ever received from anybody. I will wear it for ever until the day I die. For you. Nobody 'as ever given me so much love as you. No Italian man could be as good as you. They are different. From a different tradition.'

He was touched, but at the same time disappointed. He had

hoped that offering to marry her and giving her a ring might just have made her change her mind. It seemed as if Luciano had won. He felt tears pricking his own eyes, but blinked them back. It was too late for tears, he told himself. He had done his best to keep her. What more could he say or do, apart from kidnapping her?

'Promise me something, baby,' she sniffled, raising her head, eyes red from crying, tears trailing her cheeks.

'Yes?'

'Promise you will come to see me in Italy. At least once. Will you promise? Then I can survive, if I know you will come.'

'OK, I promise,' he said, hugging her again, choking.

'I mean soon.'

'On one condition.'

'What is it?'

'You don't marry him. I'll come as long as you're not married to him. Or anyone else.'

'I won't marry 'im soon. I'll wait for you to come, my baby. Then perhaps I'll marry 'im. Maybe I won't marry 'im. If I don't marry 'im, I will never marry anybody else-a.'

'What about me?'

'Then I'll marry you.'

'So I'm only your second choice, am I?' he teased, trying to make light of it, to ease the pain in his throat and his heart.

'You're my first choice, my baby, but I 'ave no choice. When will you come to see me?'

'I don't know,' he shrugged. He didn't know if he really wanted to. Not because he didn't love her, but because he didn't want to go through this pain again. And because there was no point if she couldn't or wouldn't marry him.

'Next montha? July? Augusta?'

'I'm working in Dublin in July and August, darling. Maybe October, during half-term.'

He didn't want to miss the summer school in Dublin – it was fun and he needed the money. Besides, it would be a good antidote to the pain of losing her. October was four months away. By then perhaps some of the pain of losing her would have eased. By then perhaps he'd be over her. By then perhaps he'd have found somebody else, though the thought sent a dagger through his heart. He couldn't imagine loving any other girl as much. He couldn't imagine life without her. The thought of tonight without her made the dagger twist in his heart. Could he really go to Italy to see her and suffer this heartbreak all over again?

'I must see you at least once again,' she said. 'I'll wait for you. You promise me you will come?'

'I promise,' he said again, wondering what the punishment would be for breaking such a promise and what the punishment would be for keeping it, looking at his watch. 'I think we'd better get up. It's eleven o'clock. The flight's at three, isn't it?'

'Si. 'old me in your arms for just a few more minutes, my baby,' she said, crying again.

He took her in his arms and held her as close as possible, caressing her tenderly, kissing her tears away, struggling to keep his own tears from mingling with hers, telling himself to memorise every moment of these last few minutes, telling his fingers to memorise every curve and surface of her body, telling his heart to remember for ever that this was what love was like, this was what love meant, this was love's and therefore life's apogee.

While she was in the bathroom, the phone rang. To his annoyance, it was Mary.

'Can I meet you today to give you those library books back?'

'I can't meet you today, I'm afraid.' Why did she want to keep meeting him? She was going to divorce him, wasn't she? Was she hoping for a reconciliation? That was out of the question now! Now that she had put him through so much grief. Now that he had found Cinzia. Even though he was about to lose Cinzia.

'Is somebody with you?' she demanded, accusingly.

'Yes,' he blurted out defiantly.

'The Italian girl?'

'Yes.'

'Is she living with you?'

'It's none of your business,' he felt like saying, but resisted. 'Just for a few days,' he said. 'She's going back to Italy today.' Why was he giving her all this information, to which she had no right, he wondered? He just didn't feel like lying or making up a story. She had no rights over him any more.

'Are you going to the airport with her?'

'I might do.' *It's none of your business!*

'That's why you can't meet me. Is she sleeping with you?'

'That's definitely none of your business,' he wanted to say, but then thought it would be better to let her know the truth, to let her know they were over, to stop her stalking him like this. 'Yes,' he said.

'I thought you said the bed was for you and me.'

'Not in the bed, on the settee,' he fibbed. She was making him feel guilty. She was good at that. Why shouldn't he let Cinzia sleep in the bed? *She* had abandoned it!

'I find that very difficult, in fact impossible, to believe,' she said, in her new, starchy voice. 'So what do you do, have it off on the floor first and then get on the settee?'

'No, we have it off on the settee, then the floor,' he couldn't resist riposting sarcastically. *As if it's any of your business.*

'I hope you haven't used the continental quilt.' *God, the things that women worried about! What the fuck did it matter? What difference would it make to the situation?* 'I hope you've had the decency not to use anything of mine. When are you going to Ireland?'

'In August.' *Not that it's any of your business.*

'Not July?'

'No.'

'You'll probably go to Italy in July?'

'I might. I'm keeping my options open.' She sounded jealous. But why should she be jealous? She had already left him!

'If somebody's living with you, then that puts a different edge on things.'

'What do you mean?' Did she mean that there had been a hope, in her mind at least, of salvaging their marriage? It sent a stab of pity through him to think so, because for him their marriage was already dead and buried. Well, the burial would come with the divorce, he supposed. He didn't love her any more. He wasn't sure if he had ever really loved her. Certainly not in the way he loved Cinzia, who he was now afraid of overhearing him on the phone.

'Has the money arrived from your father?' she demanded, ignoring his question. Not that he wanted her to answer it.

'Yes.'

'How much?'

'One thousand pounds.' This was a gift from the proceeds of the sale of his parents' house in Manchester, because they were going to retire to Ireland. In his view, she had no right to any of this money, since it was from *his* parents, even though the gift had been addressed to them as a couple, but then his parents hadn't known about their split and anyway the cheque had been made out to him. But he had decided to give her half anyway. He knew she was even more hard-up than he was. And it would help to salve his conscience.

'There's no problem about me getting my half then.'

'I'll give you half, don't worry.' *Not that it is your half.*

'When? Just transfer it to my bank. You've got my bank details.'

'I might do,' he said sarcastically, his patience snapping, because he didn't like her peremptory tone of voice.

'I'm going to speak to Molly.' Molly was his 'big' sister, a nurse, who sometimes seemed to think she was his mother.

'About what? The money? I said I'll give you half.'

'About everything. About the money. About you. I don't trust you.'

'Don't involve Molly,' he said, ignoring the insult.

'Why not?'

'It's got nothing to do with Molly. It's between you and me. It's our private business. I'll give you the money, if that's what you're worried about.'

'Do it today.'

'I'm busy today.'

'Yes, I know, taking your whore to the airport. I forgot.'

'There's no need to be offensive.' He felt like reminding her that his mother had once called *her* a 'whore', but didn't. He knew she wasn't a whore or anything like a whore. She was genuine, honest, decent, sincere, real, but injured, badly injured. By him. Though it wasn't all his fault. 'Please don't discuss my business with Molly. It'll only complicate things and make them worse.'

'They couldn't be much worse, could they?' she said, sarkily. 'I'll think about it. I can't promise I won't. I have to go and study. I've got an exam tomorrow.'

'What exam?'

'Modern English Poetry. Phone me tomorrow or Saturday.'

'I might. Good luck with the exam,' he said, but she had already put the phone down, to his relief, because at that moment Cinzia came into the living room wrapped in her towel.

'Who was thata?' she asked.

'Oh, just somebody from work,' he said, taking her freshly-laundered body into his arms and giving her a hug, wondering if the game of love was worth all this sturm und drang.

'Are you sure you still want to go?' he asked her, only half-joking.

'I 'ave to go-a,' she said, smiling up at him sadly.

'I know,' he said. 'Maybe I'll use that as the title of a novel one day: *She Had To Go.*' He smiled, but inside his heart was bleeding.

Before getting on the bus to Victoria to catch the Gatwick Express, she insisted on taking photos of each other in the local area, less than scenic as the local area was. He complied somewhat reluctantly, because now that she was definitely going, he just wanted to get to Gatwick and get it over with as swiftly as possible. Taking photos just prolonged the agony for him, especially as she looked so cute in brown, corduroy dungarees, with a red bandana around her auburn hair. Every picture he took of her was and, he knew, would for ever be a painful reminder of what he was losing or had lost. Besides, he was worried about being late for the check-in. If she missed the flight and had to come back with him, that would be – that would be both agony and ecstasy …

The 38 bus was crowded, so she sat while he stood guard

over the suitcase he had stowed in the luggage bay at the back for her. It was annoying, because he wanted to stay by her side for as long as possible. It was as if some spiteful sprite was conspiring to spoil their last few hours together, he thought angrily, though he didn't believe in such things. Half-way through the journey a man got on the bus with a pushchair and tried to force him to move the suitcase so that he could put the pushchair in the luggage bay.

'I know the rules, I work for 'em,' Pushchair pompously proclaimed. 'Pushchairs takes priority.'

'I don't care who you work for,' Frank retorted angrily, already wound up by having to be separated from Cinzia. 'You're a nobody on this bus! The conductor's in charge. If he tells me to move it, I might consider doing so.'

'I'll move it myself,' Pushchair threatened.

'You'd better not touch it,' Frank said, standing right in front of the luggage bay and blocking the man's way.

For a moment, he was afraid he would end up having some sort of scuffle or even a scrap with the man, not that he had ever had a fight in his life. But he wasn't going to let this pompous prick interfere with her luggage and to his own surprise was prepared to stop him physically if necessary – especially as the man was considerably smaller than he was, something of a short-arse in fact..

To his relief, though, the West Indian conductor came downstairs at that point and put the man in his place. For the rest of the journey he remained standing on guard in front of the luggage bay, feeling heroic but disconcerted by his own uncharacteristic truculence. It was because he was already in a highly-wrought, emotional state, he excused himself, glancing over at Cinzia regularly, and feeling a spasm of pain each time he did so, though he knew that what he was feeling now would be nothing compared with what he would be feeling tonight.

On the train to Gatwick, she cried silently most of the way. 'I'll miss all the colours in Englanda,' she sighed, gazing out of the carriage window at the midsummer Surrey countryside flashing past, a patchwork quilt of yellows, greens and browns, dotted with postcard-pretty hamlets, some of the fields containing horses, cows or sheep standing like toys in a model farm, all as picturesque as a painting by Constable. 'I'll miss London mosta. Lignano is deada. I'll be like a fish out of water!'

'I'll miss *you*,' he said simply, tightening his arm around her even more. 'I'll be like a fishbowl without a fish!'

'Oh, baby, I love you so much,' she laughed tearfully, gazing into his eyes.

'I think there's a poem in there somewhere,' he smiled, kissing her. 'The Empty Fishbowl. I'll have to write it tonight.' The thought of tonight sent an ice-cold chill through him.

'Will you send it to me?'

'Yes, if you want. I think I'll be writing you lots of poems. It'll help me to survive without you.'

'Nobody ever wrote poems for me before. I'll keep them for ever.'

'In your secret box?'

'Si. And I will read them every daya. Will you write me lots of letters, too?'

'Of course.'

'Every daya?'

'I don't know about every day,' he laughed.

'I will live for your letters. They will be my lifeline-a.'

'Very good! You learnt at least one word in my class! But you have to reply! You have to write to me, too. It'll be good practice for your English.'

'It will be my 'omeworka! From my English teacher! Who I fell in love with. Who fell in love with me.'

'Yes, who fell head over heels in love with you.'

'We were crazy. We *are* crazy. Are you sorry?'

'Sorry I fell in love with you?'

'Si. Are you sorry? I'm sorry. But also I'm glad. I think you were sent to me.'

'I'm not sorry. I'm glad I met you. I'm glad I fell in love with you. Now I know what love is. You asked me that the first time we met. Remember? In the Bell? Now I know. If anybody ever asks me again, 'What is love?', I'll just think of *you*.'

'I'm sorry, my baby.'

'Why are you sorry?'

'I'm sorry for falling in love with you. I know 'ow 'ard it is for you nowa. Because I 'ave to leave you.'

'It's not too late – we could get the train back,' he said, only half-joking.

'Please don'ta,' she pleaded. 'You will make me cry againa. I will cry again any'ow. I will cry on the plane and I will cry every day until I see you againa.'

'There are going to be floods in Italy by the sound of it!' he joked, struggling to keep tears from his own eyes.

'Si. So you 'ave to come to see me. Or all Italy will be like Venezia!'

'That's blackmail,' he laughed, kissing her, wondering if he could bear to go through all this again, but knowing that the pain of not doing so would be even worse. Or would it?

At the airport, after they had checked in, she had another cry. She asked him to buy her some popcorn to eat on the plane, so he did. 'Sweet, not sour,' she insisted through her tears.

'We forgot something,' he said, as they waited by the departure gate. 'You were going to give me a lock of hair.'

'I'm sorry, my baby,' she said. 'I'll send you some.'

'What about now?'

'I 'ave no scissors.'

'OK. Don't forget!'

'I won't forget. I can't believe this is 'appening!'

'What?'

'I'm leaving. I'm leaving you. I'm leaving England.'

'No, me neither. It's like a dream. A bad dream. I'm hoping to wake up in a moment and see you in bed next to me.'

'What will you do tonighta?'

'I'm teaching. As always on Thursday evening.'

'Will you be all righta?'

'I have to be,' he shrugged, though he was dreading it. 'Some of my evening students have got their oral exam tomorrow. Anyway, it'll help to distract me.'

'You are so good teacher!' she declared.

'*Such a* with an adjective and noun, not *so*,' he corrected her. '*Such a good teacher*. Last lesson ha ha!'

'You are such a good teacher,' she repeated, tearfully.

'You have to be professional,' he shrugged. He had thought of taking the evening off sick, or doing a swap, but couldn't, wouldn't, let his students down.

'You are the best teacher in the college,' she asserted.

'I don't know about that,' he laughed, flattered nonetheless. 'You might be a bit biased!'

'All the students say so.'

'And you're the best student.'

'I 'ave learnt a lot from you. Not just about English.'

'About what?'

'About life-a. Before I was just a little girl. Now I feel like a woman.'

'Me too. I've learnt a lot from you.'

'What 'ave you learnt from me? I'm still just a little girl really.'

'I've learnt about love. I've learnt what love is. I've learnt what it's like to really love somebody. I've learnt that it brings pain as well as pleasure.'

'Oh, baby, I'm sorry!' she burst into tears again.

'What are you sorry for?' he asked, hugging her and kissing away her tears. 'Don't cry!'

'I'm sorry for causing you pain,' she sobbed.

'It's not your fault, darling. I fell in love with you, too. It's life. It's love. You mustn't say that again! Anyway, you've given me more pleasure than pain. I'm glad we fell in love! I think it was our destiny, whether we wanted to or not.'

'I love you so mucha. I will never forget you.'

'I'll never forget you. Now, you'd better go. The gate's closing in five minutes. Last kiss.'

He took her fully into his arms and kissed her, long and deep. Then he took her to the gate by the hand, gave her a last kiss and watched as she went through, turning to look back at him every few seconds, waving with her hankie in her hand. She turned for the last time and blew him a kiss. He blew her a kiss back. Then she disappeared.

He stood watching the last space where she had been for a few moments, in a daze of disbelief, unable to move, paralysed. Even his heart seemed to have stopped, felt like an enormous, heavy stone in his chest. It was almost as if he had died, but was somehow still conscious, with all the hustle and bustle of the airport still going on around him, but he, the real, essential he, wasn't there any more, he had left his body or at least his soul, his spirit, had left his body, leaving him empty, void, hollow, lifeless, loveless, lost …

After a few minutes he came to and went into W. H. Smith's to browse for a while. Then he made his way to the spectators' gallery, feeling disembodied, like some sort of ghost. He waited until he saw the Alitalia plane take off at just after three o'clock and disappear into the sky. A huge wave of relief swept over him. The drama was over. Now he could get back to his boring, humdrum life as it had been before he met her. All he had to do now, he resolved, turning to go, was to try and forget her.

'Ah, the au pairs' delight!'

'Evening all,' he replied, going to his desk in the staffroom. He had gone in earlier than usual, to distract himself.

'Sold my bike,' Mark said, as he sat down.

'Yeah. Why?' Mark was still in his motorbike leathers.

'Bought myself a jeep. Suzuki. Four-wheel drive.' He exhaled some cigarette smoke.

'Useful for traversing the rivers and mountains around Walthamstow?' he quipped.

'Useful for picking up women and transporting them to my lair, you mean.'

'Oh, Frank, Bertha says she's got what you want,' Roy piped up, also exhaling a fag. 'Whatever that is. I don't know about you, but I'd be terrified if Bertha told me she had what I wanted.'

'I'd be running down Forest Road as fast as my legs could carry me,' Mark cracked.

'Oh, I think it's just some Business English past papers,' he laughed. *She'll be in Italy now. She'll be with him. In his arms.*

'Are you going to Dublin again this year?' he asked Roger, going over to sit beside him, though not too close because of his halitosis.

He had met Roger at the previous college, where they both worked until the EFL department had been closed down in the cuts, and become friends. He had not only got Roger a job on the summer school at Trinity College in Dublin, through his friend Charles who ran it, but also a few hours' teaching here at Waltham College, for both of which Roger was grovellingly grateful. Roger was something of a Bohemian, with long, straggly grey locks, a florid face, a rapidly amplifying paunch and disastrous teeth, usually dressed only in T-shirt, cords and sandals. But he was also an intellectual, the only real intellectual among them, who had published several books on minor literary figures and several pamphlets of his own poetry, and was working on a novel.

'You know, I still haven't heard back from Charles. Have you heard anything?' His watery blue eyes were full of worry.

'No. I'll give him a call over the weekend and ask him. I'm sure it'll be OK. He's probably just up to his eyeballs.'

'That's extremely kind of you. I'd love to go. I did enjoy it so much last year. Not just Trinity, but Ireland in general. So much literature and history to explore. Such beautiful scenery. And the people are so friendly! They actually talk to you!'

'Yes, I know. Even an Oxford-educated Englishman like you!' he chuckled.

'Oh, dear, guilty your honour!' Roger giggled, clapping his hand over his mouth to hide his derelict teeth. 'I must confess, I was a bit nervous about going last year, what with all the trouble, but you know, everybody was so friendly.'

'Oh, yes. That's what I always find too.'

'But you're Irish, you don't need to be afraid!' Roger chortled, his hand over his mouth again.

'Well, that's true, but I have got an English accent.'

'What about you? Are you going?'

'I'm not sure if I can make it this year, for the first time in seven years. I'm in the middle of buying this house.' He was also thinking about going to Italy to see Cinzia, though that would only be for a week or so – if he went. *She'll be with him now. What are they doing? Are they in bed? Are they making love?*

'Oh, yes, of course, I do understand. You need to be around. But I hope you can make it. It won't be quite the same without you.'

'Thanks, Roger. Well, I'll let you know,' he said, returning to his desk and picking up his briefcase to go to his class.

'See you in the bar later,' Mark said.

'Righto,' he said breezily, as he left.

He didn't really want to go to the bar and socialise, because of Cinzia, but he had to go tonight – some of his students were leaving. Anyway, it would save him for a short while longer from the loneliness that he knew was waiting to wrap itself around him like a shroud. It would help to distract him from thoughts of her, too – thoughts that were like darts dipped in the most exquisite mixture of pleasure and pain.

CHAPTER ELEVEN

'I've been married to the same woman for ten years, but looking round at all these seventeen-year-olds, I'm starting to wonder if she hasn't aged a bit,' Stewart – Doctor Mackay – who didn't normally attend their bar sessions – quipped in his usual waggish way, and they all laughed merrily.

'Do you know what you're teaching next year?' Frank asked him. *Is she in bed with him? Are they making love?*

'Intermediate tap dancing for all I know,' quipped Stewart deadpan and again they all laughed – this was a satirical reference to the fact that they hadn't received their timetables for the new academic year yet.

'Are you all right?' he asked Mark, who already seemed a bit drunk. *Are they doing it right now?*

'I feel great. I feel young. I might not get to Greece. But I don't mind staying in Walthamstow. Especially if I can get off with one of these chicks. Or just go on a two-month jawl for the summer.'

''Jawl' – what's that?'

'That's South African slang for 'binge'. God, are all these chicks yours?'

'In a manner of speaking,' he grinned. *Is he fucking her again?* 'Bit distracting when I'm teaching though.'

'Oh, I never get distracted in class,' Mark averred. 'But when I'm invigilating it's so damn boring I can't even begin to tell you my fantasies.'

'You can tell me later,' he laughed.

'Come back for a coffee later if you like. Are you still with that Italian chick?'

'She went home today. Took her to the airport this afternoon.'

'Never mind. Plenty more fish in the sea. All around us.'

'Yes,' he laughed. That was a typical Mark response. It would be no use telling him that he wasn't interested in any of the other 'fish', that he loved Cinzia and already missed her like hell. Mark professed not to believe in love – for him love equalled 'mutual need fulfilment' as he had once put it. *Is she – ? Stop it! Stop thinking about her!*

'You going to see her?'

'Not sure. Want to. But might just be prolonging the agony. Might be better to try and forget her. What do you reckon?'

Mark was the last person he would normally think of asking for advice where women were concerned, but he couldn't resist the excuse to talk about her – and anyway it would give him another perspective, even if a somewhat jaundiced one.

'You should go and shag the arse off her. That's what I'd do. I'll do it for you if you want.'

'I've already done that,' he laughed, 'but it didn't stop her leaving.' The though sent a dagger through him. *Should I tell him about Luciano?*

'Go and shag the arse off her, make her beg you to take her back and if she doesn't, tell her to take a flying fuck at herself. There's plenty more fish here. In fact, get grooming now! Which one do you fancy most?'

'I don't fancy any of them, to be honest,' he laughed. *I only fancy my little Italian mouse.*

'Don't tell me you're in love.'

'I think I am,' he grinned, blushing in spite of himself. 'I know you don't believe in love though.'

'I don't believe in love. Lust, yah. "I love you" equals "I need you". I need you to cook for me!'

'What about companionship?' he laughed.

'Only need companionship in old age maybe. I'll risk being lonely when I'm old. But I don't intend to grow old. Expect to go out in a blaze of glory by the time I'm sixty. That gives me twenty-five more years. Till then I prefer to be free and have fun. Except I'm not having any fun at the moment. I need a woman! I'll inflict myself on that lot over there when I've imbibed a bit more Dutch courage.' He took another swig of his Abbot Ale. 'With your permission,' he added.

'Feel free,' he laughed. *Is he fucking her? She said he liked to do it several times a night.*

'You understand my problem, don't you?'

'What problem is that?'

'My libidinal urge. It's just too deeply engrained.'

Frank laughed. 'Are you teaching tomorrow?'

'Nine a.m. City and Guilds. Bunch of mechanics.'

'Sounds like the sharp end.'

'I don't take any shit from them, I can tell you. Other lecturers might, but I don't, by Christ. Bawl 'em out. One of them raised a fist to me last week. "I'll squash you against that wall like a mosquito if you do," I told him. He backed off. I'm trained to kill, even though I haven't killed. Not yet.'

Frank laughed again. 'Sounds like he had a lucky escape.'

'You betcha.'

'So you're doing a psychology degree at the Open University?'

'Yah. Can't do this EFL bullshit much longer. Got to get out.'

'So you'll get something in the psychology field?'

'Might not. Might do something else entirely. Something more useful than this bullshit anyway. It is bullshit, isn't it? American immigrants learnt English without classes! Might become a farmer. A cabinet maker. Open a home for homeless au pairs. Or a mercenary. South American revolutionary. Do something *useful* anyway. Not this crap.'

Frank laughed. Sometimes he wondered how seriously he should take Mark. And he *was* a bit drunk.

'Just going to speak to these ladies,' Mark said, finishing his pint and turning to the girls on his left. 'See if I can work my magic on one of them.'

'Good luck,' Frank laughed and turned to the girls on his right, who he had been itching to talk to anyway, if only to distract himself from Cinzia.

'How are you, Tiziana?'

She was sitting next to him, puffing away on a fag as usual, making it obvious that she liked him. He liked her, but just didn't fancy her. He only wished he did. She was wearing the same scruffy leather motorcycle jacket as always and had changed her hair from green to orange. He wondered if he shouldn't make a date with her anyway, if only to distract himself and numb the pain.

'I think I 'ave failed the oral exama,' she said, between puffs on her cigarette, in the accent that reminded him cruelly of Cinzia, though it was even stronger than Cinzia's. There was something masochistic about talking to her, he told himself.

'I wouldn't be surpriseda, if you spoke-a like thata,' he replied, mimicking her, and they all laughed. It was the kind of joke he knew he could make with Tiziana, because she was a jolly soul and anyway was too infatuated with him to be offended.

'I think my professore is very bada, ees why,' she riposted. 'I theenk I should geev eem the sacka.'

'Very good use of idiom,' he laughed. 'I'm impressed. You've obviously been paying attention in class.'

'I know my accenta is so bada,' she said. ''ow can I change eet?'

'They say the pillow method is the best way to learn a language,' he replied, half-regretting it even as he said it.

'What ees pillow methoda?' she asked.

'Pillow. Bed. Head. Sleep,' he explained, miming.

'You are so funny!' she laughed, getting the joke.

'So, you see, you need an English-speaking boyfriend.' He knew he shouldn't flirt with her like this, but couldn't resist, because – combined with a third pint of Abbot – it helped to dull the pain. *Maybe they haven't gone to bed yet ...*

'I never meet any Eengleesh-speaking mena,' she said.

'I speak Eengleesh,' he mimicked her again.

'I weesh I could 'ave you as my boyfrienda,' she said, with a puff of smoke. 'But I know you are marrieda.'

'Well, we can be friends,' he said, feeling guilty about leading her on and guilty because of Cinzia. But he couldn't bear the thought of sitting around in his flat on his own brooding about Cinzia, feeling lonely – he had had enough of loneliness.

'You mean, we can go out together?' she asked, excited.

'Yes, of course. We can go for a drink or something if you want.' *Oh, Cinzia! It's you I want! Not this girl, likeable as she is! Come back!* 'Are you free this Saturday evening?' He tried to sound casual, as though it didn't matter to him, as though he were doing her a favour.

'This Saturday I 'ave to babysita,' she said, crestfallen.

'Oh,' he shrugged. *Bloody au pair employers!* But he was half-glad – he wasn't sure if he should really go out with her. And yet … 'What about Sunday afternoon?'

'I am free Sunday afternoona,' she said, excited again.

'OK,' he said. 'I'll meet you outside Walthamstow Central station at two o' clock. We can go into Central London and do some sightseeing if you want. Then have a drink.'

'You 'ave made me so 'appy!' she exclaimed.

'You can go and buy me another pint then,' he laughed.

'I 'ave no money,' she said, crestfallen again.

'Ah, yes, you're an au pair, aren't you? Don't they pay you?'

'Not mucha. I get some money tomorrow, Friday.'

Bloody au pair employers – they don't half exploit these girls, most of them.. Too focussed on making shekels themselves instead of looking after their own brats and cleaning their own stables. Jewish most of them. Oh, dear, mustn't let prejudices like that come out, just because I'm depressed.

'Here's some money,' he said, giving her a ten-pound note. 'Get yourself a drink, too.'

'I can't – '

'Don't be silly,' he told her. 'Go on.'

'Grazie. I geev you back Sunday,' she said, standing up to go to the bar.

He watched her as she went, short, chubby, hair like a Belisha beacon, scruffy-looking, wondering if he could possibly ever feel like having sex with her and immediately reprimanding himself for even thinking of it – then he would be as guilty of exploiting her as the au pair employers who exploited her financially. As well as guilty of betraying Cinzia. Because he didn't love her or even fancy her. He loved Cinzia. But why should he feel guilty about Cinzia? Cinzia wasn't his any more. She was probably in *his* arms right now. Popeye the sailor-man. Maybe he was screwing her yet again. She'd told him they did it several times a night. And he hadn't seen her for three months. Oh, Christ! The pain was almost physical. Like a fire in his chest. It was how he imagined a heart attack would feel. Well, it was a kind of heart attack.

'Francis, you look worried about something,' Clelia, a Spanish girl, said to him. 'You should be happy. Your holidays begin.'

'Now that I've seen you, Clelia, I'm happy,' he joked and forced himself to chat with her and the others, but couldn't stop thinking about Cinzia. Albert the Bavarian invited them all to a party at his house later and offered him a lift in his 'Owstin Sprrite', but he said he was too tired and had to teach in the morning, though he didn't, only had to go in for a section meeting.

After chatting convivially as usual for a while, he withdrew from the conversation and looked around at them through something of an Abbot ale-induced alcoholic haze, thinking what a great bunch of international people they were, how lucky, how privileged, he was to be their teacher and what a great job he had. He was also conscious of how much they liked him, not only because he was such a good teacher – as they often told him – but also because he socialised with them like this, was friendly with them, treated them not just as students or customers of the college, but as real people, in whom he was genuinely interested.

Are they screwing?

'Francis, you've gone quiet again! What's wrong wiz you tonight? What are you sinking about?' Joelle, a French girl, asked.

Sinking. That's the right word. Sinking into a slough of despond. No, mustn't. Mustn't.

'Yes, a penny for your thoughts, Mister Francis!'

'Very good, Phak!' he laughed, recalling having taught them that expression only recently. Phak was a Thai boy – quite exotic even among this cosmopolitan crowd. 'I'm thinking about how lucky I am.'

'Why you are lucky?'

'*Why are you lucky*,' he corrected, wagging his finger with mock sternness. 'Inversion of verb and subject for a question.'

'You can stop being a teacher now!' Eva, an Austrian girl, teased him.

'Oh, no!' he said, shaking his head with mock solemnity, realising he was a bit drunk. 'A teacher can never stop being a teacher. At least I can't. I don't switch off being a teacher when I leave the classroom. Just as you shouldn't stop being students when you leave the classroom. Being a teacher is part of my – my personality. My identity. For me it's a bit like being a priest. You understand, 'priest'? It's a vocation. It's not just a job.'

Oh, God, why did he have to say that? If he wasn't careful, the next thing was he'd be telling them all about his shady past and how he had nearly become a priest. And they would be asking him questions he didn't want to answer. Although part of him wanted to talk about it. The memory floated across his mental landscape like a large black cloud and he shuddered inwardly for a moment.

'Francis, are you all righta?' Tiziana asked, solicitously. 'You do seem quiet tonighta.'

God, so she's noticed too! I thought I was putting on quite a good act. Better brighten up.

'Me? Quiet?' he laughed. 'Maybe I haven't had enough to drink. If you go to the bar again and get me another pint of Abbot I might start talking. Here's some money. Get another one for yourself. Anyone else want a drink?' He gave her another ten-pound note – he was feeling flush tonight because of the thousand pounds his father had just given him – even though his wife – or ex-wife as he thought of her now – was trying to claim half of it.

Oh, God, how many times will they make love tonight?And tomorrow night? And the following night. And ... Stop!

Tiziana went to the bar, brought back a tray of drinks and gave him his change. 'You're an angel,' he said to her, giving her a kiss on the cheek and distributing the drinks to the company. 'I'll have to reward you.' *I hope she doesn't misinterpret that. But then again ...*

'Eet's my pleasure,' she said. He could tell that she would do anything for him. Anything. But …

'Cheers, everybody,' he announced, raising his pint of Abbot. 'Or slainte, as we say in Irish.'

They asked him to teach them how to say it – 'slawncha' – and taught each other how to say it their various languages including Phak's – 'chaiyo' it sounded like. They then asked him about Ireland and he happily held forth on one of his favourite topics as if he had kissed the Blarney stone, glad of the distraction, glad of at least a few more minutes' reprieve from the torment that he knew was waiting for him.

'Wanna come back for a coffee?' Mark asked him a while later.

'It's a bit early to leave, isn't it?' he said, glancing at the clock above the bar. It was only just after ten and the bar didn't shut till eleven.

'I'm missing my dog. Bit worried about her. Not been well lately. Besides none of these chicks seem to be falling for my charms. Prefer the dog's company if I'm honest.'

'OK, just let me finish this pint.'

In fact, he would be glad to escape, because he was finding it such a strain to keep up a cheerful front. Also he was having his ear chewed off by a middle-aged Iranian student, a simian little man in a short-sleeved pullover, a refugee from the mullahs, who was telling him all about his tribulations – how he had sent his wife back to Iran to sell their house, but she had become depressed and been hospitalised there, but because she was in danger, he had had to spend a lot of money to get her transported back to the UK, so now he was broke. How their house in Iran had been appropriated by the government, so he had made no money from it, but their house here was too small for them and their kids. How he had written to Khomeini personally but got no answer. How he had even written to Patrick Jenkins, the British Social Services minister, who had helped him because his own wife suffered from depression. How he had just failed his law exams in England because of the language barrier. And so it went on, one calamity after another.

Normally he was a sucker for such hard-luck stories and would have lent a sympathetic ear, but tonight he could hardly bear to listen. This in turn made him feel guilty, because this man's troubles were obviously considerably greater than his own, which were trivial by comparison, he supposed. And yet …

'Still,' Mohsen said, after reciting his litany of woes. 'Allah is good.'

'Have you written to Allah?' Frank couldn't resist joking, fuelled as he was by three pints of Abbot.

'I pray to him every day,' Mohsen replied. 'He helps me in his own way. He gives me strength and courage.'

'Well, I'm very glad to hear it,' Frank said, half-envying him his faith in a beneficent God, a comfort he could no longer avail of himself. *His* God had let him down badly, turned a very deaf ear, when he had needed help! Which was why he had cut all communications.

'You don't vant to come to my house?' Albert enquired, in between puffs on his pipe, when he started to take his leave. 'I gif you lift in my Owstin Sprrite.'

'Not tonight, thanks, Albert,' he said, trying not to sound too tipsy. 'Mark's giving me a lift home. Maybe we can have a little get-together at your house next Thursday?'

'Zis sounds like an excellent idea,' Albert agreed, always ready for a bit of fun, especially if there were a few girls involved, as there would be. 'Next veek ve haf a party at my house. Everybody vill come.'

'Did you hear that, everyone?' Frank announced, standing up to go. 'That's an order! See you all next week! Good night!'

'See you! Good night! Thank you!' they all chorused.

'See you Sunday,' he whispered to Tiziana, giving her a kiss on the cheek as he left.

Much as he loved being with his students, tonight he was glad of an excuse to escape. As soon as they went through Mark's front door, the dog was all over Mark, yelping with delight and licking him. Frank almost felt jealous.

'What's he called?' he asked, following them into the living-room.

'Inja. That's Zulu for dog. Take a pew. No food I'm afraid. Except dog food. I live on take-away crap. How'd you like your coffee?' He went into the kitchen.

'Strong. Black. Sweet.'

'Just like your women?'

'Not exactly,' he laughed. What was she doing now, he wondered? Was she - ? *Don't!*

The dog – apparently a mixture of husky and chow – lay panting on the rug, gazing with eyes full of love at the kitchen where Mark was making the coffee.

'Now I know why you've got a dog and where the panting comes from,' Frank called out.

'You betcha,' Mark said, bringing the coffee in. 'When desperate women phone me up in the middle of the night, I just put the receiver on the floor and let the dog at it. Really gets them going.'

Frank laughed, as usual not sure how seriously to take Mark.

'Just got a card from a friend,' Mark went on, picking up a postcard from the coffee table. 'Saying he's found Jesus, the way, the truth and the life. Inviting me to join him.'

'I know you're a seeker, Mark,' Frank quipped.

'The only thing I'm seeking for is flesh,' Mark riposted. 'I noticed that other Italian making eyes at you in the bar. What's her name, Tiziana?'

'Yeah, I think she fancies me,' he said, uncomfortable.

'Lose one, gain one. Do you fancy her?'

'Not really to be honest. A bit too plump for my taste. Not sure about the orange hair either.' *Anyway, I only fancy Cinzia.*

'You can pass her over to me if you don't want her. I'm not fussy. None of the other bints are taking the bait. Still, summer school starts next week. Should be some new talent. Only reason I'm doing it. Well, need the dosh too. You doing it?'

'No. I usually do a summer school in Dublin. But might give it a miss this year. I'm buying a house. Got to stick around to deal with that. Might pop over to Italy though. Can't make my mind up whether to go or not.'

'Does she want you to go?'

'Oh, yeah. But she's got a boyfriend there who she says she has to marry, even though she doesn't want to.'

'Why not?'

'Family pressure. She doesn't actually love him. If I'm allowed to use that word! Should I go? Would you go?'

'You betcha.'

'What about the boyfriend?'

'I'd tell him to fuck off.'

Frank laughed, wincing inside, wishing it were so simple.

When he got back to his flat, there was a message on his answerphone. Reluctantly, since it was after midnight and he was tired and drunk, having imbibed some of Mark's whisky as well as his coffee, he picked up the receiver, thinking it might be Cinzia. But it was Molly, his big sister, in bossy, big-sister, staff-nurse mode.

'Why have you done this to Mary? You promised me you wouldn't do it again! She cares deeply about you. People who think like you are unstable. Are you making up for what you missed when you were seventeen? You know physical desire diminishes in men! She's bound to be suspicious. Why did you take her back? You need counselling! Have you seen a counsellor? You're immature and selfish! Don't you realise you're hurting other people with your behaviour, not just Mary? Dad was about to get in his car and drive through the night when he heard, but he didn't know your address. You're not an island, you know, Fran! No one is an island! Did you tell her your marriage was a charade? If your marriage is over, you don't tell your parents something like that on the phone! Get on a train up there and face them! Do you realise Mum is very ill? She has a thrombosis. She could have a stroke and die any day. That's something we all have to face, Fran, death. Do you ever think about that? About dying? And after death there will be a judgement. Are you ready to face that? To account for yourself and your actions? You may think you're tough, but you're not. I see death every day in my job. I see even the hardest cases crack on their deathbeds and beg for the priest. I've faced the near death of my child. I'm not worried about my own death. When I'm old I don't want to be lonely. I just want companionship. To share common interests with somebody. To have a bond with my husband. A bond you form over twenty, thirty, forty years. A history of shared experience. That's very important, Fran. You can go with all the women you want to, but you won't have that shared experience, that bond. That's a mistake mum and dad made – they never developed common interests. I'm not one of those who believe marriage is necessarily for ever, it's unbreakable. I know my husband could leave me when I'm fifty. I know divorce has to happen sometimes. I understand that. But you two had such a good thing together. Why are you throwing everything away? Destroying everything? Destroying yourself? Destroying her? It seems foolish! I know I didn't go to your wedding and I know Mum and Dad didn't. But that's only because I was in America. Do you even know where or how she is? You're still responsible for her, you know! She's still your wife! If you do divorce her, you have to make sure her interests are taken care of. I will make sure anyway. Because I know you're wily. As wily as a fox. You have to give her half of that money from Dad. You've taken it under false pretences. It's fraud! If you don't give her half, I'll take you to court, if she doesn't! You need counselling. You need to see someone. You have a problem. Remember, we all have to die and pay our taxes. Including our debts to society and the people who love us. Now go to bed and be good! Behave yourself! Goodnight. I love you.'

When he came to the next morning, he wondered if the events of yesterday – Cinzia leaving, the trip to the airport, the tirade on the phone from his sister – had all just been a bad dream. But it was all true, he realised, a black cloud of depression descending on him, smothering him, as if it had been hovering over him all night, just waiting for him to wake up. His mood wasn't lightened by the fact that he had a hangover. It was made even worse when he remembered that there was an EFL section meeting that morning. He hated meetings at the best of times. He wondered if he should skip it and call in sick – as in a sense he was – but quickly decided not to. He prided himself on never missing work and on his professionalism. One day in years to come, he supposed, the college would reward him for his dedication to duty. If only with a carriage clock.

The only glimmer of light in the darkness was the date with Tiziana on Sunday. Thank goodness he'd invited her out, he thought. She obviously liked him. He liked her, too, though he didn't fancy her. So he'd be doing her a favour as well as himself. He might even tell her about Cinzia. It'd be good to be able to talk to somebody about it. But not to Tiziana – no, that wouldn't be a good idea, he corrected himself, getting gingerly out of bed, because his head felt twice as heavy as normal. As did his heart. He sat on the edge of the bed for a few minutes, his head in his hands, not daring to stand up.

After a few minutes, head lolling, he glanced down at his watch, which he had been too drunk to take off last night, wondering what time it was. He stared at it in disbelief, wondering if he was imagining things. It had done something it had never done before – it had stopped during the night. And not only had it stopped, it had stopped at exactly midnight.

CHAPTER TWELVE

At the section meeting next morning, he couldn't stop thinking about her. As always – just like EFL in general – it was dominated by the women in the section, who seemed to love talking for the sake of talking. Sometimes, he thought, they called meetings just so they could have a good old natter. Once last year, Ken, the Head of Department, had crashed in and shouted at them: 'Stop meeting and start working!' He smiled to himself at the memory.

'Well, Frank seems to find it amusing,' Harriet remarked, in her waspish way.

'What was that?' he said, suddenly hearing his name and coming to, not knowing what she was talking about.

'Associate Lecturers not needing their own desks next year,' she said. 'Ken says there's a shortage of desks, so you'll have to share.'

'Oh, really? That's ridiculous. One solution would be to chop up that presidential desk of Ken's. We could get three desks out of that.' A ripple of nervous amusement went around the classroom.

'I'll second that,' Mark said. 'He doesn't need a desk, does he?'

'Why do you say that, Mark?' Bertha enquired. She was sitting on the edge of her seat with her legs splayed as usual, tent-like dress pulled up onto her ample thighs, specs dangling from a silver chain on her even more ample bosom.

'Well, he doesn't do anything all day, does he?' Mark said. 'I mean, he certainly doesn't have any lesson preparation to do, does he? He's usually reading a travel book when I go in there.'

Another ripple of amusement went around the room.

'I think we're digressing, aren't we?' Bertha said, ignoring Mark. 'What's next on the agenda?'

Frank glanced down at the mimeoed sheer of paper containing the agenda and groaned inwardly: class programmes for next year, lecturer timetables, option classes, ESP, departmental duties, exam results, exams, re-organisation of 16+ education, YOPS and TOPS, whatever the hell they were, Section 11 funding, whatever the hell that was, urban aid, SPD funding ... *Oh, God, I give up* … AOB … *Are they still in bed? Are they – ?*

'Do you want to share a desk with me if necessary?'

'What? Oh, yeah, sure,' he whispered back to Mark while the women warbled on about option classes. 'I'll be bloody furious if we have to though. It's disgusting.'

'You betcha.'

On Saturday morning he went out to do some shopping and laundry. He had to keep busy, he told himself, to stop himself thinking about either Mary or Cinzia. But when he had finished, as the weather was so good – cloudy but warm with a balmy, playful breeze – he couldn't resist going for a sit in the Walled Garden of St. John's Church, though he knew he shouldn't. It was one of his favourite places of refuge from the worries and woes of everyday life, apart from the pub – though he usually ended up thinking about both anyway.

He was able to distract himself for a while by observing his surroundings – crimson and yellow rose bushes, plane trees, cypresses, daisies, a bedraggled-looking sparrow, a mauve-bosomed wood pigeon – but he couldn't avoid his thoughts returning to Mary for long. She had phoned him yesterday and they had arranged to meet on Monday evening, so that she could return some college library books to him and he could give her a cheque for her share of his father's gift – though he didn't really want to, didn't want to see her at all or have anything more to do with her. As for Cinzia, the thought of her and who she was with – Luciano – was like a slab of stone on his spirit, crushing the life out of him – just like one of those slabs on the tombs in the churchyard behind him. As always, he didn't know whether to envy the dead in their tombs, since all their troubles were behind them. Or at least above them ha ha. Whereas here he was, having just lost both his wife and his girlfriend, the girlfriend he actually loved more than he had ever loved his wife, so that now he had nobody.

Even his sister Molly seemed to be on his wife's side against him. He was still shaking from the tirade she had fired at him the other night. Maybe the rest of his family were on Mary's side too. None of them had contacted him anyway. Not that his parents were likely to. Not that he had any right to expect them to. Oh, God, what a depressing predicament he had somehow got himself into. Again! Maybe there was something wrong with him, as his sister said. Maybe the seminary had screwed him up. Maybe he was damaged goods. It might be his fault that he had lost Mary, but it wasn't his fault that he'd lost Cinzia, was it? Maybe it was his punishment from the gods. To have found happiness and then had it snatched away. There was always a price to pay. Not that he believed in God or gods any more. That was another crushing thought – that it all had no meaning, this was it, his life had no more importance than the life of that pigeon foraging in front of him or that squirrel scampering up and down the trees or even the ant scuttling along the arm of the bench where he was sitting.

He turned to look at the little plaque on the back of the bench:

IN LOVING MEMORY OF LILIAN ETHEL EVANS
1908 – 1969. A WONDERFUL WIFE AND MOTHER

As always, he found the memorial, simple as it was, painfully poignant. Lily – as she was no doubt known to her family and friends – had probably sat on this bench herself till quite recently, just as he was sitting here now, and reflected upon her life, just as he was doing now. Had she had a happy life, he wondered? Was there any such thing as a happy life? Probably not. Maybe all you could hope for was snatches of happiness and at worst boredom. Had she really been a 'wonderful wife and mother'? Maybe she had actually been abandoned by her family and this memorial was their way of salving their consciences. Maybe she had sat on this very bench where he was sitting now, feeling as lonely and disappointed and defeated about life as he felt. There was a story, a whole life story, encoded in those dozen words or so! Maybe he'd write it when he got home. *The Woman on the Bench.* Anyway, at least all her troubles were over, the lucky old bag, just like all the other cadavers lying in the overgrown, grandiose, semi-derelict tombs behind him. God, it put life in perspective! It put *his* life in perspective! Life was a bitch! Life was a bastard! It kept knocking you down. He was down. But he wasn't out. He was far from out. Don't let the bastards grind you down! He suddenly knew what he should do. Should he do it now? Or wait till Monday?

BONNNNNG!

The church bell suddenly clanged out, deafening, stentorian. God, it was loud enough to wake the dead ha ha! But it was a wake-up call for him too. A signal from the sky. He jumped up, grabbed his shopping and headed straight to the travel agent's before he could change his mind.

On Monday afternoon he had to invigilate a maths exam, which his maths teacher colleague said was far too difficult and had obviously been set by an 'armchair academic'.

'It's all Greek to me anyway,' Frank joked, having distributed the formulae and log booklets. 'In fact, I'd have a much better chance if it was Greek!'

One girl fled the room in tears after a few minutes and he had to go out to calm her down and persuade her to return to the exam hall, telling her they were going to make an official complaint about the paper. He felt strangely sorry for her, perhaps because he was under such emotional strain himself and she seemed so fragile, so that he found himself thinking: 'That could be *my* daughter one day.' Except that I'm bloody infertile, he reminded himself, with a wince.

'You OK?' the maths colleague asked, noticing.

'Sure, just got a bit of a crick in my neck,' he explained, embarrassed, rubbing his neck. 'Must have slept awkwardly on it or something.' Afterwards though, he thought, what he should have said was: 'Sure, just got a bit of a broken heart, that's all.'

That evening he met Mary as planned and they went for an Indian in Hoe Street, Walthamstow. He gave her a cheque for £500, told her he didn't want to buy the house jointly with her any more and asked her to sign a letter withdrawing from the sale. 'I'll have to think about that,' she said starchily, to his annoyance. This was the new, hard-nosed Mary, was it, negotiating everything like some sort of worldly-wise street hustler? He felt like asking her for the £500 back but didn't.

Like the last time they had met, she insisted on talking about their situation as if trying to negotiate some sort of reconciliation, but he made it clear that was impossible now, though trying not to be too blunt about it to save her feelings. 'Too much water has flowed under the bridge,' he repeated several times, sadly, all the time an image of Cinzia hovering at the back of his mind. He was afraid she would confront him about Cinzia – or Cinzano as she sarkily called her – and he braced himself, but she didn't. Instead, she said something that really took him aback:

'I think you deliberately engineered our break-up.'

It took him a moment to register what she meant. 'That's the most fatuous thing I've ever heard!' he expostulated, unable to contain his annoyance any longer. 'We broke up because we became incompatible. We were, we are, opposites.'

'Because you wanted to fuck other women, you mean,' she hit back boldly. 'If you had put as much energy into fucking me as other people, we'd still be together.'

'I think we'd better go,' he said, biting his tongue, not wanting to hurt her by telling her what he really thought was behind their break-up. 'Unless you want a coffee?'

To his relief she said she didn't, so he got the bill, which he paid, and they went outside.

'By the way, I'm going to see Molly tomorrow,' she said, springing it on him.

'Oh, how are you travelling?' he asked, knowing that what she really wanted him to ask was 'Why?' and wondering if it was some roundabout ruse to try and get him back.

'By coach,' she said. 'I can't afford the train.'

'Well, have a good journey,' he said. 'Goodnight.'

He paused for a moment, wondering if she expected him to give her a kiss on the cheek or if she was going to say goodnight to him, but she didn't – she turned her back and walked away without a word, limping as always, presumably to go to her friend Lisa's, where she was staying.

He stood on the pavement for a few moments, watching her go, shocked by her attitude, but with pity in his heart, not just for her but for himself and the whole damn world too. Then he turned to walk to the station to take his train home, back to his empty flat, but deciding he'd have a pint in Flanagan's opposite the station first, just to anaesthetise some of the pain.

When he got home there was a message on his answerphone. He picked it up nervously, hoping it was from Cinzia., but it was his sister, Molly, again, crying. 'I'm sorry about the way I spoke to you the other day, Fran. Can you forgive me? I've done some ferreting. I know something happened when you were away. I know you've been damaged. I know you don't want to talk about it. You mustn't tell Mum. I haven't told her. It'd make her suicidal. I was in a rage the other day. I'd been harassed by the kids all day and I had hay fever. I hope you can forgive me. You've always been a kind brother. I always stick up for you. I used to get a tongue-lashing from Mum and Dad for defending you. "You always had a soft spot for him, no matter what he does," they said to me. I think they know it was a mistake letting you go to that place. I'd never let my kids go away from me. I want to keep in tune with my kids. I go to parents' day to inspect the teachers, not find out about my kids' work. A lot of the teachers I came into contact with weren't fit to teach boys, not necessarily for *that* reason. I want to protect my children. Make sure nothing happens to them. I know you've been damaged by that place. It's when it's subconscious it's most dangerous – this is what I'm telling you, Fran. I'm not a complete simpleton! I want to ask you something. Will you see a counsellor for my sake? I can't go back to America with this on my mind. I can't help worrying about you. Worrying about everyone. It's my nature. If necessary my husband and kids can go back without me. You were on the scene long before them. You know, Mum used to cry into the kitchen sink after you'd left to go back to the seminary with Dad. She didn't want you to go back really, but she didn't want to show you that. What do your friends think, the boys you've known for many years? I know I've got my faults. I know I'm domineering. Mary's very loyal to you. I've come to love her dearly. You could be so happy, the pair of you, in your new house. That's why I want you to go and see a counsellor. I'll go with you. I know you always were a great experimenter. Mum idolised you and I dare say you idolised her. Mary's coming here tomorrow because she doesn't want to be a burden on her family, that's all. I'm not siding with her against you, don't worry. I know there's two sides to every story. I don't blame Mum and Dad. Mum thought you were in the next best place to Heaven. Please don't blame them, Fran. They didn't have any idea. You must never tell them though. It would kill Mum. Promise me you'll see a counsellor. Will you promise me that? I love you. Goodnight.'

A few days later he had a drink at Young's on the river with Terry and Serena. He fancied Serena like mad and now half-regretted letting Terry – an A-level geography student at the college – get off with her. But Terry was an all-round good guy and anyway he hoped to get Cinzia back by going to Italy next month, so told himself to keep his thoughts platonic. However, that was difficult when Terry and Serena turned up at the pub patio, where he was waiting for them, in motorbike leathers, in which Serena looked so sexy she might have just walked off a film set, a James Bond film set perhaps.

'Ciao!' he said, getting up to kiss her on both comely cheeks with a fluttering heart as she shook her shampoo-ad hair out after taking off her helmet, then shaking Terry's hand. 'So you've got rid of the car then?'

'The jam jar?' Terry was fluent in Cockney rhyming slang, which was reasonable enough, since he *was* a Cockney, though he referred to himself as Irish. 'Couldn't afford to keep it. Get twice the mileage out of the Dick Van Dyke.'

'I see,' he laughed, guessing Dick Van Dyke meant motor

bike. 'Let me get you a drink. Pint of Guinness?'

'Better make it a cow n calf. Don't want to get Brahms and Liszt, do I?'

'Serena?' he laughed, hardly daring to look at her, she looked so drop-dead gorgeous.

'Just a cow and calfa for me too,' she smiled lethally.

'You see, she's picking up the lingo fast,' Terry commented.

He went to the bar, almost glad to have a few minutes of relief from Serena's devastating gorgeousness. She was the only girl that could possibly tempt him to forget about Cinzia even for a moment. What a lucky bugger Terry was, he thought, as he waited to be served – not only had he bagged Serena, she was going to stay with him and probably marry him. Whereas – he tried not to think about Cinzia. Or Grazia. It was too painful. Italian girls! They certainly had something special. And as if to rub salt into the wound, at that very moment Rod Stewart came on the jukebox singing 'Italian Girls' ...

Terry told him that tomorrow they were off to Plymouth, where he had obtained a place to do geography at university, to finalise a place to stay and ferry some of their belongings. In the light of his dealings with landlords there, he reckoned Plymouth people must all be 'fucking Tories', they were so mean and greedy, which made Frank laugh. He also said they were taking the 'Dick Van Dyke' to Italy next month for a last holiday. That was the cue for Frank to tell them that he was going to Italy next month himself.

'Oh, yeah, got a bit of skirt there, have you?' Terry quizzed.

'Actually, yes,' Frank admitted, uncomfortable at the term, and told them for the first time about Cinzia.

'You are a dark horse-a!' Serena laughed.

'You see, she can speak English too,' Terry joked.

'She must have had a good teacher,' Frank grinned.

'So why haven't we been told about this before?' Terry wanted to know.

'Yes,' Serena chimed in. 'You are a naughty boy!'

'Well, I've only known her properly for a few weeks,' he said, embarrassed despite himself and wondering why he hadn't told them. Was it because he still fancied Serena and didn't want to – no, no, he loved Cinzia and wanted her back.

'So what's the plan?' Terry asked. 'Are you going to stay there?'

'Oh, no, I'm hoping to persuade her to come back to London,' he said. 'But there's a problem.' He told them about Luciano.

'Do you want us to bump him off?' Terry joked.

'Er, no, I don't think I want to go that far, though you look like a pair of assassins in those outfits,' he laughed, taking a slug of Guinness.

'More like a pair of plonkers,' Terry chuckled.

'I wouldn't say that,' he laughed, glancing at Serena, who looked anything but a plonker. She looked like a – like a Bond girl.

'Yes, you speak for yourselfa,' Serena reprimanded Terry.

'Scusami cara,' Terry said, putting an arm round her, pulling her towards him and kissing her, sending a stab of jealousy through Frank and making him miss Cinzia even more.

'So, it's all over with Mary, is it?' Terry asked, giving the knife a twist.

'Yes,' he said, guiltily, taking another slug of Guinness. 'It's all over. It's all over now, baby blue.'

Now that he had decided to go to Italy and bought the ticket, waiting was torture. The torture was made worse by having to go into college for meetings and seminars, both of which he found excruciatingly boring as well as largely a waste of time. One seminar, led by Bertha, the 'Section Leader', was about some 'New American Method', which involved coloured cards on a magnetic board and struck him as childish – appropriate in a primary school perhaps, but not a college of further education where the students were all adults. It was all part of a plot to 'dumb down' the subject even more, as he whispered to Mark beside him.

'Too right,' Mark whispered back. 'It's because EFL is dominated by women. They love all this crap. That's why they love EFL. Fancy a drink tonight?'

'Where? College bar?'

'There won't be any birds in, will there, now that classes have finished? I need some action. How about the Green Man again? It's Friday, so there'll be a disco. Plenty of skirt. Can go hunting.'

'What about that bouncer? If he's there, he might not let you in.'

They had gone to the Green Man disco a few weeks ago and Mark had had an altercation with one of the bouncers.

'That knob-head? Don't worry about him. I could take him out with one hand. You game?'

'OK,' he agreed, though a disco was the last place he wanted to go, being interested in neither disco music, dancing or hunting for a piece of 'skirt', as Mark put it.

'You going to Italy, by the way?' Mark asked.

'Well, I've got a ticket. Not sure I'll use it yet.'

'Hey, if you decide not to use it, I will.'

'You'll be summer schooling,' he laughed.

'Can't wait for it to start. There's got to be a few fuckable ones among 'em.'

'Mark? Frank? Any suggestions?' Bertha suddenly addressed them, obviously having noticed that they'd been 'talking in class' and not paying attention.

'Yah, I've got a suggestion,' Mark said under his breath to Frank. 'Why don't you go and take a flying fuck at yourself?' Then he said aloud: 'How about we have a coffee break? All this linguistics is doing my head in.'

At last the next day what he had been eagerly waiting for arrived – a letter from her. The colourful Italian stamps with a picture of a bearded Giuseppe Garibaldi in red shirt and blue trousers sent through him a thrill more intense than any work of art. Eagerly he ripped open the envelope to find in fact four letters and the lock of auburn hair she had promised him. His heart lurched with pleasure at the sight of it. He went into his study and sat down at his desk to read the headily-perfumed pages:

Lignano, Friday, 18.6.82

My dear baby,

Here I am sitting at my desk. It is time to go to bed for little girls, but how can I suffer less than this ... Everybody has got to learn something and I am now trying to live in this reality which seems so unkind, it looks a sad dream to me.

I will try to make this situation not too hard, living in a funny way perhaps, smiling if it's possible.

Since I've arrived I've been crying. I'm saying to myself to change my heart ... please don't cry, stop your tears, dry your eyes, Cinzia.

Francis, do you still exist? Are you really by my side? Or has our story been just a dream? There is nothing better than writing actually. It helps to relieve the pressure in myself. I wonder where I've been and who I am. Listening to music on my own, I would like to stop my thoughts. I think of you as one of the easiest people to get close to and I confided in you because you are a compatible person of tried integrity. That's why I've shared with you my most intimate secrets.

I imagine there is no country and no friends except London and you. You may say I am a dreamer, but I think I'm not.

I believed in yesterday and suddenly I've lost all my treasure of yesterday. Cinzia is still living with you. I'm always looking at you, only my shadow is moving in this house; my body requires food and sleep but my spirit needs to feel you next to me and hear your voice.

Francis, don't leave me!

I start writing to you again in the early morning: it is 11 a.m. and I've just got up. "Oh Cinzia!" Oh Francis, I didn't go to bed before 1 a.m. yesterday evening because some of my friends came to see me at home and they talked until one o'clock. Do you believe me if I say to you that I just answered their questions as quick as possible? My Francis baby I'm trying to do my very best but ...

Please, if there is any God, may I have some help? Francis come, come into my arms and stay because I really don't want you to go. I need you now so much and this doesn't mean that I depend on you completely: I just need you because I love you and you made me really happy.

I still don't know but I will probably spend a couple of days by my aunt who lives in mountains. More than anything I want to spend all my nights into your arms, you are my sunshine my love and I'm going to wait in my little town for my sunshine. I've now our photograph in my left hand, which was taken from Christine in the classroom and I want just to stop my sight on you, especially on your hands. However, I will probably leave this photograph and most of the things that remind me you in my drawer until it will be time to go to the sea. I will sit near the pier or along the sea speaking to you and asking you if you wish to come to me. I will kiss you more than ever and I will love you more than I did. My Francis I miss you!

I'm now going out to have some lunch with my friends and in the evening I will go to visit my young sister in hospital where she is waiting to be operated on Monday morning: we love each other very much! She says hello to you.

A lot of love from your little girl and so many kisses to someone special,

Cinzia xxxxxxxxxxx

It's Saturday night and I've been out until now 2 a.m. I've spent the whole evening talking and listening to my doctor and I can't now remember all the things he told me, but the most important was to put a bridge between me and my past and to start a new life as I believe.

Another drink, another pint of Guinness, another pub, another park, smiling, making love, crying, working and now I'm alone. I want my dream back which could be my true reality. Time flies on and I still feel your breath close to mine, I hear your kisses into my ears, ti amo sempre.

Francis I need to see you! I want you to cuddle me all night long and let me stay cooking for us.

Everybody has found me changed. Someone is surprised, someone else is disappointed, another one is really satisfied with my new maturity. But what is really important to me is my tomorrow: my tomorrow having breakfast with you. Oh Francis, I'm tired!

I wouldn't leave you and I kiss you even if you're probably kissing somebody else. Do you think of me sometimes?

Sunday morning.

The last words before going out to send this letter. The phone rang when I was still in bed: somebody wants to see me and I was suffering speaking on the phone because I do not want this meeting. However we'll see each other next Sunday.

Don't leave me Francis.

I love you very much,

Cinzia

P.S. I'm going to leave Lignano at the end of June and this is my address at the sea. I will probably stay here until the end of the summer dreaming of you.

He was drunk with joy. How strange that simple words on a few flimsy pieces of paper could exert such power! No doubt the perfume helped too, he thought, brushing them past his nose and breathing in the scent voluptuously, in an agony of longing for her. As for the lock of hair, sellotaped to one of the pages, which he held to his lips and kissed tenderly, it made him ache with desire for her. There was only one thing that bothered him – she hadn't mentioned Luciano at all. Or was that who the meeting she had referred to was with? But hadn't he met her at the airport, wasn't he with her right now? Was she keeping something from him? He turned back to the first page of her letter to read it again. He would read it many more times, he knew, so as to squeeze every last drop of meaning and pleasure from the words, like a desperately thirsty man who had been given a single glass of water. Then he took out some A4 loose-leaf paper and began to write his reply.

CHAPTER THIRTEEN

Lignano, Tuesday, 22.6.82

My hello to you at 11.30 a.m. of Tuesday. I can see you sitting there in your study, while I cook something for us: I never thought that I could be so happy with you. At the same time I'm thinking of other things. I will never see my grandmother again because she died suddenly 3 days after my departure to London and yesterday, even I knew she wasn't there waiting for me, I got upset when I didn't find her. Besides, my young sister doesn't feel well at all and our doctor, who phoned me a couple of minutes ago, asked where she is because he didn't find her in bed at the hospital. She shouldn't be moved for any reasons because she has been operated yesterday morning. I wonder where she is.

Francis, I feel so down. I am young. I want to live my life enjoying myself and doing what I wish. My friends have seen my eyes and they have understood my mood. That's why maybe they're helping me inviting me out and since I've arrived I haven't spent an evening at home. My parents are very angry for this reason and we didn't miss a big argument this morning because I was very late yesterday night. They have told me that I have to go back home before 12.30 a.m. because this is the law in my house. If I accept this everything will be all right for them, otherwise they say I can go back to England.

I feel so bad and also your Cinzia wants you! I'm now sitting next to my sister, who is very weak and weary and I have to look after her until evening. I'm looking through the window and I find a foreign sky, which is completely white. A long tear on my face is telling me all the pain I'll suffer till I'll be obliged to behave myself as the others want.

One o'clock. I've just come in and I'm not going into bed without saying goodnight to you. If you could see me here! New clothes, new hair-cut, new food, but one thing will never change I hope: my feeling toward you and London.

I wonder if you would still like to see me ...

Baby love, as a matter of fact I've spent most of my life at home living with my family and home environment has been perhaps the most important responsible of my character. Now I feel ready to leave my parents and cope with life having my pain and my joy.

Write to me, please, just to tell me that ...

Sorry Francis I was saying to you something wrong. Then let me only say "write, if you can".

I always love you.

May I give you a kiss?

I would kiss you for 24 hours.

I would love you for 24 hours.

I would join you for 24 hours.

After my dream, I come back to my reality and I really don't know what to say to you, because every time I write to you I have never your answer and sometimes I'm confused. I would like to tell you something and I haven't got the courage because I know our situation. I know you are not free. That's why I'm so uncertain. How can I come back to you? How can I forget what you told me?

Francis, I love you. I love you so much, but I will never be able to come back to London if you don't come to see me once. Or at least let me know that you won't come to Italy because of your new house, if it's true!

I'm now waiting for one of my friends. He is a good boy and tries to give me some help. I will try to be happy. I have to look happy even if my heart is crying because I feel you so far. I need you near me!

And for this time I've promised to be home before one o'clock. I will keep my promise!

I give you a kiss my treasure.

Your Cinzia

P.S. Please give me your suggestions in your next letter and say hello to Chingford, especially Epping Forest, and Hackney. I didn't know to live in paradise when I stayed with you!

Lignano, Saturday, 26.6.82

It's another day and since I opened my eyes I think of my last Thursday, my last day spent with you. Then I cry. There is something that has to be settled inside of me and at the moment I don't want to give any answer to people who ask me which plans I've in my mind. Yet there is plainness in my feelings: you are maybe the only one who knows how much I would like to come back to London and how hard and sad my life is without your suggestions.

My baby, I don't want to be plaintive, but how can I throw away my anxiety? I should now hang some pictures that I bought there with Christine. I should iron some clothes I used to wear when we were together. I should also lay the table because lunch is nearly ready, but I haven't enough strength to leave you.

I said to you I'll write and that's what I'm doing. I'm really feeling down. I miss your home, your bed, your kitchen, your voice. My mum is calling me and I can smell something wonderful. However, I'm still thinking of my Kentucky! By the way have you tasted a Kentucky kiss with salt? I haven't yet, Francis. I wouldn't kiss anybody else than you and when my friend gave me a cuddle yesterday I stopped my tears with difficulty. Then I wondered what will happen when I meet Luciano. I might close my eyes and forget my true reality, but it is not fair and I can't do this to him.

I'm in love with you!

I can see you joking with your friends, drinking your lovely Guinness, eating spaghetti or your usual boiled egg: I know your kind of life and I know that you're not as horrible as I used to say. Your Cinzia kitty-cat is going to love you more and more if you behave yourself well with her. When I feel you so close to me, I would have the freedom to go straight to the airport, take the first plane to Gatwick and give you a call telling that we could have another drink tonight. Maybe all this will be just a dream, maybe we won't meet each other any more because you want your freedom more than anything else.

It is OK Francis, but please be honest. I'm only asking you to be honest with me. If you have changed your mind, it doesn't matter. I will suffer, but I won't be angry with you. If you don't want to give me your understanding, your love, your patience, it's all right. I love you anyway, because you gave me so much. Now I'm going to save a lot of money for this summer and ... I will probably phone you before meeting Luciano or maybe tomorrow.

Say hello to Albert for me."Viele uber Grube an meinen Freund!"

A lovely kiss,

Cinzia

I'm going to take some pictures at the sea. Be patient!

Lignano, Thursday, 1.7.82

Dear Francis,

Since I phoned you I've been thinking of your possible holiday with me and I can't still believe to see you in Italy.

I really hope you've been serious on the phone! I'm now writing to you laying on my bed and I'm a little bit tired because I've been exposed to the sun all day long: I'm getting brown more and more.

At the moment my mood could be described positive and I'm only looking forward to receiving your letter in which I hope to read something nice about you. It's not simple for me to understand the profundity of real friendship, yet our relation has a sense to me: I could phone, visit you and call upon you for help if we lived near each other, but I wouldn't intrude on you because I know you expect the same consideration.

I miss you and I miss our open discussion of mutual interests and when I consider our story I become happy by noticing how well we shared our thoughts. I remember you reserved at our first meetings because you prefered to stay in the background until you got your bearings, that is a summing up of me. I used to listen to you carefully, because you're constructive and idealistic and I like your idealism, which is ruined sometimes by your lies!

I could be able to ignore a divergence of views with a fast friend, you can't as a rule because it's the principle that counts. Am I wrong, Francis? My doctor would say to me: "For as long as possible you'll tolerate such a big divergence, but eventually your own nature compels a break-down."

My baby love, I know I always want to get to the bottom of things and I'll carry on doing this because it's right. I'm also keenly aware of the need to keep fit my English through exercise and if I'm intensely chatty you're not less than me (or a little bit less maybe!).

I always think of you and I already dream of you here.

Cinzia xxxxx

Recco, Sunday, 4.7.82

Hello Francis,

I'm on the beach at Recco and I'm alone while I wonder when your letter comes.

I've spent my day listening to one of my friends playing guitar, singing and talking. I would say to have had a lovely day spent in perfect harmony with everybody, but eventually someone asked me why my eyes look so sad. Is it so evident my sadness? An answer is not necessary.

At the moment I would like to write to you: "Francis love, if you're wondering how you'll manage to do everything here, stop wondering. Let me be your guide."

Then all of a sudden I open my eyes to look for somebody giving me some help. I would be pleased to accept any kind of help from any people, because I don't want to suffer too much. I miss you much more than before and I'm not trying to "hide my love away".

How can I forget you and when will I be able to look at the planes without crying? Will you answer me? And now let me tell you something about Luciano. First of all he hasn't arrived in Recco yet and I can say to have been lucky once again; he is still working and he should arrive in a few days I suppose. I know he will try to know all the truth about London without trying to understand why I did all that and obviously I will be told to go to hospital because of my madness.

And where are you, Francis? I want your kisses! I want you now here to give you all my love and I know, I'm quite sure, you won't come to see me because of him. However, I won't die, don't worry, my Francis baby!

I always think of our days full of everything. Your little girl will never say to you Goodbye. You'll live inside of my mind, in my heart, anywhere I will live. I love you Francis.

A lovely special kiss,

Your Cinzia x

Recco, Thursday, 8.7.82

I've just received your letter in which you give me every detail about your arrival in Italy.

I would like to have enough time to tell you everything I've done since I'm living at the sea ... However, I've been looking for a place where to spend most of our time and I think to have found a lovely place, which is also next to other nice cities. Our room is really small, that's why it's very cheap! So we will be able to visit Italy as much as possible with all the money that will be saved.

I would be so glad to go to Venice or Florence or Rome, but you don't know how much money we should have! They are also very far from Milano and Genova. However, I think it will be possible to visit Venice once!

I'm now going out to send you this letter.

I'll meet you at the airport MILAN-MALPENSA on your arrival.

I always love you.

Your Cinzia gives you lots of love and kisses.

See you soon!

Recco, Monday, 12.7.1982

My dear Francis,

I'm now sitting in my living-room and I'm looking at the sea, that's not blue today, it looks unhappy, as much sad as me. There is no sun, the sky is grey and the weather is as cloudy as my mood.

What's happening to me Francis, where did I loose my smile and why?

Sometimes I prefer a voice that's telling me to forget our love, because this is the best solution for those people who love us, but at the same time I feel such a bad feeling that lets me down. I have not the courage to do anything. Is it possible? I realise sometimes that my actions have no sense and my words are not sincere.

Actually I'm spending most of the time with Luciano, who has arrived a couple of days ago and I'm trying to do my very best with him. I'm doing everything for him and I'm nearly forgetting myself. How can I carry on living in this condition? I really need to see you and I wouldn't leave you any more, but I have something to decide here and now and it's taking me a lot of time.

It's Monday afternoon 3 p.m. and Luciano was supposed to meet me a couple of hours ago to have some lunch together but he hasn't arrived yet. So I had something to eat on my own and I took time to look at our photograph for 2 hours. I can feel your lips kissing mine ... I love your eyes most than everything else because they speak to me in a special way ... All the love you gave made me different and it is still inside my heart and nothing of you seems far away to me because you're always by my side my Francis baby. Your letters are so lovely. I will never be able to write to you such marvellous novels! You're a writer, I'm not.

Francis your name sounds so sweet and dear. It includes goodness, kindness, love and a little bit of sadness. If I could I would join you "for ever" until you don't want me any more. If I could get a job in London very soon, I would be there at the end of the summer. Maybe I would stay in your arms whenever we can ...

I really hope to spend a lovely week with you giving you all

my love.
Cinzia

He loved her letters, even the paper they were written on, which were always redolent with perfume and reminded him painfully of her. The only fly in the ointment was her mention of Luciano. It seemed as if it was going to be a tug of war between Luciano and himself for her. Or between Luciano, her family, the whole of Italy and himself!

Sometimes he couldn't wait to get on the plane and go to her, show her how much he loved her, force her with the power of his love and his words to come back to London. At other times, though, he felt like ripping up the air tickets he had already bought and once in a state of drunken depression almost did so.

'Maybe we won't meet each other any more because you want your freedom more than anything else.' Why had she said that? What had she meant? How those word annoyed him! How they wounded him! Hadn't he given her enough love and affection in the short time they'd known each other? How could she say such a thing? If that was what she thought, maybe he shouldn't go.

But now he had told her he would go, so he would. He always kept his promises! And his threats ha ha. He would go and show her how much he loved her and that she was even more important to him than his so-called freedom. Besides, the rest of her letters were so full of love. So full of words of love. Just like the Buddy Holly song. How could he resist them? They filled his heart with love and longing for her.

And yet, always there was that fly in the ointment …

CHAPTER FOURTEEN

Tuesday 20.7.82
3.55pm flight from Gatwick to Milan Malpensa Airport. Read Memoirs of a Dutiful Daughter by Simone de Beauvoir on flight. One of the few female writers I like. Fantastic, picture-postcard views of Alps. Fantastic cloud formations too. Malpensa small compared with Gatwick. Saw her through doors of arrivals. Wearing short white dress with 'Roman' style sandals. She looked as brown as a nut. The white dress set off her tan sexily. Fell in love with her all over again! Hugged and kissed each other in the crowd. 'Ti amo,' we both said shyly. Bus to Milan. Kissed each other on bus. 'You were shy at the airport,' we told each other, laughing. Then a metro. Looked for Hotel Virgilio. Had to leave passport and ID card with reception. Annoying. Shown up to room by young porter in white shirt and black trousers. Room had two single beds pushed together, wardrobe, sink, balcony. View from window squalid! Milan looks squalid. Very humid. Gave Cinzia present of Charlie perfume. Pleased to see she was wearing the Claddagh ring I gave her in London. Delighted with perfume: 'You remembered I like perfume!' Noticed she was wearing sanitary towel. 'Just finished my menstruation, but kept it on just in case,' she said. 'Where can I get rid of it?' Litter bin on balcony? Looked at London photos. Went out. Had sandwiches and wine outside at bar. 'Milan is grey,' she said. 'What do you think of it?' 'Interesting, because new to me, different.' Went for walkabout. Corso Buenos Aires. Expensive shops. Expensive-looking furniture. C: 'Will you buy a new house for me?' 'Of course, as long as I can live in it with you.' Back to hotel. C. had shower. Made love properly for first time. C:'I am glad to make love properly with you.' Afterwards: 'Ugh – you are dirty! Let me wash you.' Hot night in more ways than one!

Wednesday 21.7.82
Made love again in morning before got up. C. mad for it! Walked around Milan. Breakfast outside. Tiny Italian coffee! C. had coke. Looked very sexy in short skirt. To Duomo. Up to roof in lift. Her first time too. Took photos. Down by stairs. C. not allowed into church because of short skirt. Went in alone. Then walked around piazza. Stage going up for pop concert tonight. Bloke playing piano! C. said Pope says Mass in church, speaks in piazza. Went to Galleria Vittorio Emanuele shopping mall. Bought bottle of mineral water. Sat on shop step, drank it and chatted. Asked her if she'd come back to London. Said she couldn't decide. To leave Italy, family, Luciano ... Big decision. Disappointed with her response. Made her promise to think about it. Didn't ask her about L. Don't want to know! 4 pm train to Genoa. In carriage put her legs over mine. So sexy! Young mother with small daughter in carriage too. Old woman. Young girl. Little girl looking out of carriage window whole journey. Kissed. C. not so shy any more! Red-tiled roofs. Fields of grain. Maize? Poplars. Arrived Genoa 6 pm. Hotel la Posta. Very old-fashioned. Room at back of hotel. C: 'My grandmother must 'ave slept in this bed!' Tiled floor. View of squalid courtyard from shuttered window. Had dinner in hotel. Soup with pasta in. Wine. Good. Wanted go for walk but C. said too tired. 'You go on your own. I tell you where to go. Not red-light district!' Not happy about it. C. came out anyway. She likes playing these games. Walked down to port. Japanese cruise liner. Kissed on steps. Dusk. Warm. Traffic mad! Bought bottle of beer to take back to hotel. Drank it in room. Made love. Fellatio. Could hear row between couple in next room. C. explained she a prostitute and he wants her to change her job and make more money. C: 'It's an Italian conversation.' Row continued into middle of night. Made love several times!

Thursday 22.7.82
Made love most of morning. Got up late. Brunch in bar near station, sitting at bar. Rice, tomatoes with mozzarella, beer, bread. To old part of town. Narrow alleys with tall, squalid-looking flats. Washing hung out. Scooters. Communist fiesta

on. Dancers in street. Kids' disco. Traders selling junk. Wine stall. Mussels stall. Book stall. Sweet stall. Bought some nougat. Funfair. Tried punchbag. Singer singing song about war. C. said it was stupid. Roast pig with legs tied up as prize in lottery. Ugh! Told C. I found it disgusting. She agreed though not vegetarian. Spoke about poverty, hunger in third world. India for example. C. said she wants go to India. Surprised. But said people in India hungry because cow is sacred. Non sequitur? Laughed at her. Slightly offended. Saw some sandals she liked but shop closed. C. had to go into back yard for pee. Prostitute in arcade. Deep cleavage. Guard with gun. Her pimp, protector? Repulsive, obscene sight! Bought gelacho – ice lolly. To port again. Japanese sailors laughed and waved because saw us kissing on steps. Sat on harbour side. Took photos. C. reluctant for some reason. Women so moody! Talked about her school days, exams, qualifications, marks. 'Maturity.' Said she was good at German, English and art. Her English pretty good certainly. In evening took train to Arenzano. Hotel Delfino. Tomatoes growing in garden. C: 'We'll steal some during night if we're starving.' Joke. Tiny room! Filled by double camp bed wall to wall. Wardrobe. Sink with one tap. Dirty mirror with tiny shelf. Glass door and green shutter. C. laughing at my shocked expression. C. put cases on top of wardrobe. No room anywhere else! Had dinner in hotel. Walked along seafront. Snazzy and jazzy. To beach. Port full of yachts and cruisers. Japanese cruise liner again. Seems to be following us! Gate to Beach Three. Deckchairs. Lay on sand. Made love on sand, under stars. Very romantic! Idyllic! Sublime! Fantasy come true. But annoyed by other couples doing same. C. shy at first. Went in for swim. C. scared of water, only paddled. Water warm and lovely! Played in water. Enjoyed teasing her. Sat on deckchairs. C. said beach was private during day. Lights from cigarettes in dusk. Fireworks. Palm trees. Had beer in Pino's Beach Bar. Back to hotel. Bed. Made love. C. pretended didn't want to make love again but did. She likes playing little games!

Friday 23.7.82

Woke up early and made love. Got up at 10 am. Hot outside again. Went to beach. Collected some rocks. Went for swim.

Swam out to raft. Windsurfers. Pedalos. Topless women sunbathing. Sunbathed. C. put cream on my back but not back of my legs. Kept her bikini on. But tiny! She's got beautiful breasts though not big. Told her I don't like big breasts. She was surprised. Thinks all men like big boobs. Not so. Has large freckle at back of her knee not noticed before. Lunch at hotel. Bed. Siesta. Made love. Afternoon walk along seafront. C. wearing blue slacks and one of my shirts. C. went for paddle in water again. Sat on beach. Kids playing. On 'colony' holiday. Back to hotel for dinner. Walked to port. Boats, yachts, fishing boats. Told her I don't like rich people. Wouldn't like to live among them because not one of them. Said I felt contempt for them even though sometimes I wouldn't mind being rich myself. C. agreed. Sat on harbour wall. Two lads fishing. Kissed on steps. Had drink in Pino's Bar again. Back to hotel and bed. Made love again though tired!

Saturday 24.7.82

Made love, got up late, went to beach, swam, sunbathed. Had lunch at hotel, went to bed, made love, had siesta. C: Why are you so wonderful when you make love? I've learnt so much about making love with you. You know everything! I won't make love for ten days after you've gone. Masturbation? Joke about Kamasutra. Talked about suppression of sex by Catholicism. Puritanism. Sex with her so natural. As natural as eating. Afternoon walked to Pineta, posh holiday resort for rich people near Arenzano. Had drink in square. Lots of girls larking around, esp. one blonde in brown shorts. C: 'Silly rich people. They hang around doing nothing all day.' Saw what looked like yacht owner reading 'La Republica', communist paper. Dressed in jeans and T-shirt. C. said car regs beginning MI means Milan, GE means Genoa. Had flower in her hair and red silk dress on. Pretty! Girls making up in ladies' offered her some make-up. Told her I didn't like make-up. Except on her! But she doesn't really need it. Got gorgeous tan. One street cordoned off. C. angry: 'So different from Britain!' Full of rich people. Beautiful houses and gardens. One garden with hammock. Path back to town. Followed by sexy girl on scooter. C: 'Do you like her? Do you want me to leave you so you can pick her up?' 'Yes, I like her, but I *love* you.' Gave her big squeeze. C: 'Ti amo.' Back to hotel for dinner. Discussed going to Calypso disco. No, too far. Went for walk along seafront instead. Had drink in Pino's Bar. C: Why do girls like you so much? Girls at college like you. Girls here like you. Do you like Italian girls? Told her I'd always had a thing for Italian girls, but she was the only Italian girl I liked now. Back to hotel. Sunburnt on back of my legs! C. rubbed cream on. Made love. C: I prefer be on top because I can move myself like this. Did you come? Yes, twice! Is it enough? Oh, yes! Told her some women never come. 'You know everything. You should be sex teacher not English teacher!' Laughed. Said why not both?

Sunday 25.7.82
Morning made love. To beach. Had picnic: tomatoes, cheese, focaccia, bananas, peaches, coke, beer. By boat to Portofino. One and half hour trip. Scorching hot! Several tankers on sea. Portofino full of impressive yachts. Another rich people's playground. But beautiful. Like walking into a postcard. Used tons of sun cream. Expensive boutiques around harbour. Pretty pastel houses. Street artists. Mopeds. Bought bottle of beer and drank while walked around. Men glancing at C. because looks sexy in hotpants. Annoying but flattering. C: I hate some men. A black man tried to touch me up in station. You know when they're doing it. 'Sesso' Italian word for sex. Sounds strange somehow. Up back street to church of St. Martin Divo Martino. Castle Brown, museum. On boat back to Arenzano sea very swelly. Felt sick. But didn't throw up thank goodness. Lay with head on Cinzia's lap. Survived. Had dinner at hotel. Conversation about prostitutes. I said there seemed to be a lot of them in Italy. Not used to seeing them in London. C. said normal in Italy. Said Luciano had been sent to one by the captain of his ship but he couldn't perform! Didn't ask her about him. Don't want to know. C. wearing red gypsy skirt with white polka dots. In bed C. played at being prostitute. What do you want? How long do you want? Played along. Funny game! How much do you charge signorina? Game didn't last long though. Both exhausted!

Monday 26.7.82
Our last full day together. Made love in morning as usual. Went to beach, swam, sunbathed, picnic. Jumped off big rock into sea. C. too scared to do it. Pretended to throw her in. Screams. Walked around crooked back alleys to escape sun. Had drink in bar surrounded by youths and kids. C: You will make such a good father. You know how to teach your kids right way. You're always reasonable and clear. You have strong character. You are the most positive person I've ever met. You have such a positive attitude to life. Told her because I believed this was the only life we had. C. agreed but said she wanted believe in 'paradise'. Told her *this* was paradise. C: I love it when you say something clever and amusing. Tearful. Went to station to enquire about train times for tomorrow. Stopped at church. Two priests standing talking outside in cassocks and birettas. Wanted to go in but C. said she wouldn't be allowed because of bare legs. She has hot legs! Went in anyway. Priests didn't stop her. Funny to think I almost became one myself. Have mixed feelings about them now. Comforting familiarity mixed with revulsion. And incredulity that anyone can believe such nonsense. Base their whole life on it! Church very impressive. Baroque style. Back to hotel. Made love. Siesta. Had dinner at hotel. C: Why are people looking at us? Because we are in love. And they know what we have been doing! Everybody wants to be in love. Everybody is searching for love. To beach. Lay on sand in each other's arms. Our last evening together. Conversation about loneliness. Purple sky studded with stars like sapphires. Sound of sea like a lullaby. Music of the spheres. Discussion about origin of universe and meaning of life. Both agreed no meaning beyond here and now. All the more reason to enjoy it. C. crying: I love you completely. How can I live without you? I will suffer. I will always remember these moments. You are inside me like my spirit, my soul. Our bodies fit together so good! Last drink at Pino's Bar. Told her if she didn't come back to London it would probably be the end. Wanted to shock her into making a decision. More tears. 'I'm not free. But I love you. I will always love you.' I said sorry. Didn't mean to upset her. Both ended up crying! Why spoil our

last evening together? Stupid! Hoped to force her to commit, decide. But felt depressed. Bad feeling. Melancholia. Will I *ever* see her again? Is this our last ever night together? It can't be! Surely love conquers all?

Tuesday 27.7.82
Made love for last time. Got up at 8am. Packed. C: Goodbye room! Had breakfast in hotel. Went to bank to get cash. C. had underestimated hotel bill. Went back to hotel to pay. To station. Train packed. Sat in corridor. Later found seats. C. in her red frock. So pretty. Pain in the heart. Milan overcast, dark, thunder and lightning. Symbolic? Left bag in left-luggage office. Went out for walk. Told C. rain reminded him of Manchester. Had lunch in restaurant. Bread, tomatoes and mozzarella with chopped cabbage and mineral water. Pinched some bread from next table! Walked to Luna Park but closed. War monument. Told C. joke about book of Italian war heroes. C. a bit offended. Stupid joke but because felt tense. Advert for film All You Ever Wanted To Know About Sex But Were Afraid To Ask by Woody Allen. So 'sesso' is the Italian word for sex? C. joking: There you go again, all you ever think about is sex! Train to air terminal. Sat in air terminal. Checked in. Tried to kiss her but she seemed embarrassed. Asked her what was wrong. C: Everybody is watching us. Men walking past glancing at her. Told her I suddenly wished we could make love one last time. C: They should have special rooms at these places. Told her she needed to be more individualistic, not go with the crowd, do something creative or constructive, write, draw, paint, learn an instrument, study. Said people only wanted her to conform to justify themselves and make themselves more important. C: Always I learn something from you. I am always surprised by the things you say. You are always looking at everything and everyone. You like to observe, especially people, how they are dressed, their mannerisms, how they behave with each other, react to each other. Told her it was part of being a writer. Told her to keep her English up. Suggested she write 'our' story in English with title: Seven Days and Seven Nights. C: I am too lazy. It's one of my faults. Tell me my other faults. Told her

she was a bit dogmatic in her opinions sometimes. And messy, disorganised, untidy. C: I will try to change. Told her to tell me my faults. C: There is not enough time! Had to laugh. Suggested she could write them to me. She said several pages would be required! Collected bags from left-luggage. Went to Departures. Heart heavy like stone. Gave her present of A PORTRAIT OF THE ARTIST AS A YOUNG MAN which I'd brought from London. C: Can I open it? Sure. Told her it was my favourite book. She opened it and read the poem I'd written for her on front page. She started crying. 'I've never had words like that before from anyone.' Hugged and kissed her. Dried her tears. Told her to read first few lines. C: It's quite easy. Explained that was because it was deliberately written in childish language. C: So you think I am a child? Laughed and told her it wasn't all like that. Last long kiss. 'Ti amo.' Tears. Bye. Ciao. Through departure gate. Turned to wave but saw her walking away fast in her red dress without looking back, crying. Felt like crying too. Cop with gun, surrounded by girls, showing off to them. Don't blame him! Sat in departure lounge. Tried to read Memoirs but couldn't concentrate. Sorry Simone. Not your fault! Plane fifteen minutes late just to prolong the torture. Kids playing football. Working-class English. Blue Sky Holidays. Sky not so blue today literally or metaphorically. At last boarded plane. Took seat. Put seat belt on. Seemed unreal. Like a dream. Surely would wake up any moment and be back with her again, making love, walking, chatting, laughing, lying on beach, eating, drinking ..? Surely I wasn't going to just fly away and leave her? Physical pain in chest. Pain in throat too. As if being slowly strangled. Noose getting tighter every minute. I can't do it. Can't leave her! Don't *have to* leave her! Why not just get off? It's not too late! Plane doors are still open. They can't stop you surely? Go on! Just undo your seat belt and get off! Go on! Now! Quick! Do it! Now! Go!

'Don't give you much room, do they? Now I know what a sardine feels like! A teacher eh? Me? Retired engineer. What part of London? Hackney? Can't say I know it. Me?

Portsmouth. Wouldn't fancy living in London. Not that Portsmouth's much to write home about. Bit of a dump if I'm honest. But home is home. Been on a package holiday for two weeks. Been to Italy a few times. I like Italy. Like the people. Don't speak the lingo though. Why not? Too lazy. If I had to, I would do. Got no motivation. Got a flask of whisky here. Fancy a drop? No? Always take my own. Wouldn't buy any duty-free because I'd only drink it at home. Do you speak the lingo? Bits and pieces eh? I'm not well-educated myself. Left school at fourteen. I knew what I wanted to be and got there. I was in the navy during the war. I did lots of courses. Had to, to keep up. I was technical advisor for the council – lifts, central heating, all that malarkey. I bluffed my way through most of the time. I was one of those who always just managed to scrape through exams. Not a brainy bod like you, I suppose. I do like reading though. I've done a lot of reading. Must have read all Charles Dickens. Simone de Beauvoir? No, can't say I have. Doesn't sound like my cup of tea. You did a degree, did you? What, English? Sometimes I wish I could've gone to university myself. Something I regret sometimes, not going. I think two weeks is too much. Might just do one week next year. Do I look a bit bleary-eyed? Had a long day today. Had to be out of my hotel by ten and hang round for hours. Then had a long coach ride to Milan. Hope I can get a train home tonight. Had to sleep in Gatwick once. Used to park my car at the airport, but it's too expensive now. What about you? You got your wheels at the airport? No? Train? Well, let's hope this thing's got some wheels to land on anyway. No, just the one bag. Always travel light. Passport and toothbrush. Funny when you think about it, isn't it? We're just ships in the night …'

At first he was annoyed with the man sitting next to him, one because he was so corpulent and two because he kept up a virtual monologue throughout the whole journey, fuelled by frequent slugs from his whisky flask. Must be a nervous flyer, he supposed. After a while though, he was glad to let him jabber on, and even encouraged him by prompting him with occasional questions, because it helped to distract him from thoughts of her, and Simone de Beauvoir was certainly no help.

It especially helped to distract him from one particular,

melancholy thought, which seemed to have invaded his brain, his mind, his very soul, like a virus – that was the thought that he would never see her again.

CHAPTER FIFTEEN

Recco, Wednesday, 28.7.82

My Dear Francis,

Should I give you a ring as I promised? I think so, but I haven't got the force to do it. I know a long time will pass before meeting each other again and the consciousness of this makes me passive. Actually there is no way to change this situation because of my insecurity. I feel you into my arms. I can still hear you calling my name and the sound of your thousand of kisses makes me smile, but all this lovely world of love is not enough to leave Italy today. I haven't the courage to let my sister down because she needs me now more than anybody else. She just speaks to me about her problems and she thinks I'm the only one who will help her at any time. What would you do in this situation? Would you do what you like and wish without considering the requirements of other people?

Francis, I'm on my own and I can imagine our next meeting when I will run into your arms. We will look the same, nothing will seem different to me, a sort of sadness will wrap me and you together while the sun goes down. Do not be sad, my baby. I will always be the sun of your life! And now let me say to you a few words really important: "I will love Francis for ever." It's so true, my Francis baby!

I'm now laying on my bed and I'm going to write our story, just the beginning, because my friend is coming soon. By the way, Luciano has gone away with one of his friends and nobody of his family told me where he is. I really wonder what will happen in the next year. Francis, believe me, since you left me I feel very depressed: everything around me reminds me you, every man sitting at the table drinking beer makes my heart cry. Then I cry walking around on my own in the evening. I dream you always day and night while I give you my hand.

I love you baby.

A very big kiss from

Cinzia

Seven Days and Seven Nights 1

It was supposed to be the greatest Tuesday of the summer 1982 because somebody was coming to Italy to see me. I was already up at 7.00 o'clock in the morning, although I felt tired enough to sleep longer, but I couldn't resist any more, I couldn't wait ... My Francis was supposed to arrive by plane at 6.40 p.m. at the airport of Malpensa and it was arranged in our last letter to meet each other there.

I wondered if it could be really true what happened in London when I was just a student sitting in front of my teacher who was become actually my loving lover.

'Hello, Roger! How's it going over there in the Emerald Isle?'

'Oh, dear! I'm not in the Emerald Isle!'

'You're not? Where are you?'

'I'm in Hammersmith Hospital!' he chortled, no doubt with his hand over his mouth.

'What do you mean?' he asked, shocked. Roger was supposed to be teaching on the summer school in Trinity College, Dublin, as he would normally be doing himself if he wasn't in the middle of house purchasing.

'I've broken my hip.'

'You've broken your hip? How?' This sounded bad, though Roger seemed to think it was all rather amusing, which perhaps was the best way to look at life's travails.

'Oh, I was knocked down in Bunratty by an Irish nurse!' Roger chortled again, as though it were a great joke.

'Oh, God!' he exclaimed, not sure whether he should be laughing or not himself. 'When did this happen? And how did you get back to Blighty?'

'Three days ago. We were on a trip with the students. It was my own fault, I know. I stepped off the pavement without looking.' *Well, he is as blind as a bat and won't wear glasses out of vanity.* 'The poor nurse had no chance to stop!'

'Well,' Fran risked joking, 'I suppose if you're going to get knocked down, better to be knocked down by a nurse!'

'Oh, gosh, yes!' Roger giggled heartily. 'Though I think she was as shocked as I was!'

'I bet she was. So how did you get back here?'

'Yoko came straight over to Ireland when she heard. She's an angel, that girl. No hesitation, you know. We came back from Dublin by Aer Lingus ambulance.'

'Well, I'm really sorry to hear this,' Fran said. 'Can I come to see you?'

'Oh, yes indeed, that would be nice. Very kind of you.'

'I'll come tomorrow.'

Recco, 1.8.82

Hello my dear Francis!

I phoned you this morning and now I'm still here thinking of you. Where are you, my Francis baby? My lovely boy, you can't imagine how much I think of your voice, your hands, your feeling towards me. I've been with Christine all day long and she still can't believe me when I say to her that you really came in Italy. She looks so surprised! You should see her face! You know, I didn't want to take her to Portofino, but at last I found enough strength to go there ... it was amazing, you were holding my hand, cuddling me, giving all the love you could. I would hear your breath. I wanted you so much!

My Francis darling, you're in the air ... Since Christine arrived I've missed you more and more because we always mention your name and sometimes I leave Chris and Luciano alone to stay a few hours just with you.

It happened yesterday night when they were dancing together and I left the lounge where we were sitting. I went out walking along the shore of the beach asking for one of your kisses. I loved you again and I felt so much inside ...

two lovers can hear the sound of their kisses flying on the surface of the sea from Italy to England, two persons who would like to stay together again, maybe for a long time.

Seven Days and Seven Nights 2

In a sunny day, as it was that Tuesday, the heat of the sun could burn a very white, delicate skin and as I love the sun, which is the source of life, I wanted to expose myself for a short time ... but my world of memories was saying to me to be ready the soonest: my dear friend was coming and as one month had gone since I left London, I wished to please him as much as possible. I remember he used to come along with my thoughts, my dreams, and he was able to let me know every truth. In fact, speaking to me and looking into my brown eyes, I could understand the meaning of his truth, which is the highest principle of the human mind. So my next destination had to be the airport, where I expected my heart jumping fast and where I had to meet my true soul.

Why he had become so important to me I didn't know. I just felt a sort of happiness mixed with anxiety and I can actually see the same tension in this handwriting which is the reflection of my character.

And now here I am sitting at the table of this small room full of light and looking at the sea. I can feel nonsensical sensations such as home-sickness and loneliness and in this mood which doesn't sound very happy, I carry on doing my work ...

Just a few words to you Francis love: I would you here into my arms while you kiss me and I say to you "Ti amo sempre!"

Your sweet, sweet Cinzy baby

He went to the hospital to visit Roger with Pavlo. Pavlo was Serbian, a short, skinny, fair-haired fellow with stubbly Slavonic features, an ex-student of Roger's, whom Roger had recommended to him to do the building work on his new house in Walthamstow. Pavlo was sporting a white leather jacket, tight blue jeans and white moccasins and carrying a white motorbike helmet. Apparently he had a degree in agriculture from Yugoslavia – not all that useful in the crowded and traffic-choked streets of North London.

The first thing he noticed when he arrived at Roger's bedside was the spike through the calf of his plaster-encased leg, from which his leg was suspended on a sort of gantry over the bed. There was a bit of dried blood around the entry and exit holes of the spike, which made him feel slightly nauseous. Roger himself was sitting up in bed in an operating gown and was as upbeat as ever, despite his broken hip and ruined summer.

'Well, at least you've got some pretty nurses to look at,' Frank commented. 'And tend to your every need.'

'Oh, yes, that's true – though they don't tend to one's *every* need!' Roger chortled, blushing, his hand over his mouth.

'They're giving me a temperature already,' Pavlo said, which amused Roger even more. 'Maybe I should go and lie down on that empty bed.'

'Are you learning Spanish?' Frank asked, noticing a Spanish Made Simple book on Roger's bedside locker.

'Yes. I thought I'd better do something while I'm stuck in here,' Roger nodded. 'It helps to pass the hours, you know. One of the nurses lent it to me actually, a Spanish girl.'

'Well, at least it's not Orthopaedic Surgery Made Simple,' Frank quipped, giving Roger the giggles again.

They chatted for a while, including about some Serbian poet who had just been jailed for 'insulting the state', according to a newspaper cutting Roger had, and about corruption in Yugoslavia. Roger and Pavlo spoke a bit in Serbo-Croat, since Roger had spent time teaching in Yugoslavia and Serbo-Croat was one of the many languages he spoke. The sound of the language, as well as Pavlo's accent when he spoke English, reminded him of Marina, his Yugoslav ex-girlfriend of ten years ago, who was also Serbian. What was she doing now, he wondered? Maybe she was working in a hospital herself, since she had been a medical student …

'Who's the chap in the next bed?' he asked Roger, putting Marina out of his mind.

'Oh, that's Aldo – he's Italian!' Roger declared. 'He crashed his motorbike into a bus. I practise my Italian with him occasionally.'

'No visitors?'

'Oh, his girlfriend's usually here with him. I don't know where she is today.'

'Is she Italian too?'

'Yes. Yes she is, acksherly. Gorgeous-looking girl.'

'I like Italian girls,' Pavlo averred. 'They are so warm. So hot. So passionata. Don't you agree, Frank?'

'Yes, I do,' he agreed, glancing with horrified fascination again at the bloodied spike through Roger's leg to distract himself from thoughts of Cinzia.

'Does it hurt?' Pavlo asked.

'What?' Frank said, thinking for a moment Pavlo was talking to him. 'Oh, this.' *This is only physical pain.* 'Does it hurt, Roger?'

'No, I have no feeling at all,' Roger said.

'Sometimes is best way,' Pavlo said. 'Do you agree, Frank?'

'Yes, I suppose so, sometimes,' Frank smiled ruefully.

'Oh, dear, I didn't mean it in that way!' Roger exclaimed.

'No, you speak the truth, oh wise one,' Frank said, with a mock obeisance, which sent Roger into such a fit of giggling that a nurse came over looking alarmed.

'OK, we go now,' Pavlo said, when Roger had regained his composure.

'Are you going to that Yugoslav restaurant?' Roger enquired.

'Yes,' Pavlo said. 'I'm going to buy him pasulj bean soup. But without the smoked sausages.'

'I think he just wants to see the Irish waitress who works there,' Frank remarked to Roger, with a wink in Pavlo's direction.

'Ah, yes, the lovely, flame-haired Galway girl,' Roger enthused.

'Bunratty Castle. English teacher. Broken hip. Yugoslav restaurant. Galway girl. Bean soup. Serb builder. There's a short story in there somewhere,' Frank observed.

'Yes, you should write it,' Roger declared.

'Well, maybe I will,' Frank said. 'Maybe I will.'

But will there be any room in the story for an Italian girl as well?

Seven Days and Seven Nights 3

I felt in London, the city of many contrasts, historic and modern, brash and dignified, sports loving and culture supporting, foggy, rainy and sunny, modest and extravagant, quiet and clattering and ever more spectacular scenery, a vista from every window.

All facets of this fascinating city folded me and now my Irish lover was arriving from London. At last my Francis baby, in this way I used to call him, waved and coming to me he made my eyes shining and holding my hands made my love deeper and both of us got red. I realised that nothing had changed in between and our merry memories followed us making our meeting very special. Francis and Cinzia were together again: I never ever had such a big event in my life! I did not know what to say and I felt even shy to cuddle him until when he gave me a long kiss on the coach, which was supposed to take us to Milan, where we had to spend our first night. It seemed really unreal to travel on the coach cuddling each other and looking around we asked ourselves if it could be true all that.

Was that just a dream or it was all reality? I still don't know the answer to these questions because the time, which is going by so quickly, mixes everything together and anything we did belongs to the past, almost like a delightful dream ...

I love you Francis as ever and I'm sure that I miss you as much as you miss me. My lovely Francis, where are you now? Please give me a little bit of your beauty! I look at me in the mirror and I can see my weary eyes. Why are they so deeply sad? You are my harmony, my Francis baby! I'll write to you again as soon as. I love you and I thank you for your photographs. Please write to me to Lignano where I'll work.

Cinzia xxxxx

It was a strain trying not to think about her while getting on with all the mundanities of life. At least he was on holiday so didn't have to teach, he thought with relief. He dreaded the thought of going back to work at the end of August more than ever – it was always a gloomy prospect, even though he loved his job. He tried to console himself with the thought that there would be other girls, including no doubt Italian girls – but he didn't want any other girl. He only wanted *her*. He was in love with her whether he liked it or not. Other girls didn't exist for him now. Only *she* existed. She was the only one. It was almost like an illness, a mental illness.

He couldn't get her out of his head. Even when he was talking or listening to Pavlo discussing the building work on his new house, or to his sister on the phone, or to his wife, or to friends, he was thinking about her, hardly listening to them, hardly able to concentrate on anything. It was developing into an obsession.

He went to Birmingham to see his sister, but he was still in Milan. If he saw a church it reminded him of the Duomo. He walked around Eccleston Square. There was a convent of the Franciscans of the Sacred Heart of Jesus with the usual gory depiction of a bleeding heart. Even that reminded him of her and his own bleeding heart. He talked with his sister and American husband – an affable Texan guy – about family, including the new baby they were expecting, about the local area and local lingo, their jobs, American literature, Ireland … All lubricated by copious bottles of Guinness and a few whiskey chasers. But he could hardly bear to listen. He could hardly bear to be there. He didn't want to be in Birmingham. Even *they* didn't want to be in Birmingham, which they regarded as a bit of a dump, which it probably was compared with Texas. But he didn't want to be in Birmingham or Texas or anywhere else. He wanted to be in Milan! His head and his heart *were* in Milan.

His sister told him an interesting story about some Irishman who had organised a mutiny on a British warship in World War One, was put in the Black Hole of Calcutta, escaped and fought in the Irish War of Independence and Civil War, fled to the

USA, refused on principle to claim a pension from the Free State government and died in the gutter. It was a great story. One he'd like to explore further. Maybe it'd make a good novel. But all he could think of was Cinzia, Milan, Recco, Arenzano, Portofino …

He forced himself to socialise as much as possible, to try and get her out of his system. He went for a drink with an old seminary friend called Patrick, who was a professor of 'anthropology of religion' at King's College. Patrick proudly showed him around King's and the splendid view of the Thames from the balcony at the back.

'A good place for ornithology, this,' Patrick commented drolly. For a moment, Frank didn't register that it was a joke and he was referring to 'birds' of the non-feathered variety. He chuckled, secretly embarrassed at his own slowness, but putting it down to the fact that he had no interest now in 'birds', as Patrick amusingly referred to women – although he was once the keenest of 'ornithologists'. Now he felt priggishly uncomfortable talking about women in this way, though he tried not to let Patrick see it. It was as if all other women were invisible to him, he reflected wryly, because he could see only her. How he wished he could get her image out of his head!

'Enough bird-watching,' Patrick said after a while. 'Let's go for a drink and something to eat.'

Frank suggested a congenial-looking pub on The Strand which he had passed on his way to King's, but Patrick dismissed it. 'That pub's no good,' he decreed pompously, in his somewhat pretentious Oxford voice, 'because it's full of spies. South African, Asian, Irish, all sorts.'

Frank felt both amused and miffed by this and was inclined to argue, but told himself it would be petty. What did it matter where they drank? After all, this was Patrick's 'turf', so he should know the best places anyway. He was only feeling argumentative and irritable because of *her*. Because he couldn't get her out of his system. Because he resented everyone and everything. He especially resented all the romantic young couples strolling or lolling about the place. It seemed as if Fate had just been playing a cruel trick on him, giving her to him, then snatching her away.

They ended up at the Lyceum pub on The Strand, where at least they served a decent ale in the form of Webster's and the garden was good for 'bird-watching', according to Patrick. But he quickly tired of Patrick's company and just wanted to be on his own to mope and lick his emotional wounds – a sensation he was ashamed of and annoyed with himself about. It was part of the 'illness', he told himself, and tried to take an interest in what Patrick – a genial fellow despite his pretensions – was talking about: his bad back, his recent stay in hospital, where he had to 'piss' and 'shit' on his back, the laminectomy operation he was going to need, so he had to cancel a holiday in Rome, his marital problems, even Mary …

'Mary has a lot of good points, you know. She's a nice person. Not so many of them around these days. I don't want to screw women necessarily – I'm happy with a good conversation. If my marriage breaks down, I think I'll just go it alone. It takes too long getting to know someone again. I've been with Maggy for nine years now. I just worry about my little boy if we do split. Wouldn't want him to be hurt …'

He wondered if he should tell Patrick about Cinzia, especially since he claimed to know Italy and Italian women well, having spent a year studying theology and, he claimed dubiously, Dante, at the Gregorian university in Rome. As well as doing a lot of 'bird-watching'. But he didn't. He didn't want to talk about her. He wanted to keep her secret. A guilty secret. A shameful secret. A precious secret. A painful secret. A sacred secret. Like an arrow in his sacred bleeding heart. An arrow which he wanted to remove but didn't want to remove. *Couldn't* remove!

That was the Webster's talking, he told himself, realising that he like Patrick was slightly drunk. But he didn't want to get drunk and spill his heart out to him or anyone else. So he was relieved when, after their third pint, Patrick rather abruptly and self-importantly said he had to go – as was his habit – and they parted company cheerfully on The Strand, promising to repeat the exercise next week.

He was relieved because it meant he was free to go and

get drunk on his own, for which purpose he stumbled off into Covent Garden, feeling lonelier than ever among the tourists, the magicians, the mime artists, the violinists and the courting couples …

Recco, 1 agosto 82

My dear baby,

I am now sitting where my daddy usually works and I've just put the phone down after our long conversation. Sorry for the paper, which is not nice but it's usually used for business and this is the only one I've got at the moment. I'm looking around and I'm looking for you as if I couldn't controll myself.

Listening to you on the phone a couple of minutes ago, I felt so much love for you that I really wanted to take the first plane to London and spend a lot of time with you, but, as you already know, I'll start working soon and at the moment I'm not free to come to London. I would ... you know how much I would come to see you, but I can't hurt some people so much! My mum was even crying the last evening when I was speaking and telling her my ideas about my future life. I was just saying that I would like to live on my own without getting married. To be honest with you, I must say that my parents are driving me mad: they wish to see me married as soon as, because they think that marriage is the best solution for every woman. They will never ever understand the meaning of freedom and independence.

Luciano is the only one who understands me a little bit more and he agrees with me about my idea to get a job and to stay on my own until I'll decide to do something more definite. My baby love, I haven't stopped thinking of you since I got up this morning, today it's an important day for you and now listen to this please: each time a birthday greeting is sent from me to you, you can be sure kind thoughts are sent, along with wishes too. And each time one year closes, another opens wide with endless opportunities to fulfil each dream inside.

I love you always.

Baby, tell me everything about your new house, how big it is, how many rooms there are in it, its colours, its shape and so on and one day when I come to London you'll show it to me, I hope. If you can, otherwise I'll be happy to stay with you in your flat, if you can keep me. My darling, are you still waiting for our love story? Be patient! You know I'm always so 'busy' (I'm laughing) that I'm writing down our story slowly.

Never mind! I keep my promises and when I finish our Seven Days and Seven Nights, I'll come to you and we'll read it together.

Always a lot of love for you and many long long and sweet kisses.

I love you,

Cinzia xxxxxxxxxx

'They've taken the pin out!' Roger declared triumphantly, as soon as Frank arrived at his hospital bedside.

There was a long dribble of blood on his floppy, glabrous calf where the pin had been removed. Roger explained that to put the pin in they had drilled through the bone with only a local anaesthetic and similarly for its removal.

'That must have hurt,' Frank sympathised, struggling to keep his mind off Cinzia.

'Yes, it was rather unpleasant,' Roger agreed, with what sounded like something of an understatement. 'The nurse kept saying, "What strong bones you have!"' he chuckled. 'He was a Cork man, though I thought he was Welsh, because his name was Mineth. Mineth means 'hill or 'ridge' in Welsh, you know. But he definitely didn't want to be Welsh! Must have been a Welsh family originally though.'

'So does this mean they'll let you out soon?' Frank asked, amused and impressed as always by Roger's enthusiasm for everybody and everything.

'Oh, yes, next week they say. But you know, I've no way of getting home to Shepherd's Bush. They won't give me any transport. I'll be on crutches apparently. Yoko will collect me, but I don't think I could negotiate a bus and we can't afford a taxi. We're broke, alas.'

'Broke in more ways than one, eh?' Frank quipped, making Roger giggle. 'Well, don't worry, Roger, I'll pick you up.' He was glad to be able to help, out of friendship, but also partly because it gave him something to do, something to help him take his mind off her.

'Would you? That's awfully kind of you, old chap,' Roger effused. 'I really do appreciate that.' Somehow his cut-glass Oxford accent and public school turn of phrase – even though he had never actually been to public school – sounded out of place in this demotic hospital ward.

'My pleasure, Roger,' he said and noticing a paperback on the bedside locker observed: 'I see you're into Icelandic Sagas now.'

'Oh, yes, just a bit of research for something I'm working on,' Roger said.

'You've learnt Spanish Made Simple then?' he joked.

'Oh, dear, not quite,' Roger giggled, his hand over his mouth. 'It should be there somewhere.'

'Ah, there it is,' Frank said, upon further investigation, and picked up another book. 'So who's this Amanda McKittrick Ros?'

Roger, eager as ever, proceeded to give him a mini-lecture about Amanda McKittrick Ros, a long-forgotten but apparently once popular, romantic, Northern Irish novelist and poet of the eighteen-nineties – Roger's specialist subject – and early twentieth century, whose biography he said he was working on. How typical of him to write about somebody nobody's ever heard of, he reflected wryly!

'I'll have to read a bit of her,' Frank commented.

'Oh, dear!' Roger sighed. 'I don't think you'd enjoy it much. It's very turgid stuff. It's just that she is, you know, a rather fascinating character in her own right. And she was once extremely popular. Tastes do change, you see.' He nodded sagely.

'Yes, well, I hope your book will be a bestseller,' he said, tongue-in-cheek.

'Oh, dear!' Roger sighed again. 'It used to be much easier

to make money by writing.' It was the first note of despondency he had heard from Roger, despite his somewhat sorry situation.

'You'll just have to give it a raunchy title,' Frank said, only half-joking.

'My working title is *Ships That Pass in the Night.'*

'Not sexy enough,' Frank asserted. *For God's sake, don't start talking about sex!*

'Oh, dear, I'll have to think of something better then!' Roger giggled. 'How's your writing, by the way?'

'Oh, I'm still plugging away,' Frank shrugged, as always not wanting to talk about it. And to distract Roger from further enquiry, as well as himself from thoughts of her, asked him another question about Amanda McKittrick Ros, whose name he would now never forget, who despite her obscurity had somehow assumed an odd significance in his mind.

After visiting Roger he went for a drink in a pub nearby. He had intended to have just one pint, but couldn't resist another, then another. It was fatal, he knew. He missed her so much, it hurt. He hoped the alcohol would anaesthetise the pain, but it only made it worse.

Then, to make matters even worse, the plangent strains of 'Hey Jude' by the Beatles came on the jukebox and to his embarrassment he found himself crying – crying, almost literally, into his beer …

Recco, 7 agosto 1982

My Darling Francis,

I lay down in my bed and after having read your book a little bit (thanks for your 'ti amo sempre', I love you too) I start to wonder if and when I have forgotten our nice paradise. Everything seems so dark to me and I've lost my smile for many reasons.

First of all, as I already told you in my last letter, there is no more understanding between my parents and me and arguments become more and more. Fortunately my family left Recco yesterday evening and as Luciano works now in a factory, I can do whatever I like: walking on my own along the beach I remember our paradise that I've lost when you left me in Milan at the air-terminal.

Francis, I always see you around me, you're like the shadow of a tree, you follow me everywhere even when I wouldn't. A few days ago, I was nearly desperate and crying in my bathroom. I called your name so loudly that maybe you heard me! I asked you to cuddle me and you didn't say no. Oh my baby, sometimes I really would start to walk up to London and join you just to show you how much I love you. I cry, Francis, I still cry for you and I ask your english God to make me sure that you are well.

I would like to know when you start to teach again and if you heard anything about my exam. I hope that your God looked after foreign students! You know that I don't believe in many different Gods, don't you?

Francis, tell me something about London and its colours and are the prices still going up? I remember when I lived with my pocket money and it was really very difficult to me to survive.

And now that I'm at the end I will tell you something not too nice: I am in bed because I am not fine. I've got temperature every night and I didn't say anything until this morning when my aunt saw me very depressed. Now we are going to call the doctor and soon I'll go home. NOT TO WORRY BABY FRANCIS!

I love you really very much,
Cinzia xxxxx

He was always thrilled to receive her letters, but after reading them always felt depressed, especially if there was any mention of Luciano, whose very name went through him like a dagger. He wrote long romantic letters back to her, but always regretted doing so, always hesitated about posting them, yet always did. It was like a masochistic game that he couldn't resist playing, an addictive drug that brought euphoric highs and depressing lows.

It was the middle of August, when he would normally be teaching on the summer school in Dublin and having great craic, especially in the evenings, going to pubs and concerts with the students. He would probably be having it off with a sexy French or German girl by now – not that he wanted to do that any more, since he was in love with *her*, could think only of *her*. But that just made it all the more frustrating! Because he knew that if he was in Dublin, he'd be just as miserable, would be missing her just as much.

Here he was, stuck in London in the middle of August, in love with a girl who loved him but who couldn't or wouldn't come to him. A girl he knew he should forget about, but couldn't. A girl who had unexpectedly captured his heart in a way no other girl ever had. But a girl who was also breaking it *slowly*, squeezing out his lifeblood drop by drop!

Ironically, he started wanting to go back to work, but that was two or three weeks away. At least he'd have his teaching to distract him and there'd be new students to socialise with and get to know, including no doubt lots of pretty foreign girls. But he didn't want any other girl. The very thought revolted him. He only wanted *her*, the one he couldn't have!

Sometimes he thought he should just get on a plane and fly back to Italy and *force* her to come back to London with him. But apart from anything else, he couldn't afford another trip to Italy, especially as all his spare cash was being swallowed up by the house. And anyway, how could he *force* her to return with him, against the wishes of her family and this Luciano, this lucky Luciano? He couldn't! Besides, she seemed to have *chosen* them over him. So love didn't conquer after all! He should just try to forget her. Or at least try to cure himself of his obsession.

He was glad to have the distraction of his house conveyancing, which he was doing himself with the help of a solicitor friend, another ex-fellow seminarian, and which required several trips to the vendor's solicitor in Epping, which in turn gave him an excuse to take long reflective walks through Epping Forest or across the Marshes – not that he needed an excuse, since these were two of his favourite places. Whenever he did go to the forest, he couldn't resist going to High Beach, where he had gone with her on that last day before she left, though he knew he shouldn't, because the memories always filled him with more pain than pleasure.

It was a relief when the house purchase was completed, because it meant he could throw himself into clearing it out for Pavlo to start the refurbishment – it had been lying empty for a couple of years and was semi-derelict, both house and garden full of rubbish which he needed two large skips to dispose of. It was only a small, Victorian terraced house in a Walthamstow side road, but he felt proud to have acquired his first bricks and mortar. He would sometimes stop work to survey whatever room he was in and visualise how it would look when the work was finished – and try to keep out the thought of how wonderful if would have been if *she* were going to be sharing it with him …

Recco, 14 agosto, 1982

Hello my Francis,

It's a cloudy afternoon today here in Recco and sitting up in my bedroom I'm thinking of your letter that I've left at home in Lignano. In fact, I was with my family a few days ago just to check and renew some documents.

I'm fine now and everything is all right with me. Don't worry, baby! The only thing which doesn't please me is that I'll start working very soon at the beginning of September maybe as a receptionist. However, this is not the only job I've found and by the time I'll get the possibility to choose another job.

I feel sorry, but at the moment I've decided to stay in Lignano because my parents have missed me too much when I was in London. Oh my dear! I can't believe I've been in London for so long. Was it a dream? You know, every time I have something from London or from Christine I smile, her words make me remember and I so often become blue. Why is it so hard? I never expected so much difficulties!

Christine as well feels down and she is also pregnant.

Her boyfriend left her even knowing she will keep the baby. What a cruel reality!

Francis, you're always on my mind and I'll visit you for Christmas if I have my own money. In fact it bothers me to ask my daddy for the money of the journey. I really hope to see you for a little while. I always love you and Luciano knows this. I often speak to him about you and I'm allowed to visit you in London for a few days.

Your sweetness is in my heart and I'm sad all the time I'm thinking of you. Do you ever cuddle your pillow? I do it very often and I feel a bit more good when I think you're there next to me. I touch your hand, which is warm and lovely and I would never leave it. Then morning comes and reality as well: I'm alone! I feel lonely, but life carries on and it's nice to remember the good time we had together.

Love from your
Cinzia xxxxxxxxxx

CHAPTER SIXTEEN

'We're still floating re desks, I'm afraid,' Roy said sourly, when he walked into his staffroom for the first time in eight weeks. 'I've already spoken to Ken about it. I told him it was intolerable. I told him I can't teach if I don't have a desk. But all he wants to do is talk about his trip to Baffin Island in Greenland. I've a good mind to go on strike. You're a union rep, aren't you, Frank? I think we should make it a union matter, don't you? They'll have to give us desks if we all down tools, won't they? Do you know what Ken said? He said why don't you take a desk in the room opposite, since there's a spare desk in there? I pointed out that it was a room full of women. I've got nothing against women, but I don't want to be the only male in there. And I'm not going to have the operation! It'd be like joining a coven. I'd rather sit in a nest of vipers! How can you cope with a man like that? I'm going to see him again right now and give him another piece of my mind.'

'That was a crock of horse shit, wasn't it?' Mark commented, when Roy had left the room.

'You mean, Roy and his nest of vipers?'

'No, the principal's address.'

'Oh, Fullofhimself? I gave that a miss. I knew it would be a load of guff. Can't stand the arrogant bugger anyway. Nothing interesting at all?'

'Nothing positive. The bar's gone.'

'What do you mean?'

'The poly's already moved out, so they've closed down the bar.'

'They've closed it? Already? During the summer? The sneaky bastards!'

'Yah. They're turning it into a science lab apparently.

Haven't got their priorities right at all.'

'But if the poly's moved out, there should be lots of extra space in the block at the back, shouldn't there? I don't get it.' He was outraged – even more outraged than at the loss of his desk.

'Apparently the council have grabbed that, so we've got even less space than before, since we had a few offices in there.'

'This is a disaster! So they just ignored our petition completely?'

'Yah. But we've still got the Bell. We can carry on our extra-curricular activities in there, can't we?'

'Yes, I suppose so,' he laughed bitterly. 'How did the summer school go? Get off with anyone?'

'You betcha. I'm shagged out. I'll give you all the lurid details over a pint tonight if you like.'

'OK. So you didn't get to Greece?'

'Nah. Was too shagged out. Having too much of a good time here! Besides I need to save some shekels to pay for my psychology degree. How about you? Go to Italy?'

'Yeah, I did in the end.' A cloud passed over him.

'And? Did you shag her arse off and entice her back?'

'Well, we had a good time,' he laughed, secretly cringing. 'But I couldn't persuade her to come back.'

'Never mind, mate. Plenty more where that came from. New intake next week. So we're gonna share this desk, are we?'

'I suppose so. What about that one over there?'

'Some new feller coming in, so he'll be sharing it with Roger. Where is he, by the way?'

'Oh, didn't you know? He got knocked down and broke his hip in Ireland. Was in hospital here most of the summer. I took him home just the other day. He's still on crutches. I don't think he'll be able to come to work for a few more weeks.'

'Unlucky bastard. Mind you, that Nip wife of his is a cracker. He struck gold there. Don't know what she sees in him.'

'I think she loves him for his mind, Mark,' he smiled.

'Well, if she's looking for some diversion while he's incapacitated, you can tell her I've got an IQ of 140 and a nine-inch dick.'

Suddenly, the door opened. For a moment they both froze, fearing it might be Bertha. But in breezed the diminutive figure of Tony Holloway, dressed as usual in a white safari suit.

'Ah, the au pairs' delight!' he exclaimed, beaming from ear to ear.

Recco, 27.9.82

Dear Francis,

How are you? Here in Italy summer is still warm and plenty of people lay down on the beach. I'm sure you would enjoy a long swimming into the warm water, wouldn't you? Do you remember our lovely plunge: one ... two ... two and a half ... two and three quarters ... and three: PLUNGE! Wasn't it beautiful?

That time seems so far away or maybe it's not completely true and right what I've just said. In fact, I can remember every moment we spent together as it happened yesterday and I can hear your voice saying to me, "I must go now," at the air terminal where you left me definitely.

Francis, my love, are you still thinking of me? You know, the last 6 nights I saw you in my dreams: I was walking along the street when I saw you sitting on a bench with a girl. I stopped walking and I pretended not to see you. I sat on the opposite bench and started to read the book you gave me as a present. When you saw me, you thought that I hadn't seen you yet, which was wrong and you got up in a hurry escaping from me with your girlfriend.

Francis, this is a very sad dream and it could become real, I'm afraid of that. Please never escape from me, my baby, even if we meet each other with somebody else.

At the moment I'm still in bed and many people are visiting me (Luciano as well) but nobody is able to make me happy as much as you. I love you with all myself even if I'm not with you.

Darling, I've received one letter from London today. Pilar, the other au pair girl, wrote to me telling me that she is going to leave Vivien at the end of September, because she can't stand her any more. I feel sorry for Pilar, who sounds to be a nice girl. However, Vivien is now far from me and I will never see her again, I promise.

Francis, I would like to give you a ring, but I'm getting shy! Silly girl! I'm a bit shy and I'm also afraid of hearing your "Hello, Cinzia!", which is always so nice and reminds me all the love I still feel for you.

I give you lots of kisses!

Ti amo sempre,

Cinzia

Seven Days and Seven Nights Ctd. 4

... but my wish is to keep my dream alive because it's a source of life, it is joy and tenderness, a little bit of pain and very much love.

So, full of happiness, we arrived at the air terminal and Milan looked so different from the last time I visited it. I could laugh for hours if somebody tells me that Milan can be nice and very romantic for tourists, but that evening on our arrival the city seemed changed to me: maybe it was a little bit romantic! I didn't even know where to find a room without booking, so we asked immediately the booking clerk where we could spend one night: we wanted something cheap and not too bad and we had a very nice room which we paid quite dear.

I can still remember every road we walked down to reach our hotel which was called "Virgilio" and it was not easy to find it, so that we asked pedestrians more than once for information. At last we found ourselves inside our bedroom and we layed down next to each other and although the air were very warm, our bodies, our hands, our mouths wished a physical contact and there we made love properly for the first time and it was so much lovely and I felt so happy that I will never ever be able to forget my nights with my Francis baby because it was delightful to sleep near him.

I loved him when he was smiling and laughing at me, when he was playing with me as a funny child, when we had our bath together, when we walked down the streets cuddling each other and holding his hand I couldn't resist from giving him a kiss and then another one and another one again.

My heart is paining for you. I still feel to love you as much as before, but life is cruel sometimes and here I am thinking of you my love!

I send you a lot of kisses with all my love,

Your Cinzia xxxxxxxxxx

The 'new boy' turned out to be an ex-monk called Edmund Dollier. They met while enrolling the next day and introduced themselves to each other. Edmund was about six and a half foot tall and broad, with a rough, pock-marked face and a haircut that looked as if it had been self-inflicted with a pair of blunt scissors. Frank thought he looked like Boris Karloff in *Bride of Frankenstein*, except that he wore a tweed jacket, with regulation leather elbow patches, a woollen tie with a rather grubby-looking check shirt, dark green cords and leather brogues on his boat-like feet. He had been a monk at Downside for two years, he told him, but left several years ago, because his mother had terminal cancer, to become a school teacher.

'What was the monastery like?' Frank asked, disingenuously.

'The cuisine was five-star,' Edmund informed him, in his RP accent, while puffing on his pipe, 'and the monks used to leave their shoes outside their cells every night to be cleaned by the servants or 'johns' as they were called. But it was a hard life. It was no picnic. One monk committed suicide by jumping out of a window. Ex-commando, he was. Hadn't slept for five nights, he told me. Must have thought he was on exercises. Everyone knew he had problems, but nobody tried to help him. There was no affection there – that was the thing I couldn't abide. Difficult for somebody like yourself to understand that, I suppose.'

'Well – ' Frank was about to hint that he might have some insight into that particular situation, but Edmund was loquacious.

'Don't be fooled by my Surrey accent, by the way,' he said. 'I'm a Paddy. Can't help my accent. Was brought up in Surrey. So don't try to tell me any anti-Irish jokes. That's what I always say to anyone who tries. “I’m a Paddy, so watch it!”. Are you Irish yourself, by any chance?’

‘Well, yes, as it happens. I was born and brought up in Manchester mostly, but my parent were Irish.’

‘You went to school in Manchester, did you?’

‘Yes, Xaverian Grammar, same school as Anthony Burgess, run by Xaverian brothers, but then I – ’

He was about to divulge that he had also been in a seminary – information that he released to virtually no one, except that he already felt a rapport with this ungainly-looking but imposing and impressive fellow – but Edmund cut him off again. It was ironic – here he was about to share his darkest secret with somebody for virtually the first time in his life, but he couldn’t get it out!

‘Ah, brothers!’ Edmund exclaimed. ‘I was educated by the ICB.’

‘The ICB?’

‘Irish Christian Brothers. Or International Child Beaters, if you prefer.’

Frank laughed. ‘The Xaverian Brothers were fond of the cane all right. Mind you – ’

‘I think we’ve got a lot in common, you and I. We Irish have to stick together! Up the rebels! Been a bit of a rebel all my life, I have.’

‘Me too, in my own subversive way,’ Frank laughed, warming to him.

‘I was in the Irish Club in Eaton Square the other night, for the first time in my life. Don’t know if you know it. Bloody big crucifix over the bar! I said to the barman, “Either that goes or I go. It’s blasphemous!” They ushered me out. I was happy to leave. Place was full of obscene language. I don’t do language. Sign of illiteracy in my book.’

‘So why’ve you come into this game?’ Frank asked, amused, remembering his many visits to the Irish Club with the Sugawn Players. ‘Did you get fed up with school teaching?’

‘I was at a really rough school in Hackney. Enjoyed it for a while. But it grinds you down. Wasn’t doing any real teaching. That was the trouble. Just minding. Warehousing as they call it. The kids were feral. I remember my very first day one of them spat at me. Sputum on the lapel of my jacket. I said, "If that happens again, I shall call the police." They just laughed at me. In the end I just walked out in the middle of a lesson and left.'

'Really? What happened?'

'I was writing something on the board when I heard air pellets whizzing past my ears. That's it, I thought. I'm not going to be shot at. I'm not in the military. It's not supposed to be a war zone. But it was, in a way. Funnily enough, I quite liked the kids. Had a certain admiration for them. Maybe respect would be a better word. They had spirit. On an individual basis at least. Together they were like a pack of wild animals though. Of course, they called me 'Frankenstein'.'

Frank wasn't sure whether he should laugh or not. 'Well, I think you'll find it's very different here,' he said, risking a chuckle. 'Welcome on board.'

'Glad to be here. Glad to have a job the way things are these days with that hag Thatcher in charge. Looking forward to it. A bachelor like me needs the structure of work. I'm not married. I'm not intending to get married either. I mean, not yet. I've got no one in mind. My flat's nice and cheap but untidy. I'm not lonely but I'd rather not live alone. I'm not gay, mind you. Are you married yourself?'

'Well, yes and – '

'Some nubile-looking young ladies here, I see.'

'Yes. In fact – '

'Is one allowed to fraternise with them? If 'fraternise' is the correct word.'

'Well, yes, of course, they – we – are all adults.'

'I hope they don't find me too scary.'

'I don't think so,' Frank smiled, though he wasn't so sure. He did look a bit scary. But he liked him, he decided. He was predisposed to like almost anyone who had been in a monastery, described himself as a 'Paddy', had an aesthetic appreciation of young ladies and hated Margaret Thatcher. Maybe he'd rope him in to their soirées at the Bell. He wouldn't provide too much competition for the girls. But even if he did, so what? He wasn't interested in the girls himself. There was only one girl he was interested in, wasn't there? Except that he couldn't have her …

'So did you manage to get away anywhere during the summer?' he asked Edmund, to make conversation – not that it was difficult to make conversation with this chap.

'Just came back from five weeks in a French monastery. Place I always go. Don't worry – it's nothing like Downside. The monks are all dressed just like you and me and they know how to enjoy life. Good nosh. Good wine. No women of course. But we'd be dancing on the tables at three in the morning sometimes! How about you?'

'Ah, Frank, there you are!'

He looked up with an inward groan to see Bertha barge into the classroom, where the students were doing their entry test – an apparition far more scary than Edmund, as far as he was concerned. But at least it saved him telling Edmund about his summer.

'Can I have a word with you about your timetable?' she demanded, plonking her voluminous bulk down on a chair next to him and throwing open a folder on the desk, scattering several of his own papers in the process. 'I don't think I'm going to be able to give you what you want.'

'Oh, why not, Bertha?' he asked, biting his tongue. He imagined what Mark might say to that and wished he could be as forthright.

'I'll go and see what this young lady wants,' Frankenstein said, rising up to his full six and half feet and striding Karloff-like towards a female student with her hand up. I hope she doesn't run away, Frank thought, gritting his teeth to listen to Bertha.

'I hope you don't think I'm being unfair to you, Frank,' she said, 'but you know you're the only one who's fussy about his timetable …'

Oh, Cinzia, why can't you be here? Why couldn't you have stayed? It would have made my life so much easier! Come back, please! I love you! Ti amo!

Lignano, 11.10.82

My Darling,

Many thanks for your long and lovely letter, inviting me to come and live in your new house with you, which made me cry. My dear Francis, I'm crying even now! It's not a joke, you know when I'm joking, don't you?

My baby love, I would like to stay in your arms for a long, long time, to have your cuddles and kisses and to feel happy with you: I would leave Italy in this moment if I could. I wonder where you are reading my letter now ... Are you sitting in your study or maybe do you lay down on your settee? I'm with you, even when I'm very tired, like now ... I've just come in after a long day of work. In fact I'm the secretary of an important director, who is involved in the famous theatre "La Scala" in Milan. Have you heard of it?

Today I've been sitting inside my office for 5 hours and during this time I've been using a standard electric typewriter. Then, I told myself to stop doing that and I decided to go upstairs to have just a drink ... unfortunately the phone rang and people from Germany required information.

At the beginning we tried to understand each other speaking English and it was lovely for me: I felt happy! Then, a woman wanted to speak German with me and problems arrived to me!

However, let's go on and let me kiss you, my love. Ti amo sempre. XXXXXXXXX

Lots of people telephone from England and France and Germany all day long and they are used to confirming their next arrivals in Italy and they also require plenty of theatre seats. I usually give them facilities.

And now shall I forget my job?

Tomorrow is another day and I shall get up at 7.00 a.m. as usual. What about you, my Francis?

Please don't ask me to come to you, because as you see it's impossible to me to leave my office now. I'll have my next holiday in summer, after June, and that's a very long time far away.

So what can I do? Darling, don't think of me too much, don't miss me, it must be painful for you. Have a drink, but not too many! Enjoy yourself if you feel to do it and be happy as much as possible.

I love you as much as before, nothing has changed between

you and me: believe me! Good night. I'm actually at work and I'm having a rest, so I'm going to finish this letter because I want you to read it as soon as.

I'll be working this weekend and the next one as well. Poor Cinzia!

Tell me everything about your new house and how you feel, what you do, where you eat and when you go to bed.

Love from

Your Cinzia xx

An attractive Danish girl caught his eye while he was enrolling a few days later, so when he had finished marking her test, he chatted her up. She told him she had only been in London two weeks and, predictably, she was an au pair, with an Orthodox Jewish family in Gant's Hill, but already couldn't stand it and wanted to change. She also told him that London was too big and she felt homesick.

'So when are you planning to go back home?' he asked her.

'When I miss my mama too much,' she said, childlike, though she was nineteen years old. As was Cinzia.

He was touched, but his interest had evaporated. She was too young and innocent. Not to mention boring. He would only be using her if he asked her out. Besides, he felt guilty just talking to her, because he was still in love with Cinzia, still lovesick for Cinzia, still obsessed and besotted with Cinzia.

'Fancy her, do you?' Mark asked, when he had sent her off to the office with her forms to enrol.

'Not really,' he laughed. 'A bit too young and innocent.'

'That's the way I like 'em. The more virginal the better. I hope you've put her in my class.'

Frank laughed. 'I've put her in Evening Advanced. She's a bit too good for First. Speaks English better than a lot of natives, being Scandinavian.'

'I know, you put all the good-looking chicks in your class, even if they can't speak a word.'

'You've rumbled me,' Frank laughed, trying to ignore the pain in the coronary area of his chest.

'Anyway, it looks as though we're getting our desks back.'

'Yes?'

'Twin-pronged assault on Ken by Roy and Bertha. Roy bored him into submission while Bertha sat on him.'

'That's good news,' Frank laughed. 'Of course, if Fullofhimself hadn't taken the old staff common room for his office suite, we'd have plenty of space. Not to mention Ken letting the Gen. Ed. offices go to Catering and grabbing a whole staffroom for himself. They're all bloody egomaniacs, aren't they?'

My Darling Francis, *Milano, 17 ottobre 1982*

Did you receive my last letter? I hope you did, otherwise I should write to you the same letter once again. You know, since I wrote to you that letter, in which I explained a lot about my job, I'm worried.

Maybe you're actually thinking that I'm very interested in my job and I'm happy with it. No, Francis, believe me, that's not true. Of course, I'm a little bit interested in my work, especially because everything is new for me and it's nice to learn and have more experiences, but eventually I feel so much tired that I would like to give up with it. And it would be so lovely to have 2 days of rest every weekend: at least every Saturday and Sunday. But I haven't been very lucky this time ... in fact I will be obliged to work when other people usually enjoy themselves, for instance on saturday afternoon and sunday afternoon because plenty of students (and not just students of course) like to spend some hours listening to very nice music.

Francis, this first part of my letter could be an answer to your letter. In fact, I've stopped writing for a while and I've read your letter again: your words hurt me and every time I read that you want to come and meet me in Italy, I would say to you: "Oh yes, come to Italy before Christmas and stay with me for 7 days and 7 nights." But baby, don't feel so down! I'm not by your side and that's the worst thing that can happen for you and me because we want to see each other very often.

Oh dear Francis! What do you expect me to do? Shall I

leave my office? Shall I come to London for a week during Christmas holiday? Darling, the thing is that I won't have holiday at all until the end of the theatrical season, that is until the next summer.

You will know how difficult it is to get money today and it is for me as well, because I never finish my work at 6 o'clock like the others do. I always carry on until 7 p.m. on Saturday and Monday. So if one day I become rich, I'll buy for you the best present that you would appreciate: a lovely boat!

Baby, I'm getting weary more and more, please forgive me if I leave you now, but my bed is calling me and I can't resist. I'm not strong enough!

Love from your Cinzia: ti amo sempre.

I'm still in Milan my Francis and I've just looked at the Duomo. I've also looked at the photographs that you sent me of the last Summer and I feel really very sad: I wonder where you are and all the times I speak English I ask myself if my English is really good enough or maybe should I come back to you to improve your mother tongue? Please, send me all your thoughts and all the love you feel towards me: I'll give you back more than this.

Baby, soon I will be 20 years old! What a pity we can't have a drink together. We can only dream to more than that with all our love.

Cinzia xxxx

Many thanks for your very nice poem: I've very much appreciated it. I do love you.

It was late Friday afternoon. Most staff had left the college, including Bertha. He had stayed on to continue organising the departmental resources, of which he was in charge. Feeling curious, he sneaked into Bertha's office, which was little more than a cupboard. On her desk, among all the other flotsam and jetsam, his eye caught a memo from a colleague:

TO: BERTHA
FROM: FIONA

RE: TIMETABLE
I am really not prepared to do a class on Monday morning if you want me to do a class on Monday evening. The gap is just too long and as you know I live quite a distance from college. Also I consider it unfair of you to tell me that I am the only member of staff who is fussy about their timetable. I consider myself to be as flexible as anyone else, indeed perhaps more so than most!

What a bitch Bertha was, Frank thought, frustrated that he wouldn't be able to use this 'evidence' in 'court'. Still, he told himself, he'd keep it up his sleeve for future use, just in case.

He went into the language laboratory to continue organising the books and cassettes, but knew he was only delaying the moment of going home. Or at least back to his empty, silent flat, haunted as it was by Cinzia's ghost. He couldn't resist glancing occasionally at the booth where she used to sit, even though every time it sent a spasm of pain through him. When he saw her name in the laboratory lending log, he decided he couldn't take any more of the torture, packed up and left the building.

It was five o'clock, a sunny September evening. Still too early to go home. A bit too early to start drinking though. But as he passed the Bell, he couldn't resist, so in he went – even though he knew her ghost would be waiting for him there too. But at least a couple of pints of Guinness would soften the pain of seeing her yet not seeing her, he consoled himself.

CHAPTER SEVENTEEN

He completed the purchase of his house, with the help of his old ex-seminary solicitor friend. He kept his own desk at college. He managed to negotiate a decent timetable from Bertha. He found out that Cinzia had passed her exam in the summer and, indeed, that most of his students had passed their exams, as usual. He even got a small pay rise. His new students were delightful and as always there were some attractive girls among them. But lonely as he was, he felt no interest in them. And every letter he received from her just made the pain worse …

Milano, 24 ottobre 1982

My dear Francis,

I'm sad and all the times I feel like now I would have you here next to me.

You don't know, but some people want me to forget you and London. Why should this happen, my Francis? I'm sure it won't, baby, you and London are the best of my life.

Every time I look at the Duomo, I remember our lovely hot days. I really would like them back, my love.

But usually dreams don't come back, do they?

Don't be sad, cheer up my angel: I love you.

And now would you like to read something "very special"?

Turn the sheet of paper ... and you will fall adreaming ...

"I send you all my eternal and deep love, while I ask you how you made me fall in love with you so much.

You made me happy
You made me cry
You made me crazy for too much life.

One day I'll be back to you with all the love that I couldn't give you!

Oh my baby, we'll be one once again, when we smiled together and everything will look the same.

One day further, I'll be back to you with so much love that the green parks of London will get green even more. We'll have a drink once again and we'll be happy together as we have never been before.

My heart is open to you and it is always sincere with you, but suddenly my reason comes back and a different reality appears in front of my eyes.

This is life!

Francis, I'm now 20 (thanks for your lovely birthday card again) and I'm still dreaming and sometimes I realise that my dreams are dangerous and not just for me, but also for somebody else: this is very bad, don't you think so?

I always try to be good and I can't stand the idea of being the cause of somebody's suffering ...

Baby, I'm actually so tired even because it's late and I need to sleep. I should write to Christine because it's a long time that I don't receive anything from her and I wonder what's happening in her new life. Maybe I write a short letter to Chris tomorrow during my work time.

Good night, Francis. I'll see you in my dreams!

Many many cuddles and kisses,

Cinzia

Darling I've just stopped reading your lovely book: I like Stephen!

Francis, today it's Thursday and my Director gave me 5 hours for resting, so I'm now at home where I feel so cold!

Do you remember how cold were my hands when we were having our first drink inside the Forest Lounge of Bell pub? Do you remember how I used to get red when you asked me questions in the classroom? I felt so much happy when you came to me at the bar of the college where we had fixed our appointment! When we sat near each other, when your hands held mine, your lovely voice, words and smile were everything for me and I still remember all this with love. Let me stay with you a little bit more ... days are becoming short and grey and I would fall asleep until spring comes and then summer and then HOLIDAYS ...

I'm already looking at them!

Your babylove,

Cinzia

He threw himself into the renovation of his house or at least into helping Pavlo, his Serbian builder, with it – though like all builders, to his frustration Pavlo disappeared for days on end, no doubt to catch up with other jobs. He went for a drink with Malachy, his ex-seminarian solicitor friend, to celebrate the completion of the house purchase, and they swapped stories about their seminary days while listening to Segui in the Victoria on Holloway Road, getting drunk in the process. But most of the rest of the time, when he wasn't teaching, he spent alone in his flat, in pubs, in libraries, in parks or wandering across the Marshes on his way between his flat in Hackney and his new house in Walthamstow.

One evening he was sitting alone in the Pembury Tavern, close to his flat, nursing a pint of Guinness and trying not to think about her, trying to resist the temptation to read her latest letter, which he had in his inside jacket pocket, for the umpteenth time, when a film came on the big screen. At first he tried to ignore it, because it was a war film, and he wasn't keen on war, but slowly it pulled him in. It was called Operation Daybreak and was about the assassination by the Czech resistance during the Second World War of Reinhard Heydrich, the brutal Nazi official in charge of Prague – who appropriately became known as 'The Butcher of Prague' and was evidently a psychopath like so many of Hitler's gang.

It was a gripping and moving story – all the more so because it was based on historical fact – but he was also captivated by one of the female members of the Czech resistance, so much so that, inebriated as he was, he fell in love with her there and then, ridiculous though he knew it was. But the combination of her physical attractiveness and her inspirational courage had an irresistible romantic appeal to him. Besides, she reminded him of Marina, his Yugoslav ex-girlfriend, who he could just imagine playing such a role in real life, proud and feisty as she was …

Lignano, 7 novembre 1982

My dear Francis,

Thank you for your last letter that I'm now keeping in my hands, but Francis you make me suffer ... you shouldn't miss me such a lot! In fact your pain is my pain and I'm sure that you wouldn't see me upset. Darling, we have to try to be stronger ... can I give you a suggestion? Don't see me always nice, try to think that I can also be very bad. Francis, please be strong!!!

Your lovely London will always give you what I like very much: you can have it, I can't because even if London is always in my heart, it doesn't belong to me for real.

Baby, you're real, I know, but you're so far away that sometimes I wonder. Everytime I get upset for some reasons, I look at the wonderful world of memories that is living inside me. I can also look at another world: the world of my sweet dreams and you're my darling, the nicest person who is living in it. Francis, I wished to phone you yesterday, I would phone you today or now if I could find enough courage.

It is always so nice to hear your dear voice, but afterwards I would feel very sad and that's why it's ages since I gave you the last ring.

Should I say "I'm sorry, Francis!"? If yes, I'm sorry, but I'm not as strong as you think!

And now listen to me for a while. Suppose I phone you now for saying that I may be coming over next month to have just a weekend in London. It could be marvellous to spend some time with you, go out together all the nights and be happy.

But many tears would get to me at the end and I would be upset even more than now. Besides, today is Monday and now it's 8.30 p.m. and I'm ready to jump into bed, because I'm really so tired that I can't keep my eyes open: I'm sleeping on my feet because of too much work.

Francis, do you imagine me? Would you go out with such a

bad girl? I wouldn't!

Baby, I want to know if you are still going to college and you are still teaching? Please answer me in your next letter. I'm always a little bit happier when I read news from you.

I give you a long long kiss and a big cuddle with all my love.

I love you very much, my Francis.

Your Cinzia xxxxx

P.S. Baby I've now received a letter I sent you two months ago: the postcode was WRONG. Silly girl! Kiss, kiss, kiss.

'I'm sorry, Frank. You can't use the phone,' Cathy, the departmental secretary said, to his annoyance. 'Bertha's using it. She's been on it for two hours. She's a pain in the backside! Blocking up the switchboard.'

'It's not the only things she blocks up, Cathy,' he couldn't resist quipping, at which moment Bertha emerged from the office.

'Oh, Frank, hello, dear. Come and see me in half an hour, would you? I've got a Pakistani on the phone who wants to come on the TEFL course and I'm trying to get rid of him without being rude.'

Damn, he thought – she'd caught him! *Without being rude? Bertha?* That was a joke! Well, she could fuck off if she thought he was going to hang around for half an hour for her. What did she want though? Maybe it'd be better to find out, otherwise he'd be in suspense till tomorrow.

It turned out that she wanted him to do a third evening class – having tried to take his evening classes off him at the beginning of term to suit herself. 'Apparently Mark is doing a course in psychology, so can't do evening classes any more. He only told me last week, which isn't very professional of him, is it? It's a JMB class. Would you do it for me, dear?'

Christ, he thought, she knows how to soft-soap people! Mark would probably tell her to fuck off. He wished he had the guts to do so.

'I'm sorry, Bertha,' he said instead. 'I'm already doing two evening classes. I really don't fancy a third. Besides, I need time to work on my new house.'

'Can't you do that in the afternoons?'

'I usually write in the afternoons, Bertha.'

'Oh, yes. How is the writing going?'

'It's going.'

'Are you still working on a novel?'

'Yes.'

'Have you thought of writing an EFL coursebook?'

I have, Bertha, and I can't think of anything more boring. 'Maybe in the future. Not now.' *Please release me, let me go! I don't love you any more!*

'Well, please think about the evening class, won't you?'

'OK, I'll think about it, Bertha. Thanks. Bye.' *I gotta get outa this place!*

It was always a relief to get away from her and out of her claustrophobic, chaotic cupboard of an office. He wanted to make a beeline for the college exit, but had to pop into his own office next door to pick up some books for his class tomorrow.

'Ah, the au pairs' delight!' announced Tony cheerily, looking up from his desk as soon as he opened the door. 'You look rumpled.'

'I've just been buttonholed by Bertha, that's why,' he laughed, collecting what he needed and exiting again as quickly as possible, afraid Bertha might follow him and pounce on him again, as always amused if slightly embarrassed by Tony's preferred mode of address to him.

On his way out, he bumped into Mark in the foyer and told him what Bertha had said about him being 'unprofessional'.

'Remind me to put some warfarin in her coffee next time I see her in the common room,' was Mark's response.

'Have you got off with anyone yet?' Frank laughed.

'I think I've met the love of my life.'

For a moment Frank wondered if he had heard right or if Mark was joking, but he sounded deadly serious. 'I thought you were the great cynic who didn't believe in love,' he laughed.

'I do now. I'm besotted.'

'Tell me more,' Frank urged, though he wasn't sure he wanted to hear.

'Her name's Edina. Hungarian. In my afternoon Business English group. Tall, slim, great legs, great boobs, red hair, good brain.'

'Wow! She must be really something!'

'You better believe it. She's really something, I can tell you.'

'You're not having me on?' He still wasn't sure Mark was entirely serious. He almost might as well have told him that the sun went round the earth. 'Are you sure?'

'Yah, you betcha I'm sure. She's the one for me. And you know how I'm sure? Inja likes her. Inja's besotted with her too! That's always my ultimate test.'

'I'll have to get a dog myself,' he joked, making to go, strangely discomfited by this information.

'You still waiting for your Italian chick to come back?' Mark stopped him.

'Nah. She's not coming back.' Even as he said it, he felt a wrench in his guts. Because the first bit *wasn't* true – he *was* still waiting for her – but the second bit, he knew, deep down in his guts, *was* true: *She isn't coming back.*

'Don't waste your time, mate. Plenty of crumpet round here.'

'You're right,' he laughed, moving away. 'I've got my eye on one or two.'

'Come round for a drink some time. I'll introduce Edina to you.'

'Will do, thanks,' he said cheerfully, hurrying down the front steps, feeling a terrible emptiness opening up inside him, a cold, desolate, hungry vacuum inside where his soul had been, the source of warmth and joy and pleasure, a space that seemed to want to swallow him, suck him, into itself …

Somehow he couldn't face going to the house to work. If Pavlo wasn't there, he'd be annoyed. If Pavlo was there, he'd want to chew his ear off about religion or his bad relationship with his father or corruption in Yugoslavia or how he wanted to emigrate to Tasmania. Well, he was a lonely soul himself in his own way, working on his own all day. And no doubt he'd tell him about more stuff that needed doing, putting the bill up. So he went to the Bell instead.

Lignano, 14 novembre 1982

My darling Francis,

Chrismas is only a few weeks away and I'm sure I'll be crying the 25th of December because you'll probably be sad.

I have to say to you, "Be happy and don't be alone."

Remember the letters, maybe one or two, in which I wrote a lot about my job at the Scala Theatre? Well, I already told you that I couldn't stop working any reason: theatre uses to work when the others are on holiday. Anyway, now it's all over, because I left my job a few days ago. I couldn't work any more because I was getting too much thin. In fact, in the evening when I was eventually back home, I used to go straight to bed without eating anything: I just drank some tea with lemon, no milk. As I'm now free, I'll follow some private lessons to learn to write in shorthand and maybe I get the driving licence too. I want to do as many things as I can, at least until when the HB Pharmaceutical firm will call me and this should happen in about 2 months.

Now, there is one thing you should know: I'm not well. A few months ago doctors said to me not to eat butter, eggs, tomatoes, fry and so on. I nearly stopped eating because I was afraid of every bit I put in my mouth. A similar thing happened to me when I was 15. I was put on a diet until when I came to England. I remember how well I was during my stay in London! What I'm going to say is that I want to discover the cause of my disease, because I can't even sleep when my blood runs hot.

Francis, you shouldn't be worried, nothing bad is happening to me: I have just a serious allergy. You know, sometimes when I'm alone, I think about the food and drinks I used to have in London. It was like a dream for me: I started drinking milk, bottles and bottles, I couldn't believe it, it made me feel well. Then I ate fish and chips and one egg a week, lots of bananas and lovely Kentucky. I could eat anything I wanted: even Treets, do you like them?

When I went back to Italy, I had completely forgotten the meaning of being ill. Now, I'm suffering a little bit because some parts of my body are getting red again. The last week I went to Switzerland and a very good doctor affirmed that I'll be definitely all right one day, but it takes him quite a long time to discover my allergy. So I'm trying to understand by myself which thing is bad for me. I want to feel well!

Francis, I give you a very big cuddle, no other words, words have no sense. I just put my fingers on your mouth. I can feel your warm lips. I can see and kiss them. Please forgive me, but I won't meet you soon. It's sad our reality, but I know that your new house will never ever "belong" to me. It's like if you live in a lovely, delicious, sweet house: you would love it but you know that sooner or later you'll leave it. I know that I could love your house too much and this could be a big mistake. It belongs to someone else.

Baby, do you remember our many happy days spent together? I do very well and I wish to ... Francis, no more words.

Just close your eyes and think I'm with you,
Cinzia

CHAPTER EIGHTEEN

Thurs. 9.9.82
To Red Lion theatre pub at Angel. Good-looking, blond-haired guy in leather jacket tried to chat him up. Obviously a queer. Felt so lonely almost responded. But not quite that desperate! Could never have sex with a man anyway. Never! Liked women too much. Except didn't have a woman. Looked round antique shops in Camden Passage. Couples in restaurants. Jealous of them. Jealousy like a poison in the soul. Went to Wheatsheaves but full of teenagers. To King's Head. Blues duo on. Good stuff. Very attractive bronzed, blond girl in short denim skirt and waistcoat with bare back and arms dancing Dionysiacally. Sexy but didn't feel anything. Dead inside. Left early and went home. Put some Van Morrison on. Finished bottle of Bushmills and crawled off to bed.

Fri. 10.9.82
8.30 a.m. phone call from Mary. Coming to London from Ireland tomorrow to see her alcoholic brother in the rehab clinic. Could they meet? Told her not a good idea but in end agreed. Or was he subconsciously glad at prospect of some female company? Even that of his wife who was divorcing him? Whom he didn't love any more and perhaps had never truly loved? Was he so desperate for female company? Perhaps he felt subconsciously guilty. About the way he had treated her. Though it takes two to tango. Resolved to resist all negative feelings of bitterness, self-pity, anger etc. Have to be strong! She asked him what he had done on his birthday. Told her had stayed in on his own all day. Mary: 'I can't believe that.' She must think he was having a whale of a time!

Sat. 11.9.82
Met Mary at Euston 2 p.m. Wearing anorak and denim dungarees over black and white striped jersey and carrying a weekend case. Toe nails painted red. New look! Strolled down to Thames where some sort of festival on. Funfair, stalls, barge races, speedboats, dinghies, biplane display, West Indian dancers, magicians, clowns, Hare Krishna monks, rescue helicopter display, Lord Mayor … Had lunch in Italian café called The Florence. Ironic! Conversation difficult for him but Mary very talkative. Talked a lot about her medical problems, her studies, asked his advice. Hard to believe she was divorcing him! Was she making last-ditch attempt at reconciliation? Too late. Strolled along Embankment to Waterloo Bridge, South Bank, Westminster Bridge. Saw couple snogging on grass in St. Thomas' Hospital garden. Embarrassing! But also made him feel jealous. Had pint in Duke of Buckingham followed by dinner in Indian. Mary: 'So what sort of relationship do you want with me?' 'I don't want any relationship with you,' he was going to say but bit his tongue. 'I don't know. What sort of relationship do *you* want?' he bounced it back. 'The one I always wanted,' she said, to his surprise and discomfort. 'I don't think that's possible any more,' he said, as gently as he could. Mary: 'Are you still with that Italian one, Cinzano or whatever she's called?' 'That's none of your business,' he was going to say, needled, but again bit his tongue. 'I don't want to talk about that,' he replied, annoyed. Then to his alarm she asked if she could stay at his place tonight. 'Don't worry, I'll sleep on the settee,' she said quickly, seeing alarm in his eyes, and she did.

Sun. 12.9.82
Mary wanted to meet him again after she had visited her brother. He reluctantly agreed. They met in Covent Garden, wandered round for a while and went for drink, in his case several pints. Then had dinner in Indian again on Shaftesbury Avenue. He drank more beer – rubbish Indian beer – so ended up drunk. Reluctantly agreed to let her stay in flat again. He had large whiskey and collapsed into bed drunk almost as soon as got back to flat. She went to sleep on settee. But during night to

his horror she crept into bed beside him. Put her head on his shoulder. 'Don't say anything,' she whispered. 'Just hold me.' He was still too drunk to resist. Put his arm round her. Slept like that. In each other's arms. Till morning. New morning? New song?

Mon. 13.9.82

Got up earlier than necessary and left to go to college for principal's start of term address at 9 a.m.. Mary still asleep. Annoyed by what had happened, annoyed with her, annoyed with himself. Felt guilty because of Cinzia. Even though they hadn't actually had sex. Like a weird dream! Shouldn't feel guilty about Cinzia though, since she wasn't coming back, but he couldn't help it. Arrived at college at 8.30. But didn't go to principal's speech. Can't stand the rude, arrogant bastard! Jack Fullofhimself. Departmental meeting in lecture theatre. Ken Cameron, HOD, in suit and tie as usual though boiling hot. Indian summer. All the usual suspects there. Patrick Glass, union chair, after two minutes: Speak up, Ken, we can't hear you! Jim Pollock: Is anyone listening? Big laugh.

Tues. 14.9.82

Enrolled gorgeous Italian girl called Pina. Would fancy her if not still in love with Cinzia. Said she liked folk music. Chatted to Vaughan, American exchange lecturer from Mississippi. Ex-fighter pilot in Yank Air Force. Discussed relative merits of Faulkner and Joyce. Told him he'd never been able to get into Faulkner. He said same about Joyce! Gave him a pointer or two. Genial enough fellow. Evening went to concert by Irish supergroup Moving Hearts at National. Brilliant but too lonely and depressed to enjoy it. On way home bumped into Rubik, mad Russian student. Claimed he was doing a Ph.D. in astrophysics at Queen Mary College under a Professor Young, funded by Russian government. Having done astrophysics at Lumumba University. Claimed he was an officer in the Russian army. Had bought a flat in Hackney for £130,000, paid for by the Russian government. Was having a court case with his landlord. Had just had an operation for cancer and been cured. His mother was a heart specialist in Russia. Had to finish his course or he'd be sent to Siberia to do hard labour. Invited him to go and teach in Russia. 'If you come to Russia, you will have a good life, everything you need, everything taken care of. You will have a privilege card.' For a fraction of a moment he was tempted by the thought. But the poor fellow was as mad as a hatter. Felt sorry for him. As well as himself.

Wed. 15.9.82
Enrolling. Moaned to Chris Hanson about Bertha giving him grief over his timetable. Chris: What's the matter, Frank? Did you get on the wrong side of her? Mark: Is it possible to get on the wrong side of something so round? Laughter. Bruno Italian student not very bright came in and gave him big thank you hug because passed FCE exam. Another feather in his cap in front of Bertha. Bumped into new teacher Edmund, aka Frankenstein, in Bell. Said had been to West End to deliver his pipe for cleaning. £40 to buy, £4 to clean. Odd bod but likeable. Especially since bought him a pint. Slightly embarrassed about being seen drinking alone but glad of company. Edmund told joke about Prince Charles and Princess Diana being held up while driving through St James Park in Range Rover. Princess Diana hid her rings up her vagina. Prince Charles: Pity my Aunt Margaret wasn't with us – could've hidden the Range Rover too. Told him another joke about pope hugging smelly, tattered vagrant in St Peter's Square and whispering in his ear, "I thought I told you to fuck off yesterday!" Amusing. Good company. Told Edmund about Mary. Very simpatico. "Sometimes I wonder if women are worth it."

Fri. 17.9.82
Section meeting 10 a.m. Boring as usual. Couldn't stop thinking about Cinzia. Tempted to read her letter again surreptitiously but resisted. Bertha sitting at front with black skirt up and adipose thighs splayed. Bosoms bursting out of grey silk blouse like bazookas. Said she had been forced to make changes to timetable by 'force majeure'. Bertha in panic about enrolment figures and need for publicity. He agreed to

design/type up new leaflet and arrange distribution. Two hours of yap yap yap. The women love it! He just wanted to get on with teaching. Bumped into new Italian student Pina on way out. Gorgeous even though wears glasses. Had pleasant chat with her in foyer. Said she was interested in folk music. But didn't let on he was into Irish folk music. Didn't want to start anything with anybody. Cinzia's last letter burning inside jacket pocket.

Mon. 20.9.82
Student induction day. Bertha addressing new students. Bemused looks on their faces. Comical! Took group of new ss round college. Pina among them. Had coffee with her and a few others in canteen. She seemed to like him. Would definitely fancy her if not in love with Cinzia. Her letter in his pocket to remind him. Every letter drained a bit more hope from his heart. Yet with every letter, his heart leapt joyfully. Until he opened it and read. A slow death. Death by a thousand cuts. A kind of emotional strangulation. Every letter another nail in the coffin. Every letter an epitaph.

Thurs. 23.9.82
Took group of students to folk club at Empress of Russia in Angel. Unfortunately Pina not among them. Or perhaps fortunately. Pub crowded. A lot of Sadler's Wells patrons. Singer an Australian guy called Martin Wyndham. Quite a good performer though some songs a bit boring. Drank six pints. Got a bit drunk! Hope ss don't get wrong impression! Great bunch though. As always.

Fri. 24.9.82
Another boring section meeting. Bertha still messing about with timetables. Bertha: Frank has ended up with a dog's dinner of a timetable, I'm afraid. Enraging but bit his tongue. Would have to have it out with her. Problem about Associate Lecturers' hours being light. Huh! Just bad management. Had big confrontation with her after meeting in staff common room. She agreed to give him morning Proficiency class which she had nabbed for herself. "I'm making a big sacrifice, you know,

Frank." Obnoxious cow! Asked him to cover another class for her on Monday afternoon because it was Day of Atonement so she was off. What a cheek! She needs to atone all right. But he had to agree. Bertha to porters: Could you try to be a bit quieter?! Got headache, sore throat, cough. Usual September back to work cold. If only Cinzia was at home to look after him!

Sat. 25.9.82
Dealt with conveyancing. Did some shopping. Sat in walled garden of St John's Church in afternoon. Resisted temptation to read her letter again. Too depressing. Sunshine and cloud. Still some blood-red roses. Last rose of summer. Wished had somebody to give one to! Blue and silver dragonfly flitting about. Beautiful yet somehow repulsive creature. Usual down and outs and winos around. Went to White Horse on Liverpool Road to see Connolly Folk Group with Terry and Serena, his gorgeous Italian girlfriend. His own ex-student. She looked drop-dead gorgeous as usual. Can't help fancying her a bit. Wearing her white trouser suit with glittery scarf. But Terry a good mate now so no go. Couldn't help feeling jealous of him though. Should have invited Pina. Group very good. Brilliant singer from Galway. Great fiddler too. If only Cinzia was there!

Mon. 27.9.82
Bertha still mucking him about over timetable. First evening class. Proficiency. Glad to be teaching again. Strain to appear cheerful when feeling so lousy but managed it. Have to be professional!

Thurs. 30.9.82
Took students for drink to Bell after evening Proficiency class. German Albert back. Several French assistantes. Good group. High level. Had very pleasant chat. A few fanciable women but ... Lift to station by Albert in his 'Owstin Sprrite'. Felt lonely going home to empty flat. Miss her so much.

Fri. 1.10.82

Saw Tiziana leaving college. Followed her. She saw him but pretended not to. Had chat with her at bus stop. Invited her for coffee. Accepted immediately. Wearing black sweatshirt, white anorak, denim skirt, knee-length boots. Hair now dyed purple! Said she wants to go to see dogs at Walthamstow Stadium. Offered to take her tomorrow but said she was baby-sitting. Invited her for drink this evening but said was going for Indian with friend Emmanuelle. Emmanuelle! Invited her out Sunday afternoon. Accepted. Don't really fancy her. Too chubby. But like her. Good fun. Need some female company. Especially Italian female company.

Sun. 3.10.82
Met Pavlo at new house. Gave him keys. Discussed work to be done. Pavlo gave him lift to Piccadilly Circus with his new Portuguese girlfriend Lucinda to meet Tiziana, Lucinda feeding them both from a bag of grapes as they went. Waited for Tiziana on Eros steps. Forty-five minutes late. Annoyed with her. Just about to go when she arrived. Black anorak today, same denim skirt, bare legs, short white socks and trainers. Shoulder bag. Asked her what she kept in it. "My diary." Walked through Green Park, to Buck. Pal., St. James Park. Ducks and geese. T. said wanted to get Italian newspaper at Charing Cross Station but not there. Got one at Victoria. Had pizza in Pizzaland. Drink in Ebury, Victoria. Told him she was in rock group in Italy. Likes Genesis. Ugh! But also John Martyn, so OK. Put his arm round her shoulder but she seemed distant. Yet warm and friendly. Something wrong. Something reserved about her. Like himself perhaps? Maybe she realised he didn't really fancy her. Maybe suspected he was using her. Which was half-true perhaps. Or maybe she was afraid he wanted to seduce her. Which wasn't true! Put her arm through his and read her paper as they walked. Saw her off at tube. Went home on 38 bus. Somehow an unsatisfactory meeting. Felt bad. Regretted inviting her.

Mon. 4.10.82
Taught morning Proficiency class for first time. Good group but small. Hope Bertha doesn't try to close it. Wouldn't put it past

her out of spite. No Tiziana in class. Had drink with Albert after evening class. Talked football. Bayern Munich supporter. Affable fellow. Must mention the war to him some time! Lift to station in his 'Owstin Sprrite' as usual.

Tues. 5.10.82
Saw Tiziana by chance in library. Gave her list of gyms as requested. She was with Birgit, German girl. Very nice looking. New girl Phoebe from Hong Kong in class. Suspect she liked him. Kept bumping into her or vice versa. But not interested. Told him she taught Chinese to kids. Studying maths as well as English at college. A bit skinny. A bit geeky.

Wed. 6.10.82
Phoned Tiziana. Invited her out but said she was babysitting. Always the same. But had pleasant chat. Just fancied some female company. Not sex. Only wanted to have sex with Cinzia. Went to KELTIC bookshop in Kensington. Had lunch in pub opposite. Home by 4 p.m. with bag full of books. Tired out. Long lonely evening. Got phone call but only from Gwen, friend of Mary's, looking for her. Had to explain not together any more. Depressing.

Thurs. 7.10.82
Roy Bunting in staffroom. Says he's given up smoking. Droning on about anti-smoking propaganda. Said he wasn't 'susceptible' to it, even though given up. 'You see, Frank, having been through the war and the blitz and all that, I've still got a "here today, gone tomorrow" attitude to life.' Gossiping about other members of staff. Bit of a backbiter. "That Elizabeth Evans, never see her do much. What does she do?" Chewed his ear off for about ten minutes. "Nice to have a chat sometimes, isn't it, Frank?" More of a monologue than a "chat"! Feel sorry for him. Seems lonely. Even more so than he. An odd bod certainly.

Sat. 8.10.82
Hoped for phone call from Tiziana but nothing. She obviously didn't fancy him any more. Or even like him. Seems a bit cool,

distant now. His own fault probably. She could probably tell he didn't really fancy her. Women's intuition. Maybe he should tell her about Cinzia? Or did she already know? They'd been quite pally. Sat in walled garden for a while in afternoon. Mellow autumn sunshine. Leaves turning brown and tumbling down. Pleasurable melancholy. Nothing to look forward to tonight. Phoned a couple of people for a drink but nobody available. Ended up going alone to the Pegasus. Or the "Pee Jasus" as Seamus at Sugawn used to call it. Good music. Mixture of rock, jazz and RnB. But miserable on his own. Had six pints of Guinness. Got home and finished off with whiskey to sound of Van the Man. Missed Cinzia worse than ever. Like a physical pain in the guts. *She's not coming back. Get used to it!*

Mon. 11.10.82
Met Rosamaria, Spanish beginner, near Central Station on way home. Invited her into Flanagan's for a drink but she declined. Felt rejected/offended. Silly. Had drink alone in Flanagan's. Pub rough. And dead. Dismal, depressing place!

Tues. 12.10.82
Met Pina at bus stop. Said it was her birthday today. Invited her for a drink to celebrate but said she was going out with friends. Invited her to Fureys concert Friday. Said she couldn't afford it but would think about it. Nearly offered to treat her to ticket for her birthday, but fed up with her. Felt rejected again. Like rubbing salt in the wound. Wound of loneliness. Gaping hole where Cinzia should be! Torture. Yet in a way he was glad. Didn't want to start anything with anybody. He was still in love with Cinzia! Still hoped she might come back to him. Hope against hope. Usual crap takeaway for dinner.

Wed. 13.10.82
Roger came in afternoon to collect some books he had been storing for him. Walking stick, plastic anorak, cords, pullover, red slip-on shoes. 'I hope I'm not being inquisitive, but am I right in thinking you and Mary have parted?' He

thought the whole world knew by now! 'I'm sure you've got something to do, but you're too polite to say so,' he said, rummaging through the boxes. Talked about Terence de Vere White and other literary matters. Said he was hoping to get compensation for his accident in Ireland. 'It happened just outside Bunratty Castle! You know, I was just crossing the road to have a cup of tea in Nellie's, although it's an obvious tourist trap. I decided a cup of tea was just what I needed. And I was knocked down by a nurse, of all people!' He giggled with his hand over his mouth as usual to hide his catastrophic teeth. 'If only I hadn't wanted that cup of tea, I wouldn't be in this situation.' 'So drink was your downfall!' he quipped and Roger went into hysterics. Felt sorry for him but just wanted to be alone even though was lonely. Roger had his sexy Japanese wife, whereas he had no one! Off he went with his booty in his kit-bag, which he complained had got covered in urine in hospital. Hoped he hadn't seemed too unfriendly. Went out for drink on his own later. Graffito on toilet door: *Life is a sexually transmitted disease.* Not the sort of thing he wanted to read in his present state of mind. Bought some chips for dinner on way home. Stood in shop doorway to shelter from rain and eat them. Remembered eating chips with Cinzia. *Come back, Cinzia!* Suddenly so depressed started crying. Or were they just raindrops rolling down his cheeks?

Thurs. 14.10.82
Posted a birthday card with £10 in to Mary on way to college. Bertha wreaking havoc with photocopier. Gave him hassle about "DDs/departmental duties" and "CT/course tutoring". What a pain she is. Always trying to exert her authority. Always trying to show who's boss. Really had to bite his tongue. Told her he was already managing resources, wasn't that enough? Not to mention lots of other stuff. Drink with Albert after evening class. Talked football as usual. West Germany just beaten England 2-1. Said his brother was in police. Loves maths. Father dead. Had always been ill. Gave him back the Proficiency exam paper he'd marked for him. Lift to station in his "Owstin Sprrite" as usual. Had a long

wait for the train. Railway platform a lonely place late at night. The world a lonely place!

Fri. 15.10.82
Took group of students to see the Fureys in concert at the Dominion Theatre in Tottenham Court Road. Had played them The Green Fields of France in morning class, told them some history. Chatted to Pina after class. Yellow anorak, white trousers, hairy pullover, specs. Intelligent girl. She seemed to like him. Asked her if she was coming to concert but said she had to babysit. Sickener! Told him about her "difficult" family life at home. Said she was the baby of the family. Parents always rowing. Said her daddy used to hit her. He was shocked. Felt like putting an arm round her and giving her a hug. That was why she had come to Britain, to escape. Said she needed freedom and independence. Told him her au pair family treated her badly, for example made her clean the kitchen on her knees because they were too mean to buy a mop. He said it was disgusting. Told her they were exploiting her, to change family. Though he knew they were all the same. Said she wants to be a journalist, a foreign correspondent. Needed to save all her money for that. Invited her for a coffee but she declined. Said she was going to the library to study. 'Enjoy your concert.' Another rejection. Won't invite her again. Just as well anyway. Want to stay faithful to Cinzia. Even though ... Maybe he should go to see her again at Christmas. Just turn up without telling her. But. But. But …

Sat. 16.10.82
Phone call from Grazia in Bolzano/Italy. Another Italian girl! Another one that got away. Another one who had let him down. She wants to open an au pair agency and send girls to Britain. Asked him if he wanted to work with her. Said he'd think about it. Thought of inviting her to London but didn't. Couldn't face thought of another lonely Saturday night so phoned Tiziana and invited her out but said she was babysitting. Damn these middle-class people and their brats! Why can't they look after their brats themselves? She said they were going to a Neil Sedaka concert. Neil Sedaka for God's sake! Mind you, Cinzia

liked Barry Manilow. Not that he fancied Tiziana. Just fancied some female company. And there'd be no danger of being unfaithful to Cinzia with her. But she wasn't taking the bait. She obviously sensed that he didn't really fancy her. Well, he wouldn't ask her again! That was it! Over before it had started! Ended up going for drink and getting drunk alone as usual.

Sun. 17.10.82
Went to the Pegasus alone. Nine-piece band called The Republic. Afro-Caribbean music. Girl singer in trilby, baggy jeans, waistcoat. Bongos, trumpet, guitar, marimbas, saxophone etc. Very good sound. Saxophonist in red jacket. Trumpeter wearing black plumed cavalry cap. Shako? Walked all way home, one hour. 'Loneliness gnawed at his heart like a rat …'

Mon. 18.10.82
Saw Roy Bunting but avoided him. Wearing plastic mac. Just didn't feel like listening to him droning on today. Drink with Albert and a few others after evening class. Albert told him that as student in Germany each student in the house had to make it with daughters of local tradespeople to get cheap goods or pay the difference!

Wed. 20.10.82
Overheard Harriet Jenkins and Jane Dawson wittering on about fireplaces and gas fires in staff common room. Then a big discussion about whether fireplace is one word or two! Cathy secretary suddenly bustled in: Harriet, Ken wants to see you. Harriet: Tell Ken I'll see him in my own good time. Later had chat with Clem, Guyanese law lecturer in panama hat, polka dot bow tie, brown suit and carrying Malacca-cane. Very urbane chap. Somehow ended up talking about Genesis. Clem said it was 'a masterly account of passing the buck'. Clem told joke. God: Why are you hiding, Eve? Eve: I am naked, Lord. God: Who told you you were naked? Eve: Adam told me, Lord. God: But where is the fig leaf I gave you, daughter? Eve: Adam took it off me, Lord. God: Why did he do that, daughter? Eve: He said he wears the plants in this family. Good one! Amusing chap. Went to house. Not much work done. Annoyed with Pavlo. But

at least grant money from council came through. Pavlo won't have that excuse any more. Can't refuse to take out chimney breasts now. Wish had Cinzia to share new house with. Invited her often enough. Forget Cinzia! Went for drink alone at Favourite. Blues guitarist with accompanist on mandolin playing to almost empty pub. Scotsman and Dubliner both drunk arguing about 'Gaelic culture'. Dubliner: That's a load of shite! Scotsman: How can you argue with a man who's irrational? Walked to Highbury Corner in rain to catch 38 home. Blue all right!

Thurs. 21.10.82
Ten minutes late for work for first time in years because had to go to building society first thing, where there was a long queue, then just missed train. Hated being late. Not professional! And to make matters worse, Bertha was waiting at classroom door for him to ask if trainee teacher could observe his lesson. No advance warning. Furious but couldn't refuse esp since he was late. Lesson went well thankfully. And trainee a rather pretty Scottish girl! But not teaching so well lately. Have to get a grip.

Fri. 22.10.82
Bumped into Birgit, German girl, Tiziana's friend, in Hoe Street. Looking at fancy cakes in baker's shop. Told her she mustn't eat them. "Vy not?" she asked seriously, in her sexy German accent. "They'll make you fat!" he joked. Very attractive. Tight jeans, woolly pullover, brown suede jacket. Said Tiziana was in Amsterdam to his surprise. Wonder if she has a boyfriend there. That would explain why she was a bit funny with him. Wanted to ask Birgit but didn't. Didn't really want to know. Not that he was interested in her any more. If he ever was. Tempted to invite Birgit for coffee but didn't. Said she was going to Soho to meet friend anyway. Said Soho was her favourite place in London. Oh well, another lonely weekend ahead. Later though he regretted not trying to make a date with her. Interesting programme about Seamus Heaney on TV. Grazia supposed to phone again but didn't. Typical of her. Felt irrationally angry with her. Can't take much more of this loneliness and frustration!

Sat. 23.10.82
Walled garden. Trees all brown now. Still a few tatty-looking roses. Sunshine. Toddler to mum next to gravestone: Is there someone in there? Innocence of children! Winos swigging and singing. Went to Hare and Hounds on Upper Street. Group called 'Alive and Picking'. Country honk, bluegrass, Cajun. Pretty good. Then to White Horse. Three months since she went. Three months of loneliness. Can't take much more. Home. Whiskey. Dylan. I'll be your baby tonight. No, I won't. To bed drunk.

Mon. 24.10.82
Cinzia's birthday. Sent her a card but don't know why. Nearly lost the plot in class this morning. Have to pull himself together! Mustn't let his emotions affect his teaching. Had to hang onto job at all costs. Mustn't give students any excuse to complain. Bertha would love that of course. She'd have an orgasm.

Tues. 25.10.82
News from Northern Ireland so depressing. Kidnappings and assassinations. Why can't the Brits just get out and give Ireland back to the Irish, as John Lennon said? Let the Prods go mad and shoot the shop up. They were already mad anyway. Bloody nutters! Fanatics! That Northern Irish girl on his first day at uni when he told her his name: Are you a papist? Pronounced 'pappist'. Bigoted little bitch! Not that he'd want to live in Catholic Ireland himself, much as he loved it. Archbishop McQuaid and all that. Gang of fascists! Prince Andrew's girlfriend Koo Stark in town for secret meeting with him. Lucky over-privileged bastard. Not that he fancied Koo Stark himself. What a stupid name! But somehow it just rubbed in his own loneliness. How stupid to be envious of a tosser like Prince Andrew! But that was how desperate he was.

Wed. 27.10.82
Anthea Harcourt in staff common room: Bertha had the cheek to ask me to teach JMB. I said no, thank you, Bertha –

I'm a literary person. I don't do graphs and pie charts. Ha ha! Stuck-up old biddy but she's right. It is a load of codswallop. Like EFL in general. Mark is right – no content. But he liked teaching it because it left his brain free for reading and writing. And also because there were lots of pretty foreign girls! Except that there was only one pretty foreign girl he was interested in. But she wasn't interested in him. Bad attack of cabin fever in the evening. Went out on private pub crawl. Rolled home drunk. Finished off with whiskey. Fatal mistake!

Thurs. 28.10.82
Terrible hangover. Just about got through morning class. Discussion with Bless, Presbyterian Nigerian girl, about God. 'God is here and everywhere! God is inside you!' How can people be so irrational? Sheer superstition. After class had to help Phoebe, Hong Kong girl, with her UCCA application. Wearing denim waistcoat over check shirt, blue jeans, blue mac. Almost pretty but not quite. Liked her though. Nice kid. Only eighteen. Must be massive culture shock for her. Went for drink after evening class with Albert, new boy Walter from Austria and a few others. Talked about 'High German' v 'Low German'. 'Sieg!' Albert left early because said he had to go to Germany in morning because mother in hospital. No lift in the Owstin Sprrite. Walked to Central. Kids collecting for Guy Fawkes. Hate going home to empty flat. Like a tomb.

It was a rainy Saturday. Almost the end of October. Three full months since he had seen her and that idyllic holiday in Italy. He had just finished writing his diary when he heard the rattle of the letter box. He rushed to the front door and saw the familiar envelope with three pretty, colourful Italian stamps with pictures of castles on them and his name and address in royal blue ink and her schoolgirlish handwriting on it. He picked it up, smelt the familiar perfume, grabbed a knife from the kitchen, sat in his study and sliced it open, his heart trembling:

Lignano, 21 novembre 1982

Darling Francis,

I read your letter a few hours ago and I say thank you for your words full of love and tenderness. Francis, every woman would feel happy after having read such a beautiful letter and I am as well, but ... I love you, baby, but ... as you see, there is always a bad BUT. What does it mean for you?

The truth is that I won't come back to live in London with you because there are important reasons that don't allow me to leave Italy. Let me tell you now what's happening to me. The first thing that you must know is that I've been obliged to leave my work because I'm not well. I didn't want to tell you the truth, but I actually think that it is necessary. At the beginning doctors said to me not to eat a lot of foods, so that I nearly stopped eating. Now I'm thin and I feel bad because my skin is getting red again. Then I've been to see the doctor once again and now I know that my blood is wrong sometimes, because I've a serious allergy.

Every time I eat or drink the thing which is bad for me, my blood starts running hot and some parts of my body become red.

Darling, I'm sure I'll be all right one day, but it takes quite a long time to discover my allergy.

Did you understand all my saying? I hope that my english is still good enough to let you read my thoughts!

You don't know but I gave you a ring yesterday afternoon. Were you having a drink in the pub? Then I phoned you again in the evening at about 9.00 p.m., but you were still out. Maybe I phone you now when my daddy goes out. Darling, it's a freezing Sunday morning and if everything is all right you should move into your new house soon. Remember, I love your house and it is nice. It is nice because it belongs to you.

The last night I've been dreaming of it. It was large and there was green all around. I know that you love trees and leaves and I always remember our walks through the parks; I could see you walking on your own in my dream. The forest was cold and some men were riding across it. What a lonely place! Too sad.

Francis, never walk through the forest in winter, you would feel too lonely. And now I suppose that you could say to me: "I've never dreamt of doing that, Cinzia!"

Francis, I like to say your name out loud, it sounds so dear to me!

Please forgive me once again, but I can't keep writing. Just think that I'm happy here and I want to stay here. Don't suffer please! I would like to think of you with a nice woman by your side. I'm sure Mary is very nice: be good with her.

If by chance I don't send you my kisses and my caresses any more, this doesn't mean that "my love for you is over".

NO forget those last six words!

It's hard for me to finish this letter, but I must go.

Today is Sunday and I'll have a nice chat with my friends tonight.

Don't be angry with me. My tears are falling.

Cinzia

Can I give you a kiss? One more! One last kiss ...

He folded the letter slowly, put it back in the envelope with the royal blue writing and three colourful castles on it, placed it reverently on his desk, leant back in his chair and shut his eyes. For a while at least he wanted to pretend he was somewhere else, the letter didn't exist, it hadn't just dropped through his letter box, he hadn't just read those earth-shattering words: "I won't come back to live in London with you." It was all just a horrible dream. For a while he was in Portofino with her again, they were strolling with their arms around each other through that sunny, picturesque, pastel paradise, young, happy, laughing, in love ...

When he opened his eyes though, he was still in his study, the letter was still lying on his desk and it was still raining outside. Was he hoping it might have magically disappeared? He could see his name and address in the blue handwriting and the three stamps with their castles on the envelope. It looked so pretty, so appealing, so intriguing! How excited he had been when he had first seen it just a few minutes ago! He could even smell the perfume on it. How could something that looked and smelt so pretty be so – so poisonous, so lethal, so devastating?

After all, it only contained *words*! "I won't come back to live in London with you." Yes, they were only words, ten little words, but each word was like a dagger through his heart.

One last kiss. Yes, one last, cold kiss.

He didn't feel any pain yet though. It was as if he had gone into shock. Emotional shock. Were there such things as emotional endorphins? Pain would come later no doubt. Meanwhile there were things to do – library books to return, food shopping to do, a launderette to go to. And maybe, he thought, jumping up and leaving his study, maybe when he came back the letter wouldn't be there ...

CHAPTER NINETEEN

'So, your full name is Dolores Marietta Ursulina? That's quite a name!' he exclaimed, returning with two pints of Abbot.

'Si. Gracias. I mean, thank ju,' she said, exhaling some Fortuna cigarette smoke.

She was wearing a black leather jacket and those awful denim dungarees again, over a hairy, multi-coloured jumper, with white pop socks and sandals, even though it was raining outside. They were having a drink in the Ferry Boat Inn on Forest Road, otherwise known as the FBI. He hadn't wanted to meet her in the Bell – too many memories of Cinzia. He noticed that one of the straps of her dungarees was loose.

'You're losing your trousers,' he joked.

'Oh,' she laughed, readjusting it over her shoulder, blushing.

'That's better! Cheers! Salud!' he said, raising his glass to hers and taking a first pull of the amber nectar.

'Cheers!' she smiled.

'You've just finished university?'

'Si.'

'What did you study?'

'Pedagogia.'

'Ah, you studied feet.'

'Feet?'

'In English, 'pedagogy'. From Latin, pes, pedis, foot. So you studied feet.'

'You are joking? Is it wrong, what I said?'

'I'm only kidding. It's Greek, from pais, paidos, meaning child. So you're a teacher?'

'Yes. Ju are bad!' she laughed, giving him a playful slap on the wrist.

'Ouch!' he said. 'You know corporal punishment is not

allowed in Britain?' Not that he wouldn't mind giving *her* some corporal punishment, he thought naughtily.

'I'm sorry if I hurt ju,' she joked, rubbing his wrist where she had slapped it.

'That's nice,' he said. 'Don't stop!'

'Ju are bad,' she laughed, giving him another playful tap and taking her hand away.

'So, you're a teacher,' he said, taking another quaff of Abbot. 'That's good. So how old are you?'

'I hab twenty-three.'

'I *am* twenty-three,' he corrected.

'Sorry. I am twenty-three. Gracias. Thank ju.'

'You look younger.'

'How old ju think I am look?'

'About sixteen! Like a schoolgirl.'

'Por qué? I mean, why ju think so?'

'Your hair.' She wore her hair in two plaits, with a red ribbon on each. She blushed again. She blushed a lot.

'Ju don't like it?'

'I never said that. I just said it makes you look young. It's very nice. You're very nice.'

'Gracias. Thank ju.'

'I think you need to demist your glasses.'

'Qué?'

'Clean your glasses,' he mimed.

'Ah, si,' she said, taking off the gold-rimmed glasses she always wore, breathing on them and wiping them with a hanky.

'You've got beautiful eyes,' he remarked, noticing they were brown like his own. Liquid brown. Would she become his brown-eyed girl, he wondered, hearing Van Morrison in his head?

'Gracias, thank ju,' she said, blushing again. 'Ju hab beautiful eyes too.'

'Thank you.' Their first meeting was going very well so far, he thought. 'And thank you for your letter,' he added.

'It's first time I've ever written such letter. After I gave ju, I felt silly. Like a sixteen-year-old!'

'I'm glad you did.'

'Do ju like me?'

'Yes, I like you.'

'I like ju.'

'I know you do. You said so in your letter. I like you too.' He took hold of her hand across the table and caressed it softly, noticing that she was wearing a somewhat cheap-looking black signet ring with a gold D on it. He couldn't help feeling excited. It was the first time he had touched a girl for four months. But he couldn't help feeling guilty too, because of Cinzia, irrational though it was. Cinzia had left him. Told him she wasn't coming back. He had to forget her. It was easier said than done. But if he had a relationship with this girl, maybe it would be easier to forget. 'What's the ring for?'

'My boyfriend gave it to me.'

'Your boyfriend? So you have a boyfriend?'

'Si. He is in Spain.'

'He doesn't mind if – if you have a boyfriend here?'

'To be honest with ju, we have separated. That's why I hab come to London. It's like a – I don't know how to say in English.'

'A trial separation.'

'Si. Gracias. Thank ju.'

'What's his name?' he asked, cradling her hand between his own hands. He suddenly felt sorry for her. And for her boyfriend. Relationships!

'His name is Herrero.'

'Where did you meet?'

'In sociology class at the university.'

'I see. What does he do?'

'He is a priest.'

'A *priest*?'

'Si.'

'What kind of priest?'

'He is Jesuit priest.'

'A *Jesuit*?' He was so shocked that he laughed, removed one of his hands from hers and took another quaff of Abbot, which seemed an appropriate brand of beer in the circumstances.

'Don't laugh!'

'I'm sorry. It's just that I thought priests – especially Jesuit priests – were supposed to be celibate.'

'Perdon?'

'Celibate – meaning no sex. Do you – did you – have sex with him?'

'Si, of course. I am – I was his girlfriend.'

'He's a Jesuit priest and he has sex with you?'

'Si. Is normal,' she said, with the accent on the second syllable. She seemed genuinely surprised that he was so shocked.

'So how often do you – did you – use to have sex?'

'Every night.'

'So what did he do in the mornings? Did he get up and say Mass?'

'Si. Sometimes I go with him to the church to help him say Mass. But I don't really believe in it.'

He couldn't help a wry smile. The Catholic church really seemed to have moved on since he had left. Maybe he shouldn't have left! Maybe he'd missed a trick …

'Does he – Herrero – believe in it?'

'I don't think so. I think he wants to leave and marry me.'

'Ah, I see.' God, he could imagine all too well the mental and emotional torment that this Herrero was probably going through.

'You don't want to marry him?'

'I'm not sure. I think I am too young for him. And he is too serious for me.'

'How old is he?'

'He has – he is – thirty-eight.'

'And you're twenty-three. It's not such a big age gap. I'm thirty-five! Maybe you should marry me instead.' As always, the alcohol was loosening his natural reserve.

'Si. I'll marry ju tomorrow.'

'Ha ha! Let's not rush things! Anyway, I'm busy tomorrow,' he laughed. She must be joking, he thought, though she seemed genuinely disappointed by his reply. She obviously liked him. He was starting to like her too. Well, he had already started to like her. But Cinzia's ghost was all around him. It wasn't too late to stop this before it went any further. Then an annoying thought crossed his mind – maybe she liked him because she liked priests and she could somehow sense that he had once almost been one. Surely to God the odour of sanctity didn't still hang over him, did it?

'Why would you want to marry me?' he asked. Even as he asked the question he regretted it – she might say: *Because you are like Herrero. Because you remind me of Herrero. Because I can smell incense on you ...*

'I like ju,' she shrugged, exhaling some more Fortuna.

'Why do you like me?' he asked, a tiny bit disappointed at this less than passionate declaration of infatuation.

'Ju make me laugh.'

'I see,' he smiled. 'Maybe that's as good a basis for marriage as any.'

'Pero – but – I can't marry ju, can I?' she said.

'Why not?'

'Ju are not free.'

'Who said I'm not free?'

'Are ju married?'

'I'm divorced,' he said, taking another quaff of Abbot. Well, it was half-true. The decree absolute should come any day now.

'Why did ju get married?'

'It's a good question,' he shrugged. 'Why do people usually get married?'

'Did ju love her?'

'That's another good question. I'm not sure.' A spasm of pain shot through him.

'Have ju got children?'

He was relieved that she didn't ask any more questions about his soon-to-be ex-wife. He didn't want to talk about her. She was sensitive enough to see that, he was pleased to notice.

'No children as far as I know,' he grinned, remembering uncomfortably that he was supposed to be infertile, his failed operation ...

'Ju don't want children?' She seemed to have missed his little joke.

'Not yet. But *she* did. That was one of our problems.' He took a quaff of Abbot. 'What about you? Do you want children?' He half-hoped she would say no.

'Perhaps in the future. Not now. I'm too young to think for that!'

'Would you like to have children with me?' That was a leading question if ever there was one, he chuckled to himself, trying to forget about his operation and the doomed attempts to conceive with Mary.

'Si. I think it would be good. But not yet.'

'You mean, not tonight?' he joked. The alcohol had definitely loosened him up. But she was easy to chat to anyway. He liked her more and more. Even though she wasn't Italian. But Spanish was the next best thing!

'Do ju want to make love with me tonight?' she asked. He wasn't quite sure whether she was expressing shock at the idea or actually inviting him.

'Yes, I do,' he said, boldly, 'but I think perhaps it's too soon. Let's get to know each other first.'

'Ju are good man.'

'Am I? Maybe I'm not as good as you think,' he laughed, emptying his glass of Abbot. Perhaps she thought he was too well-mannered or too moral to go to bed with her on their first date. Well, he was. But the thought of Cinzia was also stopping him. If he made love with this girl, or any other girl, it would be like the final nail in the coffin of his love for Cinzia. He wondered if he would even be able to do it with another girl. He wished he could get her image out of his mind.

'Can I ask ju something?'

'Sure, but let's get another drink first,' he said. 'Do you want another drink?'

'Si. But I pay.' She took some money out of her purse and put it on the table. He took it reluctantly, knowing she was only an au pair and paid peanuts, and came back with two more pints of Abbot. She seemed to like beer and was able to hold it, which was another big plus in her favour.

'Cheers!' he said, touching her glass with his and taking a first sip of the amber nectar. 'So, what do you want to ask?'

'Can I go to the Christmas party with ju?'

'Yes, of course. But that's nearly three weeks away.' In fact, he was the organiser, so knew exactly when and where it was.

'I mean, will ju invite me as your girlfriend?'

'You want to be my girlfriend?'

'Si, if ju like.'

'OK, but you'll have to apply for the job, like everyone else.'

'Qué?'

'I'm joking. Why do you want to be my girlfriend?' Why was he playing games with her? He liked her. Liked her honesty and openness. She obviously liked him. He was lonely. He was frustrated. Why didn't he just take advantage of her? Because he was still in love with Cinzia, that was why, he told himself ruefully.

'Because I like ju. And I'm afraid of the other girls.'

'Which other girls? What do you mean?'

'The girls in the class. Some of them like ju too.'

'Really? Who likes me?' This was very flattering!

'They all like ju. They think ju are good teacher and nice man.'

'You forgot to say handsome.'

'Ju are handsome too.'

'Thank you. So who likes me exactly?'

'Anna likes you especially.'

'Anna from Barcelona? Really?' He pretended to be surprised. He *was* surprised.

'Do ju like her?'

'Not specially, no.'

'I hope ju don't receive a letter from her!'

'It's too late now. You've already got the job!'

'I can be your girlfriend?'

'Yes. You've passed the interview!'

'Dame un beso.'

'What?'

'Give me a kiss.'

'Oh. Well, come and sit beside me. I can't reach you from here.'

She stubbed out her cig and came and sat beside him. He put an arm around her, pulled her towards him and kissed her on the lips. Their tongues touched briefly.

'Te quiero,' she smiled.

'Meaning?'

'I love ju.'

'Te quiero too.'

'Do ju love me?'

'I think I'm starting to fall in love with you.'

'Dame un beso.'

They kissed again, slightly longer. He felt the first stirrings of desire for her. He broke the kiss off because he was self-conscious about kissing in public and didn't want to get too excited.

'I wish ju are free,' she said.

'I *am* free,' he insisted, ignoring the grammatical error, thinking guiltily of both Cinzia and Mary nevertheless. Free but not really free in both cases, he reflected ruefully again. 'No, actually you're right, I'm not free. I'm very expensive.'

'Dame un beso,' she laughed, getting the joke, and he did so.

God, she was good at kissing, he thought, though he didn't much like the smell of smoke on her breath. Maybe he *should* go home with her tonight. Strike while the iron was hot! He had had enough of loneliness. Get Cinzia out of his system …

'I wish I am somewhere else with ju,' she sighed, when the kiss finished.

'You mean, somewhere private?' He kissed her forehead.

'Si.'

'What time do you have to be home tonight?' he asked, gazing through her glasses into her liquid brown eyes.

'I am free tonight.'

'What do you mean?'

'The family is away on holiday in Spain, so I can go home when I like. But they will come back early in the morning so I hab to be there. Do ju want to come home with me?'

'Yes, if it's safe. Where do you live?' He could invite her to his flat of course, but didn't want to, because it was still haunted by Cinzia's ghost. And it would be tricky for her to get home.

'Is safe. Is in Gant's Hill. But ju hab to leave by eight in morning. Why do ju want to come home with me?'

'Why do you think?' He kissed her nose.

'Do ju want to make love with me?'

'No, I just want to play Scrabble with you.'

'Qué?'

'Scrabble. It's a game. I'm joking. Yes, I want to make love with you.'

'Dame un beso.'

They kissed again and this time he slipped a hand under the bib of her dungarees, jumper and T-shirt up to her breasts. She wasn't wearing a bra, he noticed, to his surprise. He squeezed each of her breasts gently in turn while their tongues played together.

'Te quiero,' he said, breaking off, afraid of getting too excited.

'Te quiero,' she agreed.

'We better wait till later,' he whispered, nuzzling her ear and caressing her neck between her plaits. 'It's too public here.'

'Do ju want to go now?'

'Let's have another drink, then we can go. I'll get them.' He gave her a quick kiss on the nose, stood up and went to the loo before going to the bar. He needed a few minutes away from her, he thought, just to calm down. God, she was sexy! And she seemed even keener for it than he was, which made a change. Yet even here in the loo Cinzia's ghost was looking at him disapprovingly. He ignored her, left and went to the bar, but she was there as well.

'Can I tell ju something?' she said, exhaling some Fortuna, when he had returned with the drinks and they'd clinked glasses again.

'This sounds serious,' he joked, taking a swig of Abbot to fortify himself. 'Go on. Tell me.'

'I am a virgin.'

'You're a virgin? But I thought you and Herrero ..?'

'We have sex but we don't – ju know – '

'He doesn't make love properly with you.'

'Si. I am complete virgin.'

'It's not a problem.'

'I am worried about it.'

'Why?'

'I want Herrero to break me. Is the right word?'

'I see. So you don't want me to – ?'

'Is it problem?'

'No, of course not.' He couldn't help feeling a bit deflated though. And a bit jealous. Shades of Luciano! 'But I thought you didn't want to stay with Herrero?'

'I don't know. I'm confused. I want to find myself. It's why I hab come to London. I'm sorry. Now ju don't want me.'

'Don't be silly. Of course I want you. I don't have to – fuck you. It's not just about fucking!' Might as well use some Anglo-Saxon, he thought, even though he felt uncomfortable about it – the Abbot gave him courage and anyway he was her English teacher.

'I know it is important for men. Men are more animalistic.'

'I assure you I'm not an animal!' he joked. 'Don't worry about it. We can just – you know – play Scrabble.'

'Te quiero,' she laughed.

'Te quiero too.'

'Dame un beso.' They kissed and he slipped his hand under her T-shirt again.

'We can still have a nice time, can't we?' he said, squeezing a breast. Her breasts were small, but that didn't bother him.

'Si. I will make ju happy.'

'I'm already happy. To be here with you.'

'I am happy too. Thank ju for this time with ju.'

God, what a charming thing to say, he thought, caressing her face tenderly with the back of his hand. She had a touch of class. Or was it just a Spanish thing? He felt a sudden surge of protective affection for her. He would look after her, take care of her, be good to her, never hurt her, he vowed to himself. Maybe it was the beginning of something like love. Yet he could feel himself struggling subconsciously not to fall in love with her, because of Cinzia. But Cinzia was gone. Forget her, he told himself!

'It's my pleasure to be here with you, Dolores,' he said, planting a kiss on her forehead.

'Ju hab made me so happy,' she whispered and there was something about the way she said it that really plucked at his heartstrings.

'Weren't you happy before?'

'I think I hab never been happy.'

'What? Never? Not even as a child?' He was shocked.

'Maybe I was happy then. I don't remember.'

'What about school?'

'I went to special school.'

'A special school?'

'A school where ju study and ju sleep.'

'A boarding school?'

'Si. Boring school.'

'No,' he laughed. 'Not *boring* school. *Boarding* school.'

'Boarding school,' she repeated. 'With sisters.'

'Oh, nuns? I see. So why weren't you happy there?' As if he couldn't guess!

'I was always lonely.'

'You missed your family?'

'Si. But I saw my family at weekends. Not just that.'

'What were the nuns like? Were they cruel?'

'Cómo?'

'Were they nasty to you? Did they treat you badly?'

'Some of them were bad. But I just didn't belong in that place. There was too much religion. I don't believe in it.'

'Well, me neither.' It was funny, he thought – you always naively supposed Spanish people would be very Catholic.

'Ju are atheist?'

'On bad days, yes. On good days I'm an agnostic. Do you remember that word – we studied it in class a few days ago?'

'Si. Is Greek. It means ju don't know. The a is a negative prefix.'

'Well done!' He gave her another kiss on the forehead. 'So, didn't you have friends at school? Or at home?'

'Not really friends. Somehow I've always been different.'

'Did you have boyfriends?'

'Si. I had boyfriends. But not like that.'

'You mean, no sex?'

'No sex. I didn't need sex when I was fifteen! I didn't know about sex then!'

'What about now?' he asked, putting his hand under her T-shirt and squeezing one of her breasts again.

'With ju, yes,' she murmured, giving him her lips and they kissed while he secretly fondled her breast.

'What about girlfriends at school?'

'How do ju mean?'

'Did you ever fall in love with another girl?'

'No. But some other girls did. I never felt like that.'

'I'm glad to hear it!' he laughed. 'I went to a boarding school too.' *Damn! Why did I say that?* It was the Abbot …

'Ju went to a boarding school?'

'Yes. It was a seminary.' He might as well go the whole hog and spill the beans, he thought. In for a penny, in for a pound.

'A seminary? Ju wanted to be a priest?'

'Yes. For nine years. From the age of twelve till twenty-one. Then I left. Otherwise I wouldn't be here with you!' Or I might be, he thought, if Herrero was anyone to go by.

'Why did ju leave?'

'I stopped believing in it all. And I wanted to be normal. You know, have girlfriends, get married, have kids. *Eventually* have kids.' A shadow flitted over him. 'So you see, Herrero and I have something in common.'

'Do ju want to tell me about it?'

'About what? The seminary?'

'Si. Your life before.'

'I don't like talking about it, to be honest. I'm writing a book about it.' *Damn! Shouldn't have said that either!*

'Ju are writer? Can I see it?'

'Yes. On one condition.'

'What condition?'

'You have to take all your clothes off.'

'I don't like this change!'

'Not now, don't worry! Later, when we get home.'

'Ju can take them off for me.'

'OK, it's a deal!'

'I tried to write something last year.'

'You did?'

'I wrote one hundred pages. Herrero said it was good for me but had no literary value.'

'He might be wrong. What did he mean, *'it was good'* for you?'

'I was depressed for whole year last year.'

'Depressed? Why?'

'No se. I don't know why. My personality changed. I had problems with Herrero. I felt life had no meaning.'

'Maybe life has no meaning. I mean, other than this. The fact that we are here, happy together. I hope.'

'I am OK now. Ju are right. I feel happy with ju.'

'I feel happy with you, too.'

'Dame un beso.'

They kissed again, tongues playing together, his hand under her T-shirt. God, he really was in danger of falling in love with her, he thought. She had aroused his protective instincts. He *would* look after her and take care of her. It felt good to have somebody to love again, to look after, to devote himself to! He had been missing that as much as having somebody to love him, as much as sex, maybe more. *I'm sorry, Cinzia. I'm sorry!*

'Te quiero,' she said.

'Te quiero,' he replied, kissing her face, caressing the nape of her neck with his fingertips.

'I wish I can stay with ju. I feel so happy with ju.'

'Let's just enjoy tonight. Don't worry about the future. The future will take care of itself.'

'Do ju live alone?'

'Er, yes. At the moment. Why?'

'What about your wife?'

'My ex-wife. I told you, I'm divorced.'

'Where is she?'

'I don't know exactly. With her parents I think. Or a friend. I don't want to talk about her.'

'I would like to live with ju.'

'Yes, you can come and be my live-in slave if you like,' he said, hoping to deflect her by joking about it – much as he had started to like her, the idea of her moving in made him nervous.

'No, not your slave! Maybe I can be your au pair?'

'I can't afford an au pair. I'm a teacher. Teachers don't have au pairs!'

'I will work for free for ju.'

'But you need money.'

'Maybe I can find job.'

'What kind of job?'

'Teaching Spanish.'

'Yes, that's a possibility. For the future. You can start by teaching me perhaps.'

'I am happy to teach ju.'

'OK. You teach me Spanish, I teach you English. It's a deal.'

'I like this idea.'

'Me too. It's called the pillow method!' He had to explain the joke. 'We can start tonight. Well, we already have started. Te quiero! Dame un beso.'

'Te quiero,' she agreed and they kissed again.

'Can I ask ju something?' she said eventually.

'I suppose so,' he laughed, taking a slug of Abbot.

'Could I have my letter back?'

'Why?' he asked.

'I was naïve. I feel silly.'

'Maybe. On one condition,' he laughed. 'You make mad passionate love with me tonight!'

'No. If I make love with ju, it's not for that. That would make me prostitute.'

'I'm only joking,' he said, kissing her on the nose.

'So ju will give it back to me?'

'I'll think about it. I might want to use it to blackmail you.'

'What is 'blackmail'?'

This was where he really wished he did speak Spanish. He explained.

'Ju are bad man.'

'You see. I warned you!'

'Te quiero.'

'Te quiero.'

They kissed, tongues playing with each other, his hand gently squeezing her breasts in turn.

'Let's go,' he said at last.

'Si. Vamos,' she agreed, exhaling and stubbing out her cig.

When they got outside it was still raining and they had missed the last bus, so they had to walk all the way to Gant's Hill in the rain. But he didn't mind too much – it was romantic, walking if not singing, in the rain and the wind and the dark with their arms around each other, sharing her tiny umbrella, fuelled by beer, chatting, laughing, kissing, tickling each other, knowing that they were about to become lovers. And by the time they had passed the college, with its imposing colonnaded front, even Cinzia's ghost seemed to have stopped following them, as if knowing that she had finally lost him …

'Thanks for bringing me on this nice walk,' she said, as they stopped after half an hour for a rest and some shelter at a petrol station.

'My pleasure!' he laughed. 'We can get some petrol here ha ha!'

'Te quiero,' she laughed, kissing his rainy face. 'But I think I'll be too tired to do anything when we get home except sleep.'

'Oh, no,' he laughed. 'We must have some fun and games first!'

'But you must be out by eight o'clock. OK?' She seemed worried about it.

'Don't worry, I will be,' he said. 'I'm used to getting up early. Come on. Let's go.' And off they plunged again into the wind and rain, arms around each other, he struggling to hold onto the flimsy umbrella.

'Ah, beautiful Gant's Hill at last!' he exclaimed, when they finally arrived, after an hour of walking, both drenched almost to the skin but happy. 'So this is your street? The trees are lovely!' It was a typical, leafy, suburban street of smart semi-detached houses, as the name, 'Abbotswood Gardens', suggested.

'Ju should say it in Spanish!' she laughed.

'Los arboles son hermosos!' he obeyed. The trees *were* beautiful, even though it was late November and they were almost bare.

'Bien,' she said, kissing him. 'Ju are improving.'

'Gracias Profesora,' he said, kissing her. 'Let me see if I can guess which house is yours. This one? This one? This one?'

Eventually they stopped in front of an imposing mock-Tudor semi, she opened the castle-style oak front door and they went in to a colour-supplement, beautifully-tiled, spacious kitchen. Dolores disappeared into the bathroom next door and re-appeared a few minutes later in a blue and white striped bathrobe, drying her hair with a hairdryer. She signalled him to go back into the bathroom with her, where she helped him to take off his wet outer clothes, gave him a bathrobe to wear and dried him off all over with the hairdryer. Then she led him into the lounge.

'I sit there, Calvin sits there, Marge sits there,' she said, pointing to two fat, green Chesterfield-style armchairs and sofa.

The décor of the room struck him as vulgar and pretentious, like some fake seventeenth-century French château with its chandeliers, antique-style furniture, gilt mirror and enormous marble fireplace, on which sat a huge ormolu clock. But he had to admit the armchair he was sitting in was comfortable! Dolores went back into the kitchen and made coffee and cheese on crackers.

'They want to buy a new house,' she told him, while they munched the collation. 'They think this one is too small!'

'Some people!' he shook his head. 'They're just never satisfied.'

'Are ju jealous?' she asked, teasingly.

'Jealous? Of this house? You must be joking!' he retorted, offended by the question. 'I suppose they both work like dogs for this, don't they?'

'What does mean 'work like dogs'?'

'Work very hard. Too hard. And hardly see their own children, I suppose. Pay someone like you peanuts to look after them.'

'Ju are right. They are like that.'

'I could make plenty of money if I wanted, by going to teach in Saudi Arabia or somewhere. But I'm not that interested in money.'

'I know ju are not a materialistic man.'

'I certainly don't have any aspirations to own a house like this,' he said, mollified. 'I don't think material goods make you happy.' He always felt a bit phoney when he came out with something like that, even though he believed it. Or was it just that he felt uncomfortable saying it because of his past, because it sounded a bit sanctimonious?

'Anyway, can we view the bedrooms now?' he asked, pulling her onto his knee, slipping his hand under the bathrobe and feeling for her breasts.

They kissed and cuddled there for a while, then she led him

upstairs by the hand to her bedroom, showing him the three other bedrooms on the way, including the en suite master bedroom. Even she had a double, en suite bedroom, with huge, white, built-in, mirrored wardrobes and white wall-to-wall carpet. A large lion soft toy lay on the double bed.

'You won't need that tonight,' he laughed, taking off his bathrobe, jumping into bed and throwing the lion onto an armchair.

'Por qué non?' she asked, slipping into bed beside him.

'Grrr! I'll be your lion tonight!' he laughed, taking her into his arms and untying her bathrobe.

CHAPTER TWENTY

'Will you do something for me, Frank?' Bertha buttonholed him as he was about to enter his office after teaching, much to his annoyance. 'I know you're a practical man.'

'Sure,' he agreed, following her into her office, feeling magnanimous after his night of passion with Dolores. 'What is it?'

'Unpack this notice-board for me.' She handed him a large cardboard box, which he broke open without too much trouble to reveal a smart new wood-framed, cork notice-board.

'Thank you, dear,' she said. 'Do you think you could put it up for me?'

She was in smarmy mode, he noted, but didn't mind too much – he was looking forward to meeting Dolores for lunch later. 'Can I do that tomorrow?' he suggested. 'I'll need a hammer. I can bring one from home.' *Maxwell's silver hammer maybe.*

'Yes, that's fine, dear,' she said. 'Are you on your way home?'

'Er – yes. I've got a few things to do here first though.'

'Have you got a few minutes? Shut the door – it's what it's for.'

He did as he was bid, in a mood to humour her for once, though he was immediately on his guard and could have foregone the sarcastic observation about the door's purpose. As always, he felt claustrophobic, because her office was so tiny and so chaotic and she herself displaced a large proportion of its cubic capacity.

'Pull a chair up,' she invited him, though her invitations always sounded more like orders.

'I'm all right, thanks, Bertha. I prefer to stand, if you don't mind. I do enough sitting down. And I do have things to do.' He was already regretting his compliance, feeling trapped, already longing to escape. Sometimes he even wondered if she secretly fancied him and wanted to get closer. The thought made him feel slightly nauseous, so he banished it quickly.

'I would like to see more of you, you know,' she said.

Oh, no, she does fancy me! Horror of horrors!

'Well, you know where to find me usually, Bertha,' he said, trying not to sound too caustic himself.

'What I really meant was, I suppose, I'd like *you* to see more of *me*.'

Oh God, that's the last thing I want, to see more of you in any sense of the word!

'Well, Bertha, here I am,' he said, trying not to sound too flippant, not bothering to add, 'And who's like me?'

'I'd like to have a proper chat with you. Why don't you come and have lunch with me on Monday?'

'A chat about what?' he asked cagily, ignoring the invitation for the moment, desperately trying to think of a good excuse – the last thing he wanted was to have lunch with her, especially as her table manners were so revolting. 'Is there something wrong? Has there been a complaint?'

'Quite the contrary, my dear! Your students all love you and I know you get on well with your colleagues. I know you're doing an excellent job. I'd just like to have a general chat, you know.'

'Oh, OK, thanks,' he said, touched in spite of himself by this generous testimonial. 'I'll let you know tomorrow, if that's all right. When I come to do the notice-board.' That might give him time to think of a get-out clause, he reckoned, turning to open the door and make his escape.

'Oh, just before you go, dear, are you free on Friday afternoon?'

'Er – yes, I think so,' he stammered, immediately furious with himself, knowing she was likely to lay something on him, having allowed himself to be softened up by her compliments about his work.

'Do you think you could teach my JMB class for me? I have to go to a seminar in Cambridge.'

‘Er – I’m not sure. I think I have a dental appointment, actually.’ In fact, he had an appointment with his solicitor about his divorce, which he definitely didn’t want her to know about. ‘Can I get back to you tomorrow on that as well?’

‘If you can’t do it, I’ll have to ask Mark,’ she said.

‘I’m sure Mark would love to do it,’ he was tempted to say, mischievously, but bit his tongue. ‘I’ll ask him, if you like,’ he said instead.

‘Could you, dear? In fact, could you ask him to come and see me?’

‘If he’s there,’ he said, opening the door and making his escape, furious with her and himself, and at the same time amused at the thought of Mark’s reaction if she asked him. He’d better do the decent thing and warn him, he decided, going into his own office next door.

TONY: Ah, the au pairs’ delight!

CHRIS: How yer diddlin’ Frank? Fallen foul of Bertha again?

FRANK: She’s just asked me to teach her class for her next Friday.

MARK: I hope you told her to go take a flying fuck at herself.

FRANK: Not quite in those words. I told her I had a dentist’s appointment. She wants to see you. I think she’s going to ask you. She’ll try to butter you up first of course.

MARK: She can fuck off. The only butter I want applied to any part of my anatomy is by some sexy chick. Preferably to my dick. I’ve got my car mechanics on Fridays anyway. And my weekends begin at three pm precisely.

FRANK: She might ask you, Edmund. Be warned!

EDMUND: I told her I didn’t want a birthday card, but she’s given me one anyway! Ask me what?

FRANK: To teach her class next Friday afternoon.

EDMUND: Out of the question. I have an appointment at the barber’s. But thanks for the warning.

FRANK: That’s a good one! I never thought of that! Which barber’s is that?

EDMUND: Chap down the road. On Hoe Street. He chops it about a bit, but he’s cheap.

MARK [Under his breath]: He must be fucking blind too.
FRANK: Chris, you'd better have your story ready.
CHRIS: I've just remembered, I'm going for a lobotomy that day.
FRANK: Tony, beware!
TONY: I'm a history bod. Unless she wants me to tell them all about Adolf Hitler and the causes of the Second World War.
FRANK: Better not. Might be one or two Gerries in the class.
MARK: I've got several Krauts in one of mine.
CHRIS: I think they'd probably benefit from a bit of history.
FRANK: I've got a German fellow in my evening class. Genial chap. Get on well with him. But I'm scared to mention the war!
MARK: Have you not asked him what his father did?
FRANK: Not yet. We stick to football, beer and women. Not necessarily in that order.
CHRIS: So how is the leg over situation with the au pairs, Frank?
FRANK: It's hard work, Chris. I could do with some help. I'm fighting them off.
TONY: He's not called the au pairs' delight for nothing!
CHRIS: Can't help you there, mate. I'm spoken for.
MARK: Me neither. I'm out of the game. Now that I've met the love of my life. What about Ed over there?
EDMUND: I think they're all scared of me. I don't know why. Anyway, toodle-pip chaps. I'm off. Have a good weekend.
CHRIS: I think it must be that trench coat and trilby, Ed. Make you look a bit sinister. Like a mobster or something.
EDMUND: Because I look like Frankenstein you mean.
FRANK: Doing anything exciting at the weekend, Ed?
EDMUND: Yes, indeed.
CHRIS: Tell us more.
EDMUND: Going to the dry cleaner's.
CHRIS: Is that on Hoe Street too?
EDMUND: Yes, just next to the barber's actually.
MARK: Which is just next to the massage parlour I bet.
CHRIS: You make Hoe Street sound like Sunset Strip.
FRANK: Bye Edmund. I'm off myself. Have a good weekend all.
CHRIS: You too, Frank. Going to get tanked up?

FRANK: You seem to think I'm a regular rakehell, Chris!
MARK: He's just jealous!
CHRIS: We're all jealous. We all live vicariously through you, Frank.
MARK: I'm not jealous any more. Now that I've found my soulmate.
FRANK: We all look forward to meeting this paragon, Mark.
MARK: She is a very special lady, I assure you.
FRANK: She must be if she's tamed you!
MARK: I tell you, when I look at the chicks in my classes now, I don't see them. They're invisible to me. That's how special she is.
CHRIS: So when do we get to meet this goddess, Mark?
MARK: At the Christmas party, I suppose. But it's strictly look, don't touch.
CHRIS: We all look forward to worshipping at her feet, don't we, Frank?
FRANK: We do indeed!
MARK: Had to warn a student in the class off her the other day. Pakistani fellow. Been bothering her.
CHRIS: What did you say to him, Mark?
MARK: Told him I'd have his balls for breakfast if he went near her again.
CHRIS: You really shouldn't beat about the bush like that, Mark. You should have given it to him straight.
MARK: I think he got the message.
FRANK: Right, on that cheery note I'm off. Bye all! See you Monday. Have a good one.

'Hola. Como estas?'

'Estoy bien, gracias, señorita. Y tu?'

'Muy bien, señor.'

'Te quiero.'

'Te quiero.'

They kissed and went to the Greasy Spoon café near the college for lunch. She was wearing an embroidered suede coat, tight white cord trousers and red wellies, since the streets were slushy with melting snow. He was glad to notice she'd ditched the dungarees, perhaps because he'd told her they made her look like a farmer last night. She lit up a Fortuna.

'So how am I doing, profesora?' he asked her.

'Bien. Ju are a good student!' she exhaled.

'I told you the pillow method was good. I've got something for you?' He handed her an envelope.

'Is it my letter?'

'No. Open it.'

She ripped open the envelope eagerly and read the letter he had written for her that morning while his students were doing an exam practice. He watched her normally pale face reddening as she read.

'It's beautiful,' she said, when she had finished. 'Now I am happy.'

'You weren't happy before?'

'I was worried.'

'You were worried? Why?'

'I was worried ju only wanted me for sex.'

'I was worried you only wanted *me* for sex.'

'Ju are bad,' she blushed again, smacking his hand, which was holding hers on the table.

'Hey, I told you, corporal punishment is not allowed in Britain. Except in bed.'

'Ju are so bad,' she laughed, smacking his wrist again. 'Te quiero.'

'Te quiero too. So, did you enjoy yourself last night?'

'Si,' she blushed. 'I want to do it with ju again.'

'I'm free this afternoon.' He was only half-joking.

'I hab to take the children from school.'

'Ah, yes, one of the au pair's little chores. While *they* are out busily making even more money. What about tomorrow evening?'

'I hab to babysit. They are going out.' *Damn them!*

'Saturday?'

'Si. I am free all day. What shall we do?'

'We can go for a walk on the Marshes. Then go for a drink and something to eat. Then go back to my place.'

'Por qué?'

'To play Scrabble of course.'

'Ju are so bad!'

'Don't you want to play Scrabble? Good for your English!'

'Ju are naughty! Ju make me feel like a lover. I don't want to be a lover.'

'You don't love me?'

'Si. Te quiero. Do ju love me?'

'I think so.'

'Ju know when you are love someone. Ju feel it.'

'I'm only joking! Te quiero mucho.'

'It's nice to be loved by anyone.'

'I agree.' *Even if it should be 'by someone'.*

'Dame un beso.'

He leant across the table and gave her a quick kiss. 'Now, shall we order?'

'Si. What do ju want?'

'There's only one thing possible for me – Spanish omelette.'

He invited her to join him in the Bell that night with his evening students and she eagerly accepted. He was amused to see that she was jealous of the other girls in the group. Afterwards, they sneaked off to the back of the town hall, next to the college, and spent a few minutes canoodling in the doorway of one of the outbuildings on the edge of the playing field, even though it was a cold December night.

She gasped his name over and over again and a faraway look came into her eyes as he made her come with his fingers. Then she started to do the same for him.

'Do ju like it strong?' she asked, as she did so.

'Not too strong,' he groaned.

It took him a while to come, because this was a new experience for him, but eventually he did. Then they hugged each other tightly for a while.

'I don't want to go,' she said, clinging to him.

'No, me neither. But we'd better go or you might miss the last bus,' he said, releasing her and kissing her forehead.

'Si,' she agreed. 'Tonight I will talk to my pillow.'

On Saturday afternoon they went for a walk on the Marshes as planned and had a late lunch in the café opposite the marina, next to the rowing club, from where they could see skiffs racing up and down as well as the occasional narrow-boat or cruiser chugging by on the river. The sky was an icy blue and there was an equally icy wind blowing through the bare trees and ruffling the murky water of the river, as well as the feathers of the waterfowl, so it was just as well that she was wearing a bright-blue puffer jacket.

They ordered, she lit up a Fortuna and for some reason told him that her father had died of a heart attack last year at the age of forty-nine and how much she still missed him, that she had had a special relationship with him, had been a 'daddy's girl'.

'Maybe that's why you like older men,' he said, giving her a hug and a kiss on the forehead, feeling a surge of sympathetic affection for her – this girl wasn't just a plaything or a sex object, but somebody's *daughter*. Not that he thought of her or any girl in that way.

'I think ju are right,' she said, exhaling.

'What was he like, your father?'

'He was a very nice person. He was very sentimental. Just like me.'

'Are you very sentimental?'

'Ju don't think so?'

'I don't know. I don't really know you very well yet.'

'It's true. We don't really know each other well.'

'I still love you though.'

'Why do ju love me?' she exhaled.

Maybe just because I need somebody to love, he thought, but didn't say – somehow it didn't sound like the right thing to say. Nor did he say: *Because I've just lost my wife and my girlfriend, who I truly loved and wanted to marry. Because she left me and wouldn't come back to me. Because I'm on the rebound. Because I'm lonely. Because I'm frustrated. Because I'm scared of being in any way abnormal. Because you're pretty. You're sexy. You're Spanish ...* 'I don't know. As you said, love is a feeling. You know when you have it. You can't necessarily explain it. It's a mystery. Love is a mystery.'

'That is very romantic.'

'I am romantic. Maybe not sentimental, but romantic.'

'Dame un beso.'

He gave her a quick kiss on the lips. 'But I know why you love me,' he said. 'That's not a mystery.'

'Por qué?'

'Because I make you laugh! That's what you said!'

'Not only that.'

'I know. I'm only joking. Don't get all serious on me. Does Herrero love you?'

'I think so. But he is not very friendly. Not very affectionate.'

'I see. That's probably because he's a priest. A Jesuit.' He immediately regretted saying it.

'What do ju mean?'

'Priests – especially religious priests like Jesuits – are trained to suppress all such feelings. It's all part of the celibacy thing. You know, no sex.' God, he thought, what a state of mental and emotional anguish this Herrero must be in! He had been there himself once. Had the T-shirt …

'Pero – but ju are not like that.'

'Aren't I? Do you think I'm friendly and affectionate?'

'Si. Ju are different from him, anyway.'

'Well, that's a relief to hear! But I never actually became a priest. I left before. I was in the seminary for nine years though.' He was surprised to hear himself talking so openly about it to her – but that was probably because she was so direct and honest, he told himself. And Spanish. 'I had to fight hard to undo all the brainwashing and conditioning. Not just at the seminary. The whole Catholic thing. I think I'm still fighting fifteen years later.'

'What do they tell ju?'

'At the seminary? That you have to renounce all normal human affections. Not just sex. Even affection for your family. Or friendship. You weren't even allowed to have friendships with each other. There was something very cold and unnatural about it. That's part of the reason why I left.'

'Herrero is cold.'

'But he likes sex?'

'Si. That is natural, I suppose.' She exhaled.

'Of course it is. It's normal and natural. You don't think I'm cold, do you?'

'Sometimes ju seem a little bit cold. In class.'

'Really?' He was always shocked to hear this.

'Si. But ju are friendly. All the students like you. They think ju are a good teacher.'

'Well, I'm glad to hear that. Of course, as the teacher I have to keep a little bit of distance.'

'Yes, of course. Everybody understand that. Ju can't be too friendly.'

'Except with you perhaps!' He gave her a kiss.

'That is different.'

'Some people think a teacher should never have a relationship with a student.'

'That is stupid. We are all adults, not children.'

'Yes, of course. That's my attitude. Otherwise I wouldn't be here with you now.'

'I'm glad ju are here.'

'Me too.'

'Dame un beso.'

He gave her another kiss. Their food arrived and after eating they walked back down the river, stopping for a pint of Guinness at the Robin Hood, followed by a pint of Fullers at the Anchor and Hope, followed by a pint of Young's at the Prince of Wales by the bridge on Lea Bridge Road, where they caught a 38 bus to his flat.

As they ate and drank and laughed and chatted and strolled along with their arms around each other, keeping close for warmth against the icy air, he realised that for the first time in months he felt happy, felt fully alive again. At the same time, he also realised that happiness such as this was all too fragile and fleeting, so resolved to enjoy it to the maximum and make it as memorable as possible, for both himself and her, despite the words of the Dubliners' song that suddenly started running through in his head:

For love is pleasin' and love is teasin'
And love is a pleasure when first it's new;
But as it grows older sure the love grows colder

And it fades away like the morning dew …

They made love on the floor in front of the gas fire, while sipping whiskey and coke. He undressed her slowly, kissing and caressing each part of her body as he did so: sweater, T-shirt with the motif 'LA TOJA ISLA DE LOS SUENOS', black cords, white pop socks with pink rings, white bra and finally pale blue knickers. When she was naked, he got her to tell him the Spanish word for various parts of the body, touching each one tenderly with a finger: face – la cara, nose – el nariz, mouth – la boca, tongue – la lengua, ear – la oreja, shoulder – el hombro, arm – el brazo, neck – el cuello, tit – la teta, stomach – el estomago, cunt – el coño …

'So it's masculine?' he enquired, slipping his finger inside.

'Si,' she murmured pleasurably.

'How strange,' he mused aloud, fingering her for a while to excite her, then removing his finger and exploring the rest of her body, asking her for the Spanish word as he went, including her legs – las piernas – and feet – los pies – and toes – los dedos del pie – then letting his hand surf back up her body to her stomach, where for the first time he noticed a faint scar, which she told him was from an appendix operation.

He also noticed on his travels that she had a small wart on the side of her 'rodilla' or knee and that she had rather hairy legs, which she admitted she was self-conscious about. He told her he didn't mind, because his were even hairier. She laughed and undressed him, continuing their anatomy lesson, teaching him the words 'polla' for 'dick' and 'cojones' for 'balls', though he already knew the latter word from reading Hemingway. And as their hands explored each other more and more hungrily, he suddenly realised that he didn't need to be quite so envious of Hemingway any more – at last he was having his own Spanish adventure, though not in quite such a dramatic or dangerous setting as the Sierra de Guadarrama in nineteen thirty-seven.

CHAPTER TWENTY-ONE

'This is for ju,' she said, handing him a small gift-wrapped package and lighting up a Fortuna.

They were in the Greasy Spoon. He hadn't seen her for three weeks, because two days after the Christmas party she had gone back to Spain. They had spent the night before she left together at his flat and he had gone to the airport with her. He made her promise to send him a postcard. She made him promise to write her a letter. 'If ju don't, when I come back I will kill ju!' she had joked. 'Perfect first conditional – very good!' he had congratulated her on her grammar, laughing. He had missed her.

'Gracias,' he said, opening the package. It was a cheap-looking novelty bookmark. He gave her a peck on the cheek. 'Thank you.'

'Ju don't like it.'

'I do! It's the thought that counts.'

'It's a silly present. I want to disappear.'

'Wait till we've had lunch!' he laughed.

'Dame un beso.'

He did so, though he was uncomfortable about it, because there were a few other college people in the café, both staff and students. He had gone there reluctantly, because she had said the other café was too far and she had to go home to work soon. In other words, to do a load of ironing.

'So, did you have a good holiday?' he asked, nervously.

'Si,' she said, then dropped a mini-bombshell on him. 'I spoke with Herrero. He asked me to marry him.'

'What did you say?' Had she had sex with him, he wondered, but didn't dare to ask, didn't really want to know.

'I said yes.' She exhaled some Fortuna.

'Oh.'

'Ju are surprised?'

'Yes,' he shrugged.

'Por qué? Why?'

'Well, from what you told me, you didn't sound very happy with him.' He was trying his best not to sound gutted. Not that he saw her as the love of his life, but he had started to fall in love with her. And thought she was in love with him …

'I could not refuse him. I know he loves me.'

'Do you love him?'

'No se. I'm sorry, I'm still speaking Spanish! I don't know.'

'You know if you love somebody. You can feel it.'

'Si. Perhaps I will love him eventually.'

'What about me?'

'Qué?

'Do you love me?'

'Si. Te quiero.'

'Yo tambien.' But he wasn't quite so sure any more.

'Could I have a word with you, dear?'

To his annoyance, Bertha had come into the language laboratory while he was giving his class a listening comprehension.

'Yes?' he said, taking his headphones off.

She pulled a chair up beside him and sat down, dropping books and papers as she did so, which he helped her to pick up. He could tell she was in busybody mode and immediately started organising his defences.

'There's been a complaint,' she said, fixing him with an accusatory stare through her jam-jar glasses.

'About me?' he asked, reddening in spite of himself, a sick feeling creeping into his stomach.

'Yes,' she said.

'What kind of complaint?' he asked, trying not to redden any more, wondering if it could have anything to do with Dolores, furious with Bertha for approaching him in front of a class like this. Of course, she was loving it, the bitch, he told himself. 'Who?'

'Someone in the Proficiency class.'

'What's the problem?' he asked, inwardly seething.

'They've said the class is too slow.'

He felt a mixture of relief and anger, quickly tried to think which stupid cow might have complained. It could only have been one of the women. Blokes rarely complained. Nobody *ever* complained about his teaching! Not that there were more than a couple of blokes in the group. There was a bolshy German cow called Monika though. *Bet it was her.*

'What do they mean, too slow?' he asked, knowing it would be no good trying to get the name of the complainant out of her. *And why couldn't the stupid cow have spoken to me first, instead of going to Bertha?*

'They said you're doing too much FCE work.'

'But half of them are doing FCE at Easter. You told me to do lots of FCE work with them. You said they were weak. They *are* weak.'

'I suggest you don't use First Certificate material any more. Too bad if some of them are doing First Certificate at Easter. Let them move down if they want to. You mustn't work a class too slow. Always keep a lively pace.'

How humiliating to be told how to teach by Bertha! 'But they've already bought an FCE book,' he said, biting his tongue. 'The one you recommended yourself.' *You stupid cow!* He forbore to mention that she had only recommended it because it had been written by one of her cronies. And wasn't much good.

'I suggest you try to use as little of it as possible in future.'

'I don't use it much. It's not very good, anyway.'

'Oh? What's wrong with it?'

'It's got no grammatical exegesis. It's overweighted with reading passages. It's actually not very suitable.' *An easy potboiler to knock off for a quick buck, in other words.*

'In that case, maybe they can just use it for self-study or something. If I were you, I'd teach them almost as if they were an A-level English Lit. class. Well, no, not quite A-level English Lit. Have you ever taught straight English, by the way?'

'Only on my teaching practice in Liverpool.' He could barely suppress his rage at being patronised like this, just wanted the stupid woman to go away so he could get on with his lesson.

'Anyway, try to pitch it higher and speed it up,' she said, getting up and dropping lots of papers as she did so, which he helped her to pick up again.

'I'll see what I can do,' he said, biting his tongue again, wanting rid of her. *As if it's all about 'pitch' and 'speed'!*

'Oh, by the way, are you free on Friday afternoon?'

He wasn't going to be caught by this one. 'Friday afternoon? Er, no, I don't think so. Let me check my diary.' He turned to the console. 'No, sorry, I'm not.'

'You're not teaching, are you?'

'No, Bertha, but I've got an appointment.'

'What kind of appointment?'

'Hairdresser's.' He was getting tougher. He needed to.

'That woman!' he said, going into his staffroom.

'What's she done to you now, Frank?' Chris asked.

'First she barges into my class while I'm doing a listening comprehension to tell me one of my students has made a complaint. Then she tries to tell me how to teach. And to add insult to injury, tries to get me to cover her class for her on Friday afternoon.'

'I hope you told her to go take a flying fuck at herself,' Mark said, without looking up from his desk.

'I told her I had an appointment,' he laughed.

'At the massage parlour, I hope,' Chris said.

'No, at the hairdresser's,' he laughed. 'Thanks to Edmund over there for that one. I might actually go for a haircut, anyway. I'm getting a bit shaggy.'

'As I said, he does chop it about a bit, but he's cheap,' Edmund said.

'What's his name again?' Frank asked.

'Ali Barber,' Edmund said, his hair looking as if he'd had a bust-up with a lawn-mower.

'I think I'll stay with my Greek-Cyp,' Frank laughed.

'How's it going with the Spanish bird?' Mark whispered, when he had sat down.

'She's just told me she's going to marry this Jesuit priest boyfriend of hers.'

'He'll be able to perform the ceremony himself, won't he? Do I, Sancho Panza, take this woman to be my lawful wedded wife?'

'I don't know about that,' Frank laughed. 'I don't think he believes in the religious claptrap any more, from what she says.'

'You mean, he's going to be defrocked?'

'Something like that, I suppose,' Frank chuckled. 'Since he's been defrocking her apparently.'

'So are you still going to carry on shagging her?'

'I don't know. I still like her. But I don't feel quite the same since she told me that.'

'Plenty more fish in the sea around here.'

'I'll see how it goes. How's it going with Edina?'

'I'm totally besotted. Might even marry her.'

'Wow, you really have got it bad!'

'Yah. And I don't want to be cured. I want to die happy.'

'I've got another joke for you before you go, Frank,' Edmund called over.

'Oh, OK. Not another one about the Pope, I hope,' Frank laughed.

'No, this one's about the Pope's daughter,' Edmund said, deadpan.

'I think we should all be privy to these pearls of wit and wisdom of yours, Ed,' Chris commented.

'You have to be able to recite the Credo in Latin to qualify for my audience,' Edmund said. 'I know Frank can.'

'Alas, that disqualifies me,' Roger giggled.

'Yes, but you can probably recite Beowulf in the original, can't you, Roger?' Chris remarked.

'Alas, no, I wish I could!' Roger chortled, his hand over his mouth.

'What are you working on these days, Roger?' Frank asked.

'Oh, just something about Arthur Ransome, you know.'

'Ah, Swallows and Amazons! At last, I've actually heard of one of your subjects!'

'Oh, dear, I'm sorry,' Roger giggled. 'Of course, you went

to school in Swallows and Amazon country, didn't you? Did you know that Arthur Ransome reported the Russian Revolution for the Manchester Guardian?'

'No, I didn't know that.'

'Yes. Frightfully interesting. Apparently he crossed the lines on foot from Whites to Reds and back at one point, delivering a secret message for the Estonians. He got to know both Trotsky and Lenin well. He even married Trotsky's personal secretary.'

'What put you onto him?'

'Oh, I started to get interested in him when I tutored his grandson as a vacation job while I was at Oxford.'

'I see.' Trust Roger to come up with some killer connection! 'Well, I'll look forward to reading all about it when you've finished. How's the hip, by the way?' Roger had been left with a serious limp after his accident in Ireland.

'Oh, still a bit stiff, alas, but I soldier on.' *Typical Roger understatement.*

'Well, I'm sure it'll get better with time,' Frank said, making for the door. 'Bye all. I'm off.'

'You don't want to hear the joke?' Edmund asked.

'Keep it for the pub tonight. Are you coming?'

'The one on the corner down there? The Bell?'

'Yes, that's the one. Bring your intermediates. It'll be good for them to mix.'

'Do you always go to the pub after evening class?' Edmund asked, innocently.

'Frank lives there, don't you, Frank?' Chris remarked.

'Not quite!' he laughed uncomfortably as he left the room.

Funnily enough, sex with Dolores was better than ever after she told him she would marry Herrero. He couldn't quite work out why. Was it because he hoped she'd marry him instead? But he didn't want to marry her! Was it because he could have sex with her now without worrying about having to marry her or being responsible for her – NSA as they called it apparently? Maybe. Was there even an element of revenge in it now, revenge for her 'betrayal' of him? Possibly, he admitted to himself. Whatever it was, it seemed to have added an element of spice to their lovemaking, which now became even more frequent and more uninhibited.

She liked playing rough, even violent, games in bed, games that involved hair pulling, biting, scratching, spanking ... At first he was reluctant, such behaviour being completely out of character for him, but he soon learned to let himself go and found he enjoyed it. Then one afternoon, while they were making love in her bedroom in Gant's Hill, she asked him to do something they had never done before. At first he was reluctant, but it didn't take much persuasion on her part for him to oblige, and he found that it gave him a feeling of excitement, and closeness, even more intense than 'normal' intercourse. It was called 'anal sex', he later discovered. One particular variation that she liked was for him to use his finger.

Sometimes late at night they had sex at the bus stop, if there was no one else there, or in a shop doorway – or at least she insisted on making him come while they stood waiting for the bus after having a drink with his evening class students. He was always nervous about being seen and sometimes tried to stop her, but could never resist her unbuckling his belt, slipping her hand inside his trousers and expertly manipulating him until he came while he held her close. Somehow the risk of being seen – especially by one of his other students or even a late-working colleague – added an extra spice to these intimacies. Waiting for a bus had never been so much fun.

Because they both knew their relationship was not going to lead to marriage or be for life, he felt entitled to meet other women. He was hoping to meet his future wife or, at least, his soulmate. Tiziana continued to appear interested in him, kept approaching him after classes or 'bumping' into him in the college foyer or at the bus stop. However, after her frequent excuses for not meeting and especially after the anticlimax of their date in central London, he played it cool with her, though he remained friendly. He liked her, but didn't fancy her any more, if he ever had.

One day he met her at the bus stop near the college – a bus

stop that was rapidly acquiring something of an invisible romantic aura for him. She was in her scruffy leather motorcycle jacket as usual and to his shock had a ring in one of her nostrils, so was looking more punkish than ever, a look he didn't find attractive at all. But she was with Birgit, the German girl from Dusseldorf, whom he found very attractive indeed – Birgit was slim, unlike Tiziana, with blond ringlets, and she was wearing a flowery blouse and tight black trousers – so he couldn't resist chatting her up. She told him she was twenty-one, though he already knew from her application form, which he had secretly consulted.

'Boys of nineteen and twenty ask to sleep viz me after five minutes – they're babies!' she laughed sexily, during the course of the conversation.

'We must go for a drink some time, then,' he was about to say, but was too embarrassed to do so in front of Tiziana and anyway just then, to his annoyance, the 123 came – a bus that you could normally grow old waiting for – and they had to jump on.

He never managed to make a date with Birgit, because she was always with Tiziana, who seemed to want to keep her away from him – some sort of sour grapes, he supposed. He did make dates with several other girls over the spring and summer terms, but for one reason or another it never progressed to sleeping with them. There was a Swiss-German girl called Pia, a Turkish girl called Emine, a French girl called Sylvie, Cristina from the Canary Islands, another French girl called Véronique and a Yugoslav girl called Vera.

He liked Pia, the Swiss girl, because she was young – eighteen – and girlishly pretty, with dark, glossy, pageboy-style hair. She usually wore tight jeans and sweaters with a white anorak. She was vivacious and friendly. She told him she had been brought up on a farm.

'What kind of farm?' he asked, having treated her to a Malibu with orange.

'Cows and pigs,' she said and added joking: 'My mum looks

after the pigs. Look at me if you want to see a pig!'

'You're not fat,' he laughed, but she seemed to think she was.

He told her how he had spent childhood summer holidays on the farm in Ireland where his mother had been born and brought up. She told him she loved skiing, wanted to be a ski instructor and showed him photos of her last skiing holiday, in which she somehow looked all the prettier for being swathed in skiing clobber. She told him she had worked for two years in a sports shop. She also told him how she was a practising Catholic and loved Sunday morning Mass because it was peaceful and gave her time to think. He confessed that he was a lapsed Catholic, but that didn't seem to faze her. He even confessed to her – confidentially – that he had once been in a seminary. They talked about religion. He found it easy to talk to her, even though he was nearly twice her age. He liked her more and more. She was so fresh, so innocent, so sweet, so charming.

One evening in the pub after class she told him something that shocked him. She said that her father used to beat her and that was one of the reasons she had come to London, to escape from him. That was the cue for him finally to ask her out. He would befriend her and give her some paternal affection, if that was what she wanted. He'd look after her, take care of her, protect her. It would be like having a daughter! Yes, he fancied her too, he supposed, but it wouldn't matter if she didn't want to have that kind of relationship – he'd enjoy just looking after her while she was here, being a friend to her. She seemed delighted. He arranged to meet her at three o'clock on Sunday afternoon in front of the Town Hall, his usual trysting place.

He waited till four o'clock but she didn't turn up. He was torn between annoyance and anxiety, anxiety that something might have happened to her. He found a phone box and phoned her. Her landlady told him she had gone to the West End for lunch with a friend. Angry and perplexed, he went to the West End himself and walked around looking for her, hoping he might see her. He didn't of course. After an hour or so of wandering around among the throngs of tourists, he realised how stupid it was and went to a cinema, where he sat almost alone for two hours, then went for a pint, trying to keep a lid on his anger, trying to convince himself that she wasn't with some other man, trying to tell himself that she must have had a good reason to stand him up.

'So what happened yesterday?' he asked her pleasantly in the Bell the next evening, where he had gone with a few evening students after class as usual, as she sipped her Malibu and orange. She looked confused. 'We had a date to meet at three o'clock,' he had to remind her.

'Oh, I'm sorry, I forgot!' she exclaimed, blushing and clapping her hand over her mouth.

'Are all Swiss people so forgetful?' he asked, smiling, making the others laugh, and continued to chat to her for a while, pretending not to be offended, listening to her amiably as she told him how an aunt and uncle had emigrated from Switzerland to Canada because all their cows had been killed by disease, how her sister had written saying it was 'boring' at home without her, how she liked ballroom dancing, especially the tango, as well as skiing, how the Jewish father and son she au paired for made her work from eight to six every day while they were out making money on the Stock Exchange and didn't want to lose her because she was such a good cook. To which he said, 'Huh', told her she was being exploited and advised her to leave them.

Not that he cared much any more – she was already on his black list. Not that she would ever know that though – he made a point of being more friendly than ever towards her. You always had to be professional, as he regularly reminded himself! Which was why he didn't exclude her from the trip to the Empire Disco in Leicester Square that with the help of Albert he was organising for the following weekend.

Emine was a Turkish-Cypriot doctor, whose dress style varied between 'classic' – euphemism for 'old-fashioned' perhaps – such as long pleated cream skirt and dark-blue jersey or more modern check shirts, short-sleeved pullovers and tight jeans. Like most Turkish women she was a bit hirsute, but he found her strangely attractive – especially her big hazel eyes and her slender ankles, not to mention her plump breasts and pretty pink-varnished nails. The fact that she was a doctor, a gynaecologist, made her interesting as well as attractive. She told him that though she was from Cyprus she lived and worked in a hospital in Istanbul.

One day she turned up for class in a rather daring, low-cut, short, pearly summer dress that really showed off her sumptuous figure and he resolved to ask her out. He sensed she liked him, because she usually hung around at the end of lessons to chat to him. To his delight on this day she did so as usual, asking if she could speak to him in private and waiting for him to deal with a couple of other student enquiries as usual. His delight was short-lived though – she told him she had to return to Istanbul suddenly because of her job and asked him if he could help her get a refund from the college. She had only been around for two weeks. He took her to the office to get the requisite form and helped her fill it in. She thanked him, gave him a kiss on the cheeks and said goodbye.

'Ah well, we're just ships in the night!' he smiled sadly and had to explain the expression for her before she left.

Sylvie was a Parisienne and like most of the girls an au pair. She favoured short-sleeved pullovers, blazers, skirts and high heels. She was sexy but shy. She told him she loved reading and wanted to be a librarian. That really turned him on. She too started approaching him regularly after class. If she didn't, he felt jilted. She explained that sometimes it was because she had to rush home to pick up her charges from school. Sometimes he bumped into her at the famous bus-stop. Sometimes he made a point of doing so.

One afternoon he met her in the college foyer. She had just had a swim in the college pool and her hair was still wet. She looked as sleek and sexy as a mermaid. He asked her out and she accepted immediately. They made a date to meet outside the Town Hall at three pm on Sunday. He waited till four o'clock, but she didn't turn up. When he tackled her after class the next day, in her sexy black cord jacket, she apologised and said a friend had turned up to see her unexpectedly, but she hadn't been able to contact him. That was all right, he smiled. No problem! She went straight into his black book.

Cristina was from the Canary Islands. She was very easy on the eye and had a bubbly personality. He asked her out but she declined, saying she had a boyfriend. He told her he respected that, but carried on a flirtatious badinage with her which she seemed to encourage, despite the boyfriend. It was good fun and no harm done. Sometimes he thought she was more fun than Dolores. She had a great sense of humour – at least she laughed easily at his jokes. It made him realise again how important a sense of humour was in relationships. Just as in life. Even more important than looks or sex, he sometimes thought.

Not that Dolores didn't have a good sense of humour. But Cristina was better-looking too. There was something sun-kissed about her, with her bronzed body and bright personality. Sometimes he guiltily wished he could swap them. He was a bit bored with Dolores and she seemed a bit bored with him. Or at least she seemed a bit distant, even though they were still lovers. It was the Herrero factor, he knew, and it came as much from him as from her. Whenever they were together, especially making love, he could see the ghost of Herrero hovering in the background in a black Jesuit's habit, frowning at him. It didn't always make for fun and frolics in bed. Sometimes he thought of ending it, but neither of them wanted to enough. And he still liked her, even if he didn't love her. Besides, he didn't have anyone else.

Valérie was another French au pair. She turned up at the Town Hall, albeit fifteen minutes late, but at least she turned up, and they went to Covent Garden. She was wearing a grey cape over a yellow sweater, tight blue jeans, and maroon boots. She wore her hair in a pony tail, had star-shaped studs in her lobeless ears and several rings on her fingers. She wore no make-up and didn't need it – she had a beautiful if somewhat ethereal face, as well as a slim, girlish figure. She seemed intelligent, serious, earnest, artistic.

They strolled around Covent Garden, chatting enjoyably about literature – she was reading Siddhartha by Herman Hesse and The Good Earth by Peal Buck; about Pineapple Studios where she did ballet lessons; about music – she loved jazz; and about religion – she was a fervent Catholic. He had mixed feelings about Herman Hesse and didn't think much of Pearl Buck, even though she had been given the Nobel prize for literature, he wasn't a big fan of ballet or jazz and he certainly wasn't a practising Catholic any longer. But somehow these points of difference only made her seem all the more attractive.

She told him her parents were divorced and she had communication problems with both of them, they didn't understand her, they were against her. By now she was sipping a Martini with ice and lemon and he was supping a pint of London Pride in a pub garden by the river. She admitted she was looking for a father-figure in her life. He was tempted to say he'd be a father-figure to her, but didn't, because he wanted to be more than a father-figure. He took hold of one her hands, held it between his and asked her if she had any brothers or sisters. She told him she had a sister in Guadeloupe and had been there to see her.

He asked her how she had liked Guadeloupe. That was when she said something that shocked him to his core, changing his feelings for her in an instant from attraction to revulsion, made him let go of her hand as if it had suddenly turned into something slimy and repulsive. She said she hadn't liked it because she didn't like black people, they were lazy and stupid. Some of them might be lazy and stupid, he objected, taking a swig of Pride to cover his embarrassment, but so were some white people. They were *all* lazy and stupid, she asserted. It was in their genes. It had been proved scientifically that 'negroes' were less intelligent than white people, she claimed.

It struck him as such a stupid, ignorant and bigoted thing to say that he could hardly be bothered to argue with her about it, but he did so, trying not to sound as horrified as he felt. He laughed, took another swig of Pride and asked her where this scientific proof was, but could hardly be bothered to listen to her vague, rambling, Frenglish reply. He felt even more revolted when she went on to say how she disliked President Mitterrand and 'socialisme' – not that he knew much about Mitterrand or his policies. The voice that he had found so sexy suddenly sounded grating, the face that he had found so winsome suddenly looked mean and pinched. He had intended to go for a meal with her, but made an excuse to go home early.

In their very next class he got involved in a wrangle with Gino, an Italian student, about Mussolini and Fascism, of which he seemed to be a supporter. He knew he shouldn't have, that it was usually a mistake to talk politics in class, unless you wanted to depart from the lesson, and he could see that most of the others were bored. 'I think we'll just have to agree to disagree,' he told Gino eventually, feeling guilty about the others and eager to get back to the present perfect.

At that moment, somebody gave a sigh and said loudly, 'Now can we get on?'

He glanced around, secretly furious, to see who it was. It was Valérie. If she hadn't already been in his black book, that would have gained her instant entry at the top of page one.

Vera was that rare, almost unique, bird, a Yugoslav. She was twenty-nine years old, so more mature than most of the girls. He invited her for a drink, because she reminded him of Marina, his Yugoslav ex-girlfriend, but also because she was quite attractive and seemed intelligent. He took her for a walk down Coppermill Lane and across the Marshes and they had a drink on the patio of the Robin Hood, where he introduced her to Guinness and they chatted while gazing out across the river, the reservoirs and the lush green meadows dotted with yellow, blue and white wildflowers, a scene as pretty as an impressionist painting on this warm spring evening.

He found her Serbo-Croat accent sexy, though perhaps only because of association with Marina. Marina – to think it was already ten years ago! However, it didn't take long for him to realise that Vera was nothing like Marina and had little to say for herself, didn't seem very interested in him or anything, in short was rather *boring*, so that he found himself wishing he had never invited her out and never repeated the exercise, though as always he continued to be friendly to her, indeed made a point of trying to bring her out of her shell during class and in little chats afterwards.

Anna was a Polish girl – an equally rare bird – in his Proficiency evening class. He met her one Sunday afternoon by chance on the Marshes when he was walking alone, Dolores having told him her 'aunt' was visiting. She was wearing a black windcheater and check skirt. She had a lovely, intelligent face and full figure, with bushy black hair, and looked more Mediterranean than Polish. In fact, she was the spitting image of Kate Bush, whom he deemed eminently fanciable.

'I'd forgotten you lived round here,' he remarked, shaking her hand, pleased to see her.

'Oh, I hadn't forgotten *you* lived round here!' she smiled coquettishly, sending a ripple of excitement through him.

While they chatted, he wondered if he should invite her for a drink, but two things stopped him – she had a dog with her and, she told him, she had a boyfriend in America, whom she was going to join in September, if she could get a visa. But apparently they didn't want any more Polish people, she said, and he secretly half-hoped she would fail to get one. She said she wanted to study psychology there.

'So what are you doing now?' he asked.

'I'm helping my uncle to send food parcels to Poland.'

'What kind of food?' he asked, puzzled.

'Meat,' she said, making him inwardly squirm.

'Well, there are plenty of rabbits around here,' he joked.

'Yes,' she laughed. 'I know where to come with my bow and arrow!'

'Or you could just send the dog,' he suggested.

'Oh, we don't eat dogs in Poland,' she laughed.

'No, but he could catch some Polish rabbits,' he said, looking at the dog, which didn't really look as if it could catch its own tail.

'No, he's my uncle's dog,' she smiled, 'and we love him too much.'

'Well, happy hunting!' he said, waving cheerio, thinking with a stab of angst as he continued upriver towards the Anchor and Hope how lucky her boyfriend was and what a gorgeous girl she was, the kind of girl he could fall in love with, the kind of girl he could easily imagine marrying and spending the rest of his life with, but who like so many others was fated to be no more than a passing ship in the night ...

CHAPTER TWENTY-TWO

'Did you know Tom Mellor broke into your cassette cupboard in the lang lab?' said Roy, legs crossed, baggy grey flannel trousers riding half way up his skinny, shiny shanks. Tom Mellor was the lab technician.

'Did he? Why?' He was affronted by this news.

'Said he needed something and it shouldn't have been locked. I wouldn't accept that if I were you.'

'I won't.'

'I told him it had to be locked because I keep my plastic mac in there.'

'I don't think anyone will nick that,' Frank laughed, though he was disconcerted by what he had heard.

'I hope it's still there then,' Roy said.

'Anyone want to proof-read a psychology paper for me?' Mark suddenly asked.

'Have you asked Bertha?' Roy enquired.

'*She* can't fucking spell,' said Mark.

'I'll do it for you,' Frank volunteered. 'What's it about?'

'How to break the begging habit in dogs by progressively reducing the reward. Break the pattern. Learning codes. Susceptibility to illusions caused by the colour of the eyes.'

'There you are.' Roy said, exhaling smoke. 'Frank will proof-read your paper and you can proof-read his novel.'

'Where is Bertha by the way?' Frank asked.

'Apparently at an academic board meeting,' Roy exhaled. 'Nothing academic about it of course. Sorry if I sound cynical.'

'Can't be academic if Bertha's on it,' Mark remarked.

'The room numbering in this college is very confusing, isn't it?' Roy exhaled. 'Don't you think so, Frank? Especially for foreign students. They often come to me looking for you. I mean 141 is very confusing. Why not call it Y room, anything?

Or Frank's Room. I mean, foreign students may not know their numbers if they're beginners. I always take them back to the office. That's my principle. People on the academic board won't argue with the principal because he's useful to them. They're looking for promotion, aren't they? Don't you agree, Frank?'

'I'm sure you're right,' Frank said.

'I'm going to see if my mac's still there,' Roy declared, shuffling out of the staffroom, leaving a haze of smoke behind.

'He must have fuck all to do,' Mark muttered under his breath.

'I think he might be retiring this summer,' Frank said.

'I don't suppose anyone will notice if he does,' Mark commented cruelly and Frank chuckled, though he felt sorry for Roy, a man out of place and out of time if ever there was one.

Tony Holloway breezed into the room looking dapper in a smart blue suit and tie, rather than the safari suit he usually wore.

'Ah, the au pairs' delight!' Tony declared, in his nasal cockney voice, going to his desk.

'Where have you been?' Frank asked. 'You're looking very natty today!'

'Just been to a job interview. For a company. Very hush hush though, so don't say anything. Lots of commercial and political secrets at stake apparently. They tested me by mentioning one. Very right of centre. Basic rate not very good but lots of overtime.'

'Will you take it if they offer it to you?' Frank asked.

'Told them I'd need to think about it overnight. Be good to get out of this place.'

'Might be out of the frying pan into the fire though,' Frank said.

'Can't be worse than this madhouse,' Tony riposted.

'Message for you from our revered leaderene,' Chris said, bustling into the staffroom and handing Frank an internal, or Wells Fargo as they called it, mail envelope.

'That's got to be bad news,' he groaned, opening it.

'Well, don't shoot the messenger!' Chris said, sitting at his desk.

'Oh, fuck!' he cursed under his breath, reading Bertha's memo. 'Pardon my French.'

'Feel free,' Mark said. 'What's she done to you now?'

'I'm taking the students to Cambridge on Thursday, so she agreed to cover my class Thursday evening. Not that I want her anywhere near them really. Now she says she can't and wants me to teach Thursday evening after being out in Cambridge all day with the students.'

'Lazy cow!' Mark muttered.

'Tell *her* to take the students to Cambridge,' Tony suggested.

'And pay the coach driver to leave her there,' Mark said.

'Maybe arrange a punting accident?' Chris suggested.

'Bertha in a punt?' Mark snorted. 'You'd need a fucking Thames barge!'

'You won't do it, will you, Frank?' Chris asked.

'She can go and take a flying fuck at herself,' Frank swore.

'Attaboy!' Mark exclaimed. 'You're learning.'

'She'll try and rope in one of you lot, so be warned,' Frank said.

'Big Ed could do it, couldn't he?' Chris suggested.

'What could Big Ed do?' Edmund enquired, opening the door at that very moment with his electrified hair. He was so big he nearly filled the doorframe.

'Teach Frank's Proficiency class next Thursday evening for him instead of Bertha?' Chris replied.

'You can't because you've got a hairdresser's appointment, haven't you, Ed?' Mark said.

'No, I've got a dressmaker's appointment next Thursday evening,' Edmund quipped, going to his desk. 'Sorry, Frank, old boy.'

'Didn't know you were a cross-dresser, Ed,' Tony remarked.

'I can be very cross when I choose to be,' Edmund riposted, taking out his pipe for a smoke.

The door burst open again.

'Oh, dear!' Roger exclaimed, barging in with his duffel bag full of books over his shoulder as always, long grey locks flying behind him.

'What's up, Rog?' Chris asked.

'Claudio Forte has been sacked!' Claudio Forte was a colleague in the staffroom next door, who taught Social Sciences or some such – nobody was ever quite sure.

'Sacked?' they all asked. 'What for?'

'Apparently he's been growing cannabis in the staffroom!' Roger collapsed into a fit of giggling, hand clapped over his mouth, already florid face becoming even more inflamed.

'Where will I get my supplies now?' Ed enquired, puffing placidly on his pipe, after Roger had recovered his composure and sat at his desk.

'I can give you the number of my supplier if you want,' Mark replied, not looking up.

'I thought you got yours from your barber, Ed,' Chris said.

'I think I'll stay with my usual Old Shag, thank you,' Edmund puffed.

'What's *her* name then?' Mark asked.

Before Edmund could riposte, the door suddenly opened again.

'My mac's missing!' Roy announced, rushing back in.

'Shall we call the police?' Mark asked him, straight-faced.

'Are you sure?' Frank asked, struggling not to laugh. 'Have you checked everywhere?'

'I've made a thorough search,' Roy said. 'There's no sign of it.'

'Maybe Tom Mellor's taken it,' Frank suggested.

'Why on earth would he take my mac?' Roy almost wailed.

'Maybe he goes to Soho strip clubs too,' Chris suggested.

'I don't go to Soho strip clubs,' Roy rebutted.

'You don't?' asked Chris.

'No, they're far too expensive,' Roy smiled, playing along with the jape.

'Yah, you stick to Chingford strip clubs, mate,' Mark said.

'There aren't any strip clubs in Chingford, unfortunately perhaps,' Roy replied. 'Unless you know something we don't, Mark,' he added.

'I don't need strip clubs any more, mate – I've got all the flesh I want at home now.'

'Ah, yes, your Hungarian lady friend,' Roy said, lighting up.

'She's not a 'lady friend', she's my live-in lover, mate,'

Mark corrected him. 'Why should I go out for burger when I've got steak at home, as Paul Newman supposedly said?'

'Just before he got divorced,' Edmund chipped in.

'Have you got a 'lady friend', Roy?' Chris asked Roy.

'Yes, but she's in Austria,' Roy divulged with a puff of smoke, to Frank's surprise.

'I bet she's an ex-concentration camp commandant, isn't she, Roy?' Chris pursued.

'Oh, she's not that exciting, I'm afraid!' Roy said.

'You mean she doesn't wear her jackboots in bed, Roy?' Mark asked.

'No, and I don't wear my plastic mac in bed either!'

'I'll have a look round the lab for it,' Frank offered, feeling sorry for him.

'Would you? That's very kind of you, Frank. But I know you're a kind chap.'

''The Mystery of the Missing Mac',' Frank joked. 'There might be a detective novel in there somewhere!'

'There you are!' Roy agreed. 'Your next novel! I don't think there's ever been a detective novel set in a college of further education, has there?'

'It might turn into a murder mystery if Bertha keeps annoying everyone the way she does,' Chris said.

'It won't be much of a mystery,' Mark said. 'I'll confess right away. Fair cop, guv.'

'Maybe you should write it, Mark,' Frank suggested. 'So you would be both murderer and author. That'd be a first I think.'

'Make a change from writing pornography anyway,' Mark said.

'Well, on that pleasant note I'm off home for lunch,' Frank laughed, leaving the room to a few desultory goodbyes.

To his surprise, Dolores was waiting in the corridor, looking sexy in a yellow shirt and tight white cord trousers, with yellow sandals.

'Hola,' he said brightly, pleased to see her. 'Qué tal?'

'Can I speak with ju? Are ju free?' she asked, anxiously.

'Sure,' he said. 'What's wrong?'

'Can we go outside? I tell ju.'

He drove her down Coppermill Lane to the Marshes, past the gunmetal-blue reservoirs and filter beds, and parked at the end, just before the railway line. Then they walked across the level crossing, along the path by Coppermill Stream, and across the silvery-black river by the metal bridge towards the café opposite the marina for lunch. It was a warm though overcast June day and he was happy to see the Marshes a glorious riot of greens, the ripe grasses sprinkled with buttercups and daisies, an occasional butterfly dancing prettily above them, the hawthorn bushes still laden with foamy-white, sweet-perfumed blossom, swallows swooping about like mini-jetfighters.

However, he wasn't so happy with what Dolores told him. She told him she had been chucked out of her house for breaking a mirror, though she knew it was really because Marge, her landlady, suspected that her husband, Calvin, was 'doing something' with her. So she had decided to go home to Spain next week, a month earlier than planned, and wanted to know if she could stay with him till then, to which of course he readily acceded. He was unhappy only because he had hoped to have her around for another few weeks until he went to Dublin.

'Te quiero,' she said, when he agreed to her request, and gave him a beso.

'Te quiero,' he reciprocated, returning the kiss.

'Ju don't mind?' she asked.

'Of course not. The house is still a bit of a mess though.' He was still spending most evenings and weekends renovating the house he had bought the previous year, the house that he had once hoped he might share with Cinzia …

'I will help ju,' she said.

'Gracias. You can be my au pair for a week!' he laughed, though the sudden memory of Cinzia pained him.

'I prefer to be your lover for a week,' she said.

'You can be that too,' he laughed, caressing her throat with his fingertips and giving her a kiss on the cheek.

They were sitting outside the café, on the river bank. An occasional skiff slid by on the water. Some kids were oohing and aahing at a mother duck and her fluffy brown and black ducklings on the bank. People ambled past chatting gaily, or lolled or messed about on their narrow-boats, all dressed in their summery clothes. All was right with the world! He felt a sudden access of happiness or at least contentment, sitting there after a good lunch with an attractive Spanish girl, a girl he had become very fond of and liked a lot, even if he didn't love her. That was the only fly in the ointment, he thought sadly – he didn't love her, he couldn't love her, because she was going home to marry another man, she wasn't the one …

'Calvin didn't try anything on with you, did he?' he asked her later, when they were lying in the deep grass and each other's arms.

'I know he likes me, but he didn't do anything,' she said. 'Ju can do something if ju want.'

'You mean here? Now?' He had already unbuttoned her shirt and was squeezing her breasts gently, her arms around his neck.

'Si.' He could tell she was excited, wanted more.

'Are you sure?' He was a bit nervous about making love in public, even though they were well-secluded in the long grass in the middle of the meadow, but he was suddenly excited by the idea himself.

'Si. Te quiero,' she whispered, putting her hand on his crotch.

'Te quiero,' he murmured, kissing her, doing the same for her, then unzipping her trousers and pulling her knickers down, while she unzipped him.

'Fuck me, Francis,' she urged him, pulling him on top of her, and he did so, though he had to clap his hand over her mouth to stop her cries disturbing the wildlife.

As always, making love in the open air like this gave him a thrilling sense of liberation, of release from society's artificial rules, of a return to nature, even a return to the Garden of Eden …

After she had come, she relieved him with her hand, they re-arranged their clothes and lay in each other's arms. Then suddenly, with a shock, he saw that she was crying. He had never seen her cry before.

'Qué pasa?' he asked, wiping her tears away from her pale cheeks with a finger and kissing her eyes.

'Estoy triste,' she said.

'You're sad? Por qué?' he asked, caressing her face gently, though he could guess.

'I don't want to leave ju.'

'Por qué non?' he asked, expecting her to say perhaps, '*Because I love you*'. But her answer surprised him.

'Because ju love me. Don't ju?'

Do I love her? 'Yes, I love you,' he said, kissing her on the forehead, suddenly realising with a lurch of the heart that maybe he did love her, certainly didn't want her to go, didn't want to lose her. 'How do you know I love you?' he asked, as if seeking confirmation for himself.

'I can feel it,' she said and he knew that she was right, that almost in spite of himself he *did* love her.

'Do *you* love me?' he asked, though he knew the answer in advance.

'Si. Te quiero.' She said it matter-of-factly, so that he knew it was true, as true as the grey, overcast sky above them.

'Oh, God!' he laughed, shaking his head above her, staring down into her deep brown, almost black, eyes.

'Why do ju laugh?' she asked.

'I thought we were playing a game. A game of love. Pretending to love each other. Just for fun.'

'Ju don't love me?'

'That's what I'm saying. I do love you. But I didn't realise it.'

'I love ju.'

'But you're going to go home to Spain and marry Herrero.' This was just like a like a replay of Cinzia and Luciano, he thought, with a silent groan.

'Si,' she said, twisting the dagger in his guts. 'I hab to go. I hab promised him.'

'Even though you don't really love him?' he asked, gazing down at her.

'I know he loves me,' she sighed, evading the question. 'So I hab to do it. Lo siento.'

This is incredible, he thought, gazing down at her, suddenly stricken by a sickening feeling of déjà vu, trying to sort out his emotions, trying to decide whether or not he should be angry, with both her and himself, or sad, or even amused that the Fates should have played such a cruel trick on him again and he had fallen into the trap. But better to laugh rather than cry, he decided, lying back in the grass and doing just that, laughing up at the pearly-grey sky, at whatever gods dwelt up there beyond the clouds, gods to whom he and she were obviously of little more importance than the insects that shared their grassy arbour with them.

'Why do ju laugh?' she asked him again, propping herself up on her elbow to look down at him, stroking his face with a slender, crimson-nailed finger.

'As flies to wanton boys are we to the gods, They kill us for their sport,' he declaimed to the sky. It was one of his favourite quotations and came in useful surprisingly often.

'What does it mean?' she asked, frowning.

'It's a quotation from Shakespeare,' he smiled. 'It means the gods just play with us for fun, without caring about us, the way small boys kill insects for fun. It's from a play called Antony and Cleopatra. About the Roman general, Antony, who falls in love with the Queen of Egypt, Cleopatra. But in the end they fall out and Cleopatra commits suicide with a snake.' Actually, it was from King Lear, he suddenly remembered. Oh, well, no need to tell her – why spoil a good story?

'I think I will not do that, even for ju,' Dolores smiled.

'Yeah, well, there aren't any snakes around here,' he joked. 'At least, I don't think so.' Joking about it was one way to deaden the pain, he thought. Or at least delay it.

'I hope so!' she declared, with a shudder.

'You mean '*I hope not*',' he corrected her.

'I hope not,' she repeated.

'Good! Como se dice en español '*snake*'?' he enquired.

'Serpiente,' she said.

'Oh, my God, there's one behind you!' he exclaimed, pointing.

She squealed and turned round, but he pulled her down and pinned her to the ground by her arms, laughing and kissing her.

'I hate ju!' she exclaimed, trying to push him off, but he was too heavy and strong for her.

'I hate you, too,' he said, holding her down, kissing her face, her throat, her chest. 'How do you say it in Spanish?'

'Te odio.'

'No te odio, pero te quiero,' he said, kissing her lips, letting go of her.

'Ju are improving,' she laughed, throwing her arms around his neck.

'I've got a good teacher,' he grinned.

'Yo tambien,' she said, pulling him down on top of her.

The following week they had their end-of-term party, which he organised as usual and which was attended by over a hundred students, including Dolores. It was held in two of the top-floor EFL-suite classrooms, with the dividing partition opened. These end-of-summer-term parties especially were always fun, but always tinged with sadness, because many of the students would be leaving to go back home or move on, probably never to be seen or heard from again – even though they often exchanged addresses. It was a chance to say goodbye to them, as well as get to know them a bit better, even if it was late in the day. Students usually gave him a farewell card, or even a present and a card, individually or from the group.

One such card was given to him by a black student called Gerard, from the Ivory Coast, whose reading skills had improved dramatically after he had introduced him to Agatha Christie, of whom Gerard was now a fanatical devotee. He opened the card and read the words Gerard had written:

Thank you Teacher.
You brought out the best in me.

'Thank you, Gerard!' he shouted above the loud disco music, to which most of the students were gyrating enthusiastically, touched almost to tears, and embraced Gerard. 'That's one of the nicest things anyone has ever said to me!' And it was, he thought, as he continued to observe the scene from the back of the room, feeling privileged to be here with these people and to have been able to make some small difference for the better to their lives.

'A penny for your thoughts?' It was Edmund, looking somewhat out of place in his tweed jacket and brown cords, even though it was a warm June evening and the room was sweltering.

'That we've got the best job in the world!' he replied.

'Better than dodging airgun pellets in Hackney, anyway,' Edmund chuckled, puffing on his pipe. 'Or being an assassination target when I worked for the Ministry of Defence.'

'You're not dancing?' Frank asked, somewhat rhetorically – he couldn't imagine Edmund on the dance-floor, but then he didn't like dancing himself.

'I'm more of a ballroom man myself.'

'Some nice young foreign ladies out there, if you're looking for a wife.'

Like me, the thought suddenly struck him like an epiphany. Why hadn't he realised it before? *That's what I want, what I've been subconsciously searching for – a wife! I want a wife and kids. I want to be a father. It's time to stop playing around. Time to stop pretending to be a playboy. Time to be serious.*

'I'm thinking of becoming a deacon, actually.'

Frank wasn't sure he had heard right above the din of the music and distracted as he was by his own thoughts. 'A deacon? Does that mean you have to be celibate?' Sometimes he thought he just didn't understand people at all!

'Not necessarily,' Edmund shouted back. 'But I may choose to be so. I'm celibate by default anyway!'

Frank laughed uncomfortably, feeling sorry for him and grateful that he had Dolores, who was letting it all hang out on the dance-floor, though only for one more night.

'Are you doing anything for the summer?' Frank asked, deliberately changing the subject, because he couldn't understand why any man would make such a lifestyle choice, if that was what it was, and it reminded him uncomfortably of how he had nearly taken a disastrously wrong road himself once, or had done so but turned back in time – and in his own case The Road Not Taken was one he had no regrets whatsoever about.

'Going on my annual retreat next month.'

'You mean, to Downside?'

'Good heavens, no. My French monastery. Much more civilised. The monks at places like Downside and Ampleforth are all Tories, upper-class types. They've got nothing to do with the Gospels. They just teach the children of the rich. They were sadistic too. Apart from the corporal punishment, they used to make fun of me because of my acne. It was deeply hurtful. Dom Butler was a disastrous abbot. I'll never go back there. Left me with deep psychological scars as well as physical scars. All ex-priests, monks, nuns are left with psychological scars. Well, you know from your own experience. We have quite a lot in common, don't you think? Catholic schools and seminaries are full of sadism, of course. They're not Christian at all. Especially Roman Catholic public schools like Downside, where I went.'

Frank didn't feel entirely comfortable about Edmund claiming him as some sort of fellow 'victim', nor did he particularly want to be earwigged by him, but he seemed to need to talk to someone, was probably lonely even though they were at a party with lots of 'talent', as Mark might put it. Mark, he noticed, was sitting demurely with the love of his life, his Hungarian girlfriend.

Edmund carried on: 'Talking about young ladies, I went out with a judge's daughter once. "Come into my office, old bean," he said one evening after dinner. "Got this particularly vicious rape case. I think seven years. What do you think?" "Oh, give him nine," I said. "I'll give him eight, then." Next day there were headlines in all the papers: JUDGE LASHES OUT IN RAPE CASE. That's British justice for you! But I know these types from my previous incarnation in the Ministry of Defence. I'm used to these fascist types. Teaching's much better, I agree. Not in Hackney though. Riotous classes there! Class in my first school howled me down as soon as I walked in the door. Head of Department had to come and assume command!'

'Dance with me!' Dolores suddenly appeared in front of him, slightly drunk, as many of the revellers were, and tried to pull him towards the dance-floor.

'Edmund will dance with you,' he laughed, resisting.

Dolores tried to grab Edmund and drag him onto the floor, but he rebuffed her too and she went back to the dance-floor, though not without a knowing glance at Frank, who gave her a wink.

'Now there's a young lady who could lead me into temptation!' Edmund declared.

'Yes!' Frank agreed. 'Me too!' And later, he hoped, she would, though for the last time.

'Mister Walsh! I want to tell you something – you are the best teacher!' It was Bless, a large black girl from Ghana, come to pay her respects, accompanied by Gerard. She was obviously a bit drunk, but he felt flattered by the compliment anyway. 'This is for you,' she said, handing him what looked like an ebony carving of some sort.

'Thank you, Bless!' he shouted, touched, giving her a hug. 'And you're the best student!'

'I will always remember you!' she declared, swaying alarmingly, so that Gerard had to hold her, grinning in embarrassment.

'And I will always remember you, Bless!' he shouted, as Gerard led her away tipsily into the corridor.

'How about that?' he said to Edmund.

'Don't get me wrong, I'm not racist or anything, but I've never particularly fancied black women, especially when they're drunk,' Edmund said.

'She's a very nice lady when she's sober – a nurse or midwife or something, I think. She'd make a good deaconess I reckon!'

'Have to lock up the altar wine though,' Edmund chuckled.

'Frank! This is for you, to say thank you.' It was Yiorgos, a Greek student, with Regina, his German girlfriend, and a couple of other Greek boys. They handed him a bottle of seven-star Metaxa, which they told him meant it was seven years old.

'Wow, thank *you*, that's great,' he said, taking the bottle, admiring it and shaking hands with all of them, giving Regina a kiss on the cheeks.

'You must come to Athens one day!' Yiorgos said.

'I will, I promise! I have to see the Acropolis before I die!'

'You will be welcome,' Yiorgos said.

'You can invite me to your wedding,' Frank joked – students of different nationalities often teamed up together, but it didn't usually lead to marriage.

'Ve vill be married next year,' Regina pronounced.

'Really?' Frank said, hoping he hadn't put a foot in it. 'You're getting married? Seriously?'

'She has tamed me!' Yiorgos joked, repeating a word they had learnt in class only recently and putting a proprietary arm around Regina.

'That's brilliant!' Frank laughed, shaking his hand and kissing Regina again. 'Congratulations!'

Yiorgos, a keen photographer, insisted on taking a few photos and then gravitated back towards the dance-floor with Regina and his mates or 'malakas' as they called each other. In other words, 'wankers'!

'Beware of Greeks bearing gifts,' Edmund said behind his hand.

'I will!' Frank laughed. 'But those boys are all great guys. Anyway, I'd better circulate a bit.'

He slipped his moorings, having had enough of Edmund, entertaining as he was in a morose way, and bumped into Tiziana, who was wearing her usual scruffy leather jacket over a red sweatshirt with a denim skirt and red stockings. He'd really fancy her, he reflected, if she just dressed a bit better, didn't dye her hair and maybe wasn't quite so chubby. But he liked her all the same. Maybe he'd ask her out again next week, after Dolores had gone.

'Ciao,' he said to her. 'You're not dancing?'

'I don't like this musica,' she said, screwing up her face, to his annoyance – he had forgotten she played bass in a punk band at home, so she wouldn't much like Culture Club, UB40, Paul Young, Spandau Ballet, the Eurythmics, Kajagoogoo, KC and the Sunshine Band, the Flying Pickets, Shakin' Stevens …

'So are you going home soon?' he asked, ignoring her remark.

'I go 'ome-a in July-a,' she said, in her best Italian accent – the accent that still made him go weak at the knees in spite of everything.

'We should go for a goodbye drink,' he suggested. 'Would

you like to?'

'Si,' she agreed, with the wry grin he found both charming and annoying.

'Good – we'll arrange it later,' he said, leaving her to join a table of his other students including Albert, who invited him back to his house in Chingford with a few others after the party, and when the time came gave him a lift in his Owstin Sprrite, with Dolores sitting on his knee.

CHAPTER TWENTY-THREE

Dolores left the day after the party. On his way home, after saying 'hasta luego' to her in Departures, he had felt a strange sense of liberation. It wasn't that he didn't love her – he had fallen in love with her almost in spite of himself. It had started out as little more than a game, a bit of fun, but somehow, somewhere along the line, had become serious without him even realising it until that afternoon here on the Marshes a few days ago. It was almost as if she had deliberately laid a trap for him! Yet why would she do that, if she was never going to marry him, was always going to marry her Jesuit instead? It didn't make sense! Maybe for her it had never been more than a game and she had just been playing with him, using him?

These were some of the thoughts that ran through his head on the evening of her departure as he sat on the patio of the Robin Hood, nursing a pint of Guinness, looking out across the river over to the very field where they had lain together less than a week ago, the field of long grass speckled with yellow, blue and white wildflowers, with a row of poplars in the distance just in front of the railway line, along which a blue and white electric train occasionally rattled on its way to Cambridge. Later, he thought, he'd go back to the spot and lie down there on his own, just to recapture the moment, even though he knew he shouldn't, it was just torturing himself. Across the river and into the trees, he chuckled wryly to himself, and took another slug of the black nectar. He was going to get drunk, he supposed. It was the only way to anaesthetise the pain he knew was going to kick in sooner or later, like delayed shock, if not today, tomorrow, or the next day, or next week.

At least I've got my date with Tiziana to look forward to tomorrow, he reflected. Not that I expect anything to happen with her. Knowing her she probably won't even turn up. And then in August the summer school in Dublin. Might meet someone there. Well, I *always* meet someone there. But I don't just want an affair, a fling, enjoyable as that might be. I want to meet my future *wife*! Someone *for life*. Someone to settle down with and have kids with. A *soulmate*. After all I *am* thirty-five! It's time to settle down isn't it? No I want a wife not an affair! Suddenly realised it at the end-of-term party. Maybe because of Mark and his missus. Talk about Damascene conversions! Why has it taken me so long to realise it? But maybe I should stop looking for one among foreign girls. They always leave! Even Cinzia. And now Dolores. But Mary left too. And she wasn't foreign. Unless you count Irish as foreign. Or I left her. Well it takes two to tango. No I don't believe for a moment that Dolores was playing a game with me or using me. Her tears in the terminal earlier were too genuine. I was almost in tears myself. 'Tears in the Terminal'. Be a good title for a short story! Or a song. Maybe Glen Curtin could sing it. She told me again she loved me but couldn't let Herrero down. In a way it displays an admirable loyalty I suppose. Just like Cinzia with Luciano. That doesn't help *me* though. Feel as if I've fought a love duel twice and lost out twice! Been rejected twice. Maybe I'm just doomed to be a loser in love. No can't allow that to happen. Didn't leave the Ghosters to be a bachelor for life! Or a celibate! Or any kind of loser … The party last night went off really well as usual. Got the organisation of it down to a fine art. Like a military exercise! Enjoy organising it even though time-consuming and something of a hassle. Especially when that prat of a premises superintendent Patterson – or Pratnose – tries to stop it at ten pm, having agreed it could go on till ten-thirty. Ex-military policeman and sour, surly, chippy Scot, that's why. Luckily Bertha the Battle-axe was there to put him back in his box. Good for her! She's gone up a notch in my estimation. Though admittedly from a low baseline. In the end we didn't actually get out till eleven pm since it took half-an-hour to clear up. Dolores was really good the way she – and a few other students – mucked in to help. It was great to see the students enjoying themselves so much. They really knew how to too judging by the way they were dancing and drinking and chatting and laughing and mixing with each other. What a great bunch of people! People from all over the world from literally every continent. Except perhaps the Arctic and Antarctic. Though there was that Icelandic girl in my class. That's why I enjoy the job so much. Love meeting people from all over the world, teaching them, learning from them, finding out a bit about them, helping them, helping to make the world a better place in my own small way I hope. Great to receive their words and tokens of appreciation. *You brought out the best in me.* That was the best one. That really made me feel what I was doing all year was worthwhile. Aah, that's a great pint of Guinness! Funny to think she'd be in Madrid now, no doubt with Herrero. She said he was going to meet her. Will she tell Herrero about me, I wondered? Confess her sins to him ha ha? God I'm going to miss her! She asked for her letter back again this morning, before we left for the airport but I didn't give it to her. Pretended I couldn't find it. I want to keep it. Might come in useful one day. She made me promise to burn it if I found it and I promised I would. 'It'll burn in Hell with me anyway,' I joked but she didn't laugh whether because she didn't get the joke or was too angry. Come to think of it, it was the only thing we ever really clashed about. She was a bit obsessive about it. Can't quite understand why. 'After all,' I told her, 'I could just make a photocopy of it, couldn't I?' In fact I'd already done so, in case she somehow found it and took it. 'Anyway,' I said to her, 'you shouldn't be embarrassed about it. After all, it was what led to a beautiful friendship, wasn't it?' 'Te odio,' she fired back at me. Made me laugh. God I'm going to miss her! Miss her already. Albert the Kraut's an amusing fellow: 'It's not good for me to see all zese girls in zeir summer dresses.' Good of him to invite us back afterwards. I got a bit drunk on that German wine, what was it, Mosel? So did Dolores. So when we finally got home at three in the morning we were too drunk and tired to do anything in bed! Luckily Albert gave us a lift home in his Owstin Sprrite even though he was drunk too. Decent fellow. That German pop music pretty rubbishy though. Enjoyed the French onion soup made by Véronique. Albert seems to fancy her. Maybe they've already got something going. He certainly likes talking about football! Reckons England is 'inefficient'. Felt like saying they were efficient enough to win the war but resisted. Seems to be a bit of a fan of Maggie Thatcher and anti-trade union. Still a likeable fellow though. Said he had a heavy day today because some German industrialists were visiting his factory here. He must have had a humdinger of a hangover this morning after all the beer and wine he sloshed back! Still a bit hung over myself. Well hair of the dog. It seems to be working. I think I'll have another one though just to make sure. Can't go home on one pint!

Aagh, that's good! Strange to think Dolores was here this time yesterday and today she's there. In Madrid. Might as well be on the moon. Strange to think I'll probably never see her again too. That's a painful thought. *Like a corkscrew to the heart.* How long has it been – eight months? She's very sexy in her own way. Likes a bit of the old sadomasochism. You'd never think so to look at her! Looks a bit innocent, a bit schoolgirlish, even a bit geeky with those specs and plaits. Turned me onto it! Somewhat to my own surprise. Turned me onto anal too. Which I hardly knew existed before. God we had some good fun! And not just in bed. I really got to like her. She's intelligent, has an intellectual side to her. Well so she should being a teacher or would-be teacher. Some teachers are dimwits though. One of my own colleagues once admitted she never read a book! I didn't just like her – I fell in love with her. Took a while but it happened. Fell slowly and softly. Landed so softly I only realised it last week. Killing me softly … Couldn't believe what Edmund told me about wanting to become a deacon. Why would you leave a monastery to go and become a deacon? If you were a deacon you might as well be a priest surely? Except perhaps you could get married as a deacon. In that case why not become a Church of England vicar? Not that he's ever likely to attract a woman the way he carries on. Admits he's lonely. He should've been chatting up the women at the party but he seemed to want to spend all the time chatting to *me*. Which was a bit of a bore amusing as he can be. Going on about how he used to have a house in Surrey and how the mortgage was a millstone so he couldn't afford to drink. About how he's a member of the discalced Carmelites and had been to some church in Kensington of all places to hear a homily by the prior who was 'a fine man', a Donegal man. About how Ireland is fascist – which I can sort of agree with. About corporal punishment in Catholic schools and how sadistic priests and brothers and nuns are – which I can definitely agree with. How he'd applied for a job with NATO in Brussels and had to sit a six-hour exam translating French to English. How people laughed at him when he told them if Britain left NATO there'd be a military takeover. How Monsignor Bruce Kent was a brilliant public speaker but poor conversationalist on a one-to-one basis. Unlike himself who could hold his own in any company he boasted. Which was probably true. And all very interesting. But not really what I wanted to listen to at a party. Although the joke he told about the Pope being mistaken for Elvis made me chuckle and somehow sounded even funnier in Edmund's Surrey accent:

The Pope goes into his hotel in Las Vegas. The female receptionist says: Oh my God! It's Elvis. You're alive! The Pope says: It's not Elvis, my daughter. It's me, the Pope. Look at my white robes. The receptionist says: I'm sorry, Holy Father. Of course. The bellboy comes to pick up his bags and says: Oh my God! It's Elvis! You're alive! The Pope says: It's not Elvis, my son. It's me, the Pope. Look at my white robes. The bellboy says: Yes, of course. I'm sorry, Holy Father. The bellboy takes the Pope up to his room, where there's a semi-naked lovely lying on the king-size bed, who shouts: Elvis! I love you! The Pope immediately flings off his white cape, shakes his hips and starts singing: A one for the money, two for the show ..!

Still at least Edmund came to the party. As did Bertha. Not all my colleagues did. Not that it bothers me really. It's their loss as far as I'm concerned. Mark almost might as well not have come the way he just sat there with his Hungarian girlfriend all night billing and cooing. Last year he'd've been really putting himself about on the dance-floor with the women. Now he's even talking about getting married to her! The great white hunter trapped and tamed! Soon to be caged! The macho hard nut reduced to a teddy bear. It's hilarious. A shame in a way. I'll have nobody to talk about women with now. Or go on the pull with! Not that I want to go on the pull any more. If I ever have. Never really needed to. Meet plenty of women every day in the job. Trouble is they're all foreigners and sooner or later go home. Leaving muggins me high and dry. Like now. Like last year. Like Cinzia. I'm not going to fall into that trap again. Those letters of Cinzia! This one for example. Can't resist another little read:

I've read your last letter three times and now I do wish to read it again. Shall I go to take it? No, because it hurts me and I do not want to cry tonight. Sometimes I would open my heart and whisper sweet things to you, but here I sit country fool that I am keeping an eye on the street while my mind is with you.

But someone suggested me to forget you, be stronger than you and tough if necessary. Well, I want to promise you that we'll meet again and I know where but I don't know when, maybe soon, maybe not. What you should do is try to understand me and be realistic. Don't be like me! I can't stop staring at the three pictures of London that are on the walls, I always look at the bottles of Guinness extra stout and then I dream of the many pubs we visited together and you sitting inside one of them with your interesting look, nice face and lovely hands.

Where are you? I would pay a large amount of money if I could get this important information: where you are now ...

What does she mean, 'Where are you?' *You know where I am! I'm in London!* That perfume knocks me out. Sweet but sad. Put it away! Rest of it not so interesting anyway: about how she's doing some child minding and some English teaching and learning English from the BBC courses on television, about Christine and how her boyfriend has left her but she doesn't care even though she's about to have his baby, about how she's learning to type ... That bit at the end is both touching and amusing. *I bought four bottles of Guinness yesterday, but can't have a drink on my own – it's too sad!* But her letters are always touching. Have to try not to be touched though. To be 'tough' as she calls it. She's not coming back to me. She's said that herself. *I want to promise you that we'll meet again and I know where but I don't know when ...* She's always saying cryptic stuff like that. As if to tease me. As if it's all a game. Maybe she means in the afterlife! I've resolved not to even open her letters because they pain me as much as please me. I actually tore a few of them up without opening them usually because I was drunk but always regretted it the next morning and put the scraps back together with sellotape like a jigsaw puzzle. It's another kind of self-torture, another kind of masochism. I almost wish she'd stop writing to me but I know I'd be even more hurt if she did. I've even told her to stop writing but she's ignored me. I've tried to stop writing back but always relapse, can't be that cruel. Especially as she says she'll die if she can't write to me or I stop writing to her. And deep down in my heart of hearts I know I'd die myself if she stopped writing to me. I still love her in spite of myself. It's like an affliction. *I can't stop loving you, I've made up my mind ...*

'Stop thinking about her!'

Can't resist a third one, it's so good. One more won't hurt, will it? Can't face going back yet anyway.

Aah, that first sup is always the best! Why was I thinking about her anyway? I should be thinking about Dolores! But why should I think about Dolores? She left me too. She left me for a Jesuit! Imagine leaving a Ghoster for a Jesuit ha ha! Well maybe they aren't called the church's storm troopers for nothing. But Herrero isn't even as good-looking as I am judging from the photo she showed me. Gaunt, sallow, ascetic-looking. Deadly serious too apparently. Which is what you'd expect I suppose. The Jesuits aren't renowned for their jolliness are they? Gerard Manley Hopkins for example. He wasn't exactly a barrel of laughs or the life and soul of the party was he? Even though he is my favourite poet. Can't really understand why she fell for him. Or why she wants to be back with him. She was such good fun. Just out of loyalty? Saint Ignatius of *Loyola*. It's admirable in a way. Even though it leaves me high and dry. With a wounded heart and wounded ego. Can't really see it lasting though. Are they in bed by now? *Stop thinking about her!* It was decent of Ken to stick his head in at the party. 'Grey Ken' as I dubbed him myself. Well he wasn't exactly the Ken Livingstone of Further Education. A bit of an arse-licker really.

That's how he got to be Head of Department no doubt. He obviously enjoys it too. Just seems to sit at his big desk all day reading travel magazines. That meeting about staff development interviews for example. Ken insisting on introducing them even though the union's against and he a member of the union himself. 'I've been told I have to do them by the college executive, so I have no choice.' Weak character. Self-serving. What was it someone shouted out? 'Yes, you do, Ken – resign!' Ha ha! It was the same with the departmental re-organisation. He always goes along with whatever the powers that be demand without question. People just love heckling him in meetings. 'As long as you stay in control, Ken!' someone shouted out to general merriment. Seemed like water off a duck's back to him though. Probably votes Tory wouldn't be surprised. Or SDLP. Yes that would suit him – middle of the road compromise. The Tory victory in the general election last week's a disaster. Depressing. As if I don't have enough to be depressed about. That witch Thatcher's going to try and destroy the welfare state including the National Health Service and the trade unions. Going to privatise everything that moves too by the sound of it. They'll probably try to privatise *colleges* eventually. That'll be the time to get out. No why are you such a pessimist? They won't do that! Lecturers wouldn't let them get away with it. It was the Falklands that won it for her. Mind you it was good to see that Argentinian thug Galtieri get his arse kicked. That public-school English boyfriend of Nicole's going on about it in the pub! He's in the territorials or 'terrers' as he referred to it. '*Our* subs … must be a real nuclear sub there, if only for tracking and information … Argie soldiers must be cold, they're from a hot climate, even worse than *our* boys … must be five-hundred marines and SAS on the island by now, mapping, defending landing sites … thirty killed already, nothing in military terms … ' Made it sound like a game. Likeable enough feller though. Trouble is that's their attitude to Ireland as well. We come, we see, we conquer, we keep. Rule Britannia! They don't realise how arrogant they sound. How arrogant they *are*. That new teacher Janet Daltry's a pleasant lady. Attractive in a very blondey English-rose way. I think she fancies me. But I'm not in the mood. Prefer foreign women anyway. Both of us on the rebound. Just divorced from her husband of forty-one. He had vasectomy. Two kids. Sad. At least no kids in my case. Silver lining huh! Too messy to get involved. Both of us badly wounded. Though she doesn't know about Dolores. Too much of an emotional minefield. Interior designer by trade. Nice of her to do my curtains. Very Laura Ashley. Rolls up in open-top Lancia Fulvia. Italian cars and Italian girls – can't beat 'em! With two dogs. Green cord jacket, frilly blouse, check trousers and riding boots. Sexy. All Jilly Cooper and jolly super. Had a good chat with her. She obviously needed to unload. Said she caught her husband in bed in her own house with his girlfriend. Told both of them to fuck off. Stupid bastard! Still not all that clever myself. Sex makes us stupid. Said his girlfriend's husband keeps asking her out. But she still loves her husband and would have him back tomorrow. What a mess! Still divorce amicable enough. Said she didn't want alimony just a lump sum. Felt bitter though. A few tears. Tempted to make a move on her. But would've been unfair. She just needed a shoulder to cry on. Could do with one myself. Maybe I should've taken advantage. Told her she seemed very strong. Said she'd been to boarding school and when you've been to boarding school you develop a shell. Tell me all about it! School for sons and daughters of Licensed Victuallers' Association. Is victualler just a posh name for publican? Didn't tell her I'd been to one myself. Didn't want to go there. 'Have to take you for a drink to a pub in the country some time,' she says. That was a come-on if ever there was one. I'd love to, says I. But just don't want to get involved. Said she had diabetes. Maybe I should take her up though. Don't want to be lonely again. I think she enjoyed my spag bol for lunch. Both got a bit tipsy on the Rioja she brought. Finished the bottle between us. Nearly made an advance on her again! In the end was glad she had to go. To archery. Plays squash and badminton too. Hope she didn't shoot anyone.

Ah, this Guinness is good medicine! Might have a fourth. Yeah, just one more. I need it. Since I haven't got any morphine. Need something.

That Nat West bank manager who refused me the bridging loan for the house – what a pompous prat! 'Not interested. Wouldn't touch it. You're making me an offer and I'm declining. I advise you to sell it and purchase another place. Why should the bank get involved? You've no equity. There's nothing in it for the bank. Why should the bank get involved?' *Because that's what banks are for, you pompous prat!* So that's how they treat a long-standing loyal customer is it? Well, they've lost my account. Serve them right. Not that they'll miss my peanuts. That fellow Monty in the Higham Hill Tavern's a funny old codger with his dirty grey beard, grubby suit, red tie and beret. Toothless too. Ex-hod carrier. Says he's got no pension because got seven hundred quid from the government after being demobbed from Second World War. Said it was his seventy-third birthday the other day so bought him a bottle of Guinness. Wanted a rum and black chaser! *Thanks, cocker! Hee hee!* High-pitched laugh. Probably says same whenever he meets a soft touch like me. Interesting old codger though. Said he used to be one of Wingate's Chindits in the war. Fought behind Japanese lines in Burma. Was at Tobruk too. Mind you they all say that. My old man actually *was* at Tobruk. Says he was seven years old in First World War. His dad used to show him zeppelins coming over. British planes used to get above them so the zepp pilot couldn't see and strafe them with machine guns. Every third bullet was a tracer. *As soon as a bullet hit a zepp that old gas-bag went up in flames hee hee.* Ha ha. Not so funny for the zepp pilot mind you. What a way to die. Had to do snow training in Scotland. Never got beyond Aberdeen. Horse transport. Freezing cold in morning. Had to break ice for the horses. Nags he calls them. Bit of a reactionary old git. *So what do you think of Margaret Thatcher, Monty?* Thought he'd be a fan but no. *Thatcher is the first woman prime minister n I 'ope she'll be the last! Churchill was the best prime minister. Ted 'eath's bought a new yacht. Did you know that? He was the cunt that got us into the Common Market. I'd like to tell 'im that to his face. We should be like the Japs. They've got private enterprise n look where they are today! In the nineteen-thirties there was no social security. Did you know that? I'm givin' you an educashun 'ere! No paid 'olidays, dole, nothin' like that. I worked on a milk rahnd when I was fourteen. Seven days a week it were. Why? 'ad to 'elp my mother. Two n six I got. Used to be lovely rahnd 'ere as a kid. Greenery all rahnd. Open. Bags o' playin' space.* 'So, Monty, what's the secret of old age?' *Kept my body pure when I was young. Never went with prozzies, specially abroad. They give you disease n you 'ave to pay for it in more ways than one hee hee. I'm givin' you an educashun 'ere, cocker!* Why the hell am I thinking about Monty? I should be thinking about Dolores. Or Cinzia. Except it's too painful. They both deserted me. Which one would you choose if you could? Cinzia without question. Would marry her tomorrow. Oh God it's like a bloody knife. Better not to think about her. Tiziana's a funny girl. Don't quite know where I'm up to with her. Said she wanted me to take her to the dogs but then cancelled. Said she had to babysit. Always bloody babysitting. Wish these people would babysit their own brats. Or she's out with Birgit the German girl. Wouldn't mind going out with Birgit myself. Plays tennis with her. Birgit must look sexy in tennis clothes! Wow! Looks a bit like Steffi Graf. Better-looking even. And that's saying something. I'd play tennis with her any day. Love all! Went ice-skating with her too. What was the Italian word she used, 'pattinare'? Don't like that leather jacket she wears. Makes her look like a Hell's Angel or something. Says her landlord is some American actor called Don Gordon. Never heard of him though. Told me Alessandra said I was a good teacher and 'sincere'. Nice to hear. Another nice Italian girl. Maybe I should go and live in Italy. Couldn't live there without Cinzia though. So near yet so far. Italian girls! Tiziana a bit of a whinger. Says she's 'bor-ed' in Chris's evening class. Not sure I want her back in mine. That's what she's angling for I reckon. 'Tiziana's a funny girl, isn't she?' Chris remarked the other day. He's obviously noticed she doesn't like his class. Or she's told him. 'Is there something going on between you and her? Shouldn't ask you really.' Funny thing to say. Funny he should've noticed anything. Must have seen us together a few times. God it's like being a in a goldfish bowl! Not that I care. Do what I like. Free agent. Go out with a student if I want. We're all adults. Not that Chris would have any problem. He'd like to screw a few of them himself I know but can't since he's married. Or daren't. Funny what Malachy my solicitor mate said the other day about Europe never really being Christian. Not sure what he meant by that. And parishes are obsolete, church should be based on South American model. Well as far as I'm concerned the church itself is bloody obsolete! Didn't dare say that to him though. He might have refused to help me with my conveyancing. Saved me a few hundred quid. He still seems to be a practising Catholic of sorts. Goes to Mass anyway. In fact I'm not sure he's ever really left the seminary in his head even though he's married. No kids mind you. Maybe never consummated. Still has an ecclesiastical air about him somehow. Seems to be conflicted. As if he feels guilty about leaving. Wouldn't be completely surprised if he went back in. Even though he's very critical of the church. No danger of that in my case I assure you! Never had a moment's regret about leaving. It was a living bloody death as far as I'm concerned. In fact I still have nightmares about it. Thank God I managed to escape ha ha! I lost my faith not just my vocation, that's the difference I suppose. To me it's all codswallop – Heaven, Hell, Jesus, the virgin birth, miracles, the resurrection, transubstantiation … *Transubstantiation* for God's sake! All utter baloney. How on earth can any intelligent person believe such medieval claptrap clever as it may be in a Jesuitical way? And Lourdes – don't start me up about Lourdes! The Blessed *Virgin* Mary, the *Mother* of God, came down from Heaven and appeared in a crack in the rock to a fourteen-year-old French peasant girl? Do me a favour! And the water has miraculous healing properties? Pull the other one! Yet millions of people believe it. And actually go there on pilgrimage. Including me once. Twice! Yeah well I was only ten the first time. Didn't want to go the second time when I was twenty-one. Only went to accompany my mother. It was so embarrassing. I was embarrassed for her and for me. Felt so fraudulent saying the rosary in front of the grotto. As if I was at some voodoo ceremony or séance. Enjoyed the week in San Sebastian mind you. Except I was with my mother and she insisted on me wearing a clerical suit.

Not the dog collar mind you. Sod that. Drew the line at that. Especially in the heat. That Spanish waitress in the hotel restaurant. So pretty! As pretty as an angel. Probably only about eighteen, a couple of years younger than me. Used to look forward to dinner just to see her. Imagining what it would be like to kiss her. And more. Made me feel dizzy just to look at her. Had to be careful my mother didn't notice though. Drove me crazy with frustration. And despair at the thought that I'd never be able to have a girlfriend like that. Or any girlfriend. Never make love with a woman, have a wife, have children. Because of the stupid way of life I found myself trapped in. Made up for it a bit since though. Even had a Spanish girlfriend now. Sweet revenge! Maybe that's why I'm so obsessed with women. To make up for what I missed for ten years. I know that's what Molly thinks. Might be half-true. But all men are obsessed with women aren't they? Take Mark! It's biology. It's the way we're wired. Wonder where she is or what she's doing now that waitress? Will be about thirty-two or three now. Probably married with kids. Wish I could remember her name. Never even knew her name of course. If everything had been normal maybe I'd be married to her now. She doesn't know what a narrow escape she had ha ha! Since I was an emotional wreck. A screwed-up emotional wreck. Managed to sort myself out though. My God, the psychological damage that whole system did. When I think back to it! Kidnapping boys from their families at the age of twelve. The age of *twelve* for Christ's sake! Yes literally for Christ's sake. *Children!* And *brainwashing* them. Plus all the other stuff in my case. Sexual abuse. It's a miracle I'm even half-normal. Maybe I should believe in miracles. It's a miracle I'm even alive. Stop thinking about that stuff! Think about positive stuff. Think about *now*. Well, I'm down but not out. Far from out. At least I've lived a bit. Even if I have lost a wife and how many girlfriends? Sally, Marina, Sophie, Grazia, Cinzia, Dolores … That geography lecturer Alf's a nice bloke. Seems a bit lonely though. Not married, no girlfriend. Even though I always invite him for a drink in the Bell with my students. Now that the bastards have closed the college bar. A bit too old for them I suppose. Nearly forty. A bit shaggy-looking too with the long hair and the beard. Not to mention a bit short and overweight. Really nice guy though. Just shows how deceptive appearances can be. A bit like Roger in that respect. Interesting fellow too. Seems to have travelled everywhere in the world! Spent five years in Vancouver doing an MA. Good conversationalist. Left-wing Thatcher hater and anti-establishment like me. Maybe even more so! Scathing about college management too. Especially Ken Cameron. In fact seems to hate the whole college! *The principal, Jack Fullofhimself, is a shit. Ken Cameron is a shit, out for himself. Head of Catering Gladys White – or Gladys Knight as he calls her – is a bitch. The women staff at the college are all unfriendly bitches and women libbers*. Well I can agree with it all except maybe the last bit. Not the female EFL staff anyway. They're OK. Not that I'm interested in the women staff. My students are a lot more attractive and interesting! Says he's got a Yugoslav girlfriend of sorts but you never see her. Not to mention an Irish nurse somewhere in the background but you never see her either. Not the kind of bloke to make things up though. Asked me to fix him up with one of 'my' girls. Only half-joking I think. I'm happy to do that. I like him. Mind you he said the other day one of his own students had invited him to see Fiddler on the Roof. Was excited at first but then realised it was a group thing! Said he'd go anyway. Bit of a downer! More than I've got at the moment mind you. Likes cricket. Have to part company with him there. Not county cricket anyway. Don't mind test matches so much. But even they take too long. Life's too damn short! Likes football too though. Supports Man United. Got that in common. And beer. As well as both being Mancs. No wonder we get on so well together. Two grammar school boys made good ha ha! Funny what Molly said about the Archbishop of Westminster, Basil Hume. Described him as 'slimy'. I can see what she means but it sounds a bit harsh. She can be very harsh in her judgements. What did she say about Aunty May? 'She was born to be a lady but not required.' A bit hostile to me too. Told me I had a chip on my shoulder. Which isn't really true – I've got two chips, one on each shoulder ha ha! Not really. Still at least it'd mean I'm well-balanced. Which I like to think I am. In spite of everything. Said Mary had a blackout and left her briefcase at the bus stop, never got it back. A bit like me leaving the carrier bag with my takeaway for dinner in it on the station platform the other night. Hearing that about Mary made me feel really guilty. Used to protect her against such things somehow. It's not my fault she has petit mal. Blame that benevolent dictator God for giving her meningitis as a baby. Got a chip on my shoulder against Him definitely. I'll organise a revolution if I ever get to Heaven. Except He doesn't exist obviously. Molly and Mary believe in Him though. That's the irony. They can't see any illogicality. Oh I know, He makes us suffer to test us. To temper us in the fire. Rubbish! GARBAGE! Said Mary told her she wants to meet and marry someone else. But will always consider herself married to me. Secretly touched by that. I do feel sorry for her. No going back now though. Divorced! It's a kind of failure I suppose. That's life though. It's a losing battle really. It's full of failures and it always ends in failure. The failure of death. Don't get morbid for Christ's sake! Another pint? Might as well. Finish the job off properly. Better make it the last one though. What is it, four or five?

Aah, that's so good!

Feel a bit blue now. Why wouldn't I? Just lost another girlfriend. *Dolores*. An appropriate name. God I miss her! Didn't realise I'd fallen in love with her till the last minute. Insidious! She got under my skin without me noticing. Not just sex either. Though the sex was good. Wonder why Pina gave me her homework in the corridor the other day? Does she fancy me? That would be the best thing I could do now, find another girlfriend as quickly as possible. Stop me from moping. Fed up with foreign girls though. No I'm just saying that. Certainly not fed up with Italian girls. Don't just want a girlfriend though. Want a wife. Something that will last. Last for a lifetime perhaps. Not just for a few months anyway. It's time to settle down. Stop playing the field. Get serious. Have a couple of kids. Would enjoy being a dad. Yes really fancy it. Stop messing about. Would love to have a little girl. And a little boy. Look after them. God I'm getting conventional in my old age! What was it Harriet Jenkins said to me the other day? 'Where have you been all your life, Frank?' Sarcastic cow. Who does she think she is? Just because she was my tutor she seems to think she can talk down to me. What was it she said that other time in a meeting? 'Frank was a model student on the RSA course. He hung round like a shadow in the background, didn't contribute anything, but made no fuss, caused no hassle. I was almost annoyed when he passed the exam.' Back-handed compliment if ever there was one. Ron Fitzpatrick's another one: 'Still skulking in shadowy corners, Frank?' What a stupid fucking thing to say to me! In front of Ken Cameron too. Mustn't be too sensitive I suppose – I don't think he meant anything. Just fucking tactless. All to easy to fall out with people. Will be wary of him in future though. That French nurse Amélie's nice. Bit of a risqué joke by me. 'I know where to go for some TLC if I fall ill then.' She took it in good part though. After I'd explained what TLC meant. Well we're all adults. All grown up. Quite fancy her. Stop thinking about sex! You're obsessed! Funny thing the secretary Catherine said after the end-of-term staff do: 'Don't worry, Frank, they're not as uncouth as they seem.' Not sure what she meant really. They weren't behaving all that badly. Just the usual shenanigans. She seems to think I'm some sort of paragon. I make a point of being nice to her. You have to keep people like secretaries, caretakers and technicians sweet. They're the ones with the real power. They do impose on her a bit though. Especially Bertha. But *she* imposes on everyone. Bertha's no fool mind you. What was that poem she came out with spontaneously when Jane Dawson said she'd been skiing in the Pyrenees at Christmas? Tarantella by Hilaire Belloc, that was it. *Do you remember an inn, Miranda? And the fleas that tease in the high Pyrenees.* Recited the whole bloomin' thing by heart! Impressive. Likes to show off. That Swedish student Magnus was a nice feller. Shame he had to leave early. Forestry student in Sweden. Bloody Ena in admin refused to give him a fee refund. Mean, sour, wizened old bitch. Would probably have fancied him if I was gay. Which amazingly I'm not. In spite of the seminary. One hundred per cent heterosexual thank God. Or as near as dammit. That would have been one cross too many. Don't understand it. Must be genetic. I'm lucky I suppose. I wonder how many turned out gay? Or worse. Got my suspicions of one or two. Ben Geoghan's a bit poncey with that fur coat. But not gay apparently. Got a whole harem of women from what I hear. Good luck to him. Didn't think much of his film though. Pretentious like him. What was it called, 'Children of the Dawn'? Quite a coup to get it on at the NFT. Fair play to him. Even though I never liked him much. Too up himself. Thought he was the bee's knees and the cat's whiskers. Not to mention the cat's pyjamas. Especially at football. Felt a bit embarrassed meeting those priests there. Live in different worlds now. Including the token black seminarian from Ivory Coast. Samuel was it? Did he say 'senior cemetery' instead of 'senior seminary'? Too true in my case. The other one dressed as if by Oxfam. Red tie, check shirt, old mac, scruffy plimsolls. Well they do take a vow of poverty. Made a perceptive comment about the film though: 'Emphasis on imagery at the expense of character.' Pavlo's an interesting feller. Not your average builder. Intelligent. Interested in ideas. A seeker after the truth. Says Serbs are Catholics but I thought they were Orthodox. On about the meaning of life the other day instead of finishing my bathroom. Throws Plato into the conversation. And the Upanishads. Not that I know anything about them. Or anything really. Bertha's daughter another seeker. On about Brahma, reincarnation, oneness, we're all drops of water in the ocean … Maybe so. What do I know? Refers to sex as 'nooky'. Funny expression. New one on me. Stop thinking about sex! You're not allowed to think about sex! Monty's a disgusting old devil really. 'Tell us the truth now. When you're on the shit pan, where do you put your dick? Does it go inside or out? Mine goes where it 'angs. It 'angs dahn inside naturally. Where does yours go?' The other funny old joxer says, 'Mine goes on the sink.' Had to laugh. Terry and Serena tomato picking in Italy for the summer eh? Say Plymouth is boring. God she looked good in that poncho the other night at the Victoria. Could hardly take my eyes off her. Italian girls! He's a lucky bastard. Seems I drew the short straw. At least she's staying with him. Not like Cinzia. Fucked off back to Italy. Back to mama. And Popeye the sailor man. No mustn't be bitter. Still love her. Would have her back tomorrow. Maybe I should reply to her last letter. It just prolongs the agony though. Roy Bunting bored the socks off me the other day in the staffroom. Going on about his migraines and getting ionisers in his house and positive and negative ions and how the TV and nylon carpets eat up the good ions. Liked what he said about me as a teacher though when I had a moan about Bertha. 'We all know you're a good teacher and Bertha knows it too. She knows a good one. Impossible as she is.' Going on about his hay fever as well. Mind you it drives me mad too at this time of year. Cinzia too. We had that in common. Don't think about Cinzia! Those Greek lads asking for a certificate from the college to avoid military service. Happy to oblige. Thank goodness we don't have to do it. Gave both of them one with my own signature on it. Might get into trouble over that. I don't care. They're good lads. Malakas all! Enjoying the biography of Bob Dylan by Anthony Scaduto. Present from Mary. Don't think about Mary! Forget Mary! She's dead to me. So Janet's diabetic eh? She obviously fancies me. But I don't really fancy her. Even though she's quite attractive in her very English-rose sort of way. Not in the mood. She's just on the rebound from her divorce that's all. Wouldn't last. Not a lot in common really. Don't care for that trilby she's started wearing. Bit of an affectation. Prefer foreign women anyway. Especially Italian. But they're no good to me if they bugger off, are they? Maybe should have hung on to Mary. No it was no good in the end. The infertility thing was the last straw. Hope I can have children one day. The thought of not being able to is depressing. Essential life experience. One of the reasons I left. What an awful bloody irony if I can't. Doesn't bear thinking about. Roy really doesn't like the college. Says it's like a swearword! Used to work at Southend College apparently. Moved back to London when his father died leaving his mother alone. Feel sorry for him. 'Bad atmosphere, Frank. Cut-throat. Got to be careful what you say to whom.' Stands up and goes to close the staffroom door cloak-and-dagger style. 'Bertha for example. She's sowed dragon's teeth. She can be impossible at times, but only because she feels threatened.' Yes Roy you lonely old fucker. Hard to believe he's retiring. Was like a piece of furniture. Was really nervous about his speech at his retirement do. In his best tweed jacket with regulation elbow patches and cavalry-twill trousers. Was quite amusing though. As was Fullofhimself's though I hate to admit it. Having presented him with a quartz watch. 'We usually give a watch to unpunctual members of staff … The borough usually grants early retirement to those it wants to get rid of.' A bit near the knuckle really. Poor old Roy got a bit tipsy on sherry. Had to help him back to the staffroom. Holding onto the walls and pipes as he went. 'How drunk am I, Frank? Am I really drunk?' Helped him to clear his desk. 'This has always been an unhappy place. I'll miss you, Frank. You're a decent soul. You've always listened to me, always been very patient with me even when I'm boring the pants off you. Not many other people to chat to round here. You've done me a few good turns too. Thank you for any assistance you've been to me over the years. Am I boring the pants off you now? I think I'm sober enough to go home now. I'll leave this rubbish for Bertha …' I'll miss him too funnily enough. So sad about Mary's brother- in-law. Navvy. Trench collapsed on him at work. Buried alive. Digger smashed his skull trying to dig him out. Took an ear off too. Whole side of his face disfigured. Good-looking bloke too. Being buried back in Ireland. In his wedding suit. His wife said she didn't want a shroud. Shroud? Shroud of Turin a fake obviously. I think Mary expected me to go to the funeral. Wouldn't have been appropriate. 'That's my daddy's coffin,' his little daughter apparently said pointing proudly to a drawing she'd done of it. And: 'Uncle Mat will be our daddy now.' You can't get more poignant than that. Puts my problems in perspective anyway. Nearly copped it myself on Saturday. Nearly fell off the scaffolding. Just like poor old Gerry. Shouldn't go up there with my head for heights. Thank God I got that grant money from the council. They took long enough about it though. Cheque for three thousand two hundred pounds. What a relief! Got Pavlo off my back at least. One more pint? Why not. Might as well go the whole hog. Don't want to go home sober to my empty house. My empty womanless wifeless sepulchral house.

Is this pint fiveor six? Lost count. I'm not drunk yet anyway. Even though I haven't eaten. Stilll sober really. So where am I going to find a wife? In Dublin maybe. No. They're all foreign women. All right for a fling perhaps. Not that I'm in the mood for flings. Looking forward to it though. Take my mind off things. That departmental meeting – so boring as usual. What's all that guff about being a 'community college'? They've always got to come up with some glib meaningless advertising-type slogan. Just get on with the damn job! Not enjoying Darcy Dancer Gentleman as much as The Gingerbread Man. Fairly funny though. That debate on blood sports with the Proficiency class didn't go very well. That Spanish girl defending bullfighting! Trying to say it was some sort of art form. Part of Spanish cultural heritage. Well *bull*shit! Shouldn't have lost my rag with her though. Cruelty to animals always a red rag to a bull for me ha ha. Glad Dolores doesn't approve. It would've put me right off her. Too intelligent to approve of that sort of barbarity. Wonder what she's doing now? Is she ..? Stop! Enjoyed that film *The Lacemaker* on TV. Could certainly fancy Isabelle Huppert. Reminds me of Mary in the film. Got a soft spot for quiet, shy, fragile women. They bring out my protective instincts I suppose. Possibly not a good thing. Unbalanced? God it's hard work digging out the garden. Especially in the rain. Back-breaking. London bloody clay! Must try to finish the outside painting before I go to Dublin. That new French girl Béatrice looks like summer school Sophie. Huh. *She* turned out to be a bit of a tramp. Still all grist to the mill. Bloody cheek of Bertha trying to get me to go to an RSA CUEFL conference instead of her. Two nights, a whole weekend away! Don't even teach the damn thing. Very thought makes me cringe with boredom. 'An amiable eccentric,' that new teacher Keith Johnson called her. Hmm. Not sure about him yet. Seems a bit full of himself. Just a defence mechanism in a new environment maybe. Says he's Irish descent like me though his name doesn't sound Irish. From Sheffield but father from County Down. Have to give him time I suppose. Bit of a tough nut like Mark. Similar macho dress style, leather jacket, jeans, boots. Mark's a funny guy! So proud of his new house. Not to mention his new woman Edina. Nice of him to invite me. 'Mine's the one with the pretentious front door. Philippine mahogany with a brass spyhole.' His dog Inja nearly flattened me when I went in! Edina very sexy-looking in tight sweater and jeans. Lucky bastard. Calls her his 'manager'! Going on about the 'underfloor heating'. 'How does that work?' I ask. 'I burn Christians,' he says deadpan. Had to chuckle even though I found it a bit distasteful. Having once been a Christian myself. He likes to shock. Something immature about it? Well he's the psychology student. Bragging about how he plumbed in the new washing-machine himself. 'Not a single leak!' Those Hungarian cigs too strong. Not to mention the Hungarian Riesling. I drank too much of it. Says last time Bertha phoned him at home he told her: 'I can't talk now – I'm screwing.' Had to laugh. Says he's refused to give her his new phone number. Good for him. Says he once told her anonymously on the phone: 'Does your college run a course in social skills? If so, don't you think you should join it? You're very rude.' Not sure if I can believe that even from him. Wouldn't put it past him though. Not sure I like his taste in music. Peter Frampton and Yes. Prefer Pink Floyd myself. I'm drunk. Definitely better make this my last one. That Anthea Harcourt's a bit of a snob: 'I can't stand the expression!' Because I said 'nitty-gritty' to her. Couldn't resist throwing in 'brass tacks' as well just to tease her. And that new Russian student. Just because I asked her if she knew how to get out of the building. 'I'm not so stupid!' Well I'm afraid you are darling. You're very stupid and very bad-mannered. 'Pushy young lady,' Harriet called her. That's putting it nicely. Had to laugh at what Geoff said complaining about Music and Drama in the classroom above: 'Like a herd of elephants!' Bertha buttonholes me in my classroom a couple of weeks ago after my lesson. In her tweedy two-piece. In smarmy mode. Starts telling me her bloomin' life story. Used to be a telephonist, typist, furniture saleswoman. Oh really? Had to pretend to be interested. Knew she was going to ask me to do something. On about her back problem too. 'My back was locked. It was very scary. I had to lie on the bed. Couldn't move. I had to be *rolled.*' That's too much information Bertha, I thought, struggling not to snigger. 'I even had to be helped to the toilet.' Aaargh! That's definitely too much information. Then she starts criticising Mark to me behind his back. Very unprofessional. Very *bitchy*. 'He's not doing enough. Not pulling his weight.' 'He's probably under a lot of pressure with his psychology degree, Bertha,' I say in his defence, though I shouldn't have to be defending him to her. 'Yes, but one takes these things on if one chooses and doesn't let them impinge on one's work – does courses, has babies,' she says. 'That last one doesn't always happen by choice, Bertha,' I riposte with just a hint of sarcasm and add pointedly: 'Anyway one makes allowances or tries to, doesn't one?' 'One does, but … but …' she blusters then turns the smarm on again. 'I notice you've been a lot happier in your work this year after the initial hiccup with the Proficiency class.' To which I just smile and nod, irritated by the sting in the tail. 'I'm *always* happy in my work,' I feel like saying but don't bother. Then she delivers the punchline: 'Anyway I'm so glad I found you. I thought you might have gone. I wanted to ask you to do me a favour.' 'Go on, Bertha, hit me with your rhythm stick,' I say, getting my excuse ready. Well, Ian Dury did study painting at the college apparently. 'Oh, no, I won't hit you, darling, you're bigger than me,' she beams, eyes fixed on me like headlamps through those jam-jar glasses of hers. She's not devoid of a sense of humour, I'll give her that. For some reason I suddenly felt like being nice to her. I have to try not to be too nice to her though, because I have a horrible sneaking feeling that she fancies me. Ugh! 'Would you do Pat Daniel's two-to-four foundation class tomorrow?' She's so predictable, so transparent! I fell for it that time though. Still I was glad I did. It was full of Indian girls who just wanted to talk, sing and dance! I think I went down well with them. Fancied one or two of them actually. Rather sexy. Good fun. God I'm really drunk now. I must be, talking to myself like this. Can still hold it well though. And at least I'm not thinking about Dolores. Or Cinzia. Or Mary. Or any of them. Feel no pain. No heartache. Though I know I'll pay for it tomorrow. That Greek lad Yiorgos made a shrewd comment about poor old Janet. 'She doesn't have the skills. We classify teachers, you know.' Well she's an interior designer really not a teacher. Didn't bother to ask him what classification I was in. I think I know. The top one. Better bloody be! After all I do for them. Treat them like real people. Human beings. Not just customers. Monty trying to sell me a watch in the Tavern the other night. 'For your wife. I'd rather your wife 'ad it than that cunt be'ind the bar. 'e offered me five quid. Said it were cheap. She's worth ten quid ain't she, your missus? Better be quick. Might be gone tomorrer.' I let him think I've got a wife. Wish I had one! Use my imaginary wife to get away from him sometimes. 'Another pint?' 'Not for me thanks, Monty. Got to go. The wife will be waiting for me with a rolling pin.' Or: 'No thanks, Monty. Got to get back to the wife and kids.' A bit pathetic of me really. Wish I did have a wife and kids. Another pint meaning bought by me not him! Don't mind treating him. He's a pathetic old codger really. Cadger as well as codger. Probably skint as a rat. Going on about cowboys. Gabby Hayes. John Wayne. Reminded me of my old man! That was a nice little end-of-term party with the Proficiency class. Good bunch. Hope some of them pass the exam! Gerard, Anna, Marianne, Lone, Béatrice, Geneviève, Nanda, Steve … I wonder how many of them I'll remember in years to come? Béatrice maybe. Told me she'd been chucked out of her house that very morning because she was pregnant. Filipino Steve with his album of Love Songs. Such a pleasure knowing these people. Always feel a bit sad when they go. Still be a new lot in September. *Through the Narrow Gate* a depressing read. Shouldn't read stuff like that. Reminds me too much. Grimly fascinating though. Nice of the old dear next door to give me tea and cake while I was working on the garden. On a silver tray too! Very gracious of her. Have to reward her some time. Roger asking me how to get urine out of his leather kitbag. Funny! 'Why don't you just get a new one, Roger?' Got a really bad limp now. Shame. Silly bugger getting knocked down at Bunratty Castle! Hope it doesn't skew his view of Ireland. No he's too intelligent to let it do that. Admits it was his own fault anyway. What a prat that premises superintendent Patterson is! Bits of broken toilet cistern all over his desk. Trying to find out who broke it. Just like he tried to find the precise piece of chalk that wrote that rude word on the board. Must think he works for the CID. Scottish Quaker apparently. Stewart does a really good impersonation of him in the end of year revue. Better learn my part for that come to think of it. Really nice of that Greek girl Margaret to give me a bottle of Ouzo in the pub the other night. And a cassette of Greek folk music. But told me I was sarcastic in class. Didn't realise that! Felt a bit offended. Leonidas claims the Greeks came to Britain in pre-history. I find that a bit dubious. I wonder. Says he's going into his father's import-export business. Bully for him I suppose. God Serena looked sexy in the Three Blackbirds last week in her red poncho and short skirt. Especially when she was dancing. I know I secretly fancy her. Italian girls! What is it about them? Enjoyed that paglia e fieno she made. Straw and hay. I must try to learn Italian properly. As well as painted the front gate for me. Not just sexy but bright too. Bright as a button. Doing a degree at the Open University. That silky blue pantsuit she wears sometimes. Wow what a girl! Says her parents disapprove of her and Terry sleeping together. Called them 'peasants' which shocked me a bit. Lucky bastard he is! Wish I hadn't let him have her. Too late now. Can't take her back off him. He's a mate. Did paint the back bedroom for me too. She's all over him anyway. Insisted on giving me three quid for the camping stove. 'I know you're not a rich man.' What a girl! Well I am under some financial pressure at the moment it's true. She'll make a brilliant wife. Stop! Cut! Why are you thinking about her? Stupid on all counts! Listen to those cricketers in their whites behind me talking about how to catch the ball as a wicket-keeper. With hands pointed down. Yes you're right mate. I know, I used to be a bit of a wicket-keeper at school. Remember the time I stumped Father Director. He was furious. Don't think about that. Don't go back there! That hawthorn looks lovely. Lovely smell too. Better than any perfume. That laburnum – adorned with golden pendants. And those horse-chestnuts are glorious. Still in their pomp. What a fantastic place this is! You can see tower blocks in the distance, pylons, railway gantries, even gasometers. But it's like being in the countryside. In the middle of London! Well only eight miles from the West End. A veritable oasis. A sanctuary. In every sense. The grass a pastiche of green, blue, rust, yellow. Wind capering through the grass. Must be waist-high over there. Even higher in some places. River's a funny green colour. Sort of chlorophyl green. The reservoirs look like lakes. Lake Isle of Innisfree. There's a heronry over there on the islands you know. You see them flapping to and fro sometimes. Not to mention ducks and geese on the river here. And ducklings and goslings. And swans and cygnets. From Greek *kyknos* meaning swan. Narrow-boat called Stella Maris. Star of the Sea. Never thought my Latin and Greek would come in so useful! Bit of a fanciful name for a narrow-boat on the River Lea though. That cow looked at me very suspiciously on my way across the Marshes. Longhorns. Fearsome-looking. I'm glad there was a fence. Hey don't attack me Missus, I'm a vegetarian too! You wouldn't think there'd be cows grazing in the London Borough of Waltham Forest would you? Just a few miles from the West End. Horses too. Jane Dawson calls her kids 'beaver' and 'cougar'. Something very English middle-class about that. Like something out of the Famous Five. I was a big fan of the Famous Five myself mind you. 'You've no offspring yet, have you?' she asks in that posh RP voice. *Offspring?* 'No, Jane, I'm staving it off.' 'Don't stave it off too long!' she flings back. Struck a chord with me actually now that I'm in my mid-thirties. Funny to think Roy's retired. I'll miss the boring old bugger. Always chunnering on about something. Used to come to the lang lab just to chew my ear off. Lonely I suppose. Knew I'd be there and give him the time of day. 'You've a lot of tapes, haven't you, Frank? I haven't got that many for all the foreign languages! How many have I got? Let me see.' He turns his sports-jacketed hunched back to me and ponders as if it's a mystery of the universe. 'Five, six, no seven. Some of them are series though. May be more than one title in the series.' Eureka! He turns back and to my despair rabbits on, dropping cigarette ash on the carpet: 'Mind you, I think EFL tapes are far too colloquial. Too many um and ers. Sounds common. I'm one of those who thinks words are important for themselves you see. There are those who don't, but I'm one of those who do. Not just names, ordinary words too. That's something we don't teach our students, which I think we should teach them – how to say their own names clearly and distinctly don't you?' 'Yes, Roy, you're right.' 'Not Brian Mmm … and you're supposed to know what Mmm means. Why do they call it Ship or Sheep by the way? Why not Shit of Sheet?' Ha ha. Very funny Roy. 'Rena said Mister Wash is very nice. She meant Mister *Walsh* of course.' 'Ha ha. That's nice to hear.' 'Pronunciation, you see.' Yes, Roy, you're right. Now please go away and let me get on with my work! I asked him once, 'Why have you never got married, Roy?' 'Just never happened. I'm too damned awkward,' he says. 'I tell them that before we go any further. Don't put on a show like a lot of men.' Kinda sad. But he was quite humorous about it: 'So the Bunting dynasty will have to be carried on by my brother!' 'What about your Austrian girlfriend?' I asked him somewhat daringly. 'I might marry her,' he says. 'But I'm afraid marriage might weaken the bond of friendship rather than strengthen it. Besides there's a history of mental illness in her family.' 'Oh.' Well there's no answer to that is there? Gosh he told me he was going to retire at sixty three years ago and now he's done it! 'You don't know how long you've got to live, do you?' he said. No truer word. 'What will you do when you retire though, Roy?' I asked. 'No big project. I'm expert at doing nothing.' Oh dear! No wonder colleagues accuse him of being lazy. I prefer to call it laid-back. I like his style really. A bit like my own actually. I may not appear to be doing much but I am. Just don't make a show of it. Like some people ha ha. Probably something to do with the seminary. Kindred spirits in a way. Didn't like the way he refused to swap the lang lab for my classroom that time mind you. Could be a pompous contrary old bugger when he wanted. 'No way! Not Hut Four. I'm not suffering a deterioration of conditions. I'm not subjecting my students to the weather. Why should I?' Well as a favour to me, Roy. Since I *am* nice to you and no one else is. Admittedly Hut Four is a bit leaky. Pathetic having to teach in *leaky huts*. While people like Fullofhimself sit in their swanky offices. Doing fuck all. Shuffling paper. Shagging their secretaries. Not at the chalk face like us. Bears out what Chris said about Roy I suppose. 'He's very territorial. Very fearful. Very insecure. Not a good teacher. I feel sorry for him but … ' Maybe I should take the same attitude. Well he's gone now anyway. 'It's surprising how many things you use your thumb for, you know, Frank. You may not think so, but you do.' Hit his own thumb with a hammer! 'I hope the nail doesn't come off. No, it's not tingling. Not throbbing either. I don't like throbbing. That often means it's poisoned.' Bit of an old woman really. Wouldn't let me have the lab even though he was always moaning about it. Even though the lab ceiling was leaking too. Had to catch water in a litter bin on one of the consoles. How pathetic is that! 'You know, Frank, the lab's no better even though it was serviced yesterday. Of course, it's a waste of money anyway. It's just Fullofhimself showing off. Big money talk. Lang labs are not a cure-all, are they? They're very limited. I'm against computers too. Computers can't translate, can they? I mean, translation's more than just a choice of words, isn't it? They can't translate poetry, can they? I shouldn't smoke in here, I know.' God the guy could bore for Britain! Why am I thinking about *him*? I should be thinking about Cinzia! Or Dolores. No I shouldn't! That's the whole point. Try to forget about them. One more pint then I definitely have to go. Completely lost count. Five? Six? Seven? Don't give a damn. Might as well be hung for a sheep as a lamb. That rhymes ha ha! Try not fall over now on my way to the bar. Make a holy show of myself. Or bump into anyone. Love this pub. Feel as if you're on some sort of old ferry boat or liner. Especially if you're a bit tipsy and swaying about ha ha. Pint of Guinnes please. And a packet of cheese and onion crisps. Mustn't forget those. Probably have to be my dinner. "Now." Great the way they say that. "There you are, sorh." Thank you. Irish landlord. Great to hear an Irish voice here in the wild far east of London. Knows how to pour a pint. With due respect and reverence you see. Puts a shamrock on top. Lovely finishing touch. Now have to try and get back to my table outside without spilling any. Hope nobody's nicked my table on the patio. No they haven't. It's my favourite table. There we are. Not a drop spilt! So I can't be that drunk, can I?

Aagh! God, it's so good! I'll be sorry in the morning though. Just need to obliterate everything for a while. That was a good track on the juke box. Riders on the Storm. Good lyrics. True too. 'I'll marmalade yer!' Pub landlady to a drunk the other night. That wasn't a bad idea of Monty's. If the FA cup is still drawn after a replay, each team should share it for six months. Hark at those Hell's Angels types over there discussing *mortgages*! My eyes are going a bit blurry. Definitely better make this the last one. Oh Cinzia why did you have to go? Look at me! Talking to myself! How sad is that? I was a bit shocked by what Ivy the Hong Kong girl told me the other night in the pub. She told me Rajeev the Pakistani student had offered her money to sleep with him. I found it difficult to be quite so friendly to him after that. Which isn't fair but. Ah well they've all gone now so I suppose it's not my problem any more if it ever was. I'll never see any of them again I suppose. I'll never see Cinzia again either it seems. Don't! Poor old Michael Foot. That was a nasty thing that woman said about him: 'You can tell he's senile by the way he dribbles.' Irish woman too by the sound of her. Thatcher supporter obviously. I can never understand any Irish person supporting the Tories with their history. Or should we forget about history? Decent fellow Michael Foot. Even if a bit shambolic. Infinitely preferable to that hag. God to think we've got another five years of her. A woman with no soul, no hinterland. Grocer's daughter! Knows the cost of everything and the value of nothing. Sunset a gash of red over the reservoir. Wish I had a camera. Going to see that new play by Brian Friel in Hampstead with Malachy on Saturday. Not sure if I feel like it. Just want to be alone. Be good to go though. Take my mind off things for an hour or two. Force me out of myself. Funny bumping into John Pritchard from the Sugawn Theatre the other day. Says he's writing a play about Lord Haw Haw. Hoping to put it on at the Sugawn. 'Ah, William Joyce, you mean?' says I. 'Yes,' says he. 'Still Joyce you see.' He did a good impersonation of Jimbo in that play I must admit. Actually offered me a part. Always feel a bit uncomfortable around him though. He obviously fancies me. Queer as a clockwork orange all right. I just don't get it. Not when there are *women* around. Or even if there weren't women around. I can't even start to imagine doing it with a man. Very thought revolts me. In spite of what happened at the seminary. Miracle I'm not. Forget that. Don't go there! Think about Cinzia. Or Dolores. No don't think about Cinzia or Dolores. Too painful. Especially Cinzia. Maybe I should go to Italy again? No don't be *stupid* Frank! You must be drunk! She's with her sailor boy. Get over it. What about Dolores? She's with her Jesuit! Forget the past. Think about the future. Might meet someone in Dublin. That departmental meeting was so boring. Cuts cuts cuts. All you ever hear about.

YTS, MSC. All bloody irrelevant to EFL. Should just have our own department. Only entertaining bit was when Fullofhimself had a go at Gordon Adams: 'Listen to me, Gordon! You're not listening to me! You're too busy listening to yourself, that's why!' Two outsize egos going head to head. God I wish I had Dolores here with me. Somebody to talk to. Instead of myself. Somebody to go to bed with! Instead of myself. Don't want to go home. The house depresses me. It's in such a state. Like a building site. Bloody Pavlo won't pull his finger out. Messing me about. Need a wife. Wish I had a wife. You *had* a wife! Yes I know but. But what? Well I screwed up. You screwed around you mean. No I screwed around because. Because? Because *we* screwed up. What do you mean *we*? I mean we were screwed up by fate. Not being able to have a baby. That was the last straw. But before that? Before that I … Yes, go on. Before that I … It'd just run its course. Run out of steam. I was bored with her. I found her boring. You mean sexually? Not just sexually. In every way. I mean I found her so *limited*. Limited? Intellectually limited for example. Not that I'm any great intellectual or anything. But. But what? Well, she wasn't interested in books for example. We were just on different intellectual levels. God my mother said that to me. I was determined to prove my mother wrong but in the end I failed. She was proved right. Though it grieves me to admit it. My mother being a marvellous woman but also limited. By her background and all that. Yes I know we're all limited. I'm as limited as anybody. Maybe I should just say we were incompatible. Maybe that's a better way of putting it. The differences were always there and time brought them out, magnified them. I mean she was very conservative. About religion for example. Basically she was a conservative little Catholic convent girl. Believed in God and all that baloney. She seemed to be getting more and more conservative. Regressing. Whereas I. Well we all know. I'm the opposite. If anything I get more and more cynical about religion as I get older. About the Catholic church especially. So in a way we were opposites. Or became so. We always were. But as I say it didn't really show for a while. We should never have been together really. Sad to say I suppose. Not that I regret it. It's life. It's experience. It's all grist to the mill. And what does it matter in the end? We're all nonentities in the grand scheme of things. We're born, we laugh, we cry, we die. We don't matter. It's a real bummer! I wish I could believe differently but I can't. It's what separated my mother and me too. Religion. It was like a love affair, my mother and me. Yes a touch of Sons and Lovers about it. Great novel that. There goes the Cambridge train across the viaduct. 'They don't put the names of destinations on the front of trains – you've got to be bleedin' psychic to know where they're going.' Another of Roy's moans. He was always moaning about something! No destination on life's train either. Oh to have Cinzia here with me tonight. I miss her so much. It's like an emptiness inside. A hunger. Gnawing at me. Dolores was just plugging the gap. I don't want to go home without you Cinzia! I don't want to *live* without you! I *can't* live without you! I just want to fade away. Fade away in dreams of you. *That I might drink and leave the world unseen, And with thee fade away into the forest dim: Fade far away, dissolve, and quite forget What thou among the leaves hast never known, The weariness, the fever, and the fret.* Or I could just have another pint. No. Better not. I've had six. Or is it seven? I've had enough anyway. Don't want to fall in the river. Drown. Catch Veil's disease. Or under a bus. I better go. I know I'll go home and write to her. Yes! I'll write her the most romantic letter ever written. She'll have to come back to me then! It's not too late is it? She hasn't married him has she? Yes that's what I'll do. Yes. I will arise and go now. Yes!

CHAPTER TWENTY-FOUR

'Je t'aime.'

How thrilling to hear those words in his ear and from the lips of a gorgeous French girl! Especially while making love. Even if it was rather uncomfortable in one of the single student beds in Trinity College, Dublin. What a relief it was too, after so many weeks of frustration, to release all his dammed-up desire and disappointment and loneliness. For a few magical almost mystical moments he felt as if he had died and gone to Heaven. Left this earth anyway. Well, he reflected afterwards, orgasm was paradoxically a kind of out-of-body experience, a kind of death, a kind of ascension of the soul to a higher plane. Maybe death itself was like that. If only!

'What do you sink?' she asked.

"*What are you thinking?*" he corrected both her grammar and pronunciation woozily, still floating back down to earth, to Ireland, to Dublin, to cobbly, surly-faced Trinity College, House 16, the bedroom of Flat 3 with its drab décor and spartan furnishings, with Dublin rain spattering the casement windows set into the thick, grey-black, granite walls. 'Present continuous. It's happening now. We use Present Simple for habit, remember.'

'You are good professeur,' she said in her sexy French accent. 'Even in bed you teach me grammaire.'

'That's not all, I hope,' he quipped, turning to her, taking her in his arms, kissing her freckly face and squeezing one of her breasts gently, their legs entwined.

'I should not be 'ere,' she said, which really brought him back down to earth with a bump.

'Pourquoi pas?' he asked, lying half on top of her, looking into her hazel eyes.

'My boyfriend is coming 'ere next week.'

'Your boyfriend?' This was the first he'd heard of a boyfriend! 'I didn't know you had a boyfriend.'

''e call me yesterday to tell me. 'e is my boyfriend but we are not good togezzer. So now I am déprimée.'

'Déprimée' he guessed meant 'depressed'. 'I see,' he said, taking his hand from her breast and moving a strand of auburn hair from her face, caressing her face tenderly with his fingertips. 'You mean, you don't want him to come?' So this was why she'd made it so difficult for him, made him work so hard, to seduce her, he thought? Why until today she'd always said, 'I prefer stop now,' whenever he tried to have sex with her? She had a boyfriend! Well, she *was* gorgeous!

Her name was Régine. She was twenty-five and a dental technician from Paris. She was tall, well-built and busty, with waist-length auburn hair, sharp but sexy features and long, heavily-mascara'd eyelashes. Looked a bit like that French actress whose name he couldn't remember. She tended to wear tight sweaters that emphasised her bust and tight trousers that emphasised her generous hips. Her toenails, usually visible because she wore sandals, were painted a scarlet red, as were her long fingernails. He had fallen for her as soon as he saw her in his class. But she had made it difficult for him. He had finally cracked her defences on the coach trip to Glendalough yesterday, when he had deliberately sat next to her.

'So, don't you like me?' he asked her eventually, having brought all his powers of charm and persuasion to bear on her for most of the journey.

'Je trouve que tu es sympathique,' she had told him – *I think you're nice* – which coming from her was an accolade indeed, after all her rebuffs, so that he was emboldened to take hold of one of her hands, which was as cold as ice, but which to his delight she didn't withdraw, and finally they had arranged to meet here in her room this afternoon, after morning class and lunch.

He tried to make love with her again, but she resisted, was passive, so he couldn't rise to the occasion. 'You're making it difficult for me,' he laughed self-consciously.

'I make it difficult for you because it's difficult for me,' she said glumly. 'I 'ave someone at 'ome.'

'But he is there, we are here,' he argued, half-heartedly, trying not to betray any annoyance, wondering why she had let him make love to her at all if her boyfriend was an issue. 'I like you. I want you. For all we know, there's only now, no tomorrow, no next week. Let's be happy.'

But he couldn't rouse her again and so couldn't rouse himself. And he knew deep down that it wasn't just because of her – somehow it felt wrong, knowing she had a boyfriend, no matter how bad their relationship was. He wasn't even convinced himself by his own words about there being no tomorrow. They sounded like blarney even in his own ears. Well, they were in Ireland …

'What's wrong?' he asked, seeing with a shock that there were tears in her eyes, making her mascara run.

'Je suis déprimée,' she said. *I'm depressed.* 'It's not funny for you to be wiz me, I know.' She meant 'fun'. It was a common French error.

'It's OK,' he said softly, wiping her tears away with a finger, suddenly feeling sorry for her. 'It doesn't have to be fun. We can just be friends if you want. It doesn't matter if you don't want to make love.' He meant those words, they weren't just blarney, even though it pained him to say them, because he wanted more than friendship, he loved her a little bit at least, wanted her, had worked so hard on her.

So they spent the rest of the afternoon sipping wine and talking, talking about her boyfriend, who turned out to be Egyptian, about science, about psychology, which she said she was studying, about novels – which she admitted she didn't read much – and about religion, which somewhat to his disquiet she seemed to be very interested in.

'Ze soul is more important zan ze external,' she asserted.

'What do you mean by 'soul'?' he enquired ingenuously.

'Sais pas. It's someseenk inside of us,' she shrugged Gallically.

'You mean, something not physical? Something inside our bodies but separate from our bodies?' *Leading question!*

'Oui. Inside ze body but not part of ze body.'

'I see. So do you think it survives when we die?'

'Oui. Ze body dies but ze soul does not die.'

Oh, dear, he thought. The same old irrational, dualistic nonsense! How could people believe this? He didn't want to contradict her, because he still hoped she might be amenable to continuing their relationship after her boyfriend had gone, but he couldn't resist arguing. 'So what do you think happens to your soul when you die?' he enquired.

'Sais pas,' she shrugged. 'I don't know. It goes somewhere uzzer.'

'Heaven? Hell?' *Please don't tell me she believes in that nonsense!*

'Maybe. Sais pas.' She gave another Gallic shrug.

'So you believe in life after death?' It was almost an oxymoron, wasn't it?

'Bien sûr. You don't?'

'No. I used to. But not any more.' He resisted cracking the old joke about sometimes wondering if there was life *before* death – she probably wouldn't get it because of her limited English and anyway he could hardly claim there was no life before death, even in jest, could he? Not while lying in bed slurping wine and discoursing with a gorgeous, naked French girl, having just had his way with her! Even if she had made it clear she didn't want to repeat the exercise.

'Pourquoi pas?' she asked, innocently.

Almost inevitably, his tongue loosened by the wine, he found himself confessing his secret, shady past as a seminarian to her, half-hoping it might make her change her mind about the nature of their relationship. He knew that priests, even failed priests, had a certain allure for women.

'I don't know why I'm telling you all this,' he smiled, propping himself up on an elbow, taking a glug of wine and gazing down at her still tear- and mascara-streaked face. 'You're very privileged! I don't usually tell anyone. I don't really like talking about it. It must be the wine.'

'I inspire zis,' she smiled weakly. 'People confide in me.'

'Not in bed like this, I hope,' he joked.

But she didn't laugh, didn't seem to get the joke. She didn't have much of a sense of humour, he was starting to reluctantly realise.

'You 'ave une belle âme',' she smiled again at him, which

flattered him even though it wasn't really what he wanted to hear and her idea of 'soul' differed somewhat from his – for him 'soul' equated with 'brain', including memory, imagination, emotion, but he desisted from saying so, disarmed by her compliment.

'Merci,' he smiled back at her, gave her a quick kiss on her forehead, flopped back down on the bed and fell asleep.

By the following afternoon, though, he had changed his mind about her. He felt annoyed with her, felt she had led him on only to let him down. Why hadn't she told him about her boyfriend before? Why had she waited till they were in bed and had made love to drop that little bombshell on him? And thus manipulated him into agreeing to a platonic relationship? He didn't want a platonic relationship with her! Had it all been calculated on her part? Had she thought, I'll let him make love to me once and then tell him and he won't bother me again? Was she more scheming than he had suspected? The summer school was over half-way through and it seemed he'd been wasting his time with her!

'Yesterday you were as a lover, today you are different,' she said to him accusingly, over a drink in McDaid's pub. It was one of his favourite city centre watering holes, situated in Harry Street, just off Grafton Street, not much more than a stone's throw from Trinity's 'surly face', as Joyce referred to it.

'What do you mean?' he asked, taking a sup of the extra-excellent stout – another reason for favouring McDaid's – to brace himself for what came next, annoyed with her and annoyed with himself for betraying how he felt. Of course he wasn't behaving as a lover today! Hadn't *she* insisted they only be friends?

'Today you are not friendly and gentil,' she said. She was nursing a coke – he hadn't been able to convert her to the delights of Guinness, to his disappointment. Some of the French girls took to it. The German girls took to it like ducks to water!

He took another sup of stout while he absorbed what she had said and thought of an answer, an answer that wouldn't be too sarcastic or unkind. For an irate split-second he felt like saying,

'You really are a stupid cow!', but didn't – he would never say such a thing to a woman, even if he felt it.

'Régine, I'm trying my best here,' he said, reverently placing his glass on the marble-topped table, trying not to sound as exasperated as he felt. '*You* are the one who said you didn't want us to be lovers, who made it difficult for us to be lovers, who said you want us to just be friends. I accepted it, but I'm having some difficulty adapting to it. I still love you, I still want you, so it's difficult for me. I'm trying my best, believe me.'

'*I still love you.*' Was that true, he wondered, while he waited for her answer? Well, he certainly fancied her, especially in the tight black sweater and tight white trousers she was wearing. He still fancied her like hell! Wasn't that a kind of love or at least the beginning, the seed, of love? And he did love her a little bit. He cared about her. He didn't want to hurt her. He felt sorry for her. That added up to a kind of love, didn't it?

'I'm sorry,' she said, mollifying him somewhat. 'I know I am not funny to be wiz.'

''Fun'. You mean 'fun',' he couldn't resist correcting her. ''I am not fun to be with'.' That's true, he was tempted to say, but resisted. She wasn't much fun. But she still looked gorgeous. Those breasts! Those hips! He could see other men glancing at her jealously. If only they knew how – how *complicated* she was …

'Je suis déprimée,' was all she said.

Oh, no, not that word again, he thought, taking another sup of Guinness. ''Depressed'. En anglais, on dit 'depressed',' he explained, buying time to think of a 'gentil' response. *Might as well give her some free English tuition too, while we're at it.*

'Depressed,' she repeated dully after him. 'Merci.'

'Why are you depressed?' he asked, taking hold of one of her hands on the marble-topped table and caressing it tenderly. It was still cold. 'Because of your boyfriend? Because he's coming?' Oh, God, he thought – she's turning me into her private teacher-cum-counsellor, when all I want to be is her lover.

'Oui. Because of my boyfriend. Because of my life.'

'What's wrong with your boyfriend?' he asked, ignoring the second part of her statement, afraid of getting in beyond his depth. 'Don't you love him?'

'I 'ave no feeling for 'im.'

'So why don't you leave him?'

'I can't leave 'im.'

'Why not?'

'Because 'e loves me. But I 'ave no feeling for 'im.'

'I see.' He removed one of his hands from hers, picked up his glass and took a slug of Guinness. 'What about me?' He put his hand back on hers.

'I like you. Je trouve que tu es sympathique et gentil. But I don't love you.'

But you said you loved me last night. 'Je t'aime,' you said. You don't know how happy it made me to hear those words. But now you're saying ... So it was just because you were in the throes of passion, was it? Fuck!

'Why not?' he risked asking, taking another swift sup of Guinness to fortify himself further.

'Because I 'ave no feeling inside me,' she said.

He wasn't sure if he was brave enough to ask what she meant, but did so anyway. The Guinness was helping. 'You mean – you have no – *sexual* feeling?' He hesitated over the word because ironically he wasn't used to discussing sex with women, even with a lover, with anybody. And he was afraid of the answer.

'Oui. My sexual feeling is died. It 'as been died for several months.'

'So yesterday afternoon was all a charade, was it?' he wanted to ask her, but didn't dare. Instead he resorted to correcting her vocabulary. It was easier to deal with. 'You mean, 'dead',' he said. ''Dead' is the adjective. 'Died' is the verb. You need the adjective. 'Dead'.'

'Dead,' she repeated dully after him, with a chilling matter-of-factness, almost nonchalance. The word had never sounded so – so dead. He didn't know what to say, so took another slug of stout to give himself thinking time, emptying his glass.

'Would you like another drink?' he asked her, deciding he needed even more time.

'Merci,' she shook her head.

He was disappointed. She really wasn't 'funny' to be with. He fancied another pint, but they were supposed to be going to the theatre with a group of other students and he was secretly glad of the excuse not to have to continue the conversation. They still had time to spare though.

'What do you want to do?' he asked, thinking they could go for a walk along the Liffey. It would take them fifteen minutes or so to walk to the Abbey Theatre anyway and maybe they could have another drink there. Or on the way.

'I prefer go 'ome,' she said.

'You mean, you don't you want to come to the theatre?' he asked, disappointed.

'I am not in ze good mood,' she shrugged.

'But it might help to change your mood,' he coaxed, though his heart wasn't in it any more. 'It is a kind of comedy. And you've already paid for your ticket, haven't you?' The play was 'The Playboy of the Western World'. He had spent most of this morning's lesson explaining it to them.

'N'importe quoi,' she said. 'I prefer go 'ome. You go. I 'ope you enjoy it.'

God, you're a loser, he thought, letting go of her hand. I can't help you. 'OK,' he said, standing up. 'Let's go then. I'll walk back to Trinity with you.'

'Vot are you sinking?'

'I'm thinking I'd like to kiss you,' he replied. 'What are you thinking?'

'Zat you are cold, unfriendly, reserved. You don't talk to me. Maybe ve should go our separate vays.' He found her German accent so sexy! Even when she said something so cruel.

'I'm surprised you think that,' he said, hurt, though secretly he wasn't surprised at all – he had been cold, unfriendly and reserved with her all day. It was true. Why? Because last night she wouldn't let him go to bed with her. Or rather, she had let him go to bed with her, but wouldn't let him have sex with her! Or even touch her. So they had slept together in the same bed like brother and sister!

Her name was Kerstin. She was German, willowy, with shoulder-length, wavy blond hair, big bright blue eyes and skin like a baby. He found her beautiful, even though she was flat-chested. He had met her – or noticed her for the first time – at the theatre the very night he and Régine had ended over their drink in McDaid's. He had spent the last few days of the summer school wooing her, taking her for drinks, to concerts, for walks around Dublin, to Howth Head, to Joyce's martello tower at Sandycove or the strand at Sandymount in the footsteps of Stephen Dedalus. She seemed to like him. She was interested in Irish literature and music. She enjoyed Guinness. They got on well. He hadn't tried too hard to get into bed with her. Now they were in a pub in Kilkenny, having spent their first night together in a hotel, but all too chastely, to his frustration. Why had she agreed to come on the trip with him if she wasn't going to let him touch her?

'Vy are you surprised?'

'Because I'm not the one who's cold. *You* are!'

'Are ve going to haf a quarrel?'

'Well, I just don't understand why you won't even let me kiss you.'

'You can kiss me on ze cheek.' She tapped her cheek with a slender forefinger.

He hesitated. He found both suggestion and gesture erotic and annoying at the same time. She seemed to be playing a game with him. But he decided to swallow his pride and gave her a peck on the cheek. He couldn't resist anyway. He liked her too much. She was so lovely. He was half in love with her already.

'Are ve still friends?' she asked.

'Yes, I suppose so,' he said sulkily.

'Are you upset?'

'I'm disappointed.'

'Vy?'

'I want to be more than friends. That's why I invited you to come on this trip with me. I thought you felt the same.' He couldn't help sounding disgruntled.

'I'm disappointed, too.'

'Why are you disappointed?'

'I am disappointed viz myself.'

'Why?' He looked with surprise into her eyes, those shining

blue eyes that made his heart flutter.

'I should not haf come viz you,' she said sadly, turning away from him.

'What do you mean?' he asked, perplexed. 'I thought you wanted to come. I thought you – liked me.'

'I did vant to come. I do like you. But – '

'But what?' He had a horrible foreboding that he was going to hear something he didn't want to hear, something he may have heard before …

'I feel guilty.'

'You feel guilty? Why?' he asked, though he already knew. She didn't say anything, so he said it himself. 'You've got a boyfriend in Germany?'

She lowered her head. 'Yes. I'm sorry.'

He lifted his glass to his lips and took a glug of Guinness to help him absorb the shock. Then he lowered the glass slowly and placed it reverently on the table in front of them, as reverently as a priest replacing the chalice on the altar after the consecration. *Hic est enim calix sanguinis mei.* He gazed at it piously for a few moments while he digested the information, thought about what to say, what to do. It wasn't the first time he had looked for enlightenment in a pint of Guinness!

He could hardly believe this was happening to him again. Was it some sort of karma, he wondered? But he hadn't done anything wrong! He felt like just getting up and walking out on her, leaving her, abandoning her right here and now in this Kilkenny pub. It would serve her right. It would give him a vengeful, sadistic sense of satisfaction – he had a sadistic streak in his nature, he knew. But two things stopped him.

First, she beat him to it – she stood up herself, picked up her anorak and bag and made to go. Second, at that very moment, the musicians struck up, the traditional musicians they had come to hear – guitar, bouzouki, fiddle, banjo, whistle, bodhran – and he didn't want to miss it, had been looking forward to it all day, needed this daily dose of sustenance for his soul. It was one of the reasons he came to Ireland. For Irish soul music. They sounded good too.

'What are you doing?' he asked, having to raise his voice above the music.

'I'm sorry. I shouldn't haf come,' she said. 'I vill leave you. I vill find another hotel.'

'Don't do that,' he said, gripping her arm lightly to stop her. 'Sit down. Let's talk about it.'

To his relief she sat down and they were both silent for few moments.

'So,' she said at last. 'Are ve going to make small talk?'

He smiled – he had taught her the expression the other day. He wasn't sure if she intended it humorously though. She didn't have a great sense of humour. Well, she *was* German! *No, mustn't think like that. Remember Albert!* 'It's OK,' he said. 'We can just be friends, if that's what you want.' He could hardly believe he was saying this. *Damn! The whole trip is ruined.* 'It's just that – '

'Yes? Vot is it?'

He took a swig of Guinness. 'It's just that – it's very difficult for me.'

'Vot is difficult?'

'To have a platonic relationship with a woman I like. A woman such as you.'

'It's difficult for me also. I'm sorry. It's my fault. I vill go if you vant.'

'I don't want you to go. If I wanted you to go, I'd tell you. Or I'd go myself. Dump you in Kilkenny.'

'Vot is 'dump'?'

'Leave. Abandon.'

'I must remember zis vord,' she said, taking a notebook out of her bag and scribbling it down studiously. *Very Teutonic.*

'Yes. Very useful word!' he laughed. He was trying to switch himself into jokey mode, to suppress his anger and disappointment.

'So, vy you don't do it?' she asked, not laughing at his little joke.

'Don't do what?'

'Dump me.'

'Two reasons.'

'Zey are?'

'I want to hear the music.' The musicians were really rocking.

'And ze uzzer reason?' Ah, that guttural 'r' – it was so sexy! But it was no use to him now.

'I haven't finished my pint.' He took another slug to emphasis the point, waiting for her to get the joke, but she didn't. Or at least she pretended not to. *Well, she is German.* What did she want him to say? *Ich liebe dich?* Probably not. But he wasn't sure. He suddenly realised that she was like a complete stranger to him. Yet he liked her. He liked her a lot. He could easily fall in love with her.

'Oh, there is another reason,' he said after a while, since she didn't take the bait.

'Vot is it?'

'I like you.'

'Sank you. So ve can just be friends?'

'If that's what you want,' he shrugged, taking a slug of Guinness. God, how was he going to be able to get through three more days without touching her? Even worse, three more *nights*? Sleeping in the same bed. Or at least in the same room. It'd be a kind of torture. Just as last night was torture. Try to see it as a test, he told himself. A test of what? Willpower? Chivalry? Self-control? It wasn't what he had come on a trip for! Damn!

'It's not vot I vant really,' she said, her head bowed. 'I like you. I like you a lot. I vant to be viz you. It's just that – I feel I vant to remain faithful to him. Even zough I don't love him.'

'Huh – where does that leave me?' he thought, but didn't say it. 'Your boyfriend, you mean?'

She nodded. 'I sought I could be viz you, but I can't do it. I don't haf ze right feelink. I'm sorry. Ze trip is spoilt for you, I know. You are chust being polite. I'm sorry.'

He glanced to his side and was shocked to see tears misting those big shining beautiful blue eyes. Now it was his turn to feel guilty. He wondered if he dare put an arm around her.

'Hey, it's OK,' he said, doing so and giving her a hug. To his relief she didn't recoil. 'I'm not just being polite. I'm happy to have you with me, even if only as a friend. We can still enjoy ourselves. I just need a bit of time to adjust to the idea, that's all. It'll be all right, I promise.' He gave her another consolatory hug.

To his relief she rested her head on his shoulder and he risked kissing the top of it. Again to his relief, she didn't resist. God, he thought, I could so easily fall in love with her. I'm already half in love with her! Maybe before the end of the trip she'll change her mind …

'Would you like another pint?' he asked, finishing his own. She still had half of hers left.

'It's my turn,' she said, taking a purse out of her bag. 'I vill get zis one for you.'

'You're an angel,' he smiled and watched her with mixed emotions as she went to the bar – admiration, anger, affection, disappointment, anxiety about how he was going to get through the next three days and nights, especially the nights.

He noticed that she attracted admiring glances from one or two other males as she went. Then a good-looking young local chatted her up at the bar. God, he thought, if only they knew how complicated she was, how little chance they stood. Or was there something wrong with *him*? Had *he* missed a trick? Would maybe another man – the young black-haired Irish buck at the bar for example – have managed to get off with her properly? *Fuck her!* Maybe he should walk out and leave her, now, while she was at the bar. That'd teach her a lesson! But no – he mustn't let anger or frustration take him over. That'd really turn the trip into a disaster, ruin everything. He had to somehow carry this off, hold it together, for his own sake as well as hers. Besides, she was buying him a pint. And the music was good.

'Cheers. Danke. So, can I ask you a personal question?' he said, when she had returned with his pint, placed it on the altar in front of him and he had taken his first delicious sup. Not that he was sure he wanted to know really.

'I prefer not,' she replied.

'Why not?' he asked, irked.

'It's not my vay to ask personal questions.'

For a moment he wondered if she was joking, but she wasn't. It felt like a reprimand. He felt his anger flare up again. She was so damn Germanic! God, was it going to be like this for the next three days? He wanted to ask her about her boyfriend. She owed him that, didn't she?

'I'm the one asking the question, not you,' he laughed,

trying to make light of it and taking another sup of stout.

'You can ask,' she said, relenting, perhaps sensing his annoyance, afraid he might walk out on her.

'Will you answer?'

'I vill try my best.'

He wondered for one mad moment if he should risk joking, 'Ve haf vays of making you talk,' but decided it might be a bit too near the knuckle. 'This boyfriend of yours,' he said instead, cutting to the chase.

'Vot do you vant to know?'

'I was just wondering about him,' he shrugged, as if not really interested, and took another sup of the black stuff.

'I don't love him,' she vouchsafed. 'But I still feel I vant to remain faithful to him. I did not expect zis.'

'So who is he? What's his name?'

'His name is Roland. He is married. He is German, but his vife is American. She is Jewish. He fell in love viz me four veeks after his marriage.'

Crikey! No wonder she feels guilty, he thought, taking a swig of Guinness. She's certainly not quite as innocent as she looks.

'So you're having an affair with a married man?' he asked, pointedly, putting his glass down.

'I know zis is wrong,' she said. Ah, that sexy 'r' again! 'Zat is vy I vant to finish it. Zat is von reason vy I haf come to Dublin.'

'Let me get this right. You came to Dublin to end this affair with a married man by having an affair with someone in Dublin, someone like me?' He was starting to feel used and abused.

'I sink so.'

'But now you find you can't have an affair, with me for example, because you want to be faithful to this guy you're already having an affair with but don't actually love and want to finish with?'

'You sink I am bad, I know.'

'No, I just want to get it straight. I'm in no position to judge. I'm no saint, don't worry.'

He laughed ruefully and took another swig of stout. He was

shocked though. Not to say offended. Rejection always hurt and this seemed to rub salt in the wound. He hadn't come up to scratch. Or up to the mark ha ha.

'You are not married, are you?' she asked.

'Hey, I ask the questions!' he grinned, trying to lighten proceedings up again. 'You don't ask personal questions, remember?'

'I'm sorry. I vas vondering.'

'It's OK. I'm only joking. No, I'm divorced, as I told you.' 'Divorced' – that word still sounded strange, unreal, in relation to himself. Could it be true? Of course it could. It *was* true! To his surprise the thought still sent a pang of regret through him though.

'I'm sorry,' she said.

'Why are you sorry?'

'Sorry for asking zis qvestion.'

'No need to be sorry,' he said, putting an arm round her again. 'We're friends, aren't we? We can ask each other questions, can't we?' To his relief she let him keep his arm round her.

'OK. So vy did you get divorced?' she asked, taking immediate advantage, looking at him with her big blue eyes, making his heart skip a beat in spite of himself.

'Hey, it's my turn to ask,' he laughed, taking another swig of stout.

God, how would he be able to resist her for the next three days and nights? Especially sharing the same room, the same bed? He liked her more and more in spite of the stupid, embarrassing, frustrating, annoying, humiliating situation she had put him in. Or was that just the influence of Arthur? And the music? And the great craic in the pub? Maybe tomorrow morning, in the cold light of day, he'd feel differently. On the other hand, maybe he'd be able to break down her defences if he kept trying, so that she'd let him have sex with her. Treat it as a challenge, he told himself.

'You can ask,' she said.

Well, that was progress of a sort. 'Where did you meet this boyfriend?' he asked.

'He is a colleague at ze Institute.'

She meant the Institute of Pathology where she worked as some sort of technician. She had told him about it before – about working with corpses every day; about the smell of one drowned body split open 'from here to here' that stayed in the building for days; about finding eggs in the vagina of a strangled rape victim; about seeing the corpse of a drug addict friend of her own who had hanged himself … He had a macabre fascination with such things and it had made her even more weirdly attractive to him.

'Is he a doctor?'

'Yes. He is very clever und very calm und very kind.'

'I see.' He'd like to think all those adjectives might apply to himself. But he'd still failed the test. 'It must be difficult.'

'Vot must be difficult?'

'Working with somebody, a married man, you're having an affair with.'

'Yes. It is wery difficult. But I haf told him it has to finish. Ven I go back, I vill tell him it's finished.'

Yet she still wants to remain faithful to him, he thought morosely. Women! How illogical! How annoying!

'Can I ask you somesink?' she said, laying her head on his shoulder again, which caused him a strange mixture of pleasure and pain.

'This sounds serious!' he joked, taking a slug of Guinness to arm himself. 'Go on. Shoot.'

'Can ve stop talking about zis subject?'

'Sure!' he laughed, relieved, giving her a squeeze. 'Let's just listen to the music for a while, shall we? It's good, isn't it?'

Yes, let's just listen to the music for a while. Enjoy the craic. And imagine things are different. Imagine we really are lovers. Sitting here together, with my arm around you, in this pub in Kilkenny, Ireland, Europe, the World, the Universe, Kerstin. Lovely, complicated Kerstin from Cologne. In this one particular place in this desolate damned universe, at this one particular moment in all of human history with all its horrors, tragedies and suffering. Including the Second World War, yes. It could be some recompense for that! Our statement of defiance! This moment in history, Kerstin, which will never, never, never come again. Don't you realise that? Surrounded as we are by all these happy people. Who all probably think we really are lovers. Think we are happy! You and me, Kerstin. We should be happy! Surrounded as we are by oblivion. Surrounded as we are by life's limitless loneliness. Remember the broken-winged seagull we found trapped in the rocks on the beach at Brittas Bay? How sorry we both felt for it, doomed as it was? Let us escape our fate, at least for a while. At least once. So let's be lovers! Why can't we be lovers? Grab this single chance, this gift, of happiness that has been thrown to us? It's a crime not to take it. A crime against Fate. A sin! We will be criminals, sinners, fools not to. So let's be lovers, for God's sake, Kerstin! Not strangers. Strangers in the night ...

'Auf Wiedersehen,' he said, giving her a peck on the cheek. 'It's been – interesting.'

It was three days later and they were at the bus station in Killarney. She was taking an early-morning bus back to Dublin to catch a flight home, dressed in bright-blue anorak and jeans, rucksack on her back, while he was going to drive northwards to Connemara. She had go back to work the next day. Back to the Pathological Institute ...

'I don't know if I like zat vord 'interesting',' she said, with just a hint of irony and the glimmer of a smile.

'Well, you know me,' he grinned, both amused and surprised by this uncharacteristic drollness on her part. 'I choose my words carefully.'

'Sank you for ze present,' she said, ignoring his last remark. 'I vill play it often.'

'I hope you will think of me when you do,' he smiled.

As a farewell present in the pub last night he had given her an LP by one of his favourite Irish folk singers, Barry Moore – a brilliant songwriter and guitarist – whom he had taken her to see in Dublin and whom she had loved. 'There's a track called 'German Girl' on it,' he had pointed out. 'You should listen to that one specially.'

'I vill sink of you often,' she said. 'Vill you write to me?'

Ah, that sexy 'r' sound again! But he resisted its allure. They had not become lovers and secretly, sadly, he was relieved that she was leaving him. ‘Yes, if you want,’ he shrugged.

The driver started the engine with a deafening diesel din that made the bus vibrate violently, impatiently.

‘Vell, I better go. Goodbye, Frank,’ she said, stepping onto the bus. Were there tears in her eyes? Or was it her contact lenses?

‘Goodbye. Good luck,’ he said, choking, tears pricking his own eyes, and gave her a quick final kiss on the cheek. ‘Have a good trip. Hope to see you again one day. In London. Or Cologne.’

She sent him a short, sweet letter after she arrived home, to which he replied – choosing his words very carefully – but she didn’t write back, so he never wrote to her or saw her again.

CHAPTER TWENTY-FIVE

'Got a few good jokes for you,' Edmund said, as soon as he walked into his staffroom for the first time in two months.

Edmund was sitting at his desk, puffing placidly on his pipe, reading the Times, attired in sports jacket, cord trousers and brogues though it was a warm September day.

'Go on,' Frank smiled, putting his briefcase down on his desk.

'Deaf and dumb couple go to bed on their wedding night. Chap sees his bride is tired after the wedding, so writes on a piece of paper, "If you want to make love, pull my dick once." Wife writes back, "What if I don't want to make love?" Chap writes, "If you don't, pull it fifty-seven times".'

Frank chuckled indulgently. He was glad to see Edmund and glad to be back in the familiar surroundings of the college, which after eight years had become like a second home to him. He was looking forward, in spite of himself, to the new college year, to seeing the rest of his colleagues again and, most of all, to seeing students both old and new. It was the students that made it the best job in the world.

'Had a good summer?' Frank asked, giving his desk a seasonal clean and tidy.

He'd been to his French monastery, Edmund informed him, had had a 'damned good time', as he put it, and come back with batteries spiritual and mental recharged, ready for the fray. Then he started rambling on about something in his newspaper, something to do with African politics – Libya, Chad, Togoland – which for some reason he seemed to be exercised about, perhaps because of his former employment with MI5, but which Frank had little or no interest in, so hardly paid attention.

He was half-glad, half-offended, that he didn't ask him about his own summer, though he knew he or his other colleagues would sooner or later and had his answers prepared pat. *Oh, went to Ireland as usual. Yes, did six weeks' summer school in Trinity College, Dublin. No, it's a doddle. Good fun in fact. I enjoy it. Only have to teach in the morning, then free for the rest of the day. Out every night on the razzle! Mostly French, a few Spanish, Italian, German. A lot of them teachers themselves, so very receptive. Absolute pleasure to teach. Oh, drove round the west of Ireland for a week. Enjoyed that. Beautiful scenery blah blah blah blarney ...*

He wouldn't be mentioning Régine or Kerstin. Not to all and sundry. To Mark maybe. Though he wasn't even sure about Mark any more. He wasn't sure he wanted to talk about either of them to anyone. They had both given him grief. Spoiled the summer really. Still, it was all grist to the mill, he told himself.

'Ah, the au pairs' delight!'

'Hello, Tony! Had a good summer?' It was the stock question when they reconvened at the start of the autumn term, one which he would ask and be asked several more times before the week was out. As always he felt a mixture of flattery and discomfort at Tony's invariable greeting for him, but liked him so much let it pass. Tony was one of the good guys. He was in a white safari suit as usual, a legacy of his time in East Africa.

'Finished my book on the holocaust,' Tony informed him, rubbing his hands with delight. 'Sent it to the publisher on Saturday.'

'Great,' Frank said. 'When will it be out?'

'Oh, not till the new year, if I'm lucky.'

'Congratulations,' Edmund offered, puffing on his pipe. 'I look forward to receiving a complimentary signed copy.'

'Lots of sex, drugs and rock and roll in it, I hope,' Mark, who had just come in and overheard, remarked, chucking a rucksack onto his desk. He was dressed all in denim and looked even swarthier than usual.

'Maybe not enough for your taste!' Tony chuckled. 'You'll have to wait for Frank's novel for that!'

'Not much rock and roll in that, I'm afraid,' Frank remarked drily.

'Go to Dublin?' Mark enquired.

'Yeah,' Frank nodded. 'Six weeks' summer school at Trinity College. It was good.'

'A bit of field research, eh?' Mark asked, only half-joking.

'I'll tell you all the salacious details later,' Frank laughed. 'Get to Greece?'

'You betcha.'

'With Edina?'

'Natch. Where I go, she goes. Where she goes, I go.'

'Sounds like wedding bells might be in the air.'

'Yah, but fuck the wedding bells, mate. It'll be a simple register office job. Followed by the pub. Might happen any day actually. May need you as a witness.'

'At your service,' Frank said, feeling strangely jealous. 'Lots of culture in Greece?'

'Sod culture. Pigged out on the beach for ten days, mate. That's why I look like a Zulu.'

The door flew open and Roger burst in, florid of face, grey locks flowing, duffel bag over shoulder, dressed in T-shirt, cords and sandals. 'Ah!' he declared, 'I'm the last, am I?'

'You know what it says in the Bible, Roger,' Frank remarked. 'The last shall be first and the first shall be last.'

'I didn't know I was entering the Kingdom of Heaven!' Roger chortled, clapping his hand over his mouth.

'Anyway, you're not the last,' Frank said, when he had recovered. 'Chris isn't here yet.'

'I'm not too late for the principal's address, am I?' Roger enquired anxiously – he was always afraid of incurring official displeasure.

'Unfortunately none of us are,' Frank said. 'It's in ten minutes in the main hall. I suppose we'd better go and listen to his spiel.'

'Oh, good, I've got time for a cup of tea then, have I?' he asked, turning towards the filing cabinet coffee bar behind the door.

'I'll put the kettle on,' Frank said, getting up to do so – he was always nervous about letting Roger near it, short-sighted and clumsy as he was.

'Oh, that's very decent of you,' Roger said. 'Did you go to Dublin? How was it? I missed it!'

'We missed you,' Frank said.

'Oh, dear!' Roger exclaimed. 'I'm sure you didn't! You're just being kind.'

'So did you have a good summer? Did you go anywhere?'

'Oh, just to the Fens, if you can call that somewhere,' Roger giggled, his hand over his mouth.

'More like the middle of nowhere,' Frank quipped, putting a mug of tea on his desk for him.

'Yes, indeed, I see what you mean!' Roger chuckled. 'Thank you so much. But you know, I do like those big empty spaces. Very conducive to reflection.'

'Yes, I suppose so. Did Yoko go with you?'

'Oh, dear, no!' Roger exclaimed. 'She couldn't live in those spartan conditions for five minutes! You do remember, don't you, Frank?'

Roger was referring to the summer school accommodation they had shared ten years before in fruit pickers' shacks in the middle of the flat Fenland countryside.

'I certainly do,' Frank said, remembering with amusement and even now, all these years later, a twinge of disappointment, the 'love letter' from one of the students he had found on his bunk bed on the last afternoon, a Spanish girl he fancied called Olga, but which turned out to be just a practical joke by a couple of the male students who had obviously noticed him making eyes at her …

'What were you doing there, Rog?' Mark asked.

'Oh, just a bit of summer school work, you know, and some research for something I'm writing,' Roger nodded seriously.

'Likely story, eh, chaps?' Mark joked and they all laughed.

'What are you working on now?' Frank asked Roger, always in awe of his industry and sheer productivity.

'Oh, just a little biographical thing on John Clare, you know,' Roger nodded.

'John Clare, the Peasant Poet?' Frank enquired, only vaguely familiar and unable to remember ever having read any of his actual poems, something he'd put right quickly, he resolved. 'Who went mad?'

'Yes, indeed, that's right, poor man,' Roger affirmed. 'He died in Northampton General Lunatic Asylum, where he spent the last twenty or so years of his life, at the age of seventy-one. He was born to a farm labourer just down the road from Wisbech in a village called Helpston, just north of Peterborough. But did you know that he also spent several years at Doctor Mathew Allen's Private Asylum in High Beach?'

'High Beach, in Epping Forest?' Frank asked, intrigued. 'Where Edward Thomas also spent some time?'

'Yes, High Beach in Epping Forest! Interesting, isn't it?'

'Amazing – just down the road from here,' Frank remarked, impressed as always by Roger's erudition, remembering painfully his last evening there with Cinzia ...

'And do you know, after four years he absconded and walked all the way home to Northborough, just north of Peterborough?'

'Really? That must be a distance of what, a hundred miles?' Frank suggested.

'I think it's more like ninety miles, in fact,' Roger corrected, nodding vigorously, brow furrowed, lips pursed.

'Blimey!' Frank commented.

'What's really sad,' Roger continued, 'is that he believed he was going home to be reunited with his first love, a girl by the name of Mary Joyce, whose well-off father had prevented her from marrying him years before, but whom he delusionally thought he was now married to and had children with. He has a rather pretty poem about her called First Love.'

'That is sad,' Frank agreed, still thinking about High Beach and Cinzia. 'Was he married to someone else in fact?'

'Oh, yes,' Roger declared. 'He had been married to a lady called Martha for twenty-one years and had seven children with her! And you know, when he tried to find Mary, he wouldn't believe it when her family told him she had been killed three years earlier in a house fire.'

'That really is a sad story,' Frank shook his head and glanced at the clock above the door, through which the others had started debouching for the Main Hall. 'I must read some of his stuff. I think we'd better go to assembly or we'll be late, Roger.'

When they reached the Main Hall, it was three minutes after the official start time, but colleagues were still traipsing in through the swing doors at the back of the room. Roger managed to find a seat, but Frank deliberately loitered at the back of the room with several others, ready for a quick escape. At nine thirty-five, Fullofhimelf, the Principal, tapped loudly on the microphone to silence the hubbub of conversation and announced pompously:

'When I call a meeting for nine-thirty, I mean nine-thirty, not nine-thirty-two or nine-thirty-five. How can we tell our students to be punctual, if we're not punctual ourselves? You lot at the back, move forward. There are plenty of seats in the front stalls.'

A few colleagues sheepishly obeyed, no doubt intimidated by the besuited Fullofhimself's domineering manner, but Frank and a few others refused to be bullied.

'Go take a flying fuck at yourself, you pompous prick,' Mark, standing nearby, muttered loudly to no one in particular, causing a ripple of amusement in the vicinity.

'Did somebody say something?' Fullofhimself demanded bellicosely.

'Welcome to the machine!' somebody in the audience shouted out to guffaws of amusement, defusing the situation.

'Well, let me begin by saying welcome back to all of you,' Fullofhimself boomed into the mike. 'Good to see you all looking relaxed and rearing to go. I hope you've all had a good summer …'

Frank found himself switching off already. He hated these assemblies at the best of times. A wave of melancholy suddenly hit him. Why, he wondered? Normally, he felt excited about the new academic year ahead. He was lucky to be alive, lucky to be here! It was a sunny September day. He had a great job! With mostly good colleagues. Was it because his summer had been marred by Régine and Kirsten? Because of Mary? Because he was infertile? Because of Cinzia? Because Pavlo was messing him about so much? Because of the story of poor old John Clare that Roger had told? What was missing?

Suddenly, while windbag Fullofhimself was blathering on

about the year gone by, most of it irrelevant to EFL anyway, the answer came to him in a blinding flash of light, as clear and bright as the September sunshine beaming in through the high metal-framed windows of the stuffy hall containing over two hundred people. It was the same answer than had started to dawn on him at the summer party and at the summer school in Dublin, which he knew he had been subconsciously trying to avoid, but which now hit him with the force of a religious conversion:

I'm thirty-six! I want a wife! And I want to be a dad!

'Who's rattled your cage?' asked Mark.

They were testing and enrolling new students in one of the top-floor classrooms in the EFL suite. It wasn't as much fun as usual because Mark, being an almost-married man now, wasn't interested in rating the girls.

'Memo from Bertha. She wants me to teach JMB instead of First Certificate. Two days before teaching starts!'

JMB – Joint Matriculation Board – was an English examination course for overseas UK university applicants. One of the reasons he didn't like teaching it was that the content was arid and academic, consisting mostly of scientific and technical material. The other reason was that the students were usually almost all males.

'She tried to get me to do it,' Mark admitted.

'What did you say?'

'I told her to fuck off. Which is what you should do.'

'Yeah, I will. I might not put it quite like that though,' Frank laughed morosely, wishing he could sometimes be as forthright as Mark, even though he doubted Mark had actually used those words.

'It's the only language she understands. She's a bully.'

'I know. I'll tell her.'

'Tell her to do it herself, the lazy cow.'

'I will. I might leave out the "lazy cow" bit though,' Frank laughed.

'Apparently she fell down the college steps the other day.' An impressive, broad flight of steps ran up to the colonnaded college entrance.

'Was she injured?'

'No, unfortunately, but the college steps will have to be rebuilt.'

Frank laughed uneasily – much as he disliked Bertha, he wouldn't wish any physical harm to her. He decided to tap into Mark's new-found softer side by asking him about his girlfriend, Edina, and their wedding plans.

'We've fixed a date,' Mark vouchsafed. 'Walthamstow Register Office, Orford Road. Two p.m. next Saturday. Are you free?'

'My fees have gone up, actually,' Mark quipped.

'I'll buy you a pint of Guinness in the Castle afterwards.'

'OK, it's a deal,' Frank agreed, wondering why he felt so jealous – it wasn't as if he fancied Edina, gorgeous though she was, and even if he did, would have been too afraid of Mark to betray it.

As he had predicted, the JMB class was almost exclusively male. In fact, there was only girl in the group of fifteen. She looked Indian. His heart sank when he walked into the classroom and he had to suppress the anger he felt at Bertha for wheedling him into doing this at the last minute, despite his protestations.

It was no good taking it out on the students though. You had to appear glad to see them, keen to teach them, interested in getting to know them. You had to smile and talk and laugh and joke and engage with them. It didn't matter if you were feeling unwell or out of sorts or resentful or unhappy. You had to play the part. *You had to be professional.*

As always, after introducing himself, he made a point of finding out a bit about each one and making notes on his register. They were all studying subjects such as accountancy, business, maths, and science and came from almost every corner of the British Empire and beyond: Nigeria, Cyprus, Hong Kong, Pakistan, Zimbabwe, Iran, Vietnam, Arabia and …

He left the Indian girl to the last. She was skinny but pretty with long black wavy hair, dressed demurely in a white blouse and black skirt, with gold bracelets on both wrists, gold earrings, long nails painted red and bright-red lipstick – too bright, he thought. Her eyes were bright too, big and bright, and inquisitive and humorous. Her face, he noticed, was rarely without a smile, a playful, slightly mischievous smile that revealed one gold tooth and added a welcome splash of sunshine to the otherwise rather nerdy, serious-looking group.

Hmm, he thought.

'So, last but not least,' he smiled at her. 'I hope you don't mind being the only girl in the group.'

'I don't mind, Sir.' She didn't look the least bit intimidated.

'Good.' It was unusual for his students, since they were all adults, to call him 'Sir', but he didn't say anything. Not yet. He rather liked it. 'So, what's your name?'

'Rania, Sir.'

'Rania. That sounds nice. Does it mean anything?'

'Yes, Sir. It means 'queen'.'

'Aha! So we have royalty in our midst!' he announced to the other students, indicating her with a sweep of outstretched arm and bowing slightly. They all laughed.

To his relief, she laughed too – humour was an essential tool in his teaching tool-box, but you had to be careful, because people, especially people from other cultures, could be offended, though it very rarely if ever happened to him. At least students never visibly took offence, because he always made a point of being friendly to them and besides, they were usually intelligent enough to understand that no offence was intended, that they were in a different culture themselves.

'So, do we have to curtsey and call you 'Your Royal Highness'?' he joked, doing a mock curtsey, and they all laughed again.

'No, Sir,' she laughed, again to his relief. 'Just call me Rania, please.'

'Oh, good, that's a relief,' he joked, his hand on his chest – his brief experience as an actor in the Sugawn Theatre still came in useful sometimes. 'We'll just call you Rania then.' It really was a relief, because he could sense that they were all on his side now.

'What's your name, Sir?' she asked, with a shy smile.

'My name's Frank,' he said. 'Which is short for 'Francis'. But you can call me 'Frank'. That's what my friends call me. You don't need to call me 'Sir' either. We're not in school. We're all gown-ups here. We're all over eighteen, I think.' There was a ripple of amusement and he hoped she didn't think he was making fun of her. You had to be so careful! 'You *are* over eighteen, aren't you?' he sneaked the question in.

'I'm twenty-one, Sir,' she said, unabashed. 'Sorry.'

'That's OK,' he laughed. 'Just call me 'Frank', please. So. Where do you come from? India?'

'No, Sir. I mean, no.' Everyone laughed.

'No? Oh. So where then?'

'From South America.'

'South America? Really? Where in South America?' He did a quick scan of his mental map of South America, but couldn't come up with a likely candidate country.

'It used to be a British colony,' she offered a clue.

'It used to be a British colony? In South America?' He was stumped – he had reached the end of his geographical knowledge. 'Anyone know?'

A few students suggested countries such as Brazil, Argentina and Venezuela, but she shook her head at each one. She seemed to be enjoying herself, he was glad to see.

'Morocco,' someone shouted out and they all laughed.

'The last time I looked at the map of the world,' he commented, going over to the Times Map of the World on the classroom wall, 'Morocco was in North Africa, not South America. Unless they've moved it recently. No, it's still there in North Africa.' They all laughed again. 'So go on, tell us,' he turned to her.

'Guyana,' she said.

'Come and show us on the map,' he told her, hoping she wouldn't be too shy, but she stood up eagerly, joined him at the map and pointed with a long, thin, brown finger to Guyana – a relatively small country nestling up in the north-east corner of the continent, wedged between Venezuela and Suriname, totally dwarfed by the immensity of Brazil.

'Go on, then, tell us a bit about Guyana,' he said to her, hoping again she wouldn't be too shy, and she didn't disappoint him, launching straightaway into a mini-lecture.

'Guyana used to be called British Guiana,' she said, 'because it was a British colony, the only British colony in South America. That's why the first language is English. But it gained its independence from Britain on the twenty-sixth of May nineteen sixty-six. The capital city is called Georgetown. The population – '

'Well, OK, thanks Rania,' he cut her off, suspecting the group weren't that interested in knowing *all* about the place. 'That'll do for now. You can tell us more on another day. In fact, I'd like everyone to do that about their country, prepare a little presentation on it, which we'll talk about later. Now we'd better have a look at what we're going to be studying in this class and do a bit of practice. You can sit down now, Rania. Thank you.'

'Thank you, Sir. I mean, thank you,' she smiled, going back to her seat.

'Oh, just one more question, Rania,' he said, when she had sat down, 'if English is your first language, why are you in this class? This class is for students with English as a second language. And so is the exam.'

'Mister Murray, the Head of Science, said I should, just to improve my grammar. I don't need to take the examination. Can I stay?'

'Can you stay? I don't know. Shall we let her stay?' he pretended to ask the rest of the group, all of whom nodded, playing along.

'OK, you can stay,' he smiled.

'Thank you, Sir,' she beamed back at him.

'You have to stop calling me 'Sir' though,' he wagged a finger at her playfully. 'My name's Frank. OK? Now, let's have a look at the syllabus. And later I'm going to give you what we call a diagnostic test to find out what you all know and don't know. Don't look so scared!'

'I'm not scared,' Rania declared. 'I like tests.' The others gave her a funny look.

'Good, that's the right attitude,' he nodded.

And it was the right attitude, in more ways than one, he thought, starting to explain the syllabus, trying not to look at

Rania too often, deciding he wasn't annoyed with Bertha any longer for forcing him to do this class – not that he would let Bertha know that. How ironic that Bertha might turn out to be responsible for him finding what he had been searching for for so long, even if he hadn't fully realised it himself!

'Can I speak to you at the end of the lesson?' he whispered into Rania's ear later, catching a whiff of perfume, as she was doing her test

'Yes, Sir. Oops, sorry! Yes. Why?' There was an anxious look in her eyes.

'Oh, nothing to worry about,' he said, placing a reassuring hand on her shoulder for a moment. 'I just want to ask you something.'

CHAPTER TWENTY-SIX

'What do you want to ask me, Sir?'

She stood demurely in front of his desk in the classroom, with her grey blazer on, like a schoolgirl. All the other students had gone. There was an anxious look in her eyes. She was probably still worried that he was going to try and evict her from the class. Little did she know that nothing could be further from the truth!

'Please, call me Frank,' he admonished her.

'Sorry,' she smiled shyly, obviously uncomfortable about it.

'How do you feel about the class?' he asked.

'I like it. Can I stay?'

'Of course you can. We're glad to have you.' No way would he let her go!

'Thank you, S – .' She stopped herself just in time and laughed. He loved the way she laughed, so readily, so merrily.

'Judging from your test, your grammar is a bit weak. And your writing. But not to worry – we can work on them.'

'Thanks. That's why Mister Murray sent me here.'

'So why do you like the class?' he asked, fishing.

'I like the way you teach,' she said. 'The way you explain things. It's very clear.'

'Oh, good,' he smiled, pleased. This was going well so far. 'Well, I like you, too.'

'You like me?' she laughed bashfully. 'What do you mean?'

'I mean, well, I find you interesting.'

'I'm not interesting!' she laughed.

'Oh, you are,' he contradicted her. 'To me.'

'Why?'

'Well, for one thing I've never met anyone from Guyana before. I'd like to find out a bit more about it. And about you.'

'About me?'

'Yes, about you! Don't sound so surprised!'

'What do you want to know?'

'I've got lots of questions for you! Would you like to have a coffee or something? In the college canteen?'

'I'm sorry, I can't.'

'Oh, why not?' Damn! He'd pushed it too far. But he could hardly bear to let her go.

'I've got a maths class at one o'clock.'

'Oh, I see. OK. I mustn't keep you from that. Would you like to come for a drink some time then?'

'A drink? Where?'

'In the pub.'

'I'm sorry, I can't go to the pub.'

'Oh, why not?'

'I'm a Muslim. I'm not allowed to drink alcohol.'

'Oh, I see.' Damn – she was Muslim! That was something he hadn't anticipated. This was going to be tricky. 'But you don't have to drink alcohol. You could just drink orange juice or coffee or something. Or we could just go to a café.'

'Can I ask something?' she said.

'Yes, sure.'

'Are you married?'

'No. I'm divorced. Are *you* married?'

'Of course not!' she laughed. 'I'm only twenty-one!'

'It's not too young to get married. Would you like to get married one day?'

'Of course.' She blushed.

'Maybe you can marry me then,' he joked, but he wasn't joking.

'Are you Muslim?' she asked.

'Me? Muslim? No, why?'

'I can't marry you if you're not Muslim.'

'Oh. Why not?'

'My mum wouldn't allow it.'

We'll see about that! 'Your mum. What about your dad?'

'My dad died when I was nine. Before I came to the UK.'

'Oh, I'm sorry. What happened to him?'

'He had a heart attack.'

‘I’m sorry. What did he do?’

‘He had a business. Where we lived in Guyana.’

‘I see. So how long have you lived here?’

‘I came here when I was thirteen.’

‘I see. Have you got brothers and sisters?’

‘Four brothers and three sisters.’

‘Big family! Are you the youngest, oldest?’

‘I’m in the middle. Three brothers and one sister are older.’

‘You all live together?’

‘Yes.’

‘Where?’

‘Tottenham. Where do you live?’

‘Walthamstow. Not far from the college. I’ve just bought a house.’

‘Oh, that’s good.’

‘Yes. I suppose so.’ *Except I need a wife to go with it.*

‘I’m sorry. I have to go to my maths class.’

‘OK. Would you like to have a coffee or something on Wednesday afternoon? If you haven’t got a class?’

‘Why do you want to have a coffee with me?’

‘I want to find out a bit more about you. And Guyana.’

‘All right.’

‘Are you sure?’ He was surprised though delighted that she had agreed so readily. He had thought he was on a losing wicket.

‘Yes. I’d like to.’

‘Good! I’ll meet you in the college foyer at 1 p.m. We’ll go to a local café for a coffee or something.’

‘Not inside the college?’

‘Outside is better.’

‘Why?’

‘Oh, some nosy, nasty, narrow-minded people might get the wrong idea.’ *Except on this occasion it might not be entirely the wrong idea.*

‘I can’t marry you.’

‘Who said anything about marriage?’

‘You did!’

‘I was only joking!’ *Not.* ‘You’d better go or you’ll be late for maths. See you Wednesday.’

He ushered her to the classroom door, let her out and closed it. Then he went back, sat at his desk and gazed out through the large metal-framed windows at the weeping-willow tree that almost filled it. It was strange, unexpected, unlikely, illogical and, in view of what she had told him, complicated. Yet he had a feeling. A feeling deep down inside … No, he hardly dared to even think it. It seemed just too unlikely, too far-fetched. Guyana? He'd have to read up about it. That would be his geography homework.

'Oh, Frank, there you are, old chap. One of your students came to the office but you'd gone. She asked me to give you this.'

Big Ed handed him a folded piece of paper. He was standing in the foyer on Wednesday afternoon, waiting for Rania.

'Oh, thanks Ed,' he said, unfolding it and reading:

I'm sorry I can't make it today. My mum says I have to go straight home and do some ironing. I hate her! See you in class on Monday. Rania.

He folded the paper up again, slipped it into the inside pocket of his jacket and hurried out of the building, silently cursing her mother. To his horror, on the front steps he bumped into Bertha, lugging a shopping bag overflowing with papers and books and hauling herself up the steps by one of the handrails, as if she were ascending Annapurna.

'How's the JMB class going?' she enquired, stopping, red in the face from the effort.

'It's going OK thanks,' he said, stopping too and biting his tongue. 'Not as turgid as I thought it'd be, anyway.'

'It's good experience for you, you know,' she said, her magnified eyeballs fixing him through her jam-jar-bottom glasses, challenging him to disagree.

'Yes, I suppose so,' he agreed, trying to sound grateful, though inside he was raging at Rania and her mother, not that it was Rania's fault, he knew, and now felt aggrieved with Bertha again for lumbering him with the class.

'You see, I do try to look after you, dear, don't I?' she

said. She was Jewish and liked to play the big Yiddisher momma like this sometimes.

'Yes, I know, thanks, Bertha,' he assented. 'Sorry, I've got to go.' He started down the steps again.

'How's the magnum opus going by the way?' she stopped him.

He laughed self-deprecatingly. 'More of an opusculum.'

'Opusculum?'

'Apparently that was one of the words Anthony Burgesss used to test people with at dinner parties.'

'Oh, yes, he likes using big words, doesn't he?' Bertha vouchsafed. 'He uses the word 'catamite' in the very first sentence of Earthly Powers. You know what a catamite is, don't you?' She loved trying to catch him out!

'I do, but I don't use them,' he smiled. He had read Earthly Powers and checked out 'catamite' in his Chambers.

'I should think not!' she said, pretending to be shocked.

She did have a sense of humour, he had to agree, but he wasn't really in the mood. 'You can look up 'opusculum' for your homework,' he joked, turning to go again.

'Is Anthony Burgess one of your favourite writers then?' she enquired, stopping him again. *She must be lonely. Or she fancies me ...*

'I suppose so, yes. But partly just because I went to the same school as he did in Manchester.' *Why am I encouraging her? Maybe because I'm secretly lonely too ...*

'Did you really?'

'Yes. Xaverian College. A Catholic grammar school.' *Thought I'd get that one in – it sounds vaguely impressive.* 'He went there a bit before me though. Just before the war I think.'

'So you're following in some famous footsteps, are you?'

'Yes, I suppose so, but I don't compare myself to him,' he laughed. 'He seems to be a bit of a genius, because he's a composer too.'

'You are still writing though, aren't you?' she enquired.

'Well, I'm working on my new house most of my free time, to be honest,' he said guiltily, a wave of despair washing over him at the thought that his all-too-brief fantasy of Rania living in it with him already lay in ruins. Or seemed to.

'I suppose you'll want a new wife to go in it, won't you?' she grinned, as if she could read his mind.

The question went through him like a rapier and for a gruesome moment he thought she might be proposing to him.

'Eventually, I suppose,' he laughed, squirming inside. What a bizarre conversation, he thought! She could be so tactless. Yet he knew she meant well. He was grateful in spite of himself for her interest. Though Mark no doubt would just call her a 'nosy cow'.

'I'm sure there are plenty of eligible foreign young ladies in your classes who'd be happy to share a house in Walthamstow with you, aren't there?' she grinned.

God, it's terrifying – she really can read my mind!

'Yes, there are,' he laughed, uncomfortably. 'But I only want one!'

'I should hope you only want one!' she exclaimed, pretending to be shocked.

'Sorry, Bertha, I have to go,' he said, starting to move again, finding the conversation just too uncomfortable, afraid she might ask him to carry her bag in or some other 'favour'.

'Don't give up on the writing, will you?' she called after him.

'No, I won't, thanks,' he threw back, hurrying down the steps, touched in spite of himself by her solicitude. Maybe she wasn't such a bad old bag after all.

A few of his students were sitting eating lunch on the grass under the lemon tree. They gave him a friendly wave as he passed, heading for the main gate, and he waved back. Normally, he would have gone over to chat with them, especially as they included a couple of Italian girls. But he wasn't interested in Italian girls any more, especially Italian girls sitting beneath a lemon tree. He remembered the words of the Peter, Paul and Mary song all too well.

'So you're doing A-level maths, are you?' he asked, placing an orange juice on the table in front of her.

'Yes. And biology, physics and statistics.'

'Sounds tough!' he declared, taking a first sup of Guinness.

'Not if you enjoy it,' she flashed back.

She was wearing a white blouse and tight black cords. It was Friday afternoon and they were in the Bell. To his delight, she had come to the staffroom yesterday to tell him she could go for a drink today. So here they were. It seemed doubly unreal.

'No, of course not,' he agreed. 'So are you going to university next year?'

'I've got a place at Hull.'

'Hull? To do what?'

'Maths, stats and computers.'

'I see. Well done.' *Damn! That means she won't be able to come and live with me.* 'You said you hate your mother. Really?'

'I don't really hate her. But she's over-protective. She never lets me go out. I hate that.'

'I don't blame her.'

'Why?' She sounded defiant.

'To keep you safe from horrible men like me.'

'You're not horrible!'

'How do you know?'

'I can tell. You're nice.'

'I'm glad to hear it! But I'm not a Muslim. So you can't marry me.'

'I don't want to marry you!'

'Why not? I'm looking for a wife!'

'I don't know you. You don't know me.'

'That's true.' Yet somehow it didn't seem to matter to him. He had a *feeling*. 'We can get to know each other, can't we?'

'Yes, if you want.'

'Is this the first time you've been in a pub?'

'Yes. My mum would kill me if she saw me.'

'Well, as you can see, it's not a den of iniquity.'

'What does 'iniquity' mean?'

'Evil. Wickedness. I think we'll have to do some work on your vocabulary. Do you read a lot?'

'I used to at school. But now I'm too busy with my A-levels.'

'You need to read and collect vocabulary,' he wagged his finger at her. 'As I said in class.'

'My favourite book at school was Wuthering Heights. Do you know it?'

'Er, yes,' he smiled. 'It's very romantic, isn't it?'

'Aren't you romantic?'

'I must be, because I'm here with you!' he laughed, taking a sup of Guinness.

'You look a bit like Heathcliff. The way I imagine him.'

He spluttered with laughter, spraying Guinness out. 'No one's ever said that to me before!'

'It's just because of your curly black hair,' she said, serious.

Good. So she's noticed my curly black hair!

'So what else did you read at school?' he enquired.

'I used to love Palgrave's Golden Treasury. I've still got a copy.'

'Oh, very good!' He was impressed.

'I'll have more time to read after my exams.'

'OK. I'll give you a list of books to read if you want.'

'Yes, please. I might be able to read a little bit before.'

'OK. I'll do that. Specially for you.'

'Do you mind if I ask you something?'

'No. Go ahead.' He took a glug of Guinness and braced himself.

'Why did you get divorced?'

'Ah! Well! Do you really want to know?'

'Yes.'

'I had an affair.'

'Who with?'

'An Italian girl.'

'Was she a student?'

'Yes.'

'Just like me then?'

'No, not just like you. You're different. I don't want to have an *affair* with you.'

'What do you want with me?'

'I want to marry you.' God, the Guinness was already having effect!

'Be serious.'

'I'm being serious!'

'But you don't know me.'

'I don't need to know you. I just have a feeling. That you would make a good wife. I am romantic, you see.'

'You're being silly.'

'I'm not being silly. I'm being serious.'

'Anyway, you can't marry me.'

'Because I'm not a Muslim?'

'And because you're white.'

'Because I'm white?' He was shocked.

'My mum wouldn't let me marry a white man.'

He was starting to seriously dislike Mum. 'Your mum sounds very narrow-minded.'

'It's just our culture. I don't agree with it.'

'So you'd marry me if I became a Muslim, would you? I can't change the fact that I'm white!'

'Would you become a Muslim?'

'No. I don't believe in religion. Any religion.'

'You don't believe in God?' It was her turn to look shocked.

'No, I don't.' He realised he was probably ruining his chances, but what the hell. Truth was truth! 'Religion is all fairytales to me.'

'So who created the world?'

'I've no idea. Do you know?'

'Allah, peace be upon him, created the world.'

'How do you know that?'

'It says so in the Koran.'

'So you believe it?'

'I have to believe it if it says so in the Koran.'

'The Koran, the Bible, they're all fairytales to me. I'm sorry.' *Talk about shooting yourself in the foot!* 'I used to be very religious though, when I was younger,' he added as a sop, regretting it almost immediately.

'So why did you change?'

'That's a long story,' he sighed. 'Maybe next time.'

'Do you want to see me again?'

'Do *you* want to *see* me again?' he threw it back at her.

'I asked first!'

'OK,' he laughed. 'Yes, I do.'

'Why?'

'I like you.'

'Why? I'm nothing special.'

'You should never say that about yourself. You're special to me.'

'Why?'

'Why, why, why! Because you're different.'

'Anyway, I can't marry you.'

'Who asked you to marry me?' He was quite enjoying the game.

'I'm just letting you know.'

'That's OK. We can just be friends.'

'I have to go. My mum will be waiting for me.'

'That mum of yours! She seems to be a right dragon.'

'I'm like a prisoner.'

'I'll help you escape if you want.'

'How?'

'We could run away together. To Gretna Green.'

'Where's that?'

'It's in Scotland. It's where couples run away to get married if they're too young. But we're not too young, so we could just go to the town hall next door.'

'You're funny. I have to go or I'll be in trouble.'

'OK, let's go. I don't suppose you can get out at weekend, can you?'

'I told you, I'm a prisoner.'

'OK. I'll see in class on Monday then.'

'Thank you for the orange juice.'

'Thank you for your company.'

'You are funny.'

'I know.' *But I'm also serious.*

He enticed her to the pub again the following week, not that she needed much enticing, he was glad to notice.

'Can I ask you something?' she said, when he had brought the drinks and settled down, an orange juice for her, a Guinness for himself as usual.

'As long as it's personal and private,' he said, taking a first sup of his pint.

'Funny. It is personal and private. Can I ask?'

'Fire away.' Ah, the Guinness tasted good. As always.

'You said you had an affair with an Italian girl.'

'That's right.' He hadn't mentioned Dolores or anyone else to her, had decided it would be politic not to.

'Do you still see her?'

'She left me. She went back home to Italy.' He couldn't help feeling a stab of pain even as he said it.

'Do you keep in touch with her?'

'She writes to me sometimes but I don't reply.' It wasn't totally true, but …

'Is that the only reason your wife divorced you?'

'There was another reason.'

She must have seen the shadow that passed over him as he said it. 'I'm sorry, you don't have to tell me,' she said, embarrassed.

'I don't mind,' he said, taking a slug of Guinness for fortification. 'You might as well know the truth.'

He hesitated. If he told her, it could be worse than shooting himself in the foot – it could be the coup de grâce. But what did it matter? She was never going to marry him anyway! She was never going to be the mother of his children!

'She desperately wanted children and I couldn't have children.'

'Why not? You don't have to – '

'It's OK. Apparently I'm infertile. Or subfertile, as the doctors prefer to put it.' *That's it. That's my chances gone now.*

'How do they know it was you, not her?'

'We both had tests. They said my sperm count was too low. I even had an operation. But it didn't work. Do you understand, 'sperm count''?'

'I study A-level biology,' she reminded him.

'Yes, of course. Sorry. So there we are. Apparently I can never be a father.'

'Do you want children?'

'Yes,' he shrugged. 'I'd like to be a dad.'

'I think you'd be a good dad.'

'Why do you say that?'

'You have a good personality.'

'Thank you.'

'If you have a son, he'll be handsome and intelligent.'

'Keep talking!'

'Would you like to have a daughter?'

'I'd love to have a daughter.'

'I think she'll be pretty and intelligent.'

'Just like you, you mean?'

'Not like me! I'm not pretty or intelligent.'

'Of course you're pretty. And you must be intelligent if you're doing A-level maths, biology and physics.'

'Do you really think I'm pretty?'

'Stop fishing! Yes, I do. I'm sure lots of boys tell you that.'

'I never talk to boys.'

'You've never had a boyfriend?'

'No! My – '

'I know – 'my mum wouldn't let me'!'

'I hate her.'

'You shouldn't say that. Even if she is a dragon.'

'I'm twenty-one, not a child. But she treats me like a child.'

'All the more reason to run away.'

'She treats me like a slave too.'

'What do you mean?'

'She makes me do housework all the time. She hardly even allows me time to study. That's why I might fail my exams.'

'Oh, dear, don't say that. You mustn't fail your exams.'

'I'm worried about it.'

'You have to stand up for yourself. Your education is more important than housework or anything else.'

'Thank you. But I can't stand up to her. She's my mum.'

'Hmm. What about your brothers?'

'They're worse! I mean my older brothers. They bully me and treat me like a slave too.'

'How do you mean?'

'They order me to iron their shirts for them for example. And they don't do any housework at all.'

'Can't you just refuse?'

'If I refuse, they'll hit me.'

'They hit you? How?' He was shocked.

'They slap me. Sometimes they use a belt. They call it a 'buckle'.'

'That's terrible. I can't believe it! You can't allow that! You should run away.' He felt angry as well as shocked, felt like going round there right now to confront them.

'I can't run away. They're my family. They pay everything for me. I've got nowhere to run to.'

'You can run to me,' he said, taking a swig of Guinness.

'I could never do that! I'd be looked down on by the Muslim community.'

'What about just renting a room somewhere?'

'I couldn't do that. Not while my mum's home is available. We'd all be looked down on by the Muslim community. Anyway, I haven't got any money to rent a room.'

'You can rent a room in my house. Free.'

'Why are you so nice to me?'

'Because I like you.' *I more than like you.*

'It's impossible. I'd be ostracised by the community. Anyway, my brothers would just come and drag me back.'

'Maybe you should go and see Student Welfare.'

'I know you're trying to help, but you don't understand our culture. I can never leave my family without being married.'

'So, we'll just have to get married then, won't we?' he joked.

'I have to go,' she said, ignoring the joke.

'I know – back to prison,' he chanced another joke.

'Thank you,' she said, ignoring it again, standing up.

'Thank you for what?'

'For listening to me.'

'That's all right. I'm a good listener. Would you like to come for another drink next week?'

'Would *you* like to?'

'I asked first!'

'Yes, if you don't think I'm too boring.'

'Oh, I don't think you're boring at all,' he smiled.

CHAPTER TWENTY-SEVEN

The next time they met for a drink, she asked him about his house, so he invited her to come and see it. To his surprise, she agreed and they arranged for her to come the following Saturday afternoon at three o'clock. He spent most of the day working on and then tidying up the house, which was still a building site, and waited for her. And waited. But she didn't come.

That evening he went to the pub at the bottom of his road, the Tavern on the Hill, which had now become his 'local', and had several pints of Guinness, with Monty, attired in beret, union jack T-shirt, red braces, cardigan, jeans and motorcycle boots, for company, even though he'd grown tired of Monty and wanted to be alone to lick his wounds. However, he felt sorry for the old codger and even bought him a bottle of Guinness, his favourite tipple, and let him rabbit on while only half-listening …

'… that last one was by Victor Silvester, yer know ... 'e 'ad a nineteen-thirties dance band … 'is son took over when 'e died in seventy-eight. Did yer know that? … ballroom dancing yeah ... they still 'ave it yer know … dahn at the tahn 'all … too expensive though …'

After a while, to his relief some fellow-drinkers rescued him by pinching Monty's beret and throwing it childishly around the room, so that Monty went chasing geriatrically after it and he was able to slink away to another section of the bar to continue drowning his sorrows. When he got home, he finished the job off with a few glasses of Bushmills, to the accompaniment of some Van Morrison, though he knew he'd regret it in the morning. Regret not only getting drunk, but also ever having imagined that a pretty, personable young Muslim girl from Guyana could ever become his wife.

'Oi, Mister! There's someone at your door.'

It was one of the boys next door, calling over the rickety garden fence. He was digging out his back garden, building a sizeable mountain of soil and assorted rubbish, finding the exercise therapeutic for both his hangover and his heavy heart.

'Oh, thanks,' he said, going inside to answer it, wondering who on earth it could be. Maybe Pavlo, his builder? He didn't really want to see him today and certainly was in no mood to discuss the meaning of life.

But it wasn't Pavlo. It was Rania. She was in her grey blazer, white blouse and navy-blue cords with gold sandals.

'Come in!' he said delightedly, when he had got over his surprise. 'It's in a bit of a mess, I'm afraid. Me too. I've been working in the garden.' He was in his work clothes.

'Can I see?' she asked, taking off her gold sandals at the door.

'Sure,' he said, taking her through to the back of the house and showing her the mountain of soil and rubble.

'I'll help you if you like,' she said.

'Thanks, but I don't think you're dressed for the occasion,' he laughed. He brought her back into the living room and sat her on the settee. The room had hardly any other furniture and no carpet yet, but at least he had painted the walls, a pastel red colour. 'Would you like a cup of tea?'

'I'll make it,' she offered, standing up.

'No, it's OK, I'll do it. You sit down,' he ordered her and went into the ramshackle kitchen to do so.

'I'm sorry I couldn't come yesterday,' she said, when he had brought the tea with some chocolate digestive biscuits and sat on the settee near but not next to her. 'My mum wouldn't let me go out. I cried all day. I really hate her!'

'I'm sorry,' he said, cursing her mother silently. 'Did you tell her you were coming here today?'

'No! She'd kill me!'

'What did you tell her?'

'I told her I was going to see a friend from college to do some study together. That's why I've brought my file.'

He could see a fat loose-leaf file in the bag she had placed on the settee between them.

'I can't wait to go to Hull to get my freedom,' she declared.

'You should just run away.'

'I can't do that. I want to leave home decent. Get married. In a white dress.'

'Well, I'm still available,' he said, only half-joking.

'You know I can never marry you,' she said.

'Why not?' This was becoming a familiar game.

'You know why. They would never let me. My family.'

'Because?'

'Because I'm Muslim and you're not. And I'm Indian and you're white.' She was sitting on the edge of the settee, fidgeting with a handbag, one of her skinny brown legs moving nervously.

'Maybe we should get divorced now then,' he joked. 'Save time.'

'You're funny. Would you really marry me?'

'I'd marry you tomorrow.' He was deadly serious now.

'Why?'

'I like you.'

'I like you too. I like you very much. I wish I was free.'

Suddenly there were tears in her eyes. He moved beside her and put an arm round her. To his relief she didn't object. 'Listen,' he said, 'maybe you shouldn't be thinking about getting married. You should be thinking about your education. You should go to Hull and do your degree. Concentrate on that. You'll be free then too. Forget about me. You'll find someone else. I'll find someone.'

'I don't want to forget about you.'

She was still fidgeting with her handbag. He took hold of one of her hands and again to his relief she didn't resist. Her fingernails were painted a bright crimson red, he noticed, just like her toenails.

'We can still be friends if you want,' he said. 'Maybe I can come to Hull to see you sometimes. See how you're getting on. Help you.'

'When I get married,' she said, as if she hadn't heard him, 'I never want to get divorced. I want it to be for ever.'

'Me too,' he agreed. 'I've been divorced once. It's enough.'

'I'd try to please my husband in every way always.'

'You've got the job,' he laughed. Why was she telling him this, he wondered?

'And I want to marry someone more intelligent than me,' she said, apparently not getting the joke. 'I don't want to lead.'

'I'm sure you'll find somebody,' he said. 'Maybe one of your lecturers at Hull.'

'You know if my family knew I was here they'd kill me,' she said. 'I'd better go.' She had only been there half an hour!

'Maybe you shouldn't come again then,' he said, letting go of her hand and removing his arm, starting to feel hopeless again. It seemed as if he couldn't win against so much prejudice and bigotry. Better to just get on with his gardening and forget her!

'Don't you want me to?' she asked, hurt, turning to face him.

'I do want you to, but not if they're going to kill you,' he said. 'I don't want a dead body on my hands. I'd have to bury you in the garden ha ha.' He was trying to make light of it, for his own benefit as well as hers.

'Sometimes I think I'd be better off dead.'

He was shocked, put his arm around her again, gave her a little hug. 'Hey, you shouldn't say things like that.'

'I'm sorry. I don't want to cause you trouble.'

'Don't be silly. You're not causing me trouble. I'm here to help if I can. You can come here any time.' She *was* causing him trouble, but he had invited it and wasn't going to just abandon her. Far from it. A snatch of the Horslips song flashed through his mind. Maybe he'd listen to it later.

'I'd better go,' she said again, standing and picking up her bag with the file in it.

'Shall I walk with you to the station?' he offered at the front door. 'I can't give you a lift. My car's broken down.'

'If it's not too much trouble,' she accepted. 'I've already given you enough trouble.'

'Oh, yes,' he laughed, grabbing his jacket. 'You're trouble with a capital T. But I like a bit of trouble! Let's go.'

'Don't put your arm around me in the street, will you?'

'Why not?' he asked, shutting the door behind them.

'I'm not your wife,' she said. 'There are people who know me in Walthamstow.'

'We can walk on opposite sides of the road if you want,' he said.

'Please, be good!' she remonstrated.

'Oh, I'm always good,' he laughed. 'Or nearly always!'

On the way to the station they made somewhat strained small talk and when they got there he risked a quick peck on the cheek as he said goodbye to her. She didn't scream, to his relief, especially as a West Indian ticket collector was eyeing him suspiciously or perhaps just curiously. He waved her off down the escalator in her gold sandals, then walked back home to continue digging.

She met him for a drink in the pub or the café or visited his house regularly after that, though sometimes to his exasperation she didn't turn up, or turned up late, always because her mother or brothers had prevented her going out. 'I hate them all!' she said more and more resentfully. 'They expect me to act like an adult but treat me like a child.'

'My offer is still open,' he said, laughing but serious.

'Would you become a Muslim?'

'No, I'm sorry.' *That would really be out of the frying pan into the fire.*

In fact, he had started reading the Koran out of curiosity and liked what he read no more than the Bible. It was too authoritarian, too dogmatic, too strident, too prescriptive, too intolerant, too vengeful, too fascist for his taste. Apart from which he could no more believe in Allah than God the Father, Son or Holy Ghost. It was all fairytales. Childish. Yet intelligent, educated people *did* believe in such nonsense – that was the big mystery to him. G. K. Chesterton, whom he had been reading, for example. He didn't say that to her though. He didn't want to wreck his chances completely.

'I understand,' she said, to his surprise. 'I wouldn't become a Hindu.'

‘We could just get married in a register office.’ He remembered Mark and Edina’s wedding only a few days ago. Lucky blighter!

‘I’d like a religious ceremony when I get married. I’d like to get married according to Muslim rites.’

‘Anyway, I think two people should live together before they get married,’ he said, testing her out. ‘Why don’t you come and live with me?’ Might as well cut to the chase …

‘I couldn’t live with someone without being married. Not from my background.’

Well, that idea bombed! ‘It’s the best way to get to know each other,’ he argued, feeling deflated. It seemed like an irresistible force against an immoveable object.

‘Do you still feel the same?’ she asked. She was sitting on the edge of the settee, her arms around her knees. Some sort of self-protective, defensive posture, he surmised.

‘What do you mean?’ he asked, though he knew.

‘Do you still like me?’

‘Of course,’ he said, feeling sorry for her, moving beside her and putting an arm around her. To his relief she didn’t resist. ‘I more than like you.’ It was true. He really was developing deep feelings for her. But at the same time trying not to. Because he felt he couldn’t win. Was heading for heartache. Maybe he should break it off now. Before either of them got hurt. That’s what his head said. But not his heart.

‘What about you?’ he asked her.

‘I haven’t changed,’ she said.

‘You still like me?’

‘Yes. But I can’t marry you.’

‘That’s OK. We can just be friends,’ he said, his heart giving a wrench, and removed his arm. *Oh, God, we’re going round in circles! Back to square one.*

‘If I got married now, it would just distract me from my studies.’

‘Yes, I know.’ He was flogging a dead horse! ‘But maybe not necessarily. We could work something out.’ *Have to keep hope alive somehow.*

‘Yes it would. It’s the woman who makes the home and looks after it. That’s what I want to do when I get married.’

It sounded very old-fashioned, yet charming. She was an old-fashioned girl. He probably wasn't right for her. Better to let her go now. Before it ended in tears.

'Did you watch that Indian film I gave you?'

'Yes, I did.'

'Did you like it?'

'It was funny in parts. The story's silly though!'

'I don't like Indian films either. I mean the stories. Just the music, singing and dancing.'

'I like Indian music, but classical Indian music. Ravi Shankar for example. I love the sound of the sitar and the tabla drums.'

'I'm sorry I couldn't come yesterday. My mum wouldn't let me.'

'It's OK. I understand.' He was getting used to it.

'My mum went to Guyana this morning.'

'Oh? For a holiday?'

'Yes. And to take care of her property.'

'She has property there?'

'Yes. A house and land. On an island called Leguan in the estuary of the Essequibo River. The house we used to live in. My dad built it himself out of mahogany wood. It was so beautiful! I'll bring you a photo next time. It was built on stilts because of flooding.'

'So who lives in it now?' It all sounded rather romantic, he thought: Essequibo, Leguan, mahogany …

'My mum rents it out. And the land. We had lots of chickens. They used to live under the house. And an orchard. You could just pluck the fruit off the trees if you were hungry – pineapples, mangoes, guavas, coconuts, bananas! As kids, we used to love playing in the creeks.'

'It sounds idyllic. So why did you leave?'

'A lot of the Indian-Guyanese people left when a black government took over. They were afraid they would take their property off them. The Indians owned most of the businesses so were quite well-off. Like my dad.'

'I see. So there was a lot of racial conflict between blacks and Indians, was there?'

'Yes. But I don't have any problem with black people. I have a lot of black friends.'

'I'm glad to hear that. I hate any kind of racism.' He remembered how his own father had been forced out of the pub he owned in Manchester by anti-Irish racism. The stories his mother told about anti-Irish behaviour towards her when she first came to England to train as a nurse. The anti-Irish germs that still hung in the atmosphere in England or lurked in certain crevices of English society even today … 'So, anyway, if the cat's away, the mice can play, can they?'

'What do you mean?'

'If your mum's away, we can meet more often.'

'My brothers are still at home. They try to stop me going out.'

'You really need to liberate yourself from your family's domination. They're suffocating you. Preventing you from developing.'

'I can't. You don't understand our culture. I wish I could, but it's impossible. You know, I didn't say goodbye to my mum when she left this morning. In fact, I haven't talked to her for two weeks.'

'Oh, dear, I'm sorry. Because of me?' He felt guilty.

'Not just because of you.'

'Maybe …'

'Maybe what?'

'I don't know. Maybe you shouldn't come here any more.'

'Don't you want me to?'

'I do want you to, but I don't want to come between you and your mother or you and your family. Or you and your religion.'

'I like coming here. It's a sort of escape for me. And I like you.'

'But you can't marry me.'

'You said we could just be friends.'

'We can just be friends. You can come any time you like. What's that bruise on your leg?'

'It's where my brother hit me last night.'

'Your brother hit you? What with? Why?'

'With a leather belt. Because I wouldn't say goodbye to my

mum even though she was going away.'

'Oh, my God! I'm sorry. Come here.' He moved beside her and put an arm around her and to his relief she let him hold her closer than he had ever done before. Now all his protective instincts were really aroused. 'What does this brother of yours do?'

'He works in anaesthetics. In a private clinic in Harley Street.'

'He's an anaesthetist? And he hits you with a belt?' He was doubly shocked.

'He's not a doctor. He's a technician. He likes people to think he's a doctor though.'

'I see. Well, he's a bully. And a coward. It's disgusting.' *Somebody should give him a good thumping.*

'I'm afraid to go home. He's going to belt me again.'

'You can stay here if you want.' He was horrified.

'I can't stay here. They'd kill me if they found me here.'

'Well, if you want, I'll give you some keys and you can come here any time. In case you need to escape. You shouldn't let anyone do that to you. It's criminal.'

'Would you trust me with the keys to your house?' She seemed genuinely surprised.

'Of course! We're friends, aren't we? You can use it as a refuge.'

'Thank you. Why are you so good to me?'

'Because I like you.'

'Can I ask you something?'

'Yes. What?'

'Have you got any other girlfriends?' He liked that word 'other'.

'No. I've sacked them all.'

'You are funny. It's one of the reasons I like you. But sometimes I'm not sure whether you're serious or not.'

'Oh, I'm very serious, don't worry. So does this mean you want to be my girlfriend?'

'I don't know. I have to think about it.' This was progress!

'OK. Don't take too long though. I want to have children before I'm eighty.'

'Funny! I can't live with you without being married though.'

'Let's just play it by ear, shall we?'

'I'll help you with your garden if you want.'

'That sounds like an offer I can't refuse!'

'Next time I come I'll bring some wellingtons.'

'That might be a good idea. Those high heels wouldn't last long.'

'I'm a good worker. I might not look strong but I am. I used to have to feed the chickens at home before I went to school.'

'I don't have any chickens I'm afraid.'

'You could get some! You could grow vegetables too. I can do all that.'

'You've got the job. Head gardener.'

'You really are funny, aren't you?'

'I have my moments.'

She came to his house several more times and they became closer and closer. She brought him Guyanese food and helped him with his garden. She could handle a spade, despite her flimsy build. And she let him get more affectionate with her, though she always stopped him from going 'too far', as she called it.

'Don't you think I'm too skinny?' she asked him once.

'I don't know, I haven't seen you without clothes on,' he laughed, stroking her long black hair tenderly.

'You wouldn't before we're married,' she said primly.

But he could tell she was softening up. 'So we're getting married, are we?'

'You know I can't marry you.'

'So we're just going to live together, are we?'

'You're a devil! Honestly, sometimes I just don't know whether you're serious or not.'

'I'm very serious.'

'You know I can't or go to bed with you or sleep with you without getting married. I wouldn't want to be your lodger. I'd want to be your wife.'

'Who makes these rules?'

'It's not a rule, it's the way I feel.'

'Yes, but why do you feel like that?'

'Because of my Muslim background.'

'You're not being logical or rational. Do you like me?'

'You know I like you.' They were both afraid of using the word 'love'.

'And I like *you*. That should be all that matters, shouldn't it?'

'I want to show you how I feel but I can't without being wed.' *'Wed'* – it sounded charmingly old-fashioned.

'Why not?'

'I'd feel cheap. I'd feel embarrassed if I met you again and we weren't married.'

'Why would you feel like that?'

'I don't know. Because I would. I can't argue with you. You're too clever for me. It's just your bad luck you met a Muslim!'

First a Catholic, now a Muslim. Can't win. 'You're very hard.' He had his arm around her but loosened it.

'You think I'm hard? I'm not hard! You think I'm not loving enough? I'll show you if we're married. I'll give you anything you want if we're married.'

'That sounds like a good deal. We can't get married though, can we?'

'Maybe we could get married if you're willing to have a Muslim wedding ceremony.'

'But I don't have to become a Muslim?'

'No, it's just a religious ceremony. We call it a nikah.'

'To be honest, I don't like the idea of a ceremony of any kind, legal or religious.'

'You don't like me enough to have a marriage ceremony?'

'You don't like me enough to come and live with me?'

'I can't come and live with you because of my background and my opinion.'

'Maybe we should just forget it then. Just be friends, as we said.'

'It's not a legal ceremony. I don't want to possess you or anything like that. Just a Muslim one. So my mum can give me away.' She seemed reluctant to give up the idea, which pleased him though frustrated him at the same time.

'OK. Let me think about it. Let's play it by ear. Let's not

rush it. No need to decide anything now.'

'Do you still like me?'

'No, I want a divorce.'

'You're so funny. My mum says it'll end in divorce if you marry someone from a different culture.'

'What? You haven't told her about me, have you?'

'No. She'd stop me seeing you if I did. Just in general.'

'Your mum sounds pretty narrow-minded.'

'She can't help it. It's her background and culture.'

'Don't worry, my mother's a bit the same.' *Mothers – some sons do 'ave 'em!* 'She probably wouldn't accept you.'

'Because I'm brown?'

'Yes. And because you're not a Catholic. She wouldn't even accept my first wife and she was Irish and Catholic like herself! Even though we eventually got married in church. In fact, she refused to even come to the wedding.' It hurt him both to remember it and to admit it, wished he hadn't.

'Can I see a photo of her?'

'My mother?'

'No, your wife.'

'Yes, if I can see what's under your blouse.' He started to undo the top button of her blouse.

'You are a devil, aren't you?' she said, but didn't stop him opening her blouse and putting his hand inside.

'I'm a bit of a devil, yes,' he laughed. 'But I have to examine the goods before I buy them, don't I?'

'Very funny! They're too small, aren't they?'

'Not at all. Anyway, small things are precious, like diamonds.' It was often a useful line.

'Oh, I do like you,' she said, folding her skinny legs up on the settee and snuggling up closer to him while he continued to fondle her, even planting little lovebites on her neck.

'Why don't you take your sandals off?' he suggested.

'I don't want to.'

'You'd be more comfortable. Me too.'

To his delight she did so, throwing them onto the as yet uncarpeted floor. Another small victory, he thought!

'Why don't you come and live with me?' he coaxed, holding her in his arms, kissing and caressing her. She was wearing a woolly red skirt.

'I can't come and live with you.'

'Why not?'

'You know why. Anyway, I have to do my degree first.'

'Yes, you must. That's the most important thing.'

'Are you being sarcastic?'

'No! I just want a decision.'

'Do you want me to be your future wife?'

'No, I don't want you to be my future wife.'

'You don't?' There was a wounded look in her eyes.

'I want you to be my *present* wife. Three years is too long for me to wait.'

'Can we have a Muslim ceremony?'

'Yes, all right.'

'I'll marry you then.'

'It's a deal. Shall we go upstairs?'

'What's upstairs?'

'A bed. A nice big, comfortable, double bed. Plenty of room for two.'

'It's all right, I've got a bed at home, thank you.'

He laughed and didn't try to push it any further. OK, you win that one, he thought.

'What do you do in bed?' she asked.

'Think about you!' he laughed.

'What do you think about me?'

'I think you're too skinny, which is a pity, because you're so nice. I'll have to fatten you up.'

'Funny! You don't think about your wife, do you?'

'*Ex-wife*. No. Sometimes.'

'What do you think about her?'

'What a mistake she made leaving me.'

'You should go and get her back.'

'What? And have the two of you?'

'You can't have both!'

'I don't want both. I want *you*.' He sealed it with a kiss on her cheek.

'Are you sure you want me?'

'Yes, I'm sure.'

'Can I see the photo of her now?'

'OK.' With some misgivings he went and got their wedding album and gave it to her. She sat up to look at it, his arm around her, her skinny legs over his knee.

'What do you think?' he asked.

'She's different from me. She looks nice. You cheated on her – that's why she left you, isn't it?'

'Yes.' It wasn't the whole truth, but he couldn't be bothered to elaborate.

'Don't worry. It doesn't change my mind.'

'You still want to marry me?'

'Yes.'

'Why?'

'You're lovely. I think you'd make a lovely husband.'

'And I think you're lovely. So we'll make a lovely couple.'

'Tell me if you find another girl, won't you?'

'Hey, stop saying things like that! I don't want to find another girl. I've found *you*.'

'Would you mind if I went with another boy?'

'Not at all.'

'Oh, that's nice! You know, the boys at college try to chat me up all the time.'

'Really? What do they want?' As if he didn't know.

'Last week one boy asked me for paper. He admitted he didn't really need it – he just wanted to talk to me! He's gorgeous.'

'Are you trying to make me jealous? I hope you didn't give him any paper!'

'I try to avoid them all. Especially now I've met you.'

'I should hope so. As far as I'm concerned, we're betrothed now.'

'What does that mean?'

'Engaged. I'll buy you an engagement ring if you want.'

'Oh, I feel so happy with you. I don't want to go home at all. I wish I could stay here with you. I like it here. Better than at home. I know if I lived here, you'd let me study as much as I want.'

'You *can* stay,' he said, giving her a hug.

'Promise you won't find another girl?'

'I promise. As long as you promise not to find another boy.

Hey, don't cry!' There were tears in her big brown eyes, he noticed with horror, and gave her another big hug.

'I have to go or I'll be in trouble. Will you give me a lift to the station?'

'Of course. It'll cost you though.'

'Yes? How much?'

'Ten kisses per mile.'

'Oh, you're such a devil! Are you sure it's not too much trouble?'

'The station's only a mile away. That's only ten kisses.'

'Oh, I wish it was a hundred miles away!' she exclaimed, throwing her arms around his neck.

CHAPTER TWENTY-EIGHT

'That'll be the phone!' Roger announced, coming into the office and picking it up.

It was Roger's usual little joke whenever the phone rang in the office. 'For you, Frank,' he said, waiting to hand him the receiver. 'A student, I think,' he whispered.

For some reason he had a feeling of foreboding as he stood up, walked to the end of the room and took the receiver.

'I can't come to your house again.' It was Rania.

'Oh, I see. What's the matter?' he asked, struggling to keep his voice calm and professional-sounding in front of his colleagues, even though only Roger and Mark were there.

'My brothers followed me to your house yesterday, so they know I went to see you. I had to tell them.'

'I see.' *Bastards!*

'I'm sorry.'

'It's OK. Don't worry. Did you get into trouble?'

'Yes.'

'I see. What happened?'

'They gave me the buckle.' *Bastards!*

'I see. Where are you now?'

'I'm at home. I can't talk. I have to go. My mum will be back soon.'

'Aren't you coming to class?'

'They said I can't go to your class again.'

'Oh. Oh, OK. Well, I hope you get better soon. Bye.'

She hung up without saying anything else, so he did too and returned to his desk full of fury and despair to complete his lesson preparation, hoping nobody would talk to him.

'Yoko would like to invite you to dinner this Saturday,' Roger said, leaning over confidentially.

'Oh, right, thanks,' he accepted automatically, though he didn't want to, unable to think of an excuse, his brain whirling. 'That's very kind of her.' *Sexy Yoko! Lucky Roger! Unlucky me ...*

'Oh, good!' Roger enthused. 'She'll be very pleased. I'll tell her. Do you eat fish?'

'Er, no, I'm sorry. I'm completely vegetarian now, I'm afraid. I don't eat anything that moves.'

'Oh, I see!' Roger chortled, his hand over his mouth. 'I'll tell her that! I'm sure she can concoct something.'

'Yes, OK, and tell her thanks very much, Roger,' he said. 'How's the hip these days?' *Make small talk. Try to act normal. Get into role.*

'Oh, it still gives me a lot of trouble, but I try not to let it hinder me too much, you know.'

It didn't seem to stop him tramping over half the country in his sandals, duffel bag over shoulder, researching his books, Frank had noticed admiringly.

'Are you still working on the John Clare biography?' he asked. 'How's it going?' Automatic pilot switched on.

'Very well, very well. Did you know, he was only five foot tall?'

'Really? Wouldn't have made a good goalie then.'

'Oh, dear, no!' Roger giggled, hand over mouth.

'Why was he so short? I know people were generally shorter in those days, but ...'

'Alas, malnutrition in childhood,' Roger nodded gravely, lips pursed. 'He was forced to work as an agricultural labourer as a child, though he did go to school till he was twelve. Golly, is that the time?' He glanced up at the clock above the door. 'I must go and do some photocopying.' He rushed out, book in hand, to the reprographics room down the corridor.

'Sounded like bad news on the phone,' Mark remarked from his desk.

'Oh, yeah, sort of,' he replied, not wanting to talk about it, needing to digest it himself.

'The Indian one? She got cold feet?'

'Yeah, something like that.' He tried to sound casual.

'Never mind, mate. Plenty more fish in the sea.'

'Yeah, I suppose so,' he laughed, picking up his briefcase

and leaving the room to go and teach the JMB class, fighting off waves of despair at the thought that she wouldn't be there, at the thought that he might never see her again.

'Have a good one, mate,' Mark said, without turning round, as he left the room.

'Thanks. You too,' he replied, closing the door and heading down the corridor to the classroom, feeling as if the corridor ceiling and walls were closing in on him, trying to crush him …

'Good morning!' he exclaimed cheerfully, entering the classroom, depositing his briefcase on the teacher's desk at the front and going over to the windows to pull the blinds down against the bright October sun. Then he started rearranging some of the tables and chairs that had been left in confusion by a previous class – bloody annoying, but he mustn't let such things bother him in his present mood, he told himself.

'Good morning,' a few of the students mumbled sleepily – well, it was Monday morning – and one or two helped him with the furniture, for which he thanked them.

Most of them were there, but there were a few stragglers as always, especially on a Monday morning. The seat where she usually sat was conspicuously empty, he noticed, with a lurch of his heart. How was he going to get through the next two hours, he wondered grimly? The next two days? The next two weeks, months, years ..?

'Everyone had a good weekend, I hope?' he asked, arranging his books and papers on the teacher's desk at the front, psyching himself up.

There were a few vague smiles and nods, so he didn't pursue it, didn't have the heart, was afraid of having the question returned to him. He liked them – liked and respected all his students – but they were a rather boring group, all embryonic scientists, accountants, businessmen, engineers, computer boffins … She had been the one bright star!

'Done your homework?' he asked them, when he had finished setting up. 'I'll collect it later. Ha ha – you were hoping I'd forgotten, weren't you? I *never* forget! Before you hand it in, check it and if you like show it to your partner to look at and peer review as usual. If you see a mistake in your partner's work, point it out. *Politely*!' This got a few half-laughs. 'Remember: SPG – SPECIAL PATROL GROUP – spelling, punctuation, grammar.' He wrote it up on the blackboard. 'But also look at vocabulary, word order and layout. Don't forget those. Right. What are we going to do first today? Oh, good, some grammar. Just the thing for a Monday morning.' There were a few grimaces and groans. He knew they hated grammar. 'Grammar is good for you!' he insisted, like a strict parent or a doctor about to dispense some unpleasant but efficacious medicine.

'It's not necessary learn grammar though, is it?' Leung from Hong Kong piped up provocatively.

Leung was a bit of a smartass, but he didn't mind too much. It gave him something to waffle on about before getting into the lesson proper. He could have done without it though. 'Well, it may not be absolutely necessary,' he conceded equably, 'to know grammar in order to use a language, but – and this is the point – it will make you a *better* user, a more proficient user. It's like driving a car. You don't need to understand the mechanics of how a car works to be able to drive, but if you do, you'll be a better driver. For example, if you understand how the brakes work. Agreed?'

There were a few half-hearted nods and murmurs of assent.

'So, grammar is like car mechanics. Understand grammar and you'll be a better driver. Well, a better language user. Yes? Agreed? Anyway, it's necessary for your exam. So, let's do it.'

He chalked up on the board the sentence:

'By this time tomorrow, I will have eaten my porridge.'

'Can anyone tell me what tense this is?' he asked the class, underlining '*will have eaten*'. 'First, maybe I should explain, I have porridge every morning for breakfast and I always have my breakfast at eight o'clock. Every morning. Like clockwork.'

'What is porridge?' somebody asked.

'Ah!' he exclaimed, caught on the hop. You always had to remember they were *foreigners*, from different cultures! 'Porridge. Anyone know porridge? Anyone else eat porridge for breakfast?'

He eventually elicited some understanding of what porridge

was, generating lots of useful new vocabulary – cereal, cornflakes, oats, wheat, barley, honey – and said, 'You can also *do* porridge. Anyone any idea what that might mean?'

'Make porridge?' Olusegun from Nigeria suggested.

'Good guess, Olusegun, but no,' he said and rejected one or two more guesses. 'No. Porridge is also a slang word for 'prison'. So to 'do porridge' means to go to prison or be in prison. It comes from a popular TV comedy called 'Porridge', because, I think, porridge is the traditional breakfast in prison. It's very funny. I'll show you a video of it some time if you're good.' This got a few vague smiles. He wished he'd thought of the video idea before. Too late now! Besides, it was a pain getting Media Resources to supply and set up the equipment. 'Anyway,' he continued, 'I eat porridge every morning for breakfast, but not in prison.'

This actually elicited a ripple of laughter. They were hard work, he thought, but it was all part of the fun, a bit of a challenge. Besides, the harder he had to work, the less chance he had to think about her, though it was hard not to keep glancing at her empty seat.

'So,' he rewound, going back to the blackboard, 'can anyone tell me what tense this is?'

'Past?'

'Past simple? Not past simple. Remember, we use that for something that happened in the past, yesterday, last week, before.' He pointed back over his shoulder.

'Past perfect?'

'Not past perfect. We use that for something that happened before something else in the past. Is this sentence about the past, the present or the future? We've got the word 'tomorrow', so that's a clue!'

'Future?'

'Future simple? Not future simple. OK, I'll tell you. It's FUTURE PERFECT.' He wrote it up on the blackboard in big letters, thinking *future perfect no more*. 'OK,' he turned back to the class. 'What does the word perfect mean here?'

'Very good?' Hoang from Vietnam suggested.

'No, Hoang,' he smiled. 'Not 'very good'! In grammar 'perfect' means 'finished', 'done'. It's from Latin.'

Yes, he thought morosely, writing on the board, finished, done, ended, gone, over …

Then he turned back to the class and had one of those horrible moments that happened to teachers as sometimes to actors too – his mind went completely blank. He had forgotten his lines.

Somehow he got through the week until his Thursday evening class, though it was an ordeal going into the college and even more of an ordeal walking into the classroom. It seemed as if a heavy, leaden, black cloud lay like a pall over his spirits. He tried to avoid colleagues, but couldn't avoid students. Sometimes, at the end of a lesson, he was amazed that he had managed to put on such a good act. In fact, he found himself 'performing' better than usual. It was some sort of adrenaline-fed over-compensation, he knew. But at the end of each lesson, he felt the black cloud crash back down on him, crushing him, crushing the life and spirit out of him.

At home, in his free afternoon and evening hours, he tried to keep himself from sinking into a slough of despond by working on his house. He spent the daylight hours digging out the rest of the garden – 'burying himself' in it, he laughed mordantly to himself – and barrowing the soil and rubble through the house to a skip at the front. How he missed her in her wellies, skinny but industrious! Missed sharing mugs of tea with her. Missed the Guyanese food she brought him. Missed chatting and laughing with her and teasing her. Missed her sitting on his knee on the settee.

After dark he spent some time doing internal work, mostly painting and decorating, though his heart wasn't in it. Anything to try and keep his mind off her. Afterwards, he would go for a pint or two in the Higham Hill Tavern, hoping to avoid Monty, followed by a bag of chips on the way home, followed by a few slugs of whiskey before crashing into bed, struggling for hours to sleep though he was emotionally drained and physically tired out, struggling to forget her, struggling to forget tomorrow without her and the sunshine she had brought briefly into his life.

The following Thursday night, after evening class, he joined a few of his students in the Bell as usual, though he didn't feel at all sociable. The Greek boys were there – Yiorgos, Yiannis, Leonidas, Demetris, calling each other 'malaka' – and a few of the girls: Katia from Italy, Josiane from France, Selina from Hong Kong, Mariangeles from Spain, Aysen from Turkey … But he wasn't interested in them. Not even Italian Katia. He'd been cured of his obsession with Italian girls! He wasn't interested in anybody. Except *her*.

Inside he was a maelstrom of emotions: disappointment, anger, frustration, despair, loneliness … He was even a bit worried that her family could cause trouble for him at the college. Not that he'd done anything wrong. She was an adult. She was twenty-one. He hadn't raped her! Hadn't even had sex with her properly. Didn't want to yet. Had started to like the idea of a marriage ceremony. Was happy to wait. Was serious about her. Respected her. Had even gone out and bought her a Claddagh as an 'engagement' ring!

God, he'd been stupid, mad, to think he could ever have married a girl from that background, a Muslim girl! He had to forget about her. Look somewhere else for a wife. Plenty more fish in the sea, as Mark said. An Italian girl maybe. Katia there? No. She was nice enough, but not wife material. Being Italian wasn't enough any more! He was well and truly over that obsession. Well, *two* Italian girls had let him down. They'd had their chance! *She* was different. Completely different. There was something about her. He'd felt it from the first minute. And she'd confirmed it. He'd started to really like her. Really admire her. Really *respect* her. Love her? Yes. Even though he'd never used that word to her. Yet. Never would now. The thought was like a punch in the guts. Another hammer-blow to the heart. Another kick in the – *stop thinking about her! Forget about her!*

'Sorry, Yiorgos?'

'Do you want another beer?'

'Oh! Yeah. OK. Thanks, Yiorgos.'

Great bloke, Yiorgos! He couldn't resist another one. Number four. He was drinking too much, but it dulled the pain, at least for a while. Must remember he had to teach in the morning. Nothing worse than going into a classroom with a hangover. Except going in with a broken heart maybe. Or both. Had to be really on the ball tomorrow too. Proficiency class. Go sick? He *was* sick, wasn't he? It was a kind of sickness, wasn't it? Sorry, I can't come in today, I've got a broken heart ha ha. No. *Never* went sick. Even when he was sick. Too damned professional. Always there. Always on time. Always delivered the goods. Professional pride. Sense of loyalty to students too. Respect for them. Like these ones here. Great bunch. Love them. Love teaching them. Love getting to know them. Look at them, from all over the world, chatting and laughing together. International friendship. No discord. Great job. Best job in world.

'Thank you, Yiorgos,' he said, as Yiorgos deposited a new jar of creamy-headed, liquorice-black Guinness in front of him, along with the regulatory packet of cheese and onion crisps. 'You're a gentleman and a scholar.'

'He's a malaka!' Leonidas scoffed, making him laugh.

'What ees this 'malaka'?' Katia, the Italian girl, asked.

'Yes, what is it?' one or two of the other girls enquired.

'I'll leave you to explain that, Leonidas,' he grinned, taking a first sup of his new pint.

At that very moment, 'Italian Girls' by Rod Stewart came on the juke box and he dipped out of the conversation again to listen to it for a few moments, even though it gave another wrench to his already battered heart. Maybe he should reply to the letter he'd received from Cinzia over a month ago, he thought? Maybe he'd let her go, given up, too easily. Maybe she deserved another chance. Yes, he decided, he'd do that, maybe tonight when he got home, if he wasn't too plastered …

As soon as he opened the front door, he felt a strange sensation. There was something different about the house. He had been a bit drunk when he left the pub, but the half-hour walk home had more or less sobered him up. He remembered how Pavlo had said he thought there was a ghost in the house, maybe somebody had been murdered there, certainly people would have died in it – after all it was almost a hundred years old. But he didn't take much notice of Pavlo, who was a bit of a romancer, and didn't believe in ghosts. On the other hand, the house did have a spooky air about it, because it was still largely in a gutted, dimly-lit state.

He put his briefcase down, switched the bare hall lightbulb on and went into the kitchen to check, feeling nervous but also ridiculous. Everything seemed in order. He went into the ramshackle lean-to at the back of the house and peeped through the rickety back door into the garden. On his way, he picked up the shovel he had been using to work in the garden, just in case. But all he could see was the still considerable black mound of soil that he was gradually trying to remove. There was no sign of anybody or anything untoward. But what if an intruder had got into the house and was hiding upstairs? It would be easy enough, the windows and doors being so insecure. Not that he had anything worth stealing, except maybe some tools.

He went back inside, switched the dim landing light on and gingerly crept up the bare wooden stairs, still brandishing the shovel, hardly daring to breathe, his heart fluttering nervously despite himself. It was silly carrying a shovel upstairs, he told himself, but he definitely had a feeling there was somebody or something in the house. His imagination started running. There might be more than one intruder. They might have a weapon of some sort. In which case the shovel would be some defence. Or what if it *was* a ghost, something supernatural? The whole house was eerily, spookily silent. Then the shovel would be no use at all. He suddenly felt very lonely and absurdly, childishly scared.

On the landing, he switched the bathroom light on, waited, slowly opened the door and peeked in, holding the shovel up in front of him with both hands. Nothing. Just the newly-installed bath and washbasin, newly-plastered walls, bare floorboards, one or two tools lying around. He tiptoed up to the back bedroom, which as yet had no door, reached his hand in, flicked on the light and waited, his heart now pounding in his chest. No sound. He leaned slowly in to look. Nothing. The room was completely bare except for building materials, paint pots, tools …

Heart drumming, he turned to the last room, the room he was using as a bedroom, one of the few rooms in the house which had a door, though he hadn't got round to painting it yet, and which was shut. Holding the shovel in his right hand, with his left hand he slowly turned the doorknob, pushed the door open a little and waited. There was no sound. The room was in darkness, except for the glimmering orange light from the street lamp right outside. Quietly, keeping a firm grip on the shovel with his right hand, he reached in with his left and flicked on the light. It took his eyes a moment to adjust, dim though the light was. There was somebody in his bed! He stared in shock. It was Rania, clutching the bedclothes, her eyes wide with fright. Then, in a voice that was little more than a whimper, three tiny words that would change both of their lives for ever escaped from her mouth.

'Can I stay?'

For information about Eugene's other books,
please see over.

GHOSTERS

GHOSTERS is the prequel to both *Opposite Worlds* and *Italian Girls*. At the age of twelve, Frank Walsh leaves home in Manchester and enters a Roman Catholic seminary in the English Lake District to fulfil his dream of becoming a missionary priest. At twenty-one, having lost his faith, he makes an unsuccessful attempt to commit suicide, leaves the seminary and returns home. With the help of Sally, the girl next door, he slowly manages to recover from depression and starts to feel 'normal' again. After finishing university, he leaves home yet again – and Sally – to live in London. There he tries to escape the ghosts of the past and fulfil his dream of being a writer, while teaching English to foreign students in a private school in Soho. He has a passionate love affair with one of his students, Marina, a vibrant, eighteen-year-old Yugoslav girl. They plan to marry, but a chance meeting with a ghost from the past threatens to destroy this dream too. Yet Frank refuses to be beaten, because he still has one dream left …

'I like it ... imaginatively strong ... I was riveted ... sensitively worked out ... intelligently written ... powerfully presented ... this heart-felt painful re-creation of a central hidden part of our culture.' Kate Cruise O'Brien, Poolbeg Press Ltd., Dublin

'... extremely well written and moves at a pace that keeps you captivated. Crucially, it deals with the disturbing subject of abuse in the Catholic Church in a revealing, but sensitive way, without pulling any punches, drawing on the author's own firsthand experiences ... provides a graphic and disturbing insight into the emotional traumas suffered by both the victims and ironically the perpetrators ... an informative and thought provoking book that could and should be adapted into a television drama.' John Vesey, Amazon

'... deals with some very sensitive and difficult [not to say topical] issues in a very interesting, serious, intelligent way. It's very well written. It's obviously autobiographical (or

seems so) but that in no way invalidates it in my opinion. If anything, the reverse is true. The story really carried me along and I couldn't wait to find out whether Frank (the hero) would be able to turn his life around or not. I won't give the game away by saying whether he does nor not! ... I'd recommend this book to anyone who is interested in a very good human story, well told, and who is interested in such issues as child abuse both sexual and physical, religious indoctrination, love and self-fulfilment. It is a bit slow at the start, but I found it difficult to put down once I got into it.' Orinoco, Amazon

'Christian romance' is a bit misleading perhaps, but this book does deal with the question of religious faith – specifically the Catholic faith and theology – in a very intelligent, dramatic and moving way. More accurately, it deals with the loss of faith. The main drama is about how Frank Walsh manages to recover from his drastic loss of faith, reinvent himself and forge a new life, in effect a new identity. But the story also encompasses other themes, such as child abuse [very topical] and romantic love both homosexual and heterosexual. I found the story of Frank's progression from despair at losing his faith [and therefore his vocation to the priesthood] to relative happiness as a young, carefree teacher in London to be completely engrossing. The author deals with all these themes very honestly – sometimes painfully honestly – so for me this was a riveting read.' Nena, Amazon

'Ghosters' has a really powerful emotive effect as it charts Frank's life throughout his childhood and as a young adult and is very truthful and honest ... it deals with Faith, Religion, Love and most of all Identity. It is an empowering story that allows the reader to connect to Frank, the main character. This was a thoroughly enjoyable read that grips the reader throughout.' Miss A. M. Kearney, Amazon

GHOSTERS is available from Amazon.

Amazon Average Customer Review *****

OPPOSITE WORLDS

OPPOSITE WORLDS is the follow-up to *Ghosters*. It finds Frank alone and lonely in London, having been jilted by his Yugoslav girlfriend, Marina, on their wedding day. On the rebound from this, he has a passionate affair with Kalli, a gorgeous Greek singer and belly-dancer, who is a student in his class at the school in Soho where he teaches English to foreign students. When Kalli leaves him, Frank finds himself alone again. Then one evening, in a folk club in an Irish pub, he hears a young, attractive girl singing and falls instantly in love with her. Her name is Mary, he contrives to meet her and Mary falls in love with him. Love leads to marriage – reluctantly at first on Frank's part – but their marriage proves to be a collision of two very different, indeed opposite, worlds ...

'Opposite Worlds is an extremely well written book – thoughtful, descriptive and emotive. The journey of exploration and discovery for Frank Walsh enables the reader to identify with him on a deep emotional level. As you read, you feel how Frank is thinking and feeling as if you're in that moment with him. Overall, it's a great read as it explores identity, relationships and belonging. A definite recommendation! It gives a clear insight into the life of Frank Walsh and touches the reader on a deeper level.' Miss A. M. Kearney, Amazon

OPPOSITE WORLDS is available from Amazon.

VENICE AND OTHER POEMS

VENICE AND OTHER POEMS is Eugene's first book of poetry. It includes poems written when he was a teenager to poems written recently. In other words, it covers a span of nearly fifty years, from his schooldays in the early sixties to 2014. However, the poems are in alphabetical not chronological order. Each poem expresses a state of mind or emotion at the time, an observation of a scene or a reflection upon some experience. So in a sense the poems are autobiographical, though not necessarily an exact mirror of the author's life – there may be some 'poetic licence' here and there. Perhaps it would be better to describe each poem as a prism. As well as reflecting his own life-experience though, the author hopes that in at least some of these poems readers may catch a glimpse of their own lives, past, present or even future.

'This is a very appealing collection of poems. They are well constructed with lots of descriptive, emotive language. The writer explores deep subjects such as Love, Identity and Loss. I would recommend this collection as it has a lovely selection of poems that touch you with many emotions.' Miss A. M. Kearney, Amazon

VENICE AND OTHER POEMS is available from Amazon.

You can contact Eugene at:
veseyeugene@hotmail.com

Eugene is also on Facebook

Lightning Source UK Ltd.
Milton Keynes UK
UKHW011214290319
340150UK00001B/3/P

9 781785 070884